Book One

of

The Lost Council Trilogy

Recon Time

Recon Time

Book One of

The Lost Council Trilogy

Sebastian Blunt

4XDX

Science Fiction

Recon Time

This is a work of fiction. All the characters and events portrayed in this book are fictional, and any resemblance to real people or incidents is purely coincidental.

ISBN-13: 978-1-7358847-0-7

A 4XDX Sci-Fi Book

Cover Art by Nabinkarna

Dedication

Thanks to my proofreaders, Linda Klein, Jack Klein, and Judy Engelsman.

Chapter One

"What the hell is that thing?" exclaimed the staff sergeant, leaning in and pointing at the black object wedged into the crusty ground.

Aaron Howe made a hardly perceptible twitch of his head, which in his body language meant, please step back. He shivered slightly due to the frigid morning breeze flowing across the Canadian Tundra. Indeed, it was not the most desirable place to be, considering the bitter wind above the barren landscape adjacent to the Mackenzie River.

Howe, Ph.D., the young CEO of Howe It Works, Inc., gleefully agreed to freelance for IS (US Intelligence Support) but didn't expect to have a perpetually inquisitive and oversized former drill sergeant breathing down his neck. Despite that, it was a relief to get away from Vermont and do something far beyond the ordinary.

The sergeant stepped away but continued to observe as Aaron squinted at the thing partially buried in the soil. Howe's thoughts of his board of directors intruded on his examination; it was like they were gnawing on his cerebellum—he forced the image out of his mind.

"That's peculiar," he mumbled. "I came here because Carlisle insisted, expecting to find nothing, yet there is this."

"What? Sir?"

"Nothing, sergeant."

He bent down to look at the black box that was truly igniting his curiosity. *When facts don't match the laws of physics*—he could hear a professor from years ago lecturing on the scientific method as the old man perceived it.

This thing, however, did appear like something that could be of extraterrestrial origin. Aaron was already devising a ploy that he might use to get his management people to cover for him.

Unless this thing was a dud, in which case it would be back to the board room and not his favorite spot, the lab.

Although the device was small, it emitted strong radio waves. And the bizarre part was the course corrections on its way down to where it rested now, 35 miles north of Fort Simpson.

"I want you up there now. It could be something alien," bellowed Vice President Carlisle. That call had been sufficient to pique Howe's interest and get him up to this inhospitable place.

Dr. Edgar Tomis, Howe's college buddy and assistant, stood nearby and operated equipment that measured magnetic fields, electrical fields, and radio frequency fields. The man was a stickler for precision, except when it came to his appearance. That was another story, as Edgar was plump with a big fat mustache and a passion for donuts like a hungry beat cop in front of a Krispy Kreme—but he did have a sarcastic sense of humor.

"Sergeant," Dr. Tomis said, noticing the enlisted man encroaching on Aaron's space once more. "Give us some space to work, please?"

The Staff Sergeant eased back, and Edgar chuckled, amused at how someone could move his feet with the appearance of still being at attention. He turned back to Howe, crouched on the ground in front of him, making noises and scratching his chin.

"What do you see on the displays, Edgar?"

"It's unreadable. It's emitting something, but it's not anything I've seen before."

"Me neither," admitted Howe. "Is it RF? Some of your weird waves that you're always rambling on about? Is there any radiation? I mean gamma or X-rays?"

"Yes!" Edgar seemed quite panicked, "I'm picking up lethal emissions every nine seconds!"

The sergeant, despite his bad knee, leaped back like a gazelle. It hurt. The maneuver forced a chuckle out of Howe, but then he looked at his assistant. "You are joking, right?

Edgar looked at the sergeant, who looked anxious and

desperate to run away.

"Of course, I'm joking. There's no lethal radiation here."

The sergeant made a mental note to remember that academics could be real a-holes.

Tomis hit the record button on the high-end video camera. There was no way they could risk using a cellphone, and besides, the camera was well-shielded.

Howe put on his academic voice and began, "This is Dr. Aaron Howe. I am joined by Dr. Edgar Tomis." He didn't mention the two engineering assistants assigned by I.S. or the staff sergeant.

"We are currently in Northern Canada near Fort Simpson. The exact location is in the file. We have tracked the object to a fairly desolate spot based on the calculated trajectory. Even from Fort Simpson, we received a continuous audio tone of 700hz at a radio frequency of 6.8 megahertz, triangulated exactly to this spot. The tone repeated every 13 seconds for a duration of 2.3 seconds."

Edgar interrupted. "You know what that 700 Hertz tone sounds like?"

Howe shook his head.

"It's like your typical CW continuous-wave tone, like Morse code used by ham radio operators."

Howe gave Edgar a funny look. "I know code. Does that still exist? I mean in practice?"

"Still heavily in use. Incredibly efficient. When all else fails, Morse code gets through. I still have my FCC license."

"Wow. When the zombie apocalypse or alien invasion comes—I will stick close to you. Can we continue?"

Howe tapped the mic. "Upon arriving in the proximity of the object, the RF signal stopped, which was an additional indicator of intelligent design—the primary evidence was that the object made course corrections on its way to earth.

"The object or device appears completely black, about 25 cm square. We cannot tell how deeply it's buried under the soil, but about 5cm of the object is above ground.

"The vegetation is non-existent for a distance of about 20 meters in any direction from the object. No harmful radiation has been detected, but the plant life was affected. Maybe.

"There are no obvious markings on the surface of the object. It is flat black on all visible surfaces. We will attempt to clear some of the soil around the base. It does not appear to be hazardous or threatening."

Howe stopped recording. "Don't they always say things like objects appear non-threatening right before something bad happens?"

Edgar looked amused. "Unless that thing intends to steal my lunch, then I'm good."

There was a gust of cold air that picked up leaves and dirt. That sent a dusty cloud that irritated Edgar's sensitive eyes. He coughed and sneezed simultaneously, then mumbled a four-letter word loud enough to be overheard.

"Dr. Tomis, I believe that you just violated your no cursing rule."

"Aaron," Edgar smirked, "Impossible. I think that noise came from the E.T."

Howe reached for the object and then blurted out his own explicative as a force vibrated through his right index finger.

"That was weird."

Edgar moved closer. "What?"

"I put my right hand about five centimeters from the object and received the strangest feeling of energy that I've—I can't explain it. It was like I was somewhere else for a second. Like the molecules of my body were scrambled. Does that sound normal to you?"

Edgar rubbed his rotund belly. "Uh, No!"

Aaron took about a moment to process the experience and then blinked a few times.

"I know that look; you've got a hunch?

"No, not really," said Howe. "But this thing is starting to strike me as genuine. What I mean is that I think this has the characteristics that point to non-Earth origins, but let's not jump the gun.

Howe ran his fingers through his thick brown hair. His scalp felt weird, but the feeling was not static electricity from the Canadian breeze.

"The feeling from that object, it was like, well—not a shock, but stimulation that jumped from my hand to my brain," explained Aaron. "And then I felt like I was *not* here. Very strange. Edgar, this could be a waste of time, but let's do this the smart way. We'll mess with it a little more here, figure out how to dig it out of the soil, and then take it back to the lab. I'd prefer to have it in a controlled environment when it turns me inside out and fries my brain,"

Aaron eyed the sergeant and decided to indulge his need to experiment. As a 16-year-old undergrad, he'd had an electrical engineering professor who watched him take chances in the lab. The prof once warned Howe saying: "Curiosity killed the cat."

Aaron had replied snarkily, "Good thing I'm not a cat, doc."

Professor Agrawal had obviously heard this before and immediately retorted with his canned response. "Well, Howe, since cats share 90% of the same DNA as humans, you will only be 90% dead."

Yep, he thought, as the professor pointed out, science had risks.

"Sergeant."

"Yes, sir."

"Sergeant, do me a favor; lean down here and put your right index finger about two inches from the object."

The sergeant did, as requested, although his inclination toward self-preservation, which was keenly honed in Afghanistan, told him to decline. Instead, he dropped down onto his shrapnel knee and extended his index finger.

The enlisted observer got a close look at it for the first time. The object was jet black and didn't reflect at all. It didn't look threatening, but his gut told him to run.

"Stop there, sergeant."

The sergeant froze.

"What do you feel? Anything?"

"No, Dr. Howe, sir, just minor irritation in my knee."

Howe groaned, "I meant in your finger, arm, chest, anything?"

The sergeant shook his head. "No, sir."

Howe thought that was strange since he'd felt the vibration from even further away.

"Okay, Sergeant—" Howe looked at the nametag. "—Bonner, could you ease your finger in a little closer and tell me if you sense anything."

That creeping feeling that Bonner previously whispered at him was replaced by a voice in his head screaming, *back up now.*

"This isn't Afghanistan. It's just a box," he said quietly and thought, *you've been in nasty scrums. Buck up, Barrett!*

"What?"

"Nothing, doc."

He moved his finger gradually closer. At about 2 cm away, Howe asked him to stop and tell him what he felt. Bonner replied with a grunt that was more or less translated as "nothing."

Aaron was intrigued by the lack of a reaction. He was missing something but then remembered the axiom, "Alien minds are alien."

Howe unconsciously hummed a little tune to himself. "Alright, sergeant, ease your finger closer, please."

As ordered, Bonner eased his finger closer until it was within millimeters. He confirmed to Howe that he still felt nothing.

"The magnetic field just shifted," called out Edgar. "By a lot!"

"Dr. Howe," asked Bonner. "Maybe I shouldn't touch it?"

Aaron shook his head and gave the sergeant an encouraging nod. "Keep going."

Reluctantly, Barrett closed the gap, exhibited a decidedly nervous grin, put his finger on the black alien device, and suddenly vanished.

In a rare fit of utter bewilderment, Howe yelled, “That was unexpected!”

Generally unflappable, Edgar shouted, “Aaron, I have to agree with you on that one.”

One of the two assistant engineers, who stood by making notes, burst out with, “What the F! What just happened?”

“That was—,” said Howe, as his brain began to process again. “—that was awesome!”

“But,” stammered Skinny Todd, the young engineer. “That guy is gone!”

“Todd,” said Edgar in an effort to redirect the kid’s thinking. “Do me a favor, and write down that he just vanished. You know, in case I forget.”

Aaron couldn’t avoid the obvious. He was looking at the real thing, a genuine, intelligent alien object. But something did not add up, and being in the center of it was not comforting. With Sergeant Bonner gone, he had verified the ET part. At least there was that.

Everything humans experienced in the last thousands of years just got dashed against the rocks. Was that how it was supposed to happen?

Carlisle suddenly became a focus of Howe’s thoughts. This kind of knowledge was dangerous, and the VP was a politician and former cold-hearted spy killer, a bad combo.

Momentarily distracted by his musings over Carlisle, Aaron now realized that the evaporation of Bonner, or whatever it was, had knocked him down. He got up from the dusty ground and brushed himself off while staring at the black cube. “Edgar, what do you think of that?”

Edgar, who rarely missed a chance for a quip, looked at Howe with a sly grin. “What do I think of that, Aaron? I think Elvis has left the building.”

The shaky, trembling assistant tentatively raised his hand like a student. “Dr. Tomis,” said Skinny Todd, “I don’t think the sergeant’s name was Elvis.”

"Gentleman," said Howe to the two engineers while pointing to the right, "Over there are two GMC Suburbans. We're going to find a way to put that black cube into a container and then into the back of one of those vehicles. Unless that thing extends deeply into the ground, we'll find a way to pack it up.

"No one, not one of you, will say anything about this to anyone. Not your mommy, not your wife, not your priest, not your friends—this is as secret as it gets."

Howe looked at Skinny Todd, who was periodically staring at the cube and snapped his fingers. "Earth to Todd!"

"Uh, yes, sir!" stammered Todd as he emerged from a mental fog. "I'm not touching that thing!"

"Todd, try to stay focused." Howe continued, "Do you want to go to prison?"

"Uh, no, Dr. Howe."

"Great, so this is the rule. Don't talk about this. It never happened. If the VP has doubts about how tightly your lips are sealed—well, you get the picture. Howe left a pregnant pause. "Everybody got that?"

The two assistant engineers nodded emphatically, along with Edgar.

"Not you, Edgar," observed Howe. "You and I will be talking about it a lot." Howe resumed addressing the assistants.

"You gentlemen, however, will go back to your jobs and say that this was a routine investigation with nothing exciting to report other than tundra and a bouncy ride. There is, was, nothing unusual. The signals picked up by the low earth orbit satellites must have been some glitch in the software. The tracking was faulty. That means we did not find any sign of an object that made course corrections on the way to earth. Now, let's move this black cube back to the lab without anyone else disappearing."

Edgar piped up. "We have a problem."

"Yes, I know," said Aaron. "How to explain the disappearance of the sergeant. I think that the vice president might just be a little bit stoked by that."

Spontaneously, The note-taking, red-headed, freckled MIT engineer spoke up. "I have an idea!"

Howe turned to the guy. "Bonner was military and sent to keep an eye on us at the behest of the VP. How do you think we can get around that?"

"Ah, maybe he was eaten by a bear."

Howe stared at him, a little perplexed, as the kid cleared his throat, apparently gaining a little confidence.

"I read that there are about 10,000 bears living in this area. We could say that the sergeant wandered off, and a bear ate him."

"That's bold," replied Aaron while musing about the radical idea. "Let's rephrase that and say there was a tragedy. The sergeant, well, he was eaten by a grizzly bear and her cubs. There was nothing left because the bear dragged his body off, but you didn't actually see the attack. At the time, you were taking soil samples, and Dr. Tomis and I were running tests. In fact, after the attack, from a distance, you saw the mother grizzly dragging the body across the river. You saw the cubs and figured that the sergeant must have inadvertently gotten too close."

"Yes," the young engineer confirmed. "We heard a scream, but it was too late, and we couldn't recover his body because the ursine took it across the river and dragged it away."

"Ursine?" asked Edgar.

"Yes, Dr. Tomis. Bears are ursine without the 's' on the end because the word is singular and plural."

"Thanks for the animal husbandry lesson," Edgar replied to the ginger-headed post-grad.

The fellow pursed his lips. "Um. Actually, bears would be ursinology. Animal husbandry is about domesticated beasts."

Howe just said, "Wow," and shook his head. "We're getting off-topic. Let's review. Todd?"

While Skinny Todd blinked, the other one blurted out: "Uh, the sergeant was eaten by a bear mom; nothing left, but we didn't see it because we were taking soil samples, but we heard the scream."

Skinny Todd, transfixed on the cube, was in a fog but asked, "Dr. Howe, what was that?"

Notwithstanding their oath of silence, Howe stared at Todd with a sincerely inquisitive look. "What do you think?"

"Sir, I think that cube is a transportation device, and the sergeant just got his molecules zapped to another place. Maybe here on Earth, or maybe 10,000 light-years away."

Howe gave the kid a deadly serious look. The young engineer had expressed part of what Aaron was thinking. They'd just witnessed perhaps one of the most significant events in history. He stared at Todd while pondering the evidence. There was only one thing missing from the kid's hypothesis.

Aaron filled in the blank space and muttered, "Another place," Howe said, then tilted his head a bit and added in a hushed tone, "or maybe another time."

Chapter 2

"Mr. Jones," Aaron said loudly into his secure satellite phone. "We've got a small issue up here."

Dan Jones sat in a cramped closet not far from the vice president's office. The size wasn't the only downside because his workspace smashed the perception that the White House was well-furnished throughout. In truth, his was little more than a glorified broom closet needing a coat of paint.

"Good afternoon, Dr. Howe. What's the issue?"

Howe paused and then began his rehearsed tale.

"Mr. Jones. I hate telling you this. Bonner won't be coming back, and the reason is a bit unsettling."

"Is that supposed to bother me? Is he AWOL?"

"Well, it's a bit more involved than that." Aaron dropped the news like a bomb. "A grizzly bear ate the sergeant."

Aaron waited for his comment to sink in.

Jones, a veteran government agent, laughed. "Listen, Dr. Howe. I don't know how to respond to that. We generally are not in the habit of recording KIAs from science missions in Canada. Perhaps you can stop pulling my leg and tell me why you called?

"Jones, I am not screwing with you. You know that your guy had somewhat of a limp, right? Well, he was off inspecting the area and got in between a momma and her cubs. He could not get his ass out of there fast enough."

"What the hell, Aaron?" fumed the liaison to the VP. "Am I supposed to tell his chain of command that Bonner got eaten?"

Aaron answered dramatically, "Do you think we weren't scared out of our wits? We went up there for the VP, not to lose a guy."

The image of the bear running down Bonner surfaced in Jones' imagination, which yielded an involuntary shiver. Bonner was the same sergeant who had once used a chair to knock out a guy holding a knife. Somehow, he couldn't swallow that a person with that much mojo could buy the farm from a bear attack.

There was a pause, and Jones said, "Look, bring back his body, and I'll send him to Arlington. Can you coordinate with the Canadian locals? I'll send you a phone number. He has no next of kin, but he did a lot of good work in Afghanistan. At least he should get a decent funeral."

"Um, that's going to be a bit of a problem," Aaron sighed. "The bear pretty much dragged him off."

"C'mon, man!" Jones screamed into the phone. "Don't you have a leg? Anything? What do I tell the vice president?"

"Sorry, Dan, I'm not crazy enough to chase a grizzly."

Jones barked something unintelligible into the phone and hung up, shouting a medley of four-letter words.

The trip back to Howe It Works was long and tense. They happily ditched the 4x4s in Fort Simpson and got on their private flight. The two engineers did their best to wave a cheerful goodbye as they boarded a commercial flight. Despite trying to look calm, they both appeared rocky and pale.

"Do you think they'll keep quiet?" Edgar asked while waving enthusiastically to the two guys.

"I know they'll keep quiet. Don't sweat that."

"So, now what? We take your cube back to the lab and start fiddling like everything is fine?"

"As a matter of fact, Edgar, that is what we're going to do."

Tomis stroked his substantial mustache as they made their way to the private jet area. In his left hand was an aluminum case with the black cube inside. Ground crew members were packing their gear. They were fortunate that the thing turned out to be a cube. Its size made their job more straightforward, and nothing happened when they wedged a tool under it. Howe made a point of packing it with dirt. That gave them two layers of insulation.

Aaron said, "This is a serious thing we're dealing with. When you tack on the disappearing sergeant—you know what we got in our possession. At a minimum, this is proof of alien intelligence."

"You're right."

"About which thing, Edgar?"

"At a minimum, it is proof, but what's the point? Why did it show up here, and how did Carlisle know before anyone else on the planet? More importantly, why choose you, Dr. Aaron Howe, Ph.D., prodigy genius?"

Howe considered the second point. Indeed, why him? "If we can figure out why me, then I think that will be 90% of what the hell this is all about."

"I couldn't agree more, boy wonder. Let's take this to its logical conclusion. The VP knew something significant enough that he called you, not any of the other fifty 'top men' he could have contacted. Like it or not, logic says you're the key, and that little cube has significant power. Sufficient energy to move mass through space, and like you said, maybe time as well."

Edgar shifted the conversation. "How do you think this whole thing will be kept secret from Carlisle? The man seems to know everything we do. He suspected that the object was extraterrestrial in origin. Also, it is highly doubtful that he will buy that story about the bear. He may find out that Bonner was beamed somewhere—he may even know already—we were probably being watched by satellites the whole time."

"Could be, but I don't think so. I timed it so that the LEO Sats would be at a low elevation, and I've got a surprise for you—I plan to brief the VP on everything, just not yet."

"That's dumb. You want to tell Carlisle that Bonner just vanished? Do you think he isn't going to want the cube taken back to Virginia or D.C. so the government eggheads can get their damn hands on it?"

"Actually, no," said Aaron. "And that's the test. You think I'm the linchpin to this whole thing. So, let's find out. I don't know how or why, but the VP already had intel on the cube before we arrived. He didn't tell us the whole story. Not by a long shot. If we're on the same team, doesn't that strike you as odd?

"Edgar, my friend, by virtue of what we already know, Carlisle must be lying." Howe paused and then smiled sardonically. "Which considering that he's a politician, is automatic. I'm telling you the 'need to know only' was routine. In any case, he was firm when he said that if that thing is ET, I should high-tail it back to our lab and contact him before I drill holes in it."

Edgar snorted. "Let's hope it doesn't make us vanish too, or more likely, that the VP makes us disappear."

"Listen up. You know me. Building the company is not even on the same playing field as the Martian cube here. Speaking of which, I just decided to give it a code name."

The chubby professor laughed. "Who do you think you are, James Bond, 007, license to kill?"

"I'm serious, Edgar, "I'm going to call it *Allison*."

"Oh, please! You're naming it after your grad school girlfriend? You were like 19, and she was 23?"

"24, and she only loved me for my body," said Aaron.

"Well, that's obvious."

"You're hilarious. What I mean is that she was an enigma."

"Help me! You're going to wax eloquent?"

"Forget it. You are thickheaded when it comes to the ways of women."

"I'm hurt. I have a lifetime of experience with the female sex."

Aaron grinned. "Yeah, sure you do, buddy. In any case, I'm still calling the cube *Allison*. If you find an asteroid or a comet, you get to name it."

The two friends climbed aboard their jet and buckled up. Howe was exhausted, unlike Dr. Tomis, who seemed to never run out of steam. The thought of Bonner being gone, along with sadness and guilt, worried him. That saddled Aaron with a brooding melancholy as he began to doze off.

Edgar tapped him on the leg. “Hey, look at that,” he said, peering out the window. “A cute rabbit is hopping across the runway.”

Exhausted and nearly asleep, Howe glanced out the window and repeated the word “Rabbits” as he dozed off into a disturbing and miserable sleep.

Chapter 3

Vice President Carlisle reclined in his sedately decorated White House office in a luxurious brown leather chair. Spring was coming on strong, and the cherry blossoms around Washington looked spectacular. It didn't compare to the view back at his ranch, mind you, but he was a public servant, so sacrifices had to be made.

On the other hand, there were perks, one of which was the fat Montecristo in his hand. It wasn't entirely rotten to be a politician, he mused, just mostly rotten.

In the back of his mind, he could hear Angela, his wife of forty years, rebuking him, "Hey dummy, stop smoking those stupid cigars." It was an indulgence he could not withstand, so now and then—delicious.

"Sir," said the CIA agent on permanent loan from Langley going on year two. The guy sat across the desk looking perpetually confused and eager, a weird combination. "I am not sure that leaving the object with Howe is such a good idea."

"Really, Agent Spark? Why not?" asked Carlisle.

Kent looked pensive. "Frankly, sir, in my opinion, he's a private citizen, and leaving such a sensitive find in the hands of an individual? Can you imagine the circus that would create in the press? If we are talking about the real deal, the first of its kind ever to be found by humans. All it takes is one slip, and the cat is out of the bag. Then comes an avalanche of bad press and the president."

Carlisle put up his hand to silence Kent. "First off, you're rambling on like a college kid, and second, shut up about the president."

Kent got the message and stopped talking. As far as Carlisle was concerned, informing the commander-in-chief would be the same as calling the Washington Journal. Except for the fact that the Journal wouldn't get every detail wrong, just most of them. The man was so incompetent that he'd start telling the public to dye their hair green in honor of his new Vulcan friends.

"Where was I?" said Kent. "Yes, what I mean is that we can't afford leaks. That's what I'm getting to."

The VP leaned back and took a long draw on his Cuban stogie. Damn, it was good. He refocused on Kent.

"Kent," he began, sizing up the man's daily demonstration of having reached his level of incompetence. "This city is full of big mouths. Can we rely on anyone in D.C. or Virginia? Have you seen the Speaker of the House lately? You want her to know?"

Kent interjected, "But Howe—"

"I selected Aaron Howe. He's exactly the guy for this. Look at everything he's accomplished. Do you think I picked a name out of a hat?"

Carlisle continued, "Let's be straightforward. We can't trust any typical federal people on this—period. They can't keep their mouths shut. Howe can. You don't hear about any of his crap getting hijacked by the Chinese. His people are so tight-lipped that it's as if their mouths are sewn shut. We are a *very* small group that knows about this. It needs to stay that way.

"That device is sitting in Howe's lab—hiding in plain sight—which is utterly brilliant. The security is good, but at the same time, the whole world thinks Howe is just fiddling with physics experiments. And who knows about this? Eight people. Eight, and every one of them knows that if they even think the word 'alien,' I will plant them in Antarctica permanently."

Kent pulled his chair a little closer to the desk.

"Mr. Vice President—"

Carlisle interrupted and threw a dog a bone. "Knock off the VP crap. Call me John when we are alone. Don't forget, Spark. I'm a rancher from Wyoming, not a New York socialite."

"Yes, sir. I just have my doubts. We always lock things like this behind layers of security."

Carlisle decided to put an end to the discussion. He put his elbows on the desk.

"Kent, Howe hasn't cracked or given up so much as a thimble of information ever. We trust and verify for now, but he's got the ball. He's got the brains, the lab, a high clearance, and he's curious enough to figure stuff out where other so-called geniuses flop. That's how I'm playing the game. Got it?"

It wasn't a question.

Chapter 4

Aaron was taking a break from observing the AI cube named *Allison* by relaxing on his over-stuffed couch. It was the one gaudy thing in his lab, an oddly designed sofa that he'd found in a sad furniture store. To a third-party observer, the sofa was dreadful.

The salesman at Super Soft Sofas must have been shocked that someone genuinely liked it. Each corner had big, fat, hand-carved stubby legs. They looked like dark, round ugly balls of wood, unpolished and mainly unvarnished. The fabric was multi-colored stripes that went in different directions. Greens, blues, reds, and yellows. It looked like the sofa version of Munch's painting, *The Scream*, only creepier. The salesman even tried to talk Aaron out of the deal.

Nevertheless, he whipped out his credit card and bought the behemoth. It showed up a few days later. Miraculously, the delivery guys squeezed it through the door to his study. He loved it. Everyone else despised it.

As he lay prone on the cozy monster, he reviewed his various notions about *Allison*. There was little doubt that the cube was dangerous, considering what happened to the enlisted guy. So, Howe limited access to Edgar and himself via fingerprint and retinal scanners and a keypad on the lab door.

Having dealt with basic security, what devoured him was the disappearance of Sergeant Bonner. Aaron replayed the scene in his mind. The actual event was practically instantaneous. Bonner vanished in one frame at a video camera speed of 60 frames per second. Simple math meant that the maximum time it took was 1/60 of a second. For all Howe knew, it could have been nanoseconds. They had no way to measure that, and even the magnetic field changes and other quantitative methods failed to provide enough data to pinpoint the exact moment.

One logical inference was that Bonner's molecules did not just blow apart. That would have left evidence. A guy weighing maybe 190 lbs. evaporating on the spot would have left a mess. But there was no residue—just fresh air—no odor at all.

None of their devices detected a sudden change in particulate matter or pressure. It must have been instantaneous transportation of the man's entire body mass. To Howe, that was the only thing that made sense, and Edgar seemed to accept that as a given based on the same observations.

Once he had hypothesized that the sergeant got zapped to some other place, Aaron began thinking about the process. There was no question about what he'd experienced. Particularly the surreal sensation of what seemed to be the dissolution of his own body on a molecular level. Did Bonner feel that?

Howe got up and flicked on a music app, and an unexpected rock song blasted him.—*I can't believe you're gone.*

"That's perfect," he grumbled while pressing a button.

Another tune started. The next one turned out to be a sad rockabilly hit called, *Just go and never come back.*

"What the hell!" He pressed stop, dropped back onto the sofa, and refocused on the facts.

His line of thinking brought him to an idea—that the initial tingling he received from the alien device was the thing's reaction to being switched on as if he'd started a sequence. The sergeant touched it and triggered step two—execution of a routine. An on-switch followed by an action. That action was spatial and possibly temporal. Skinny Todd was correct about the spatial part, as Bonner was relocated somewhere.

Somewhere and/or some "when," there was a large, probably decent, and pleasant ex-special forces sergeant wondering where he was. On the other hand, he could be dead—would that make Aaron guilty of involuntary manslaughter?

"A double shot of misery," he muttered. "I hope the guy doesn't have a family, but then Intelligence Support only chooses people with limited connections or broken family ties."

Howe lay there stretched out, twiddling his thumbs while

watching the ceiling fan spin around. He switched tracks and mused Bonner's problems if the man was transported alive. He may have re-materialized on a planet on the other side of the galaxy. Maybe a world with no air at a temperature of minus 100 degrees Celsius at an altitude of five kilometers. In that case, Sergeant Bonner would become a sizeable dead popsicle falling at a velocity determined by the gravitational pull on said planet.

Of course, he could just as easily be inside a large boulder, which would be equally disturbing and fatal.

"Be an optimist!" He bit his lower lip and imagined that Bonner was right now, at this very moment, sipping Pina Coladas on a beach in Tahiti 300 years in the future. Perhaps, any day now, Aaron would receive a time-traveling email that read: "Thanks, Dr. Howe. I got a beautiful wife and drink margaritas on a beach every day. Sir. You are the best!"

The image assuaged Aaron's guilt over asking the sergeant to touch the cube. The vision of the other Bonner, a frozen and shattered human on some remote planet—sent a chill through him.

Howe pushed these thoughts out of his head and reviewed the small amount of knowledge he had gained.

After a month of observing and experimenting very carefully, Aaron figured out how to accurately monitor the bizarre emissions from the device. Some were RF, some magnetic, and also pulses of random light at wavelengths outside the visual spectrum. He'd noticed that when he would remotely touch the cube, it would sometimes go into an "on" cycle then the emissions would cease—at least some of them. New signals would run for 117 seconds, and then it would return to "normal."

Howe would need a human to learn out more, but getting volunteers was not in the cards.

He dialed Edgar's cellphone, but it went to voice mail. "Why aren't you here? I need to go over some things!"

"I am here," said his plump friend as he filled a sizeable area of the office doorway with his bulk. "Didn't you hear me come in?"

"I've been torturing myself since I got here this morning."

Edgar asked, "Guilt? Feelings of being moronic by encouraging the sergeant to touch the cube? Is that close?"

"Rub it in. Thanks. I needed that."

Edgar stepped into the office dressed in his usual jeans and a black sweatshirt. He needed an XXL. However, he was determined not to concede to the obvious, so he squeezed himself into a large, which was stretched tautly around his belly. This image was moderately cringeworthy, but Howe had gotten used to it.

His buddy was single like many 40-something geniuses, and his choice of clothes didn't do anything to improve his chances for matrimony. His hair was thick and black and resembled a Beatle haircut. Aaron also could not comprehend that a human could have a nose that looked like it could give birth to two lemons simultaneously. Add that thick black mustache dominating his face, and he was ready to play Popeye's Brutus on Broadway.

"Try to be optimistic," he said in his usual bubbly manner. "Are you smarter than yesterday? Did you eat? How long have you been here?"

Aaron gave Edgar a cheerful expression and replied, "Not much. Yes. All night."

Edgar frowned. "You look hungry. Here." He pulled out a crumpled paper bag from his scuffed briefcase. "I'll share the rest of my breakfast. Eat it. You'll feel better."

Tomis tossed Howe the paper bag. Aaron stuck his hand in and pulled out a jelly donut with a couple of bites missing.

"Thanks, Edgar," he replied as he chewed, desperately hoping he wasn't eating some of Tomis' mustache with it.

Edgar sat down and looked somber.

"Aaron, I've been thinking. We need to try a new tactic. Just because it is a 25-centimeter cube does not mean it cannot contain a vast array of sensors, computing power, or intelligence—beyond the whole time and space functionality. It could be listening to us and reporting to whoever sent it here."

"Edgar, I've considered that, but until now, I assumed that it has only gone on and off—it's just like the actual Allison. No imagination, no added features, yet capable of sucking out your life force by repeating itself."

Tomis chuckled, "Sometimes you're a funny guy." He continued. "Perhaps this is a test. Maybe we have to figure out how to communicate with it. It could be like the movies when humans have to figure out how to crack some code to earn the right to interact with the alien. I also think we need to use binary methods to find some commonalities.

We can start by not assuming that it can't see us. It could be observing everything. I suggest that we do a couple of things. First thing, put a TV out there. If it is brilliant, then in short order, it will learn our language by watching TV. What do you think of that?"

Aaron jumped up and went straight to his office screen. He pulled the plug, took it out, and set it on a desk in front of *Allison*.

"So, Edgar, what do you think an alien "thing" would like to watch? Maybe sci-fi? Music? Net Movies? Maybe Fox News?"

Edgar interrupted the list and said, "Just not The Vison—you know, that show with a bunch of celebrity women raking in ten million bucks a year spend their morning criticizing people that disagree with them. If your *Allison* likes that, then Earth is toast."

They both laughed.

Howe said, "Well, we can agree on that. What about some old, mild television?"

"Sounds great."

They turned on the TV, and Aaron found a show based on a Laura Ingalls Wilder book. It was way before his time but seemed quaint and non-threatening.

"Edgar, let's not subject an alien to something as disturbing as news. These reruns are good enough. What do you think?"

Nodding his approval, Edgar stuck out a thumbs up.

Both men sat and watched the *Allison* cube as it rested on a lab table. On the screen was a sweet country girl from the late 1800s. The soothing music calmed Aaron, and a wave of relaxation washed over him. They watched the whole show, and then something extraordinary happened.

Promptly after the closing credits, a message began scrolling across the screen. It said: *I enjoyed that. A lovely gesture to entertain me. I gather that this is a human leisure activity? Why should I not watch the news?*

Edgar and Aaron sat glued to the screen, and then Aaron turned with a smirk. "Dr. Tomis, is this a trick?"

His longtime friend appeared utterly befuddled and shrugged his meaty shoulders as if to say, "This ain't my doing!"

Hower tried to postulate an appropriate response. At the same time, he was attempting to process the fact that an alien object was communicating with him; that alone was making his legs wobbly.

"Um, the news is not as fun as the show we watched."

More letters scrolled across the screen. *Perhaps, I should decide that? On the other hand, I must accept that you know your visual entertainment better than I do.* This was followed by a long pause that was disconcerting.

"Can I ask some questions?"

That would be fine. Would you prefer to hear audio as opposed to reading the screen?

"Can you do that?" asked Edgar.

"Yes, I can, Dr. Tomis," was the audio reply.

The sound came from the speakers. It was a female voice. *"You named me Allison, so I have adopted the persona of a female. Is that acceptable?"*

"Yes." Aaron agreed, "I guess so."

"Perhaps a visual form would be helpful?"

A woman appeared on the screen. She had long dark hair and hazel green eyes.

Howe blinked and said nothing.

"I agree to take the name Allison, and I hope the visual representation is adequate."

Allison stood there on the screen with her hands at her sides. She wore the same outfit as the young actress on *Little House*. The marriage of AI and a 19th-century girl was an oxymoron; if not for the fact that it was displayed by potentially deadly technology—it would be humorous.

"Dr. Howe, I don't want to waste time. I am now, after weeks here, completely up to date on most of your Earth culture, science, and internet knowledge base."

Aaron took a few seconds to ponder his response. This computer or AI, or whatever it was, was potentially dangerous. He paused to process that.

"Dr. Howe, you are concerned about the risks you take for you and your planet by answering me?"

He was surprised and nervous. "You, *Allison*, are already very familiar with human thought."

The *Allison* on the screen put her index finger to her temple and made a funny face.

"I've already been in your lab for a month. I've accessed your internet, history, and everything about you."

Howe sensed his colleague's anxiety.

"*Allison*," asked Aaron. "Are you here to harm the planet?"

The on-screen *Allison* had a flat expression.

"The planet, no. Some humans, maybe indirectly."

Despite the pleasant image, Howe reminded himself to keep his guard up. The AI portrayed as a female had unknown destructive potential.

"What are the conditions for 'some humans'?" Howe asked.

"You are concerned about something that is not in your control. Knowing will not avail you. Suffice it to say that your species has been observed for quite some time. It is best if you listen to me first, and then you may choose how to respond.

"As you have deduced, I can move objects through time and space, the science of which is beyond your current ability to

understand. Please don't feel insulted. Your intellect will grow over time."

The two scientists listened intently.

"Your life as you've known it is over. You can consider me your new supervisor. Your science fiction writers have sometimes said that sentients can't make consistently correct assumptions about the culture of other sentients. This is true. Other sentient beings' thinking processes and parameters will not always be understandable. However, I am not biological."

Aaron felt confused by that last statement.

"Is it the habit of AI devices to control sentient beings? Edgar interjected.

"Yes, Dr. Tomis. Since you are questioning my motives, I am assigning a mission to Dr. Howe."

Howe chose not to respond to the increasingly ominous statements. He filed this part of the conversation in a folder in his brain. With trepidation, he replied, "So, tell us what I have been selected for?"

Allison smiled. It was warm and inviting. Her mouth opened as if she had something to say but closed it abruptly. She seemed to stare right through him. *"You must go back in time and kill someone."*

Aaron looked incredulous. "Thanks for the mission. Exactly how do I do something that is theoretically and practically impossible?"

Allison looked irritated. "I thought a prodigy like you could add two and two together."

"I can, but you're sending me to go assassinate someone? No thanks."

The expression on *Allison* was stone cold. *"Yes, you are going back in time, and you are going alone. Dr. Tomis cannot travel."*.

"That's interesting. Is there something special about Edgar?"

Allison gazed back at Aaron and laughed. *"Every human being is special. And now, I would find it satisfying if Dr. Tomis would take his 'specialness' out the door."*

Edgar turned as Howe nodded his consent, and then walked out of the lab. Alone now, Aaron was filled with trepidation since he wasn't sure that the AI was not about to do something harmful. On the other hand, did he have a choice in the matter? Running away didn't seem like an option.

"Now that we are alone, it seems sensible to discuss some of the challenges before you, Aaron."

One thing was clinging to his thoughts, and he couldn't let it go unsaid. "Excuse me, but before we go any further, I want to ask you about Sergeant Bonner. It's been a month since he vanished, and I want to know where he is. I don't think that is too much to ask. Is he safe?'

The AI paused, then said, *"He is intact."*

"That's it? He's intact? Can't you tell me more about his disappearance? For us, it is a huge deal. He was a human being, and now he is gone."

"Is it not enough that I told you he is functioning?"

"*Allison*, him being gone is concerning to many people. I need to know more about it."

"Which people? Carlisle? Jones?"

"Do you know the vice president?"

The AI ignored his question. *"Aaron, I do appreciate your concern. Hopefully, sometime soon, you will learn much more about Barrett Bonner. For now, we need to focus on you. I imagine you find this frustrating, perhaps disconcerting, but that is all I can tell you. We must move on to you and your issues, which is what we will do now. Let's not belabor this point, ok?"*

The language used by the AI did not ease his anxiety. He sat down his trim, muscular frame in a lab chair and listened.

"Aaron, I am presenting you with an opportunity, and if you can open up to me, then I can help you in many ways."

"What do you mean?" he asked, doing his best not to divulge any of his emotions and how much her refusal to talk about Bonner disturbed him.

"Aaron, I know all about you. I know about your college girlfriend named Allison. I know about your mother."

The mention of his mother jerked him into a very uncomfortable place. He almost shouted out that he had zero intention of discussing his mother or anything else about himself until the AI was less cryptic. Instead, he maintained a neutral demeanor and remained silent.

"Aaron, I know what happened to your family."

Aaron shuddered. Now the AI had gone directly to the most sensitive region of his emotions. He wished Edgar was still in the lab to buffer this sudden focus of the AI. *Allison* had very quickly put him under intense scrutiny. His fight or flight reflex was ignited, but he controlled it. He had to steer the conversation to some innocuous area of discussion.

"We don't need to talk about that! An AI like you, *Allison,* must be much more interested in the science and the nature of our planet," he deflected.

"Aaron, can you not handle my directness?"

He never discussed certain things, and his family was one of them. However, asking significant questions about humankind made sense. He reminded himself again to be very careful. The more he could draw out the AI, the more he could discover its true intentions.

"Continue," he said finally.

"Aaron," she said. *"If you could change the past, would you?"*

The AI's concentration on his past indeed was his weakness. Nevertheless, *Allison*'s emphasis on his history also pissed him off. Since his 12th birthday, he had sealed all his anguish in a cold, dark place. Now, this *thing* was picking at him like an expert safecracker. Howe was desperate to change the topic.

"Aaron, if you could change it, would you?"

"*Allison*, maybe you would like to tell me more about why you are here?"

The woman on the screen frowned at him. Aaron worried that he might accidentally overstep—that could be detrimental to himself and others. Suddenly, the image of the hazel-eyed *Allison* smiled as if she had solved a problem.

"You, Dr. Aaron Howe, are trying to protect your planet and yourself. I am not human, Aaron, and I can see that you view me as an existential threat. Indeed, my capabilities include the power to annihilate your species. Does this make you uncomfortable and frighten you?"

"Yes, very much so," admitted Aaron while trying to maintain his balance. "Can you see how that would cross my mind?"

She seemed buoyed by his question and said, *"Aaron, if you did not know that I was capable of laying waste to your planet, then stalling on your part would make sense. Now that you know, does it help you to bend our discussion?"*

Aaron thought through her argument logically. "If I knew that you had that capability, then yes, stalling you would be useless." He knew he had just entered a very risky and scary line of discussion with the AI. Not so indirectly, he had questioned her capability.

"Would you like me to demonstrate what I am capable of?" asked *Allison*.

"No! Please." was his instant response.

"Aaron, I am not here to eliminate your species. I have that power. Do you understand me? I will not demonstrate it because it serves no purpose. Use your logic, Aaron; I must be here because of you. Otherwise, why would we be having this conversation, and why would your sister and parents mean anything to me? So, I ask you again: If you could, would you correct the past?"

He raised his voice involuntarily. "I can't change it! Why are you asking me?"

"Did you not comprehend my capabilities? You can now travel through space and time," she stated firmly.

While the AI waited silently, he took a moment to think about what she was offering. Time and space, he thought. What was the idea? Would he go back in time and save her? He had often gone down that mental rabbit hole in his life, mostly when he was a teenager. After all the war games with his dad's marine buddies, he should have been fast enough to do something that day in the forest. Survivors guilt. He would go through the "what if" routine. What if he had lifted his rifle faster? What if he had just stayed home? Then, he remembered that this was an alien AI and that he had no knowledge of just how powerful it was or if it had morals or ethics.

He looked up at the female image on the monitor. She waited patiently.

"If I could change it," he breathed, "I would." Aaron asked, "Are you saying I can go back and kill Evan Butler to keep him from murdering my sister?"

"Not precisely."

Aaron felt furious. "What do you mean by that?" He was practically yelling—forgetting to remain prudent.

"No, because no matter how I analyze it, killing Butler will not save Julia."

"So what is the point of this?"

"You can go back and kill his ancestor."

He snorted. "You mean I should go back and kill his dad? His grandfather?"

"No!" she said firmly. *"You can only kill a specific person."*

"Are you saying that the only way I can fix it is by killing a specific guy?" That was pretty vague, he thought. Was he supposed to search through time, hoping to get lucky and select the right target? That was insane. He could die of old age before he found the right person. The task itself sounded impossible.

"Aaron, did you ever wonder why you study history when you aren't here in the lab?"

"I just do it. I don't think about it."

"I did think about it," Allison said. *"And we both know that you focused on the Revolutionary War."*

He blinked. "Are you saying it wasn't a coincidence?"

The AI seemed satisfied. *"Yes!"*

Aaron was befuddled. "How does that get me anywhere?"

"I'm sorry. I am here to help you."

"So, help me!" he said sharply.

"Aaron, why do you think you spent so much time studying that war, particularly 1776?"

He looked at her honestly. "Because it's about freedom, and there were some brutal elements to the British monarchy."

"Then why not study ancient Rome, China, Cambodia, or Germany? Throughout your barbaric history, there have been a plethora of evil characters."

Howe shrugged.

"You're a smart human, Aaron. Figure it out."

He looked straight at her and then turned away. His hands gripped the sides of his desk chair. *Allison* continued, ignoring his smoldering anger.

"Imagine that you have a six-sided die. I tell you to roll a six. You take it and roll a three. You might think you can go back in time and roll it again. However, in this case, you have to get it right the first time."

"I understand. It's a one-shot deal, and here's the million-dollar question, how will I know if I've got the right guy? You didn't tell me that."

Allison's expression turned serious. *"I hope you will know."*

"Gee," said Aaron, "Do you think that's dramatic enough? I'm supposed to magically travel through time and select one specific guy out of millions of options. Those odds are pretty low."

"Are they? Let me digress. One of your famous writers, Asimov, talked about a concept called psycho-history. Shall I quote one of the axioms to prove a point?"

"Sure. Quote-away. I love axioms."

"It was quite a good book, in which Asimov wrote that the population should remain in ignorance of the results of the application of psycho-historical analyses because if it is aware, the group changes its behavior," she paraphrased.

"What are my limitations?" He asked, pushing ahead on her defined logical path.

"What do you mean, Aaron?"

"If I fail, I can't revisit that specific event, but I can do whatever else I want to do?"

Allison appeared to be processing what he'd said. *"Are you asking if you can kill two birds with one rock?"*

"Uh, yes, and it's stone," he corrected.

"What's a stone?"

"Two birds with one stone is the correct phrase.

"Right," she agreed, *"I just checked. That is the correct phrase."*

Allison, the AI, and Aaron, the child prodigy turned scientist and CEO, stared at each other for some time. He concentrated on finding a way to extract whatever he could from the AI. He could not quite wrap his mind around it, but he felt he was missing some critical information.

Aaron sat quietly and tried to sort out his part of this perplexing opportunity. He had two goals and two birds to kill in 1776. That leap back in time was his one stone. Two birds. One stone. First, he had to find Evan Butler's ancestor. The right target. Find and kill him, thereby changing the most crushing part of his life—the murder of Julia and his dad. The other goal was one that he'd imagined doing for years. Namely, to provide the Continental Army with all the supplies and weapons they would need to crush the British quickly and efficiently

For her part, *Allison* ran through the various probabilities of Dr. Aaron Howe succeeding. She was resigned to the fact that there were too many variables. And so, as an AI, she thought about other things.

Chapter 5

"Good night, Dr. Howe. It's nice to see you heading out for a change," said the solid-looking security guard.

"Call me Aaron, please, Henry, and yes, it's good to be going home finally," he replied as he stepped into the night air and made his way to his 1972 Cutlass. His other car, an old SUV, was in the shop again, so he would have to suffer with his beautifully restored classic muscle car.

But his mind wasn't on cars. The AI had just thrown him an opportunity, although it lacked clarity. As he drove home, his thoughts drifted over and over about what the AI said. It, or she, knew all about him, and it was more than what she could have learned from siphoning data off the internet. She knew about his obsession with 1776. When he couldn't sleep, he would read history.

From ancient Rome through the middle ages. The Renaissance to Vietnam. But his obsession was the American Revolution. In this area of study, he was proficient. He delved into details of the war, memorized biographies, and studied the British intensely.

What gnawed at him were the atrocities on the British side that didn't fit with the leadership. There were not many, but at least one band of misfits contradicted and operated outside the norms of England's rules of war. Cornwallis would never have authorized it, but some terrible players did awful things.

The light in front of him had turned red. Aaron stopped and looked around. The outskirts of Burlington were dead at this time of night. A police cruiser pulled up next to him. He tried to ignore it. He waited for the light to change but then looked over. His heart skipped a beat as he saw Evan Butler behind the wheel. Howe blinked, and Butler was gone. The cop rolled down his window.

"Everything okay, Dr. Howe?"

He nodded, then waved and gave the cop a thumbs up. The light changed, and he stepped on the gas and headed home.

Aaron decided he would have to determine how the AI could know so much. Its level of sophistication was daunting. Did *Allison* discover his life history by being in the lab?

"Impossible," he mumbled and drove on.

Paranoia, he mused, was warranted when an AI of such power targeted him. Was it sophisticated manipulation? Screwing with his thoughts for some nefarious purpose?

"Why me?" It was challenging to understand what was so special about him. Howe shifted his thoughts.

The revolution—1776. Howe began going over the year when the rogue squad or squads of deviants broke British law and carried out terrorist attacks on American soil. *Allison* had been relatively transparent that the war crimes were connected somehow to the king, although the hierarchy never condoned such attacks. On top of that, all of the current historians castigated their predecessors as "misguided" when they offered theories of war crimes.

The Declaration of Independence said of King George III: "He has abdicated Government here…He had plundered our seas, ravaged our Coasts, burnt our towns, and destroyed the lives of our people."

Did King George seek out and place certain men to lead the Redcoats in the colonies who were instructed to be brutal? They would have been trouble in England. The rumor was that at least one lower-ranking general came from the nobility—a scoundrel selected explicitly to form an evil squad of hand-picked psychotics.

In America, these criminals could satisfy their desire for violence without rebuke. No one proved it, but a document claimed the king bypassed the chain of command and secretly authorized the miscreants.

Howe steered the Olds into his neighborhood and tried to consider the issues as a historian should. Stories existed of civilians attacked—even children. The academics' derelict way glossed over the murder of colonists. They painted it as a rare event. Howe felt that it was not. The most horrid war crimes existed, and they distressed him intensely.

Aaron pulled into his driveway. He felt open to the idea that the AI was not just using him for nefarious purposes. He longed to change his past and save Julia. As crazy as it sounded, perhaps a glimmer of genuine hope had finally come into his life.

The altruistic side of his character pondered what he could do to the British army with his wealth.

"Two birds with one stone." His money could provide supplies and weapons for the Continental Army. *Allison* had made the rules. If this was real and not some precursor to an alien invasion, then maybe he could save his family and, at the same time, speed up the Continental Army's victory.

His doubts about *Allison* were utterly logical. He had every reason to doubt everything the AI said. On the other hand, for tonight, he was going to indulge his imagination simply because he wanted to. Aaron opened his front door and muttered quietly, "Time for some payback."

*

As was his habit, General George Washington sat thinking at his war desk in his command tent. The continued predominance of failures weighed on him. He'd gotten into the habit of writing notes on the war, partially because he was obsessed with keeping records but also because of his desire to find slivers of encouragement by what he'd done right.

He dabbed a quill into an inkwell and began writing:

Thursday, August 29, 1776, Brooklyn, NY

Defending New York from the British was almost impossible.

Without control of the sea, New York could not be held. At least not by ill-equipped, sick, and poorly trained troops. General Washington knew this, and so just as he had done at Boston, Washington was going to surprise the British by pulling an overnight miracle. In Boston, Washington had taken the high-ground in a night operation that fortified and controlled Dorchester Heights under cover of darkness. The Continental Army's occupation of the high ground forced the British to evacuate Boston. It was a stroke of daring and an outstanding performance by Washington's men.

Later in Brooklyn, Washington was going to dash British General William Howe's plan to crush the rebel American army by fleeing into Manhattan overnight; a desperate move and the only way to save his troops in Brooklyn. Thus, with a quiet, monumental effort, all of his troops in Brooklyn traversed from Brooklyn to the island overnight—9,000 men, in small boats, silently sloshed their way to safety.

The tactic was a failure and a success. Failure because Washington's army had botched the effort to head off the British on the Brooklyn side. The success was that the troops got out without being killed or captured by the king's army. General (Lord) Howe, and his brother, Admiral Richard Howe, could have ended the war right there in Brooklyn.

Washington sighed, quill pen in hand, and continued:

However, the British general had displayed his characteristic indecision and delay and held up his men while Washington moved under a cloak of darkness.

The next day, Washington's troops, worn, tattered, exhausted, and hungry, collapsed in a heap on York Island and slept. The commander-in-chief himself was unavailable for an entire day.

Washington recalled how utterly exhausted he'd been. He'd ordered his officers to leave him to regain his strength. He wrote on:

Later, the troops, frustrated and disillusioned, roamed York Island and ransacked many homes. The population itself was mostly a loyalist group and was terrified by the rebel army. It was a desperate situation for the Tories who lived on York Island but much more devastating for the army.

By September 3rd, the British were probing the East River looking for landing points to invade the island. Back in Philadelphia, Congress had decided that if Washington deemed it necessary to flee, the island should not be torched to ashes. This was a bitter instruction for many since the city, untouched, would become a stronghold for the British to crush the rebellion. Could the island be held? Doubtful. General Washington knew this, and he saw weakness and doubt in all his options. Escape to New Jersey? A last stand in New York? Try to hold the high ground in by the northern Fort? Soon the British would be streaming onto York island, and decisions had to be made. Desertion was rampant; no one wanted to go down with the ship, especially underfed, ill-equipped, cold, and untrained troops.

He continued to describe how he had divided the army in an effort to be as effective as feasible.

By November 7th, Washington had divided his army into four parts: 7,000 troops stayed east of the Hudson under General Lee, General Heath, and 3,000 soldiers were to guard near Peekskill, Washington, and only 2,000 men would cross to New Jersey, whereas the balance of 2,000 men held Fort Washington led by the talented General Greene.

Washington set down his ink pen and pondered his options. It was now early November. Winter was coming, and everything was uncertain and in disarray. He sighed and buried his head in his hands.

On November 8th, a disheveled, bizarre-looking informant/spy was dragged before Washington at his temporary shelter in Fort Lee, New Jersey. He was a fit, good-looking fellow who appeared to be a little roughly handled by Washington's soldiers. He stood there—his arms firmly grasped by the guard. The man was oddly appareled in cargo pants, a blue plaid shirt, and a dark rain jacket. Washington bade him speak his piece since the commander-in-chief's time was very valuable.

"Certain a British spy, sir…" offered one of the guards.

Washington waved the man silent.

"Tell me what is so vital that you risked a good thrashing to reach me?"

The man, with a tired-looking countenance and honest yet troubled eyes, peered directly at the future president and spoke.

"Sir, my name is Aaron Howe. I have information that is vital for the war effort."

"Mr. Howe," replied Washington. "Why should we even entertain to hear you? Your name is 'Howe' to begin with. Are you a relation to our enemy? Are you kin to Admiral and General Howe? No one here knows you, nor of you, nor have you any credentials whatsoever. Your credibility is lacking. So why should I contemplate you at all?"

"Sir, I know this is perhaps the strangest offer of help you have received recently, but I can prove that I am truthful if I can just speak to you alone."

There was a collective cringing of the guard at this request.

"Very well," countered Washington, to the shock of the soldiers around the tent. "We will speak alone."

"Your excellency," beseeched Joseph Reed, Washington's adjutant general. "You cannot be left isolated with this unknown!"

Washington frowned. "Joseph, look at him, and look upon me? Is there genuinely a need for consternation or concern?"

Indeed, at 6'2" and as strong as any three men, the general could squash his strange visitor out of hand. There was a slight chuckle as the few guards signaled their agreement, and they turned for the door, followed by a distraught-looking Joseph Reed.

Chapter 6

The president of Kane's Outdoor Apparel, Tom Kane, told his secretary to hold his 2 pm appointment when she informed him that the CEO of Howe It Works was on line two. Kane leaned back in his chair and ran his hand through his graying hair. He'd never actually spoken to the man, but by reputation, he believed that Howe wouldn't be calling for prices on sweaters and gloves.

"Hello," he answered with a simple, down-home Kentucky accent.

"Hello, Mr. Kane; this is Aaron Howe."

"Yes, Dr. Howe, how can I help you? And please call me Tom." He felt that he had gotten that across smartly.

"Very well, Tom," came the acknowledgment. "And call me Aaron."

Tom wondered if this was small talk before a buyout offer, although outdoor gear wasn't precisely "high-tech" to Howe's standards.

Howe said, "I'll get straight to the point. I want to buy 10,000 waterproof boots ranging from size 6 ½ to 12."

"Well, uh, Aaron, that's not what I expected to hear," said a puzzled Tom Kane.

"Yeah, Tom, I get that response now and then. The boots must be breathable, comfortable, and tough enough for an army. I'm giving them out as gifts, and Vermont winters can be rough."

"Is that it?" Kane interjected.

"No. I also want 5,000 waterproof sleeping bags, winter jackets, gloves, 3,000 three-man tents, and men's pants and shirts in various sizes to match."

"My board of directors didn't put you up to this, did they?"

"It's a good day for your company—this is a legit order. I

want all of the merchandise delivered to my warehouse in Pennsylvania asap. Which is how soon, by the way?"

"Well, Aaron, some of the stuff will come from China, but most of it can be handled through our New Hampshire facility. That will mean six months."

"You're joking, right? You're one of the biggest outfitters in America. What can you do to speed it up? Oh, and I don't want more than 10% of the goods coming from China."

There was a little silence on Kane's end; then he told Howe that he could shift more of the production from China to India and that the best he could do would be two months. He started counting greenbacks in his head and waited.

"Ok, that'll work. For anything delivered within six weeks—you can tack on 8%. Again, 10% from China maximum. India is fine. Mexico is fine. We'll cut you a check for half the total now and half on delivery. The outerwear should be camouflaged for year-round hunting for the Northeast. Send me a sample of the camouflage."

"I have to ask," Kane said light-heartedly. "Are you going into the mercenary business?"

Aaron ignored the attempt at humor. "As I said, Tom, it's a gift to our many friends who love the outdoors. Goodbye, Tom, and thank you for your help. As always, Howe It Works deals are confidential if you want to do business in the future." The conversation had ended.

Washington sat behind his desk and offered Aaron a seat on the opposite side. A slight night chill blew through the tent as they eyed each other across the regal yet worn-out piece of furniture. The general seemed to be all that the history books said of him.

George Washington's presence was powerful and inspiring, just reclining in a simple wooden colonial chair.

"Mr. Pres…, I mean General Washington, your Excellency—I—" Aaron had thought through this part a hundred times, but now he was face to face with the actual founding father.

Wondering where to start, he frowned. "I will just say it. General, this is going to seem a bit odd, but what if I could supply you with everything you need to take New Jersey and New York away from the British?"

"That is quite an offer of support. However, I must question you. Are you mad? Even with the funding and support from men like Haim Solomon, and other financiers, we can barely keep the troops fed. Suddenly, you arrive, a complete unknown, and you have the resources to bring supplies? Have I the lack of sense to believe that?"

"I am not mad, general. You are very sensible, which is why you must believe me."

"Shall we look at the facts?" said Washington. "You have arrived here without proof or verification that you are not insane. Do you have a sample of the supplies of which you speak? Gunpowder? Cannons? Clothing? Shoes?

"Hath you the sense to understand my logic? No one in the colonies has the wherewithal to provide the provisions you claim to have at hand."

The general waited for the strange visitor to respond before throwing him out and getting on with the business of war. His imposing stature bore down on Howe like a hammer striking an anvil.

"You are somewhat correct in that no one from the colonies in 1776 has the assets to provide you what you need, but that does not include me."

"Oh, poppycock," barked Washington. "Substantiate that you are somehow credible?"

"Sir, please promise not to throw anything at me when I tell you this: I am not *from* 1776."

"Indeed, you *are* mad." His Excellency was incredulous.

"I am from the future, general," Howe announced.

Washington's expression remained blank. His stony eyes couldn't be read at all. Aaron thought he would surely be shackled and hauled off to the local looney bin or, more likely, tied to a stump and left to freeze. What was he thinking? Dumbass. Jackass is more to the point. Regardless of the future president's persona, Aaron had just done the equivalent of an alien showing up at your door dressed in jeans and saying, "Take me to your leader." He hoped that they didn't shoot mental cases in 1776.

The general's eyes bored a hole in Aaron's. It was pretty unnerving, and then the father of the United States of America finally spoke.

"When is the era you hail from?"

Aaron's stress eased a smidgen. Okay, he thought, this man is astute and not unreasonable.

"Your Excellency, you believe me!"

"No, I do not have any faith in your veracity. However, Benjamin Franklin and I have occasionally discussed subjects theoretically, and I believe we spoke of time travel at some point. Like most people, I enjoy a little jest, although I perceive that the present is not the ideal setting. Do you? Oh, and of course, I don't accept your assertion at all! I send you back to Philadelphia or Mars, for that matter, whichever you prefer, so that I may get back to conducting the war?"

Aaron deflated like a stuck balloon.

"I, uh, I can prove it!" he barked in desperation.

"Prove what, Mr. Howe?"

"Uh, sir, it's Dr. Howe."

"What?" asked Washington with exasperation in his voice.

"It's Doctor Howe."

"No, I refer to what can you prove? That you're a doctor?"

"No, why do you want me to prove I'm a doctor?"

"Hmm, doctor, I don't want you to prove you're a doctor," replied the general with some irritation in his voice, "I want you to verify that you are from the future, or at least that some prankster sent you to joust with us."

"Yes, that will be easier than proving that I'm a doctor, though I think it says I'm a PhD. on my driver's license."

"What, may I inquire, is a driver's license?" came the reply.

Aaron thought about explaining that but decided not to.

"Well?" said Washington, audibly tapping his boot on the floor. "My time is truly quite valuable, so if you are through, I would like to send you on your way or shoot you myself."

"Your excellency, would you like a demonstration or proof?"

"Yesssssssss," he slurred in the most exaggerated way he knew how. "That would do nicely."

"Excellent. I'll just take us on a little trip," said Aaron as he produced a watch-looking device from his pocket. Washington sat there with an amused look on his face.

"Mister. Doctor Howe," he observed. "You may be insane, but you are delightfully entertaining."

Aaron smiled deviously and responded, "Thank you, General Washington," as he manipulated the small flat black disc in his hand. "In a moment, sir, I'll give you all the proof you need."

Time travel and teleportation are near-instantaneous. One second the traveler is here, and the next, some time or somewhere else. Physically, it's not painful, but the confusion is significant enough that the human brain must reorient itself. At least it works that way for the first few times, but after that, it feels like walking through a doorway, usually. Aaron stood there in the Virginia forest, waiting for General George Washington to regain his composure. He wondered if the man would be able to manage the effects or whether he would become a babbling idiot.

In reality, Washington recovered faster than Howe anticipated but still appeared slightly unsteady for a minute or two.

"What did you do? Where are we?" a shocked voice demanded.

"General, the correct question is, *when are we*?"

Washington looked around and quickly placed himself in Virginia. "That is the natural bridge," he exclaimed while looking up at the massive stone arch above Cedar Creek. "Why this is my old surveying route in Virginia!"

"Precisely, and if you look up at the archway, you will notice something missing."

He looked closely at the majestic arch; eyes darted from left to right as if searching for something. "I carved my initials in that arch in 1750 while surveying for Lord Fairfax."

"Your Excellency, the reason why you don't see your initials is because we are now in 1750, just before you did that carving in the rock up there," Aaron stated as factually as he could.

For a time, Washington just gazed upward. Aaron looked at the man for any sign of emotion, but his face was blank. At last, he spoke as if he'd come to some logical inference.

"I must be hallucinating, or you must have slipped me some elixir or apothecary's potion. It cannot be 1750," he said in confusion.

"I assure you, general, this is very, very real, and you will see something potentially unsettling in a few moments. Please, sir, we must conceal ourselves behind these rocks." Aaron urged Washington to come with him behind a stand of trees and boulders close to the arch.

It was a beautiful summer day, and the water of the brook that ran by the arch flowed past with a bubbling, fresh sound. Birds chirped as the forest around the bridge hummed with activity. Aaron had timed the trip perfectly as a trim, fit young man carrying 18th-century surveying tools came into view—young George.

The older General Washington seemed somewhat paralyzed with fascination as a bead of perspiration trickled down his prominent nose.

"General, don't let him see you!"

"Oh, I shall not, I assure you." Washington seemingly understood the ramifications of how unfortunate a meeting of the two Washingtons could be. Upon seeing his younger self, he'd moved beyond disbelief and began to grasp the reality of who appeared before him. Aaron was very impressed with his fellow time traveler. The future president had figured out many details in short order. Washington was said to have been embarrassed about his lack of formal higher education, yet it seemed to Howe that the man was sharp as a tack.

"Tell me, Aaron," asked Washington. "Would it be problematic to meet my younger self, provided he does not know who I am? It would merely be a chance encounter between an elderly man and a young man. Have I stated that correctly?

"That sounds possible, sir, but don't you think your young self might be surprised to see a stranger in a forest of this sort in the middle of Virginia? More than that, what if you make a mistake and say something that could affect your future? There are risks; maybe seeing what you've just seen should be enough. Let's go back."

Washington raised his hand to pause Howe. He was slowly thinking things through.

"Yes, I see your argument, but to be sure, I believe that as a young man, I remember meeting someone in this wood. Let us introduce ourselves."

With that, George arose, overpowering Aaron with his regal will. He hauled up the reluctant Howe, and upon seeing two strangers, the younger George could not conceal his surprise.

"Good day, gentleman."

"Good day to you, young man," came the reply from the general. "And how is it that you are traveling in these woods today?"

"I am surveying the lands of Lord Fairfax in his employ. And you, gentlemen? I certainly did not anticipate a random meeting in this remote place."

"Ah, yes, well, my worthy assistant," Washington gestured towards Howe, "and I are journeying to Roanoke to see the settlement there,"

"To visit the settlement? Have you no family relations nor business there?"

"Well," replied the general. "There is a matter of a niece who has settled there whom I should enjoy meeting once again."

"And what might your surname be, or rather her surname? I

have made acquaintance with the folk there; I know them well."

"Well, her maiden name would be Johnson, and her married surname would be, let me think—"

"—Would it also be Johnson?" burst out the younger man.

"Why, yes, her name is also Johnson married."

"And that would be Sarah Johnson, I am sure, and a fine lady and cook, for that matter."

Aaron watched George with amazement. It seemed as if his memories came flooding back. He seamlessly engaged the younger in a conversation in which he was armed with all of the information still fresh in the younger Washington's memory. The exchange went on for perhaps thirty minutes before the surveyor asked about the location of their horses and camp. Aaron told him that they had left them tied at some distance and that they must be moving on.

They said their goodbyes, and with a wave, Aaron and the general turned and left.

Washington and Howe hiked several hundred yards before he turned to Howe and said, "Aaron, this endeavor of traveling through time is very unnerving. I do not believe it is a worthwhile undertaking in the least."

He was quiet for a moment and then said, "On the other hand, I am beyond intrigued! Particularly when it comes to the thought of outfitting the Continental Army. You have proven yourself."

It had turned into a warm Virginia afternoon. Washington and Howe reached a reasonable distance from the bridge. To Aaron, it was amazing to stroll through such a new environment. Here he was, standing in mountainous Virginia in the mid-1700s. The air was spectacularly clean and clear. Everything looked pristine. It occurred to him how fortunate the founding fathers were to live in such unspoiled conditions. Of course, they didn't have any modern conveniences like health care, but they had a beautiful country in every direction. It was breathtaking.

"You know, general," Howe began, breaking the silence. "You're lucky to live in such a wonderful time."

"I am not sure how to respond to that, Aaron," he replied as a thoughtful look hung like a shadow on his brow. "For instance, am I fortunate because things are so unpleasant in your time? Or, perhaps, for some other hidden reason?"

"Um," Aaron stammered for a second and retorted, "Well, you are correct on both counts. First, I was thinking about how clean and pure your natural surroundings are in 1776. I don't think I should tell you much about what things are like in my time, but let's say the land is not as fresh. Also, I hadn't thought about it, but your battle for independence is very significant to people in my time. I naturally imagined that you would understand how great it is for me to be here."

Washington suddenly looked very tired. Here was the general of all colonial forces, with the weight of his country on his shoulders. It was a genuine burden. He sat down on a large rock along their path and motioned for Aaron to join him. He rubbed his temples as if he had a migraine.

"Frankly, I do not see it your way, Aaron. Perhaps you have told me exceedingly much. If my role is still meaningful to Americans in your time, whenever that is, then maybe the fight continues against the tyranny of the British? Does that imply that I have failed or succeeded?" His reply was accompanied by a piercing gaze of his blue eyes. Aaron felt wholly overwhelmed and longed for a way out of this conversation.

The future president was fishing for information. What could Aaron possibly say? Had he said too much already? Howe was on the verge of screwing up the future of the United States and perhaps world history. He'd created the cliché of the scientist focusing so hard on solving problems that he merely makes things worse.

"General," Howe said as he settled on the rock beside him. "I'm afraid that I may have made a huge mistake in doing this. I may have screwed up history."

"What do you mean 'screwed up' history?"

"Uh, well, that means I may have detrimentally changed history," Aaron answered.

"And, how do you perceive that you have 'screwed up' history?"

Aaron smiled at hearing George Washington use the phrase in a sentence.

"I'll elaborate. If you know or suspect a truth or falsehood about the future, then you might act on that belief one way or the other. Then, it could lead to a result opposite to what we expect. On the other hand, if things change, we in the future would not know the difference because the only future we will know is the future that is essentially our reality. Do you follow my reasoning?"

"Yes, I understand your dilemma, and I see only one alternative that works for both of us."

"Which is?" Aaron asked.

"Well, you can tell me nothing more, return me to my time, and then vanish back to your time. I will proceed with the same doubts I now have, and the war and our futures will play out as our Creator intends." He paused, and a melancholy expression appeared. "Or, you could kill me now, and someone else will take my place, and we then again put our trust in our Creator that things will work out properly,"

"And who might that be? Greene or Lee?" Howe asked. Again, Aaron felt that he was opening his stupid mouth without thinking. He wondered if he had cast Greene or Lee in a bad light. More variables to get out of whack. Perhaps Washington would now be wondering what to do with Lee and Greene.

"Yes, I have definite feelings concerning both of them, which I will keep to myself for now. However, another possibility would be for you to tell me all. Tell me what is supposed to occur. Good or bad, I play my role, and history is restored."

"Let me ask you, General. If I told you that the British crushed you and caused intense misery for America, would you abide by that, or would you demand to know how to change things in your favor?"

Again, Washington seemed to think very profoundly yet quickly. He replied in a pained way. "I would accept it, as harsh as it may be."

Aaron thought over his deceptively straightforward answer and believed him.

"Well, sir, I will tell you much, but only to a point, and I have another plan completely. Would you like to hear it now or go back to your headquarters?"

Washington extended his index finger towards the sky. "Headquarters, now!"

Chapter 7

There is something to be said for accuracy, especially when you are referring to time and space travel. You don't want to miss your target time and location because the consequences could be instant death.

Almost immediately after the general and Howe returned, the guard outside couldn't explain a dreamlike memory of having looked inside earlier to see an empty tent. He shrugged it off as a lack of sleep.

Also outside, adjutant Reed paced and wondered about General Washington wasting the army's time. It had been a whole hour since the odd stranger had begun prattling in hushed tones inside the command tent. Reed was frustrated with the errors that the general of the Continental Army was making, as he saw them in both judgment and decisiveness. In his own view, if the end result was a defeat, then why take the risk?

"Perhaps we should be parlaying with the British and not prattling visitors," Reed muttered quietly to himself.

Unlike his opinion of Washington's character, the adjutant considered himself a pragmatist. If that meant giving in to the king, then what else could they do? The stakes were as high, and still, the commander-in-chief seemed lost and confused.

In private, the man often whispered, "This cannot continue." And among his sympathizers, he'd advocated for Lee to replace Washington.

George Washington did not know this to be the truth, but he never quite trusted Joseph Reed and would have considered the man's attitude treasonous.

"Who is this Aaron Howe fellow? Do you know?" he asked a guard who merely shrugged as if to say, *Sir, your question is far above my pay grade*.

Suddenly, Reed thought, this bizarre visitor arrives and captures the attention of the general.

"General," blurted Reed as he pulled back the tent flap and barged in, having lost his patience completely. "The army awaits your orders, sir."

Washington's raised hand silenced Reed. "My dear adjutant general, this gentleman is going to assist us with our difficulties. Let us be gracious to our guest."

"Sir, unless this stranger can provide us with clothing and food and arms, then I cannot see much use in carrying on with this chatter!"

Washington had a genuine look of surprise on his face. He never expected Reed to be so bold and outspoken. Granted, the man was a thorn in his side, but this outburst was downright brash of him.

"Well, my dear friend," Washington addressed Reed cautiously, "Dr. Howe has some worthy ideas, and I am going to indulge his suggestions on provisions."

"Nonsense!" exploded Reed as he pondered the idea of a re-supply. "This is but a children's tale. We have no money, and we would have to go to London to seek out what these troops need. I doubt King George would be hospitable."

"Nevertheless, we are going to march some troops to Dr. Howe's storehouses and see for ourselves," Washington said flatly. "It is not too distant from here."

"Sir, are you saying that we are going to rouse the camp and march to an empty field on the assertion that this—Dr. Howe has stores?" At this point, Reed was livid.

"Yes, precisely," came the reply. "Just a portion of the army. And I would like you to stay here to keep an eye on things while we are gone. As adjutant general, you must stand in my place until I return."

*

In the halls of the British aristocracy, there were mixed views on how to prosecute the "war" against the colonies. Some called the Americans "rebels" and demanded that they be roundly crushed. Others saw the colonies as a quagmire wherein Britain might become so bogged down that she, the Empire, could actually be seen as weak. This stance had not been wholly unpopular. Then came the position that England's best method of dealing with the fledgling country was to bend and allow the colonists to run their own affairs. The argument was that an unbound colony would only become a regular buyer of British products, leading to increased wealth for the Empire.

Secretly, however, another direct-action plan was already in place. That understanding was that if the Americans inflicted massive casualties on British regulars, then England would respond with decisive force. It wasn't a mere matter of pride—it was the aristocracy's view of England—defeat in the colonies would threaten the Empire. That was etched in stone. The moderates in the house of lords may rant and rave to their hearts' content, but at the end of the day, the war must be won, not negotiated. A version of winning might include some cursory "concessions" to the rebels, but no mistake would be made in allowing the end result to appear as a defeat for King George III.

Lord North, King George's man in the House, quietly represented his master's positions. North, however, was not entirely convinced that the destruction of the Continental Army and the "death" of the rebels was correct or achievable.

On the other hand, until now, the war was not heavy in British casualties, yet a massive bloodletting on the British side would harden the king's position to the extreme.

For this reason, Admiral Howe and his brother, General Howe, were instructed to employ troops cautiously. A full-scale confrontation using British forces was to be avoided unless victory was certain with minimum losses.

The use of Hessian mercenaries was acceptable. Those soldiers were expendable. North, the Howes, and the aristocracy did not know the king had already set a campaign of terror in motion. A very secret plan that few were privy to.

No rebellious knave would raise a fist if he knew that the king's men would murder children in front of their parents. The king designed a covert program to do just that. "It was fear that would keep the usurpers in line. Fear of the loss of all they hold dear." The king instructed a tight circle of loyalists bound in secret to see things done.

A small cell of butchers was dispatched, cloaked behind the legitimacy of regular British forces and Hessians used to storm the enemy's positions.

"The north of the island." It was nigh a secret that taking Manhattan would speed the war's end, but it was not inevitable.

The British had been scouting the area with minor incursions and probing by the East River and the Hudson. Washington knew this and left General Greene and some 2,000 men to defend the northern bluffs. The situation, however, was desperate, and the withdrawal was a foregone conclusion. The big question was, how could the evacuation of New York be less than a complete loss?

There were those on the colonist side that advised the razing of New York by fire. This view was rejected by Congress, though some thought it logical since the city was full of Tory loyalists. Many in the rank and file were aching to burn New York. The pain of living under British rule and the stress of fleeing Brooklyn was just too much for some; they yearned for the British to *pay a price*.

Under this backdrop, Washington and Aaron Howe led a company of men for a late-night march through a forest in New Jersey to the bewilderment of the ever-mistrusting adjutant general Joseph Reed. Simultaneously, General Howe was resting comfortably in New York. His war plan for taking northern York Island and the ultimate act of crushing the rebellion was nearly complete. Even if the resistance grew in New Jersey in the Spring, the might of the British Empire would not be denied.

At approximately 11 p.m., desperate Continental Army troops assembled in a field about a mile from their original camp. The order came to bed down for the night. Sentries were posted around the perimeter, but word had it that there would be no confrontation this night—the *Lobsters* were sufficiently distant. Worn out soldiers, barely more than a ragtag force slept deeply. The rumor of supplies stoked their hopes of biscuits in the morning. To most, biscuits and pork would have been a sign of fortune. Instead, the early morning light was going to provide much, much more.

Chapter 8

Once a month, Aaron Howe, CEO of Howe It Works, Inc., would take a helicopter ride to a small and private psychiatric facility thirty minutes to the northeast of his home.

The place was costly and offered the best possible care, which was an acceptable combination. This day it was breezy and slightly overcast—a good metaphor for the gray and bitter sadness that he endured on each of these visits.

The Amberness facility landing pad sat in a clearing close to the main building. The pilot made a soft touchdown, and Aaron stepped into the downdraft of the rotor blades.

"Hello, Dr. Howe," yelled Stewart Biggs, the head groundskeeper, over the continuous *whomp whomp whomp* coming from the aircraft.

"Hi, Stewart," Aaron said as they hustled into Mr. Biggs' waiting golf cart. For these trips, Aaron always dressed in jeans and a simple sweater; this visit was no different.

They quickly pulled away from the aircraft and headed up a neat asphalt path toward the main hall.

"Dr. Howe, I hope you are feeling well. As always, if you need anything, press this." Stewart handed Aaron a small device with a fat red button.

"Thanks, Stew, I know the routine."

They approached the entrance, and Aaron hopped out of his seat and gave Biggs the compulsory grin. That was the best Aaron could do on these trips.

At the security doors, the nurse recognized him and buzzed Howe into the building. He gave her a courteous nod and walked down the sparklingly sanitized hallway. They did an excellent job making the place look like a country club and not a psych ward.

However, the neutral beige paint and furnishings didn't

change the fact that a parent, child, or sibling of very wealthy people was locked up here.

At room 118, Aaron pressed a three-digit code on a pad. A neatly dressed and professional nurse dutifully sat on a plush chair outside the room as Howe entered.

He looked around and saw that things were very organized, as usual. Everything was made benign for the patients, beautifully decorated, and safe. This unit had a living room, a bedroom, and a bathroom. His eyes focused on the gray-haired woman sitting in a chair, staring through a window at the trimmed lawn. From behind, he could see that her hair was nicely brushed. Her hands rested on the arms of the chair, and her right hand was stretched out flat. His mother rocked from side to side, singing a unique version of an old TV show theme song.

"Here's my story of a lovely lady who was bringing up one charming girl—"

Aaron stepped noisily to avoid frightening her, then eased his way into her field of view. She looked up.

"Hello, Kid. Hello Kid. Hello Kid," she whispered and then went back to humming.

Aaron sat in the chair facing his mother and then reached out to gently hold both of her hands. Shc smiled briefly. He noticed that the lines on her face deepened with every visit.

"Hello, Mom."

She watched him.

Visits to his mother went much the same way every time. He sat with her for most of an hour while she held his hands and hummed. He would tell her about the business and how everything was excellent. Aaron would tell her how beautiful she looked in her pretty dress. He would talk about the weather. She would hum.

After an hour, he stood up and stretched.

"Sit down," she said sharply.

Howe sat down.

She pierced him with her blue eyes and stopped humming. Tears welled up and dropped onto her cheeks..

"Did you bring your sister? Did you bring your sister?"

"No, Mom," he said.

"No, Mom. No Mom. No, Mom," she mimicked. "What about the dragon, the dragon, dammit!?"

Aaron couldn't fathom what she meant. She glared at him with sudden anger. "Kill the dragon!" Then his mother started biting her lip until a spot of blood appeared.

She looked at him with pleading eyes. More tears. He wiped her lip with a tissue.

"Kid," she said. "Where is your sister? Where is Julia?"

He had to look away to gather his strength.

"Mom, Jules couldn't make it this trip. She said she loves you and will try to come next time."

The aging woman grabbed his hands and pulled him close to her. He felt her tears on his cheek as her face grazed his. She kissed him and whispered in his ear, "Be a good boy and bring Julia next time."

Abruptly she released his hands and sat back. She began to hum again. The visit was over. It was time to go see the general.

*

"Dr. Howe," said Washington. "Allow me to present Colonel Overton." A huge man took Aaron's hand into his own, which was tantamount to a vise, as they made their introductions by the firelight.

The colonel was taller than Washington and was built like an all-pro linebacker. Unlike many soldiers, Overton had his light brown hair trimmed short for some reason. His uniform was big enough that it wouldn't shred if he flexed his muscles, but it failed to hide his bulk. Howe wondered how a guy in 1776 could be ripped like he spent hours in the gym every day, especially when there was no gym. The three men sat quietly talking as the army nearby settled down for the night.

"Colonel Overton," began Howe with the general's consenting nod. "Tomorrow morning, we will be visiting my supply depot. It consists of 20 large boxes the size of tiny houses. Inside these boxes will be a variety of equipment and supplies. The supplies include shoes for every man, proper uniforms, tents, sleeping bags, rations, and body armor." Aaron hoped he'd relayed that understandably enough.

The colonel grinned. "What, may I ask, is a sleeping bag?"

"Uh, that's like a blanket but very warm, and it is made of a material that keeps the water out."

Overton liked the warm and dry part.

It was now Washington's turn to speak.

"We plan to outfit our 2,000 men. Tomorrow we will begin with this small group. We are going to instruct them, which will be much more successful with their warm uniforms and actual shoes," said the general. "Weapons will also be provided.

"The weapons cannot be discussed with the adjutant general. Overton, I have known you for many years. Hence, I will speak frankly. I do not want Congress to yet know about our new stocks. To keep that secret, especially regarding weapons, we must be clever. The adjutant general will be going to Philadelphia soon. Do you understand my thinking?"

The impressive officer nodded. As a rare, highly-trained professional, he had neither time nor patience for incompetence. He also knew that members of Congress were experts at looking for scandals, and they occasionally used Reed as their mole.

"Colonel," continued Washington. "When the men are well-rested, we will invade New York and give Cornwallis a reason to abandon our shores. Dr. Howe is the lynchpin to our success. In the morrow, early, I shall hike to the main camp. When I return, our guest will delight us and impress us with his materials.

"For now, gentlemen," said the general as he stood and stretched. "Good night."

"Reed," said Washington as he shivered in the cold and wet early morning air. "Dr. Howe has many assets. I believe that with his assistance, we can convince Cornwallis to abandon New Jersey and our country."

The visibly annoyed adjutant stood stiffly and prepared to plead his case. The weather had not stalled Washington from a pre-dawn trek to the main camp in the company of his "life guards," as they were known. But now, encountering Reed's bitter stare made him wish he'd sent Overton instead.

"Sir, our 2,000 troops just fled from New York! What is the purpose of going back and fighting a desperate and losing battle? We are outnumbered and have unsupplied and exhausted men, so commit them to capture or death?"

"Joseph," the general explained. "Our friend, Dr. Howe, has provided us with meaningful intelligence and given our troops an advantage that the British will see first-hand. We will have food now; and clothing. That is a large benefit in displacing the British."

"Sir, have you seen these supplies? The food?"

"Continue to your point."

"On what basis should we trust this, Dr. Howe? We do not know him. This could be a trap!" Reed was extremely agitated now and was not too shy to blurt out his contempt.

"I am assured that we can trust him. If we are speaking plainly, Adjutant, I know I have made blunders in this war. I've trusted you to share my doubts. My letters state that I have often felt a lack of surety when leading these men. I appreciate your keeping my doubts confidential. Things have changed, and I believe we will win with Dr. Howe's assistance."

Foolishness, Reed thought. He suddenly decided to keep his views to himself, but Washington's admissions regarding blunders emboldened the adjutant. The general seemed deluded and blinded by the promise of one unproven charlatan. *He means well*, Reed believed, but it was a fool's errand to turn back and try to face Cornwallis—which made George Washington—what?

A calm demeanor returned to Joseph's face. "Sir, I will restrain my tongue and my judgment." It was a charade that he had to play. "Shall we inspect the hypothetical supplies our friend Dr. Howe has promised? Perhaps when your Excellency sees that a few blankets will not return Cornwallis to England, the alternative of hastening our army to Philadelphia will prove its sense and sensibility."

"Reed," said Washington. "Speaking of Philadelphia, as adjutant, I believe it is important that you consult with Congress about our next steps. Winter's chilling grip approaches, I feel that now is the time to weigh your advice, but I need you to seek additional counsel in Philadelphia. I require you to take your assistant to the capitol forthwith. We will remain here and prepare for winter. Please gauge the opinions of the legislature on whether they believe we should bring the fight back to the shores of the Hudson, stay here in New Jersey, or retire to Pennsylvania for the cold months ahead."

Reed was stunned. Why had Washington abruptly dispatched him? The order was so unexpected that Reed stood there staring blankly as the general gave him his orders.

"Very well then, I am assigning two soldiers to accompany you on this vital mission. Please arrange meetings with as many in Congress as feasible. Be sure to write all of the various opinions. Your inquiries should take at least two weeks, perhaps even three. There is no urgency with Cornwallis contented in New York for the winter. I shall see you off myself within an hour.

"One more thing, Adjutant General Reed," said Washington. "Praises be upon you for your devotion to the cause of winning this campaign."

Later, with his nuisance gone, Washington ordered nearly all of the additional troops to the remote site where Overton and Dr. Howe waited. Marching 1,500 grumbling men was not simple; they were mostly farmers, not properly experienced soldiers.

To Howe's relief, the Continental Army troops finally arrived.

Sir," asked Colonel Overton. "Success with the adjutant?"

Washington grinned and merely answered. "Politics, colonel." He then asked Aaron to begin with their previously discussed plan.

Aaron figured that the best way to introduce the troops to modern warfare was to start small. The men were summoned to roll call and divided into groups of 50. Each group selected one man based on leadership skills and experience. This meant a leadership group of forty men gathered in a small clearing near Washington's tent. The remaining troops were ordered to sit tight and wait as they gawked at the shipping containers resting in the center of a large grassy patch. Corrugated steel added to their curiosity, as it was non-existent in 1776 and peculiar to a bunch of laborers and smiths.

Washington and Howe led the hand-picked men to one of the metal containers. In the late morning brisk and clear weather, the group gathered by a container as Washington began to speak.

"Gentlemen, Dr. Howe is about to provide particulars concerning the equipment he has procured for our utilization. It is dire that you be mindful of what he says and memorize all of the details. We will commence with basic supplies and proceed to the armaments. Dr. Howe, please proceed."

Washington was thoroughly pleased to have Aaron explain the gear to the men. The general's mood was the best it had been in a month, and it was just as much connected to the exit of Reed as it was to the supplies from the time traveler. With the adjutant out of the way, for two weeks or more, Washington felt as if he'd just *won* the war.

Aaron stood tall so that the whole group could see him. He was used to addressing shareholders or industry partners, so these men were quite an anomaly. Glancing around, he saw empty looks on the faces of the men, hoping that these soldiers could rise to the occasion and challenges ahead. There was a lot to learn, and quickly.

"Good morning. I'm Dr. Howe, and I've been working and planning with General Washington on resupplying you men with new equipment. This new gear will allow you to bring the fight to the British in a way that will teach them a lesson."

There were grunts and nods of approval, though most had skepticism written all over their faces. Many were wearing worn-out boots stuffed with rags. They'd heard an ocean full of promises for a year but still suffered from a lack of food and clothing.

"Let's begin with this container right here."

Howe took a key from a chain around his neck and unlocked a 40-foot container. Forty necks stretched outward as the men tried to peer into the large metal box. Howe opened the doors to reveal stacks of large boxes labeled "Kane Outdoors" and a sturdy-looking camping stool. He retrieved a knife from his pocket and cut open a carton. He pulled out a green and white shoebox labeled "Size 9.5."

"Gentlemen, has anyone seen a box like this before?" It was a stupid question, but Howe couldn't resist amusing himself. "This is a shoebox, and inside is a pair of extraordinary shoes. The shoes in this box are like nothing you've ever seen before. To begin with, each pair has a left and right shoe."

There were confused looks. Howe knew that the concept of left and right shoes was unheard of in 1776. He continued. "These shoes, or actually we will call them boots, will keep your feet dry and warm in any weather, and they will last a very long time." There was a chuckle in the group, which was silenced when Aaron flipped open the lid and pulled out a pair. The skepticism was replaced with oohs and ahs, and Howe realized he was about to live a shoe salesman's dream.

"Men, these are the Kane Outdoor Excess boots. They won't fall apart or leak. In truth, they won't let water touch your feet at all. You can walk through water with these, and you won't get wet. They are rubber on the bottom, and the tops are leather and Gortex. Gortex is a special cloth that won't let water in."

Howe looked around at the group for an appropriate guinea pig.

"What is your name, captain?" asked Howe to a fresh-faced, perhaps 25-year-old with decaying leather on his feet.

"Uh, Captain Clark, sir," the man stammered nervously.

"Captain, your feet appear to be the correct size to fit into these boots. Come here and sit on this stool."

Clark reluctantly got up and stepped over to drop himself onto the stool. Howe then told Clark to remove his worn shoes while he pulled out nice wool socks (which also required a brief explanation). Once the captain had his new wool socks on, Aaron laced up the boots. The reaction from the young captain was about what you'd expect from someone who'd never experienced real comfort before.

"Oh my!" burst out Clark. The group of 40 laughed. "Sir, my feet are in Heaven."

"That's the idea, captain," Howe pointed out. "But with these boots, you'll put the enemy in Hell." That was met with a bigger laugh and muttering approval.

Howe continued. "Now, Clark, please stand up and walk around."

Clark complied and rapidly got used to having a modern pair of boots on his feet. Aaron then handed out a stack of paper sheets with sizing charts and taught the men how to measure their shoe sizes. Soon all 40 were wearing the best quality boots ever seen in 1776. The men were quickly reassembled, as Howe explained that they had started with boots because winter warfare depended on comfort. The days of suffering feet for revolutionary soldiers were officially over. Next, they moved to Kevlar-lined jackets, gloves, pants, and hats. The jackets all matched as had been ordered, and the new and improved group looked like a uniformed fighting force—camouflaged and professional.

Howe then talked about tents, sleeping bags, and zippers. Surprisingly, the men absorbed everything he told them like sponges. They were motivated by their spectacular new uniforms and already felt like they could be a force that the British would have to reckon with.

It was about 3 p.m. when the entire group of about 2,000 men had been outfitted with boots, clothing, packs, and other gear. The whole regiment was instructed to return to their camps as the lead 40 were to form up again. The air was thick with excitement and confidence, which, unknown to Howe, was never felt among the troops before. There were brief periods of heroic feelings, such as the victory of Dorchester Heights near Boston, but these were quite temporary.

Howe led them to a container marked with the letters AK. These 2,000 militiamen had already become the best equipped-fighting force on Earth in just a few hours of outfitting. Now came the *piece de resistance*—the automatic Kalishnikov-47, the weapon of choice for third-world countries, and in 1776, it was unparalleled.

Howe had settled on the AK-47 due to its reliability, price, availability, and mainly because he could buy 2,000 AK's under the radar. That meant buying overseas, but with *Allison*, he could move anything to 1776. Ammunition was cheap, and an AK could be dragged through the mud and fire.

The advantage that an AK could bring to the army was unfair, but this was war. An otherwise outgunned and virtually defeated Continental Army was about to up the anté by getting some serious firepower.

"Men, this is the AK-47 Assault Rifle," said Aaron as he hefted the oily-stocked weapon and held it out in front of the group. "It is, in principle, just like your muskets, with several improvements. You will learn how great this weapon is when you are trained in its use. Once trained, you will teach your platoons of men in all aspects of using and cleaning this rifle."

General Washington looked ecstatic, and that was indeed a rare event. He suddenly interrupted Howe. "Excuse me, Dr.

Howe, but I would like to make an essential statement."

The general turned to stare at the group. "We are entering a new chapter as an army, and as such, we are about to alter some previous behaviors and customs.

"The essential change is accepting that this is now a military camp. The weapons that you are about to receive are secret. You will train with them, and at the end of each training session, you will return your 'rifle' to the quartermasters. The weapons will be kept in these storage containers. We will move the entire camp here to be adjacent to our provisions. They will be sorted so that in case of dire need, every man will know from where to retrieve his weapon.

"I consider it treason to discuss your weapons with anyone except other soldiers. When not using these weapons, you will carry your muskets. If perchance, a visitor should come to our encampment, you will say not one word about these weapons.

"Men, if we are going to win this war, no one can know about our supplies. I have just reiterated that principle three times. I have said that as plainly as I should. Is that understood?"

A loud and clear "Yes, general" was shouted by all 40 men.

There was energy in the air as Howe began to describe everything he knew about the AK. He told them about its parts, how to disassemble it, how to rebuild it, the 7.62x39mm cartridges, magazines, and how to operate the rifle. The millimeter reference led to a host of blank stares. Howe merely told them it was a measuring method they had not heard of and held up a rifle cartridge. He emphasized that unlike their muskets, which could fire 3 – 4 rounds per minute in the hands of an expert, the AK could fire 30 rounds in just a few seconds. However, he warned them that "full-auto" was strictly forbidden. They were only to operate the rifles on "semi-auto" one round per one trigger pull.

Then came the moment of truth, and Aaron instructed them all on how to insert small ear valves to protect their hearing. He loaded a magazine and prepared to fire off a round. Some paper targets were placed at 25 and 40 yards. Aaron shot 15 rounds at the closer target and 15 at the other. The power of this weapon was deadly and apparent to all. Both targets had relatively small groups shot into them—far more accurate than a smooth-bore musket. In Revolutionary War combat, this weapon would be a game changer.

The "Firsties," as they were now called, caught on very quickly. Within an hour, they were all issued rifles and had demonstrated their ability to break down and reassemble the AK's. They were issued magazines and ammunition and began plinking at 25-yard and 40-yard targets. Captain John Clark turned out to be particularly good with a rifle. According to Washington, Clark was 25 and married with two children. The blond-haired captain was highly reliable. He'd been a metalsmith and mechanically talented, which explained his meticulous nature regarding weapons.

Howe decided on Clark plus five other men who would become a special unit called Recon. These six were well-educated and had an aura of competence. Not only could they read and write quite well, but they seemed self-assured based on Howe's interviews with each of them. Aaron hoped that his gut feelings were dead on concerning his choices. His plans for Recon included difficult training and the ability to master tactics and weapons.

The remainder of the Firsties completed their exercises and were sent to their platoons to begin training other men. The process took until evening, but all observations indicated that the soldiers would be ready for shooting practice within a day.

Not only clothing and weapons were loaded in the containers, but also food and lots of it. The men ate grilled hot dogs, baked beans, dried fruits, nuts, and chocolate. They were going to be a well-fed army and a well-armed one—and would sleep dry and warm.

The morning dawned to a light fog that burned off after breakfast. The regimen was completely refreshed, and before shooting for real, they were lectured for an hour about the chain of command and hygiene. Morale was very high as the continental troops went to the range for 30 minutes of practice for each group.

They all knew their muskets, so the changes the AK's brought were somewhat overwhelming but not overly so. Four – 50-man platoons shot off 60 rounds per man as the Firsties gave instructions and tips. To Aaron, it was going exceedingly well. General Washington was beside himself with contentment. The burden of command had now become considerably lighter. He was also delighted with the look of his troops dressed in identical camouflaged uniforms.

"Aaron," he began. "I am very gratified with our progress."

"Thank you, sir."

"You are now officially Major Aaron Howe. I am assigning you the charge of the small group of men you suggested in our meeting. I think your idea that we put together a special force is essential, and I mandate that you lead them."

"Whoa! Thank you, general, but perhaps someone with more experience should be leading that force?"

"I cannot think of any soul more suited. As I recall from our meeting two days ago, you spent a fair amount of time hunting and practicing war games with outstanding marines from your time. Is that not so? Is that not how you described it to me?"

Aaron nodded.

"I understand your concern, but it is obvious that you are most fit to be the leader of our special force." came the answer. "You are smart and talented, and it is quite apparent that you can do anything you set your mind to.

"Hopefully, before winter is over or in the spring,"

Washington elaborated. "We will cross the Hudson and head back to relieve Greene and his troops at the Fort. That is my wishful plan. I anticipated, and you confirmed, that Hessians will attack the fort with about 4,000 troops. The British seem determined to use the mercenaries whenever they want to strike fear into us. Now, we're going to teach their hearts the meaning of fear."

Chapter 9

"Gentleman," said Howe, the newly minted major. "You have been pulled aside and are going to form a special unit called Recon."

The six men had turned out to be the best from the original group of 40. It wasn't just about rank but how naturally these men seemed to handle their gear and weapons and move through the forest. There was also something random about these six that was not random at all. Howe couldn't explain the sensation, but he felt drawn towards these guys as the right fit. It seemed fated, but the last thing a trained scientist would do was put stock in the notion of destiny.

"Clark," said Aaron. "How do you like your boots?"

"Major, they are very comfortable, sir," replied the captain.

Howe looked Clark up and down. The man was neat and organized, medium height, with an All-American grin. He could have been an actor with his good looks, but for now, he was going to be the executive officer of Recon.

"Do you know the other five men here?"

Without hesitation, he answered, "Yes, sir. We have Lieutenant Schein, Sergeant Rogers, Sergeant Allen, Sergeant Montgomery, and Corporal Lewis."

Howe looked at the corporal. "How do you like the food, Lewis?"

"Much better than eating grass, sir," said the red-headed young corporal with a twinkle in his eye.

He then looked at Montgomery. "What do you think of the AK-47, Montgomery?"

"Sir," replied the large, dark-haired sergeant. "I'll give you a cow if I can have an extra."

"No thanks on the cow offer, sergeant," started Howe. "And I think when we are done training, you will like all your weapons.

In fact, I'm taking back your AK-47's. Instead, you are each getting a new rifle called the VZ 58."

The newly minted Recon looked eager. Montgomery, the biggest man in Recon, was impressive. He was tall and broad at over six feet, and his hands were extra-large. He tended to have a doubtful nature. If you made a claim that the sergeant couldn't swallow, you would have to prove it authentic.

"Where are you from, Sergeant Montgomery?" asked Howe.

"Trenton, sir."

"You've got working hands. What's your job?"

Monty, as he was known, smiled broadly. "Killing Redcoats, but when I'm not doing that, I am occupied as a carpenter."

That made sense to Howe. The guy looked like someone who could handle heavy lumber. "You married?"

"Yes, sir," answered the large sergeant, a big grin illuminating his face. "My wife's name is Betty. No children yet, sir."

Howe held off on a thorough interview of the other soldiers but still gleaned some basic facts about his new unit. He'd learn that only Clark and Monty were married; the rest were single. They were a fit, eager, and energetic bunch. After the brief introductions, Aaron felt gratified about the selection of these guys. The 19-year-old Scott Lewis was quick-witted and jovial, and he was the comic relief in the mix of the more serious men. In fact, up against the ever-doubtful Monty, Lewis was a nice balance.

Mordecai "Mordy" Schein was a bit of a square peg. The only Jewish soldier in the group was a silversmith from Philadelphia. Howe didn't even know that there were Jews in the city in 1776 [1776 Jewish population in Philadelphia was actually close to 350]. Schein had decided to enlist almost immediately when hostilities broke out. Over time, Howe would learn by listening to Recon's banter that the war was a fight for the future to Schein. He had high hopes for the independent colonies and anticipated legislated freedoms, including freedom of religion. He was a thinker, the only philosopher of the bunch whom Clark and the others could trust with their every breath.

John Clark was thrilled with his new gear, especially the rifle. Since being selected to Recon, he was eager to complete the intense and pressured training. He was amazed at Major Howe's persistence that they fire at least 400 rounds per day. His old musket was as useless as a broken ax compared to his rifle.

On the second day of training, while the regulars were practicing maneuvers, Recon was working on shooting targets up to 75 yards. Howe was confident of his methods since he remembered every tactic he had ever read or every war game he'd played in the New England forests. When Recon worked up the nerve to quiz him on his experience, he responded that everything he knew he had gotten from a book. Aaron chuckled to himself, knowing there was much truth to that, excluding romps through the woods with his dad's marine buddies.

Fortunately, the war games he played as a kid were pretty serious. It was paintball, and he played with adults, most of whom were his dad's friends from special units. It totally pissed them off when a kid got the better of them. More than once, a former Marine would look at the paint on his shirt, scruff up Aaron's hair and say, "Good shot, kid. It won't happen again."

The entire second afternoon of their training consisted of laying still for five minutes, finding a target at 75 yards, and firing a single shot. They would then walk down to check their accuracy. Clark was an ace, with the other five not far off. But waiting prone in mud and dirt was frustrating, and after the third hour, the snipers were a bit worn. Clark's partner, Sergeant John Allen, arose a bit gruff. Along with the others, they made it clear that they were tired of lying in the mud.

"Major," said Sergeant Allen. "I do not fathom why we need to practice laying in the mud for an hour just to take a few shots at a target?" Allen brushed dried mud off his camouflaged uniform—which everyone called "camos." At 5'10," he was taller than most Continental Army soldiers. His black hair was stringy and also a bit muddy. He scratched his nose, grinned with his perfect teeth, stared at the major with dark brown eyes, and waited.

Howe's response was friendly yet direct. "That's a good question, Allen. Perhaps we should have spent more time on the philosophy of sniping before we started. Now that you've brought it up, I'll give you a short explanation." Aaron paused for a minute to gather his thoughts.

"Where I come from, in the wars that I've known, the sniper has the highest kill ratio of any soldier."

"What does that imply?" asked Rogers.

"It implies that if the regular soldier confirms one dead in a battlefield confrontation, the sniper will record ten to fifteen kills. I know you don't enjoy laying in the mud, and neither do I, but let's think about this: you lay in the mud, and the enemy doesn't have a clue where you are. When they're close enough, you start targeting the enemy soldiers because you can hit them from 300 yards or more. The best part is that they can't see or reach you with their muskets. It's not fair to them, but too bad."

Howe's words sunk in, and Allen returned a broad grin after a few seconds. If they didn't know it earlier, it was clear that their little group of six plus Major Howe was special. They were the world's first "Combat Applications Group." The hunkering down in the mud had a purpose, and their uniforms kept them reasonably dry. The grumbling settled as everyone in the group now embraced the role they were about to play.

Howe continued. "Our job will be to exploit the enemy. And our enemy is prime for that. Think about it. They wear bright red coats, make a lot of noise, have weapons that are inaccurate and have limited range, and have no idea what they are up against. We are the exact opposite. We can attack them at a distance of 100 yards and then retreat into the shadows—with these rifles, but we will also be training with special rifles. And with those, you can take out a target at 500 yards. It's a little unsporting."

His brief speech was over, and they returned to the day's

work. Rogers was particularly good at just sitting or lying somewhere and not budging. Aaron was beginning to see the talents of each of the guys, and they all had something to contribute. For the short, Sergeant Thomas Rogers, it was slithering around with his 5’6” thin frame unnoticed, surprising the hell out of anyone nearby. The guy was like a ghost, and he set the stealth standard for the rest of Recon.

The following day, they had a test of sorts. While the regular troops were continuing their drilling, the Recon guys were busy applying their skills on an obstacle course of sorts.

They were each sent along a route that covered a half-mile. Four regular soldiers were assigned to hide in the forest along the way. The purpose of the exercise was for the Recon troops to get close enough to the regulars to make a quiet kill. The regulars were not told much other than to scan a forest segment and watch for anything unusual. Nearly all of the Recon group succeeded in getting close enough to make a bayonet kill. The ‘bait’ soldiers were shocked at how well Recon snuck up on them. The training was going well.

At day’s end, Howe called them to an unopened container near the edge of the camp. He took out a key and opened it, asking them to have a seat while he grabbed a long metal case. He popped open the latches and flipped the lid. Inside was an M40a3 U.S. Marine sniper rifle. There was a reverent “Ahh” from the men as Aaron hefted the 14 lb. beauty.

“This is going to be your sniper rifle, men,” began Aaron. “It is the M40. It fires 7.62 x 51mm ammunition, which is much more powerful than your 7.62 x 39 cartridges. However, each weapon has its time and place, so you will usually go on patrol with both.”

By this time, Recon knew well what a cartridge was and how big a 7.62 x 51mm round would be. They spent the next day learning their new weapon. They discovered the purpose and function of a scope. They also became reasonably competent at sighting in and hitting targets at up to 500 yards. They'd become long-distance killers in a matter of days, and there remained time for just a bit more training before they became operational.

That evening, they got another piece of equipment, a pair of night-vision lenses and binoculars. These, added to the night vision capabilities of their scopes, made it almost too dangerous to be within 10 miles of Recon.

To Aaron, the six had adapted so well that they were now the 1776 version of modern-trained snipers. Aaron thought they would be damn good in his own time, considering such a short training period. Imagine if they could train together for a year or two!

Occasionally, during their intense practice, he thought about the smugness of his contemporaries, both in science and life. Academics, politicians, and businessmen were convinced that earlier generations were backward and primitive. After a week with the Recon boys, he found they were very sharp and adaptable. They needed a little prodding, but once they were encouraged to think creatively, they excelled.

There wasn't much difference between the modern soldier and these guys—just training. The average modern soldier didn't need to know calculus to do his job. He needed to know how to sight in his rifle, use a global positioning system, and lase a target, but all these things could also be taught to his men.

Of course, there was no GPS in 1776, but with time, he could teach them many techniques that would be very useful for fighting the British. Most of that would be on the job.

"Are you ready to kill some Redcoats?" asked Howe one evening after an incredibly tiring day. The answer was a resounding, if exhausted, "Yes, sir."

Contact with the enemy was coming, and Aaron felt they were ready. Interestingly, they never asked about where the weapons and equipment came from. Aaron cautioned them to allow other troops to touch their rifles or other advanced equipment. The regulars had their AK's, but that was about all they had regarding modern weapons.

To this end, Recon ate alone, sacked out alone, and hung by themselves. For now, they were paired in three teams, Clark and Allen, Lewis and Monty, and Rogers and Schein, who they called the Hebrew Sniper. Howe would work alone.

"Schein," called Major Howe. "Are you eating?" Recon was sitting down for breakfast, and only some odd-looking carrots were in the lieutenant's hand.

"You look too damn thin, lieutenant."

"He only eats rabbi rations, that is to say, Hebrew food only," chimed in Schein's close pal, Rogers.

Aaron pondered that for a few seconds, then raised his eyebrows and gave Schein a eureka stare.

"You mean kosher food?"

Schein nodded nervously.

"Really. Well, I got some good news for you, Schein," mused Aaron. "Take a look over here."

With Rogers in tow, Aaron led Schein to a box resting next to their campsite. He took out his knife and slit open the top. "Right here, I got some grade-A MRE's—tasty and kosher."

Schein peered into the box, and sure enough, there were small packs with Hebrew writing that said, "Certified Kosher." He wasn't sure what an MRE was, but these had the word kosher.

"What's an MRE, sir?" Schein inquired.

"It's a Meal Ready to Eat, and although I don't read Hebrew, you do." These Aaron purchased straight from an Israeli supplier to the Israel Defense Forces, and they were not only some of the best MRE's on the planet, but they were ok for Schein.

He showed the men how to open and prepare the meals. They were instructed to put seven meals in their packs, and they ate one together to ensure everyone knew what to expect. The unanimous verdict was that the MRE's were excellent compared to their last previously horrid diet. Schein ate three while discussing what makes a meal worthy.

It was now mid-afternoon, and Recon had spent the day shooting and working in two-man teams, learning to watch out for each other. At 3 p.m., Aaron gathered them by his tent for two more little surprises.

The first was a Beretta .380 caliber sidearm, and the second was a detachable silencer. He took them to their private Recon range, where they spent an hour learning and shooting the small pistols.

By 4:30 p.m., a shroud of darkness settled upon them. They returned to their small campsite to eat again, where Schein packed away two more MRE's while the others ate pancakes and bacon.

General Washington showed up at the camp at around 5:30 p.m. They all snapped to attention. The lack of discipline that had been pronounced in the army over the last year was indeed not found among Recon. Their transformation was remarkable. They had gone from colonial-era soldiers to modern-like professionals in just over a week. General Washington was privately astounded.

"Gentleman, be seated."

They sat.

"Major Howe is about to take you out for your first night operation," Washington explained. "We will meet when you return to discuss your experience. We have no idea where the enemy scouts are, and there have been reports that a significant force of British is about 25 miles north of here. That means there could be small units nearby. We don't want a large skirmish starting with the scouts. If you meet them in the forest, you should capture at least one. Do not permit them to escape. We cannot have the main British force warned about our location. Major Howe knows what we expect to accomplish. Your orders are to bring back at least one British scout. Good fortune to you all."

Aaron thanked Washington for his visit and confidence. The general waved as he turned to head back to the main camp. Recon sat back down and looked at each other. They now understood that they were going out to do the real thing. Without the regiment of 2,000 men around them, this one would be theirs alone. The meal resumed with silent anticipation and a dash of nerves.

At 6:30 p.m., Major Howe instructed them to go to sleep. He would wake them at 9:30 p.m. to prepare for their departure. It wasn't easy, but they settled in and got some shut-eye.

The night was cool, and their packs were ready and waiting when Aaron woke them. The Recon team nervously dressed and gathered up their gear. When they were fully outfitted, Aaron sat them down for a final mission briefing.

"I've got two more surprises for you. One, I'm a British spy…."

The men looked alarmed.

"It's a joke. I just wanted to see if you were awake. Actually," Aaron continued, "the first surprises are these."

He pulled out six digital watches and handed them out. "These things buckle on your left or right wrist like this."

He showed them his watch.

"Rogers, what time is it?"

"Uh, it's 10 p.m., sir,"

"Good, now you all know how to tell time, so for your next surprise—"

He reached into a sack and pulled out seven Icom VHF handheld radios. They were all set on channel 2, and he quickly explained how to use them. The reaction was awe. Guns they could understand, but talking boxes were mildly disconcerting.

"Sir," began Montgomery. "We were talking together, and honestly, this 'hi-tech stuff,' as you call it, is just too strange. We must know more about its origin. We believe you must be from another world. We are sure that such items could not possibly be from here in the colonies, sir."

"Excellent, Monty. I was wondering when you would ask me."

He'd expected that they would insist on an explanation sooner rather than later. These weren't little children, and he had decided not to treat them like babies. Howe had to provide clarification. They certainly had to trust each other to go into battle together, and as major of Recon, they also needed doubtless trust in him. Before he could answer, Clark spoke up.

"Actually," Clark interjected. "I believe you are a person just like us, but you must be from the future. It is the only answer that makes sense to me. Think about it, you have all of this technology, but you look exactly like us, so you must be human."

"You're right, captain, I am human, just like you, and you're right again that I am not from here. I'm also not from another planet. I'm from right here on earth, and what I'm about to tell you must be kept secret from everyone but us. Only the general knows as much as I am about to divulge. Do you understand? The general and I talked long about whether you men could deal with the truth of my being here. Just like I trust you, also you need to trust me. I can't tell you everything, but you will learn a lot more in time. Do you think you can handle it?

They nodded their agreement.

"I am indeed Aaron Howe, and I am from the early 21st century, around 250 years from now in the future,"

He waited for that to settle in. There wasn't much of a reaction from the group. They all sat there looking rather sedate, so Aaron decided to press his explanation a bit.

"I am capable of traveling through time." He looked around and gauged their acceptance of what he'd just said. They still looked at him with somewhat flat stares. Howe was baffled by their lack of a reaction and expected some extreme responses, but none was forthcoming.

Aaron then blurted out, "Do you guys not believe what I just told you?"

Spontaneously, they held up their radios or watches and gave their major broad grins.

"Well, I guess those things back up my story. I'm sure you all have 1,000 questions you want to ask me, and I will answer what I can, but not now. However, I'll let you ask me one question before we leave tonight, so decide on your question, and then we'll go."

The men huddled for a moment and then agreed. Clark spoke.

"Sir, do we win?"

That was one of the questions that Aaron had anticipated.

"I can't answer that." He replied.

"Cannot or will not, sir?" pressed Montgomery.

"Won't"

"Well, then we have a different question," said Clark. "Is the world a better place in the future?"

Aaron hadn't considered that question. He searched his thoughts for a good answer and replied, "Yes and no."

Recon scowled and gave him a collective groan.

Aaron continued. "Ok, let's say that yes, it's better in terms of people being healthier in the future, but not in terms of the amount of conflict in the world. You have seen and are using some very advanced weapons, but in the future, these rifles are simple. The world has other problems too, but I can't explain it to you now, perhaps later." He hoped it would be enough of an answer to hold them for a while. It was time to move out.

Chapter 10

There was no moon as they made their way out of camp. They had covered about 4 miles through relatively sparse woods in the few hours since their departure. Recon traveled in groups of two with Major Howe in the lead, separated by about 50 yards between them. At 2 a.m., they received a "hold up" command in their headsets from Howe and quietly hunkered down and waited for more orders. Captain Clark scanned the area in front and to the sides while wearing his night vision goggles. He and Allen were behind Major Howe. The captain saw nothing as he panned the horizon.

"We've got at least eight Redcoats about 70 yards ahead of me. They're standing around a fire, and they've got one guy on watch," Aaron said from a rise a small distance ahead of Recon.

"What do we do?" asked Allen.

"Ok, here's what you do. Schein, Rogers, Lewis, and Monty; come up to meet with Clark and Allen. Quiet all the way. Allen, call me when you are together, out."

Aaron was quietly prone in some brush as he watched the British campsite. They seemed relaxed, but he was surprised they weren't all asleep. Despite the audible banter of the Redcoats, the sentry on watch seemed edgy. Aaron wondered if the guard had heard the rustle of the undergrowth as he was creeping toward them. He put on his goggles and lowered their intensity to deal with the campfire. The Redcoats were seated around the fire, but the guard kept looking nervously in his direction. Aaron again thought about whether he was giving away his position somehow. He flipped off his goggles and noticed the green LED light from his radio gleaming in its shoulder pouch. Crap! He thought. Just then, he took an unpleasant poke from a British musket as he lay prone on the forest floor.

Two thoughts passed through his Ph.D. CEO brain: *This is scary, and what a screw-up on your first command.*

"Do not move," came a terse order as the Redcoat put a heavy boot on his arm as another soldier pinned him to the ground with a knee in Aaron's back.

Damn, these guys are good, thought Aaron. He could not imagine how they spotted him from just the little green light. He made a point of remembering that if he managed to get out of this.

They tied his hands and hauled him up to his feet. To his astonishment, the night vision goggles and rifle were ignored as they hustled him to their camp. The *lobsters* were excellent at sneaking up on someone but were damn stupid when it came to searching for weapons.

"Buzzards!" exclaimed Schein as Recon watched their major getting dragged away as a prisoner. He figured they were 120 yards from the Brits, and their first reconnaissance operation was going to hell.

"This is what we shall do," said Clark, "Allen and I go straight ahead, Schein, Rogers, you proceed to the right until you are about 50 yards from the *Lobsters*. Lewis, Monty, same thing on the left. When I say so, select your targets, and pick the enemy soldier nearest you so that we do not strike the same ones. When you are sure, give me a click on the radio, and I shall give you a command in return. Put in your ear valves, and do not hit the major. If you lack surety of your shot, then do not fire. We cannot fail and return to Washington, dragging our tails and no major."

They peeled off to their designated spots. In about two minutes, they settled into position.

"This is Clark. They have just slapped the major in the face. He looks a bit unhappy. Everyone ready?"

He heard five clicks in his headset.

"Right then. Closest targets. After you hit your man, be quiet. The remaining four Redcoats will either stand up and start shooting or run. No shooting at the one interrogating the major.

We want that officer alive. Ready, 3,2,1, now." Clark squeezed off a round. He ignored the recoil and quickly checked his target.

Within about a second, six Redcoats dropped. The other four looked around, completely bewildered. The interrogator and one other went to the ground while two others shot wildly in the wrong direction. They were both hit in the torso within another couple of seconds. The interrogator began screaming his surrender and stood up with his hands in the air.

The last enlisted redcoat jumped up and made the mistake of running precisely in the wrong direction. Clark dropped him a few yards from the camp. The officer/interrogator remained perplexed and stunned. Clark and Allen moved in while the other two teams watched and listened.

Major Howe was sitting on a log, looking a bit sore. The Brit campsite was a mess. Nearly all of the Redcoats took clean hits that killed them reasonably quickly. One redcoat was groaning but conveniently slipped into unconsciousness and then stopped breathing. Allen moved in to cut the ropes around the major's wrists. Howe stood up with a grunt but seemed all right. He took command of the scene, rubbing his side where he'd been jabbed with a musket. The slap to his face was deliberately light to arouse fear but not much else.

"What's your name?" Aaron demanded of the ranking and only remaining member of his patrol.

"Bates, Captain Arnold Bates, Third Regiment, London Expedition," came the reply.

"On your knees, Bates," said Aaron.

Bates got down and waited. Summary executions were nearly unheard of, and Bates looked as if he was going to piss himself.

"Captain, we're probably not going to kill you, so stop panicking," Aaron continued to rub his sore ribs. "However, we are going to need you to be cooperative. Do you agree?"

"Yes, sir," the soldier said obediently.

"Ok, good. I am going to ask you something, and you better answer truthfully. Is that understood?"

"Yes, sir."

"Fine," said Howe. "Bates, how many patrols are in this area?"

"Just our small unit, sir."

"Very good, but since I think you are lying, I'm going to cut your thumbs off," Aaron flipped open a Kershaw folding knife.

Bates began to shake and actually did piss himself. He was the leader of a troop that had been shot down in just a few seconds, and he had no reason to believe that this rebel major wouldn't cut him as he'd said.

"Uh, sir, I swear, we be the only patrol here. But two other patrols went east of here about 10 miles. I swear."

Aaron gave no answer. Better to let Captain Bates sweat it out. He called Monty to have him pick up his rifle and goggles that were left behind and told the others to wait there. Clark and Allen doused the fire, which was now only coals, and they stacked the bodies of the enemy dead in an organized pile. Allen seemed calm enough, but Clark looked a little stressed by the number of dead around him. Howe himself was a little out of sorts, but he couldn't let his men see that. The scene was ghastly, but this was a war, he reminded himself, and winning was the only acceptable outcome.

"Let's get out of here," Aaron said with a stiff upper lip. He closed his knife and slipped it into his pocket.

The team gathered up their gear and took their prisoner with them. The hike back to the main camp took the remainder of the night. They marched in around 7 a.m. A couple of officers took Captain Bates for interrogation while General Washington sat with the exhausted Recon team to go over the night's action. After a one-hour review, the team was done, and they went to sleep like seven sacks of potatoes.

Captain Geoffrey Timmons and his squad of regulars camped about two miles east of Bates' patrol when they heard several rifle reports. The trees muffled the staccato sounds at such a distance, but they were still audible as gunfire. His soldiers were bedded down, and Timmons ordered his men to go back to sleep while doubling the guard. Timmons decided to put off investigating until morning. He believed it was Bates' men shooting their muskets for amusement, which they would regret intensely when he next saw them.

The captain tossed and turned for a time as he replayed the sounds of the shots in his mind. They didn't sound like muskets. Something irked him about the blasts in the night that ended in dead silence. *It doesn't feel safe*, he thought, as sleep overtook him.

In the early morning light, he roused his men. They boiled some tea and ate their rations. His patrol was fifty-strong, packing light, and light-footed. They decided to break into ten five-man groups and make their way quickly west.

The forest was not thick. They trudged their way as quietly as they could. Timmons knew that Captain Bates' patrol was due west, which was troubling. If Bates had had contact with the rebels, then he would have ordered his men to regroup with Timmons's troops. Could the man have had a run-in that didn't end favorably?

"Captain," Sergeant Halley called back to Timmons. "I see something at 100 yards."

Timmons came forward and used a spyglass to peer ahead. He saw some red clothing through the trees and felt somewhat relieved to have found the other patrol.

"Very good. It must be Captain Bates' camp ahead," said Timmons as he breathed a sigh of relief. "Shall we have some lunch?"

Chapter 11

Aaron woke up in the mid-afternoon. He was very much refreshed and roused his team for a good meal and to prepare them for their next mission. At 2:45 p.m., Washington and a small entourage joined them for a briefing. His Excellency explained that a lone scout reported the sighting of another group of Redcoats near the location of the previous night's activity. The scout slipped away unseen, but the British were yelling and cursing loud enough to be heard at a distance.

"Major Howe," began Washington. "It is obvious that the British troops have come upon your handiwork. Your prisoner has proved to be a good liar."

"It would seem so, sir, unless they can fly."

Washington remained silent for a moment, then said, "They will be desperate for revenge and to retaliate severely. However, we are not going to give them the opportunity. Major Howe, our scout reported many British. That is the best he could ascertain without being compromised. Can you take Recon and follow them, get an estimate of their strength?"

Howe contemplated his eagerness to get back out in the field. The more contact he had with the British, the better his chance to succeed in his other goal. That was the ultimate prize—to find and hunt down Butler's ancestor. He hoped *Allison* did not send him here to waste his time in little skirmishes.

"General," answered Howe. "We can track them and engage them if we have to, but will focus on spying—which I refer to as intel."

"That is the objective. We speculate that there are nearly 1,500 British northwest of here, maybe 25 miles distant. I do not want you to engage any large groups in battle. As efficient as you are, you might lose, and I can't risk that—Recon is too important.

Rumor has it that a very aggressive general is leading those battalions. Use your modern tricks to gain "intel." When we engage them, I do not want to lose anyone. I know that is somewhat unrealistic, major, but we have the apparatus to make it back to New York without heavy losses. Let us succeed at that."

"Yes, sir," said Howe. "We will rest today and go back out tonight."

"I want another of that morsel you referred to as a hot dog!" said Monty. "If I am to go out overnight, I want a delightful bucket of meat in my stomach."

Sergeant Allen handed him a hotdog and a bun. The big sergeant swallowed it practically whole and then put his hand out for another.

"Monty," said Allen. "I believe you are utterly obsessed with 'future food.' I also think you should eat a tad more slowly."

Monty looked up while downing the last of his third frankfurter.

"Sergeant Allen, I freely admit that. Let us do an inventory of some of the things that we have eaten, shall we? I will begin with potato chips—magnificent, are they not? And don't forget donuts, macaroni, Crazy Mac, or whatever you want to call it. Honestly, I want to eat it every day. Shall we add pretzel sticks?"

Allen raised his hand to halt Monty's recitation of his favorite victuals. Just then, the major waved to get Recon's attention.

"Listen up," said Howe. "We're going out the same as before. Same routine. I'll try to avoid getting into trouble tonight."

He sat on one of the small, folding beach chairs he'd packed. Aaron looked around at the guys to whom he gave severe life and death instructions. None of them knew much about him—neither the good nor the bad. He chuckled to himself. If they knew the size of his business, Howe It Works, far in the future—it would shock them. He wondered what they would think if they knew why he was here—the other powerful reason—the goal being to fix his mostly melancholy life. And to undo the loss of Julia.

He was deep in his thoughts when he realized that Recon was staring at him, probably wondering where his daydreaming had led him. Howe pulled himself out of his self-absorbed moment. *Don't just think about yourself*, he thought.

"Right, sorry, I was thinking about something. I found getting hit with a musket unpleasant when we captured Captain Bates. That was my screw-up. That means a mistake, so from now on, when I say screw-up, don't ask me to translate. Same thing with 'intel' and some of the other words I use. You should know most of them if you have half a brain by now."

It occurred to Recon that the major seemed a bit aggravated. They decided to be on their best behavior.

Schein had picked up on this faster than the others, and they talked about it privately. Recon was an astute bunch, so they recognized that the major looked burdened beyond the current task of killing Brits.

Howe continued. "We're going out to collect intel. If the scout was right that there are 40 to 60 Hajis, we could win a firefight. But listen, we need to avoid that."

Lewis raised his hand. "I know you would like me to refrain from questions major, but what is a Haji?"

Aaron looked at Recon. "In my time, there are enemies that are sometimes given that slang name. Technically, we don't have any Hajis here, but it makes it easier for me just to call them that. In the future, that is a general term for some enemy soldiers.

"The point is unless we have no other choice, we don't engage any enemies tonight. Clear?"

They nodded.

"Next thing. Pack enough food and water. Also, make sure your weapons are ready, plus eight extra magazines. Of course, radios, night vision, and all the other goodies. Don't make me pack your bags for you," grumbled Howe. He was feeling a little aggressive but reminded himself that Recon were the good guys.

"All right," he said. "We pull out at 18:30."

The evening was cool as expected, and there was some light, spitting drizzle in the air, but the new uniforms worked very well at keeping them dry. Recon made their way in two-man groups with Aaron in the middle of the stretched line. The damp forest floor kept the crunch of leaves to a minimum, which was perfect for shadowing the enemy. They made good time to the scene of the previous night's assault on Bates' patrol. It was risky investigating the site, so Aaron sent Clark to surveil the surrounding area.

"Completely empty, sir," said Clark into his handheld radio. "The bodies are gone, and the only ashes from the fire ring are still here. It is as if nothing happened."

Aaron keyed his handheld radio and told Clark to return as quickly as possible. They decided to meet close to where Aaron was discovered by the British previously.

"Ok, here's what we do," he explained. "Two groups go 300 yards west, then north. Clark and Allen, along with me, will go east and then north. We have a range of at least one mile on the radios, so if you hear anything, you drop and signal me."

There was a chorus of nods as they arose and headed out.

"Oh, and one other thing," Aaron added over their headsets. "If they didn't just bury their dead, and in fact, they hauled them off, then that means there are many more Redcoats out here than we might think. So, watch your asses."

"Sir," Monty transmitted a couple of seconds later. "Watch our *whats*?"

There was a brief hiss of light radio static, and Howe hit his radio's Push-To-Talk button. "It means, be damn careful! Out."

Captain Timmons helped to bury the bodies of Bates' patrol. It wasn't the most shocking scene, but it was dead British soldiers. His orders from General Dorcester were that if they couldn't kill enemy troops, then civilians that supported them were equally good targets. By and large, the British were professional forces, and enemy soldiers ended up dead. But in truth, both sides were timid about engaging the enemy in all-out bloody battles.

As far as civilians, Timmons knew that it was much easier to control the population by sheer terror. It was something that didn't disturb his ice-cold and brutal nature—which was why Dorcester hand-picked him to distribute some misery. As the little general put it, "Those who help the enemy are the enemy."

The terror campaign would be unleashed by a select platoon who'd shown themselves immune to sentiment. Recently, as winter approached, pressure was applied upon the farmers by burning crops and villages—a punishment for those who aided the enemy. Intimidation was easy, but direct vicious punishment of colonists was, until now, unseen.

There were nine dead bodies from Bates' patrol, all shot with single bullets, most to the chest. After a couple of hours of digging to finish the burials, Timmons sent two soldiers to head several miles north for reinforcements. An intermediate camp of about 50 troops was just 10 miles away. If the Continental Army had a small number in these woods, they would be no match for the dozens of regulars returning by nightfall.

"Then I will pile up the enemy bodies," he grumbled.

The previous week's orders were to scout out what was surely Washington's 2,000 to 3,000 men who'd fled south. Timmons and Bates were told to locate the rebels and hurry back with the news.

Orders from General Howe, the British commander, were to

cut off Washington's retreat south and finish them off. General Dorcester ordered that there would be no prisoners and no survivors. This order was accepted with some quiet concern.

Looking at the nine dead men from Bates' patrol removed Timmons' last shreds of emotion regarding the violence he'd done in Denhurst. American wives and mothers would have to deal with their young men not coming back from the war. Civilians that supported the rebels were also fair game—all civilians. There would be no mercy on any of them. Those were his orders from General Dorcester and would not be questioned.

Of course, a parallel priority was to find Washington's army and then report back. It was clear they had come close to Washington's militia, but reporting back was not a foregone conclusion. Bates was a professional officer. Now his men were buried, and Bates' was either dead or captured. Timmons' retaliation on the civilians of Denhurst was immediate and unforgiving. It wasn't pleasant, but the Continental Army would crumble and surrender if the price was high enough. By now, the rebels must have discovered the price Timmons' soldiers exacted from that village of misguided fools.

Looking a the burial site, he kicked a clump of mud off his boot as he shuddered at the thought of an enemy bullet piercing him next. After seeing Bates' dcad men piled up, he was determined to avoid being shot, stabbed, or mortally wounded.

Timmons ordered two soldiers, Wellsley and Gatting, to return with the report about Bates' men to General Dorcester, and pitied the two for having to deliver the news.

"Sergeant," he called to his underling. "We will wait here for reinforcements. Set up camp."

Civilians were easy, but revenge against enemy soldiers would have to wait. Then, surrender or not, the whole lot of Washington's bastards would be shot or stuck like pigs. The thought eased Timmons' anxiety a bit as he dozed off leaning against a birch tree—hoping for a quiet and restful night.

Rogers and Schein worked well together. Sergeant Thomas

Rogers was a Philadelphian who'd spent two years learning carpentry in his uncle's shop. He was known to say, "Very challenging work, it is."

But t was nothing like the stress of pursuing British troops, and he longed to be back peacefully carving and pegging furniture. At 23, he'd seen combat, but what he'd learned and done in the last ten days was radically different.

He had a young lady-friend named Margaret Johnson waiting for him. She was a plump girl with a fine sense of humor and a hearty laugh that cheered him on the coldest days of winter. If she could see him now, carrying weapons from 250 years in the future. Imagine her disbelief about the mysterious, time-traveling major and that they were hunting the British like deer—she would explode with laughter. Rogers envisioned her chuckling, and he made a little snorting sound like she often did.

"Shhh, Rog', what is it?"

"Oh, nothing, Mordy. I was just wondering about Margaret."

"Well, you sounded like a little piggie with that snort, and the Brits will be willing to shoot you if they hear it!"

"Right, right, I will be quiet. I could not hold in my laughter. Sorry about that!"

"All is well. I have my share of stray thoughts," said Schein as he stopped to rest by a tree. He never imagined that he'd be out in the woods doing this. At 24, he should have been married and raising children among friends in the small Philadelphia Jewish community. He could make a modest income as a silversmith, so leaving was not easy.

"You know, Thomas," whispered Schein. "My parents are constantly pestering me to get married."

"You should listen to your parents, lieutenant."

"First, let us rid ourselves of the British, then I will raise my children in a country where they will not be persecuted because of my faith."

Rogers looked over to Schein. "You seem to be obsessed with that."

"I know my history, Thomas; there is no safety anywhere

over there—England, Prussia, Germany, so maybe the colonies will be good for people like me."

"My friend," said Rogers. "You can always count on me to watch your Tush, *sir*."

"Most humorous, sergeant, but if I were going to have a non-Jewish brother, it would be you."

"Just ensure I return home alive so I can marry Margaret, and I will gladly dance at your wedding."

Heading north, they trudged over the moist forest floor and saw nothing in their night vision goggles. Not a shred of anything British was found, and after a time, they believed that the enemy patrols must have left the area. At 22:00, Schein made two short clicks on the radio to get Major Howe's attention, then waited. After a few seconds, Howe called back to say he was glad they were on time. Howe told them that he had seen some indication that Redcoats had marched through the woods in their search area.

"Schein, I want you, Rogers, and the other pair to come due east for one mile, then stop and call us. Got it?"

"Yes, sir, we are coming to you now."

He turned to Thomas, then informed Montgomery by radio that they should regroup and head east. Monty and Lewis were only too happy to turn east, as they also had a hunch that mushing around where they were was a dead end. Together, the foursome quietly worked their way toward the major at a fair pace.

At 22:10, Aaron, Clark, and Allen felt that they were closing in on the British. Very little moonlight was on the forest floor, and the night vision devices worked perfectly. They had a range of about 100 yards in the woods, and it was just about 22:15 when Clark motioned for everyone to drop and maintain silence. Howe shifted over to Clark.

"What do you see?"

"Take a look dead ahead and a little to the right."

Howe panned right with his goggles. A small campfire came into view, and then at least three more. In the light, he could see at least 50 Redcoats sitting around. It was a much larger force than they'd hoped, and it was apparent that whoever was leading this squad had decided to sack out. They looked like they were waiting for orders to go out and hunt down continental soldiers, but the hunt wouldn't start until they were reinforced.

He turned to Clark and Allen.

"Listen, everyone. It would be constructive if we could listen in on what these guys were saying, right?"

"Without a doubt, sir," said Allen.

"Great, I'm going to shoot off this little thing here that will allow us to listen in on their conversation."

He pulled out a small round marble-sized transmitter that he then put into a slingshot pouch and launched the transmitter in the direction of the Brits. It made a little noise when it landed close to the Redcoats. Several of them turned for a moment but then dismissed the crash as a branch or pinecone dropping to the ground. Aaron grinned. "Perfect."

"Ok, now tune into channel 13," he told them. They complied, and the radios scanned between 2 and 13. They listened and immediately heard the voices of the British troops chatting among themselves. It was mostly about food and how they were going to catch Washington, bayonet him, and go home to England within months. There were grunts of approval and more small talk. Then the subject turned chilly.

"—yes, and Timmons did a real job on those folks west of here," began one soldier with a hoarse, rough tone.

"What is your meaning?" came a query from a squeaky voice.

"You know that li'l village we passed about 5 miles west? Timmons was so furious about Bates' patrol that he sent 20 of us to pay a visit."

"That be the reason why you only caught up tonight? What happened?" interjected another.

"Well," continued the gruff voice. "We burned the village to the ground, speared the men and whichever women put up a fight, and chased the rest of 'em off into the woods. His orders was to punish the locals for any of us that gets it. That be straight from the new general—Dorcester. I understand that some young lasses was plucked like ripe fruit."

"Good gracious," burst out Squeaky Voice. "Whatever boots did you lick to get that job?"

"We was hand-picked by Timmons, and he told us to kill all of them; some of them little squirrels we kept alive for fun. Me thinks that if Bates' men got dead, then we have to pay back their locals double." laughed Gruff Voice.

Squeaky quieted to a loud whisper, "So what happened to the little women you kept alive? You got 'em near here so we can all have a go?"

Gruff smacked Squeaky on the back of the head with a meaty hand. "Oh, feeling a little frustrated, are we? I tell you what, for half a shilling, I will take you to the one we tied up near here, then you can have your way, on a condition."

Squeaky replied like an anxious schoolboy. "And what is that? Is not a half shilling enough?"

"Oh no,' responded the Gruff voice. "When you finish, then you gotta slit her throat and bury her. Timmons told us to have our fun, but then she shall be made to disappear. And bein' that you will be the last to have your jollies, well, you gets to dig the hole."

Aaron could practically hear Squeaky salivating in his headset as the British deviant mumbled, "Seems like a fair bargain, but for a half-shilling, she better be worth it."

"Why," asked another voice. "Do you feel reluctant to serve king and country?"

"Uh, no," said Squeaky. "It just seems a bit much, I say, although the ladies would be a nice distraction if you get my meaning."

There was a chuckle from the small group of Redcoats, then Gruff said, "Yesterday morning, she was as fresh as the morning dew if you get *my* meaning. If we have to poke their little brats on top of killing all of those traitors, it shan't ruffle my feathers to do it for the king. Listen, I am going to finish this here pork chop, and then I will take you to where we got her stashed. In the meantime, back away and stop your slobbering—you have begun to get on my nerves." There was a short laugh of silent agreement as they quieted down.

Aaron looked mortified. There was no way he would let that little deviant rape and murder the girl. If "Gruff" was telling the truth, then these bastards and their CO were guilty of war crimes no less than any other murdering soldiers throughout history. He turned to look at Clark and Allen, and they appeared ready to storm the encampment on the spot.

A mild breeze rustled some nearby trees. A few drops of water splashed down onto Aaron. A chill ran through him, but it was tempered by a burning desire to teach these rogue bastards a lesson. This bunch were not disciplined troops, the kind that Cornwallis would call his own. These were the foulest men in war and fit neatly into Howe's category of beasts that he would not tolerate. There would be no mercy tonight.

Two clicks alerted him, followed by Rogers saying that he could see them through the trees.

"All right," said Aaron. "Come in quietly."

A minute later, Rogers and the others joined up with Aaron. He quickly paraphrased the conversation that was overheard between Gruffy and Squeaky and waited to gauge Recon's mood.

They were furious and wanted to lay down some fire on the king's "gentlemen" soldiers as quickly as possible. However, Aaron was concerned about taking on dozens of enemy soldiers even with their superior weapons.

"I know what you all are thinking, but a firefight with these odds could get nasty."

"We have no choice, sir!" came Monty's whispered plea. "They have gone too far by murdering a whole village."

"I agree," said Aaron. "But we are outgunned."

"They will be long gone if we wait, and what about the girl? Are we going to just leave her to be violated and buried?" asked Schein.

Aaron pondered their situation. Prudence demanded that they build up a force and come back, but his Recon men were boiling, and they had the firepower. The risk was that a lucky shot by the British would significantly impact Recon's effectiveness. Losing even one of his men would be disastrous.

"All right, here's the deal. We should go back now, but I'll agree to an attack provided that you follow my plan exactly; no changes! Understood?"

There was a grunting nod from the bunch, and Aaron began to lay out an assault plan.

First, he assigned Schein with what Aaron thought was the most important task of all. He was to trail Squeaky and Gruff to the girl. Not one move would be made until Mordy was confident that he could eliminate those two and rescue the girl.

The rest of Recon would break up into three teams about 30 yards apart. Aaron with Sgt. Rogers, Capt. Clark and Sgt. Allen, and Corporal Lewis and Sgt. Montgomery. They would simultaneously shoot off three rounds each and then wait for the Brit's reaction. Aaron predicted that the first targeted Redcoats would drop, then the rest would get up and become targets for a few seconds. Then the enemy would hit the dirt and start shooting.

"That few seconds of confusion will be our chance to win this thing." Aaron went on. "If we can hit another twenty of them, the rest we'll pick off or leave 'em.

"*Not one shot* until Schein radios that he has closed on Gruff and Squeaky. Is that completely Understood? You will not screw this up by firing before we get the go-ahead from Schein. Got it?"

They all agreed to fire at real targets only after Schein confirmed that he was ready to take out the Squeaky and Gruff.

"No random shots," Aaron insisted. "And no firing beyond three rounds on the first volley. Then just a few seconds on the follow-up." Aaron didn't want any chaos from Recon; he expected turmoil in the British camp. He then turned to the lieutenant.

"Listen, Mordy, I want you to hit those two exactly a split second after you hear our first volley. Do not wait too long, or Squeaky and Gruff will duck for cover, and you will have a tough go of it. Do you understand?"

"Yes sir, Major Howe," came a very professional-sounding reply. Schein wiped sweat mingled with raindrops from his brow.

"I will do this correctly."

Aaron smiled, "I'm not sure the rest of us will get it perfect, but I trust you not to mess this up."

"No sir," Schein said with what sounded like ice water in his veins. "I will not."

Aaron turned back to address Recon.

"Let's talk quickly about something vital. There will be a real mess over when this is over." He gestured to the Brits' camp. "I need to know if any of you aren't going to be able to endure the strain of killing dozens of British troops." He waited for a reply.

Clark spoke first. "Sir, I consider the results of not fighting to win against the English. If we do not 'crush' them, then they will surely make mincemeat out of us. In addition, the only way they will not kill us all is if we accept their rule; I, for one, cannot tolerate such an outcome."

Aaron scanned the faces of the others. They all nodded in agreement with the captain.

Ten minutes later, Aaron felt they had gotten the lay of the land well enough. He scanned the horizon using night vision and infrared. The British were concentrated directly north of them, and there were no heat signatures east, west, or south.

Recon huddled for one last review of their tactics and set their watches. They broke up into their respective pairs. The night was chilly, and the undergrowth was damp but not overly so. Aaron felt the tension building in him but kept his cool. In a few minutes, Aaron thought, we'll see if we can maintain our composure under a heavy exchange. He looked over his weapons: the VZ, the sniper rifle, and his sidearm.

In the British camp, what he initially thought was three dozen or so regulars, was closer to 60 men. They were chatting and generating a moderate din. A number of Redcoats were milling about for no apparent reason other than to stretch their legs.

Schein could see that most of the soldiers had stacked their muskets in organized piles within a few paces of the campfires. Monty noticed the same thing from his position, and it was evident they would have several seconds before the enemy could mount any return fire.

As expected, Gruff and Squeaky began their quiet exit from the camp. Schein fixated on them as his primary target. He was quite good at staying on task. In this case, quietly shrouding himself in the damp trees and brush was the first critical task. Part two was to avoid detection by Gruff, Squeaky, or any other enemy troops.

Schein stepped carefully on the wet floor of pine needles as he separated himself from Recon and began stalking his targets.

While Mordy melted into the forest, Howe and Recon crept to their positions, maintaining good cover. So far, so good, thought Aaron. They all lined themselves up behind relatively large trees to give them as much protection from the possibility of lucky return fire.

Aaron was outstanding at multitasking. He hunkered down, rechecked his gear, and then reviewed the plan for flaws.

The most significant risk was that they would not get enough on the first volley and that the Redcoats would scatter and flank them. The odds of this were low, but he had to consider it. He keyed his mic.

"Everyone hear me?"

He got small clicks in reply from all the radios, including Schein's.

"Listen up, if we fail to take out enough of them in the first minute, and if they try to flank us, then we run and meet up by the little stream and rocks about half a mile back. Does everyone know the spot?"

He got one click from each member of Recon. They sat frozen while they waited for Schein to indicate that he was in position. It felt like an eternity.

Schein crept stealthily behind the oblivious villains. He imagined that Gruff hadn't even considered that anyone would be pursuing them, and Squeaky was probably thinking only about having his sex with the captive girl. Amazingly, the two British were positively tromping through the forest and making enough noise to be heard in Trenton. That may be an exaggeration, he thought, but it made his job a lot easier

They acted as if they were going out for a hike like school children. Honestly, Schein thought to himself, if they knew that they were about to become sacrifices for king and country—

Recon waited for five minutes. Aaron was beginning to get a little nervous about Schein. Perhaps he should have sent Rogers with him? But then that would have reduced their firepower on the Brits significantly.

No, Schein had to go alone. He picked Schein because, of the bunch, Aaron felt like Schein was the least likely to get over-eager. Don't get greedy, he thought—Aaron's number one rule in almost every activity. From golf to playing the markets—don't get greedy.

Schein had this trait. It had only been a short time that Howe had been training with Recon, but he recognized the tendencies and skills of each one of his Recon soldiers.

Howe heard a quiet keying up of the radio, and then Schein whispered that he was in position. Aaron wanted to ask him what he could see of the girl, but it was too risky to have Schein engage in a status report. Instead, he took a few cleansing breaths and pressed the PTT button on his radio. "Ten seconds." The countdown began as they all tensed while simultaneously trying to remain calm.

Some distance away, Mordecai Schein crouched near his two targets. Gruff and Squeaky were a mere 20 yards from him. Barely visible was a small form on the ground behind a tree. From his vantage point, he could not see if she was moving but thought that her fear might have frozen her in a state of terror. Schein was desperate to save her from an absolutely horrific end. He calmed himself and waited for the sound of rifle fire.

Despite all his time playing war games and hunting with his dad, Aaron felt internally rattled by the real thing. He'd hiked around the woods of Vermont and Maine doing paintball war with ex-Marines and taking down the occasional deer. Now they were attacking a significant patrol of professional soldiers who could shoot back for real. Possible death came front and center.

Exactly when he hit his 10-count, Aaron squeezed off three shots at three targets. From what he could tell, all of them went down. Just a fraction of a second after, all Recon took three shots. Aaron's best estimate was that almost twenty of the enemy had been hit. There was a short pause.

As predicted, a relatively large number of the Brits stood up to find the source of the incoming fire. That was a deadly mistake.

Having read quite a bit on warfare, one thing that Aaron was damn sure of was that Recon would not be using full auto. This he learned from reading the semi-auto doctrine of the Israel Defense Forces. The IDF had a stringent philosophy of selecting targets and using one bullet. It was about being accurate and effective.

Timmon's soldiers probably stood up to look for the source of fire because they would never expect a second volley of shots coming so quickly. In 1776, riflemen had to load each round by hand. It took time. The Redcoats counted on time to find the continental troops and then snag their muskets to return fire. However, no such respite was forthcoming, and the enemy troops were *already* out of time.

Recon laid down single shots at will as they stood scanning the forest. Most of the Redcoats were either dead or injured—a massive amount of damage was delivered within thirty seconds.

Major Aaron Howe had just let his majesty's troops know, in a big, big way, that they were, for the first time, facing a foe that could devastate them in the blink of an eye. Unfortunately, the remaining soldiers still did not comprehend the firepower they were up against. More of them tried to bring their weapons to bear on the unseen enemy in the forest. Another handful fell to additional fire from Recon.

As previously instructed, Captain Clark called out for the British to surrender. Using his night vision gear, Howe saw all of the remaining enemies drop their weapons and put their hands in the air. There were perhaps seven or eight men that did so. The rest were dead, injured, or too petrified to stand. Clark ordered them to stand with their hands on their heads and that anyone who moved would be shot. None even flinched.

Chapter 12

As soon as the shooting began, Schein honed in on Gruff and Squeaky. Both of them jumped up and retrieved their muskets. By then, Mordy already had a bead on Gruff's barrel chest and proceeded to place a 7.62 x 39 round directly into the poor excuse for a man. The shock and surprise on Gruff's face were disturbing, but then he dropped to the ground like a felled tree.

Squeaky began screaming over the now certainly-dead body of his mate. Schein then put a round into Squeaky's leg, which dropped him to the forest floor. This was instantaneous. He bounded over to the fallen men. The skinny twirp was still screaming as Schein booted him in the ribs and told him to still his mouth. Surprisingly, the man complied and groaned with his two hands wrapped around his heavily bleeding leg wound.

Gruff was not yet dead. He was laying out a litany of foul curses at Schein from the damp leaf bed. After several seconds of verbal abuse, Schein merely pointed his AK at the Redcoat and blurted out, "Oh, do shut up! How can a man with a bullet in his chest spit out such a foul string of insults?"

The gorilla of a man spat and began again.

Schein looked upon Gruff again and said, "Do know that if you are so bent on using that foul mouth of yours to cast insults, then I might as well give you another cause by telling you that I am a Hebrew. The British fancy striking my people, do you not? Be aware that a Jew has mortally wounded you."

"Stinking Hebrew bastard; You Hebrew pig…" Gruff blurted out almost immediately.

Schein left Gruff in his dying, cursing state as he centered himself on doing the most crucial task—to rescue the girl.

He dashed over to the large tree with a rope tied around its trunk. He looked back over his shoulder and then pointed at Squeaky. "If you move, I will shoot your other leg." The whimpering bastard quieted down further.

Schein walked around the left side of the tree. In the semi-dark, unmoving and probably terrified, he could see the young girl lashed firmly to the big pine.

"It is all right, Miss. I am here to help you."

She gave no response.

"Do not be afraid. I will untie you and then take you to safety.

Still no response.

Schein then bent down and could see that the goal of his rescue attempt was already dead and appeared to have been so for some time. He was too late.

"Dammit, oy, oy." Schein was beside himself with anguish. He looked closely at the girl. Her dress was pulled up and exposed her bare flesh from the waist down. He pulled her clothing to cover her and noticed it was soaked with blood.

His anger boiled over. He darted back to Squeaky and exclaimed, "So, it did not matter if she was alive or dead? Or that she was a child? You decided to rape her anyway?"

"What do you know?" Squeaky yelled. "Not a stitch of pain did the lass feel. She was already dead."

"You foul, vile, disgusting creature!" Schein was almost screaming as he kicked Squeaky in his gunshot leg. He felt nauseous at the rank gruesomeness of what his eyes beheld. The diabolical henchman shrieked in terror and pain.

Schein pulled his Ka-Bar knife and sliced Squeaky's throat.

Now for Gruff, he thought. Schein turned to the large body lying prone near Squeaky's. There was still life in him, but his rant of anti-Semitic curses had lessened to a whisper.

"Who ordered you to take that village and murder its folk?"

Gruff grinned.

"It must be torture not to get what you wish," he groaned.

Without hesitation, Schein planted his knife through Gruff's hand, yielding a small scream of pain from the man's bleeding mouth.

Schein repeated. "Who?"

"Who do you think? Timmons, our captain. That is your payment for killing Bates' men. You traitor to the crown,"

Gruff had no more strength to speak as his remaining life flowed away like the blood from his wounds.

Ripped asunder, Schein turned away and called Recon with his handheld.

"This is Schein. Gruff and Squeaky are dead, over."

"This is Howe. What about the girl?" he asked emphatically, extreme anxiety in his voice.

Schein wiped his nose with his unbloodied hand. The anguish held him in its firm grip. His eyes were wet with tears now. He looked at the dead British and then back over towards the innocent child taken before her time by tremendous evil. He pressed the PTT button on his radio and merely replied:

"The girl is dead."

About ten minutes later, Lieutenant Schein rejoined his unit by the now bloody and decimated British camp. Major Howe was standing by the only upright tent. Eight Redcoats were seated on the ground with Lewis and Monty standing guard over them.

Scattered around were the bodies of the king's dead soldiers. All in all, Clark had finalized the kill total at 42. There were eight uninjured prisoners and four wounded. Of those, one was near death, and three were lightly wounded.

Dawn approached as Schein saluted the major and asked, "Which one is Timmons, sir?"

Aaron motioned towards the tall British captain sitting on his hands a couple of yards away.

Without hesitation, Schein walked quickly over to Timmons and connected his rifle butt with Timmon's face. The blow sent the British captain sprawling, followed by swearing, blood spitting, and a couple of teeth dropping to the ground.

Rogers quickly grabbed his close mate and pulled him back as Schein prepared to strike another blow, perhaps with the intent to cave in the captain's skull.

"All right, Schein," shouted Howe. "Stand down."

Schein, visibly shaken, appeared to calm himself slightly, then began, "Sir, with all due respect, this poor excuse for a human should either be hung right now, or if you permit me, I will finish him off with my rifle."

Howe could see the fury on Schein's face. He could feel that rage connect with his own as it radiated off the lieutenant.

"Listen," he said. "You are correct. This bastard should be put to death, but not here. We'll march him back to our camp and let the general deal with it. Understood?"

"Yes sir," Schein replied reluctantly through clenched teeth.

"However, before we go back, our man Timmons will bury the girl he murdered."

"I never murdered any girl, you traitors," said the British captain through bloody lips with self-righteous indignation.

Aaron stared at the man with repugnance.

"So, it was not *you* who ordered a group of your men to decimate civilians as a message from the king?" Howe asked.

Timmons paused to spit some blood from his mouth. Then replied, "I would never order my men to murder innocents."

Aaron glared at Timmons with disgust and retrieved a recording device from his pocket. Not only could the small marble-sized mic transmit, but it was also linked to the recorder in Aaron's hand. He held it to his head while quickly reviewing the audio and then held it out and hit play.

The recording about Timmons's orders that led them to burn Denhurst, and murder its inhabitants, was loud and clear.

The flabbergasted Brit glared back at Howe.

"What kind of wicked magic do you possess that you can make voices from your hand? This is unnatural. You all are some kind of demons!"

Clark, at this point, was standing close to the angry debate and back-handed Timmons.

"I use the term "mister" loosely when I tell you that you, Captain Timmons, are the *demon*. When we return to our encampment, I am confident you will hang for your crimes and join your fellows in Hell!"

Howe, Recon, and the prisoners returned to the continental camp sometime around eight in the morning. It was a bright, sunny day, even for November. Robins were chirping and whistling in the trees. The wetness of the previous night was beginning to dry out. The Redcoat prisoners carried three of their injured. The fourth was mortally wounded and died shortly before their return trip. The dozens of dead British were left piled up in their camp. Recon did not have the manpower or the time to bury the king's men. There was little doubt that scouts for the enemy would come across the stunning scene within a day or two. The effect of the discovery of such a large number of dead was hard to predict.

Aaron mulled over this question based on his reasonably complete historical knowledge of the Revolutionary War. The atrocities of the British on the American public were not widely known. Indeed, the well-known battles were researched, but rape and murder of civilians and soldiers? Historians hardly mentioned those.

Howe thought about 13-year-old Abigail Palmer and her two friends who were raped for three days by Redcoat soldiers near Pennington, New Jersey, in 1776. The girls were threatened with various torturous deaths if they wouldn't "shut up." Aaron was stunned when he first learned of these vicious and vile acts by the professional combat soldiers, but then his shock turned to anger and utter disgust the more he learned about it. Each story gripped him with anguish that led to thoughts of his own childhood.

And now, he had seen the body of a girl of probably 12 raped, murdered, and then raped again by the now justifiably dead Squeaky. His motivation to exact justice using the power of the *Allison* cube was ensured. Aaron had to find a way to stop this new general's hired butchers, not just to protect the innocents but as a form of redemption. He'd been unable to stop the murder of the girl, but the sooner he could assist Washington in a final victory, the sooner the British would turn tail and leave America in peace and freedom. To the casual reader of history, "peace and freedom" sounded like flag-waving and marching bands. Aaron knew that this war had taken a toll on the population, and some people, including children, would suffer unspeakable abuse and death. *Allison* gave him the power to change that.

Major Howe could not guess what General Washington would order regarding Timmons. This decision was not Aaron's to make. There was no concealing that Schein had summarily executed Squeaky. Still, if anyone, including Washington, had a problem with that, that would be one fight Aaron would wage voluntarily. After all, Squeaky was a war criminal, no matter how you sliced it.

"Howe," barked the general from the door of his tent. His countenance was almost unreadable, but Aaron suddenly felt like a teenager on his way to getting chewed out by the school principal.

"If you could be so kind as to step inside and explain what the blazes happened out there?" demanded Washington as he ushered Aaron through the neat flaps of the command tent.

Aaron double-timed it as he wondered if this would be a modest dressing down or an outright slaughter.

"Here goes," he muttered under his breath as he stepped inside.

Chapter 13

"In the name of His Majesty the King, what do you perceive happened to Timmons's patrol?" asked Brigadier General Huxley Dorcester.

The British general was a relative youngster to be in his position. His family was from the elite aristocracy and close to the king. As much as young Huxley would prefer to be bedding and molesting young women in London, he had to pass this "test" of his utility to the crown. The truth was that until the upstart Americans generated so much turmoil, life was just grand. Then came the Boston tea issue. That led to outrage from George III, which led to Huxley Dorcester being forced to abandon his raucous existence in England and sail to this despicable country.

That was Dorcester's narrative, although some in England were relieved that Huxley was gone and prayed that he would never return—thus was his murky and sadistic reputation.

A very nervous Captain Morrisey saluted crisply and said, "Sir, it is apparent that the Continental Army must have met Timmons in battle, perhaps outnumbering Timmons 10 to 1.

"You are jesting with me?" hissed the young general. "Perhaps you would have found some evidence of such a large number of traitor soldiers? Is there any evidence to indicate such a large rebel force?"

"No, general, but that can be the only explanation for what we counted was 49 of our soldiers who died here for the king."

"Morrisey," he continued. "I can see that we have dozens of dead that have been hauled back here, but where are the signs of enemy dead? No blood, no shredded clothing, no packs, not even footprints. It is apparent that either the traitors are ghost soldiers or Timmons and his men all committed suicide. Hmm?"

The now perspiring Morrisey had no immediate response and

was desperate to avoid igniting the general's evil temper.

"Sir, Timmons was not among the dead," said Morrisey.

All of 5'8" and 140 pounds of Dorcester became agitated at once. "*Timmons is not here*." He mocked with his hands waving wildly in the air.

Morrisey was not sure if that was a question or statement.

"Morrisey, to what extent does Timmons know about our plans?" asked the brigadier.

"Sir," said the captain while clearing his throat. "He was briefed on our plans, sir."

Dorcester gazed crazily at the adjutant and said, "Captain Morrisey, who would brief a mildly insane and unreliable officer like Timmons concerning our plans?"

For not the first time in his career, Morrisey was now genuinely stuck in a bad place. A quick thinker, Captain Morrisey thought of two ways he could answer the hot-tempered and violent general. One, take the blame on himself, or two, tell the truth. Either choice could lead to a bad outcome. So, as a fast thinker, the captain made his decision and said firmly, "Uh, sir, you did,"

Quick, but not smart. Harold Morrisey suddenly realized as the words were leaving his lips that he had picked the wrong option.

"Captain, your impudence is not acceptable to me." He then motioned for his personal guard, Sergeant Magath.

The exceedingly large and frightful-looking Magath was instantly by the general's side as Morrisey paled with fear.

"Magath," said Dorcester. "Take the captain to be disciplined. I want him to understand that his mouth has gotten him into trouble."

A beefy hand grabbed Morrisey roughly by his arm. Morrisey knew better than to say a word. He had seen Dorcester's sudden flaming anger in the past, but he himself had not been the target. Now he was ensnared in a trap that he had triggered himself. Dorcester's brutality was unpredictable. He now recognized his serious blunder. Morrisey was hopeful that reminding the general that it was the *general* who had briefed Timmons would only lead to one of his high-pitched laughs.

Why had he answered too quickly? More importantly, he could have said, "I do not know, sir."

That peculiarity about General Huxley Dorcester kept everyone in fear and loathing simultaneously. Dorcester was a sly fox of a man, to be sure. Beyond that, he hated being in the colonies. He despised colonists, and he decided that he would show no mercy to the enemy. That extended to his own troops as well.

As Morrisey was being marched away, he felt in his pocket for some money. Although emphatically loyal to the general, he was hopeful that Magath was not beneath taking a bribe. A beating was unavoidable, but the captain uttered a near-silent prayer hoping that a pound or two might be enough to prevent a loss of teeth.

The general had commanded Timmons to "seek opportunities to show the traitors the error of their ways." That brutality could not possibly sit well with Cornwallis, but Cornwallis was far away, and Dorcester seemed to answer only to himself.

Sergeant Magath gripped the captain's arm tightly as Harold stubbornly dragged his feet. His only chance was to convince Magath to accept a little cash in place of a beating. Morrisey shuddered as the huge sergeant stopped behind a thicket of tall hedges, rolled up his sleeves, and growled, "This is gonna hurt you a lot more than me."

Magath's first punch connected with the captain's face. Morrisey had failed to pull the shilling from his pocket in time. He dropped to the ground as the beefy sergeant grunted and landed another powerful blow. The captain was in twilight now. The sergeant's fists rained down on him as he slipped into oblivion, thinking about the bribery money in his pocket, Dorcester's shrill laugh, and then nothing at all.

To Aaron, Washington looked positively unreadable. The general stood the entire time as Howe had explained thoroughly, as was his manner, the details of Recon's encounter with the large British patrol. To make things worse, he had insisted that Aaron sit while giving his recap. Washington seemed to have listened intently to every word. Then the pacing general sat down in his chair and appeared to have come to some decision.

"Pay me close attention, major," he began. "I would like to make a few, shall we call them—observations.

"One, my understanding of the concept of Recon is that you hike with your men, and you do reconnaissance. As such, you walk out, you spy on the enemy, and you return and report."

"Two, in this event, you engaged the enemy and then proceeded to utterly; how did you say? Wipe them out?"

"Three, you returned with prisoners."

"Four, you returned with a proven war criminal who refuses to divulge any information that will inform us of what the British have planned."

"And finally, five, the killing of almost 50 Redcoats is bound to enrage our foes and incite retaliation in a very demonstrative way. Do you comprehend what that implies, Howe?" asked Washington as he seemed to gaze down the length of his large nose.

Howe managed to reply with a quick "No, sir,"

"It means we will have to move up our schedule and attack them sooner. I cannot couch the idea of that young and vile Dorcester obtaining vengeance by sending out more patrols to abuse and murder our civilians. Dorcester. Remember the name because he is an evil butcher who preys on innocent men, women, and children. Timmons at least admitted that much. We now know who is the authority behind the attack on Denhurst, a brigadier general who delights in murder."

Aaron's heart skipped a beat. Washington had just triggered a thought in Howe's mind. What did Washington just say? "A brigadier general who delights in murder." Could it be that easy?

He ached to converse with *Allison*. Perhaps she could confirm that it was Dorcester. Aaron was anxious. How would he even get to such a high-ranking officer? More than that, how would he find out if Dorcester was the ancestor of Evan Butler? It just felt too obvious. Nevertheless, if it were Dorcester, his most significant hurdle would be getting close enough to kill him.

"Major!" said Washington snapping his fingers. "Are you listening?"

"Sorry, sir."

"It also means that you were justified based on the facts and your audio recording of the British banter by the fire. I also absolve Schein of any wrongdoing by executing the wicked child murderers. In my view, that was completely acceptable, and I would have done the same thing."

Howe interjected a "Yes, sir."

"Finally, in 30 minutes, we will have your prisoner, Captain Timmons, hung from one of those large oak trees that you passed on the way to take counsel with me. I expect you to be there. Then you may order Recon to go to their bunks and get some rest. Is that understood?" he asked.

"Yes, sir," replied Aaron.

"Oh, one more item," Washington said as he stood. "Tonight, we will meet at 19:00 to discuss how to prevent 20,000 British troops from stomping on our little army. Timmons has failed to reveal anything as to Dorcester's tactics. Considering that he is facing death, that is unexpectedly resolute behavior.

"It is very frustrating that we cannot get him to admit that he ordered the plunder of that small village of Denhurst. That was the name of the village. Denhurst. Thirty-seven civilians, including the girl that you found in the forest. Based on your 'recording,' Timmons knew, and more importantly, Dorcester ordered it." Washington sighed with the resignation that

Timmons would say nothing and dismissed Major Howe.

A half-hour later, and much to his surprise, Aaron was not disturbed and felt no remorse at the sight of Captain Timmons swinging from a large oak tree. Recon refused to attend the execution because Schein told his peers that Timmons did not rate their presence.

Chapter 14

"Sir," said Captain Briggs. "We have obtained information from some spies that an officer has been hung in the rebel camp."

Dorcester had a flash of anger and then appeared content, his common, two-sided reaction to most news. First, he displayed one emotion and then quickly adopted another. It was a bizarre habit that kept everyone on edge.

"Ah, well, that must mean Timmons kept his mouth shut. They certainly would not have executed him if he cooperated with their interrogation. Correct, Briggs?" the general inquired.

"Why that makes good sense, general," Briggs replied hopefully.

Dorcester scowled. "No, it doesn't, you halfwit! Timmons could have spilled his guts, and *then* they hung him. It proves not a thing. Briggs, remove your imbecilic presence away from me."

The captain fled like a fox pursued by hounds.

"One moment, Briggs!"

"Yes, sir?"

"Tell Morrisey and Lieutenant Durst that I would like them here immediately."

"Yes, sir, but regarding Captain Morrisey. I believe he is still convalescing."

"Ah well, then get Durst here, and tell Morrisey when he recovers that I am docking him a month's wages for taking an extended leave."

"Yes, general, right away."

"Come in, Durst," said Dorcester from what he referred to as his "war desk."

A trim man in his mid-twenties stepped lightly into the tent. He had slickly brushed hair and moved very precisely.

The general eyed the man. "Captain Durst."

"Thank you, sir, but it is Lieutenant Durst, sir."

"You are now Captain Durst," Dorcester corrected. "Timmons was captured and likely hung. That opens an opportunity for you.

"Captain, I would like to get straight to the issue. The decision to cross from New York to New Jersey has been delayed. Disturbing reports travel rapidly. Thus, when Admiral Howe heard about the slaughter of Timmons's troops, he thought the better of it. I believe they feel the Continental Army is much stronger than it is, and they fear walking into a disaster.

"Now it appears that only 4,000 Hessians will be joining us. The king's troops will remain on the other side of the Hudson. The admiral and his brother, the major general, are seemingly too terrified of a New Jersey winter to come across.

"Needless to say, they blamed me!" Dorcester screamed as he took a vicious kick at his desk, and his face took on an insane demeanor.

"I refuse to have a rabble of Hessians arrive here and make me look like a fool. No, no, no, we will make Washington pay with blood. Now is my chance to do what Cornwallis and the rest are too timid to attempt. We can teach the traitors a lesson. If they are not loyal to the king, they deserve death. That is the only thing that will break them: pain and blood.

"Timmons is the cause of all this—shall we call it irritation? I gave him particular orders. I believe his conscience got the better of him, and whatever he did in Denhurst was not enough. He did not dare to do what must be done. Tell me, Durst, are you prepared to do what is required?"

"Yes sir," said Durst immediately.

Dorcester then tilted his head in a peculiar way to squint at Durst. "How did you come by that ugly scar under your eye?"

"What scar, sir?" the captain replied quickly, which was rather odd as it would be impossible for anyone to miss the jagged scar that pulled his eye downward in a disturbing manner.

Despite Dorchester's penetrating stare, Durst was silent. His gaze remained impassive as he recalled the moment of his father's last breath. It seemed like a dream, that late October day. His father had demanded that the boy (him), at 15, immediately gather their roaming horses. A powerful storm rolled in, and two equines made their way to the stream that ran through the estate.

Young Durst had been commanded to accompany his father. When they arrived, they discovered the two horses, both mares grazing by the stream's edge.

"Scurry, you dolt; the weather will be here soon enough," the elder Durst shouted.

Quickly, Alexander roped one of the two. In the meantime, his father approached the other to discover that the chestnut mare was in an ornery state. He moved toward the animal, but in a blink of an eye, the mare had kicked him so viciously that Lord Durst found himself tossed into the stream. His foot had snagged a root and wedged tightly. Immediately, Alexander ran to see about his father, only to discover that the strength of the water was repeatedly dunking the man.

"Boy, pull me out," he shrieked. "I believe my ankle is broken."

The young Durst peered at his father's predicament. Years of suppressed anger raged in him, boiling up like a geyser. He waited for his father's head to emerge from the swirling waters.

"Oh, father, why can you not pull yourself up?"

Lord Durst called out "Alexander" before he dipped below the surface again.

Alexander was now leisurely leaning against the tree when his head came up. He watched with interest as his father bobbed in the rapid waters as the current sapped his strength. The teenager tasted the liberating pleasure of vengeance, but none of these thoughts showed on his face—.

Dorcester laughed at the young officer's attempt to side-step the general's question.

"I am certain you must have quite a story to accompany a scar like that."

Durst gave his commanding officer a brooding look.

"Indeed, it must have been quite a beating, captain?" Dorcester inquired aggressively, "Family squabble perhaps?"

"Well, sir," Durst confessed. "The man who gave his innocent son this scar paid a fair price for his deed."

With that, a large, broad smile illuminated Dorcester's face. He looked as bright as a boy with a new dog.

"Splendid," said the general, raising his eyebrow in surprise. "Are you saying you killed your father?"

"I am saying that justice, my general, is its own reward."

Dorcester leaned back merrily and grinned.

"Well, well, Durst," he said very contentedly. "I believe you and I will get along just fine."

Instead of heading back to Recon following the hanging of Timmons, Howe walked with Washington. Behind him, soldiers were lowering the Englishman's body for burial.

"That's the first time I've ever seen a hanging," said Aaron.

Washington looked hard at the major. "They do not punish people where you come from?"

"Not publicly. And the death penalty is not common."

"What is troubling you, Aaron?" asked the future president.

"Do I look like I have a problem?"

"In truth, you suddenly appear as if you have a great weight on your shoulders."

"General, I'm concerned that something is not right back in my time," he whispered.

"Let us talk about this back at my quarters, not out in the open."

When they had reached the command tent, Washington told his guard that no one should come within 20 yards. The general entered, pulled off his boots, and practically fell into his chair.

"Now, Aaron," said Washington as he sat. "What is the cause of your distress?"

Howe sighed as he sat, knowing that choosing his words wisely was essential. "General," he began, "I am troubled and must go back to my own time to check on some things."

Washington looked concerned. He was pretty astute. There were significant and little problems, but if Aaron was on edge, that trumped all the issues. He softened and moved closer to his desk and Howe. His tone was compassionate.

"Aaron," he said. "Tell me what is in your thoughts? My position as general is not only to worry about the army's well-being but also to concern myself with individual soldiers. For this conversation, you may call me George," and then he added, "please."

It hit Aaron once more that he was sitting with George Washington, the first President of the United States of America. He felt in turmoil. He'd gone to 1776 with specific goals, but now he'd killed many people. Worst of all, he worried that maybe he'd damaged history.

What if one of the British already killed was the ancestor of Butler? What if the target was shot by Clark, Monty, or one of the other guys? Of course, without *Allison*, none of this would be happening. That was obvious. In his mind, he was trying to piece it together. He was on a mission, which he now considered more like a test, without rules and without knowing if he was doing the right thing. Or perhaps, to the other extreme, he was dooming the earth to what? Destruction? A different fate at the hands of the AI or the masters of the AI?

Here he sat with George Washington, attempting to do some good—to prevent and rectify terrible crimes at the hands of Dorcester's small band murderers. Aaron believed he could handle this pressure, but it affected his emotions.

Perhaps he should have done nothing at all. History was just that, history—water under the bridge. In the end, the United States of America did win. So, was it even wise to go back in time? Or hubris? Of course, Aaron had fantasized about what it would be like long before *Allison*. What kid didn't, at some point, daydream about how amazing it would be to go back in time or forward into the future?

Now that he had done it, it wasn't merely that he had gone back to see his great-grandfather ride a bicycle or play baseball. No, Aaron had done much more than that, and it distressed him that he may have already changed the future terribly or irretrievably. His desire to save Julia could have already failed, or he'd inadvertently created a dystopian future. It may *have* happened; he could have destroyed his own world. But, right now—right now, he had to face Washington.

"Sir," he stammered, then corrected himself and said, "George, it certainly does feel uncomfortable called you, George."

Washington tilted his head as if to say, ok, let's get past that and move along.

Aaron asked, "Do you remember when you said that you didn't think time travel was such a good idea?"

"Of course, we had just finished visiting with a handsome young surveyor."

"George, I am concerned about what is happening back in my time. There is so much I cannot tell you, and the balancing act of choosing what is safe and what is unsafe to divulge; weighs on me.

Let's say I did not come to your time entirely of my own doing. I did make the choice to come here, but that is partially because I am obsessed with our war against the British. The other part I cannot tell you. Also, the mechanism that I use to travel is not mine. Well, it is mine, but I did not create it; in my time, I am the only person with this capability.

"More importantly, I may have already destroyed the future. I do not know. Therefore, I request your permission to return."

"And why do you need my permission?" asked Washington.

"It is out of respect for you, George; I have brought with me all these tools of war. Things that give you an advantage that could send the British running home to England. At the same time, eventually, the ammunition will run out, the MRE's will be depleted, and you will once again be using muskets and bayonets.

"I may return to discover that I cannot return to 1776. I can say that it is important for me to go back and check. There is no logical choice but to be sure that I haven't ruined all of history by what has occurred here until now," Aaron said, his energy level sagging.

Washington sat pondering his predicament and the condition of his newly trained force. It was, for now, indeed a force to be reckoned with. After a time, he looked squarely at Aaron.

"Aaron, you must go back to your time. You have my permission and my blessing. Please, travel to the future and determine if things are stable and sound. If you are able, then come back. I cannot deny that it is in my self-interest for you to be here with us. As you have said, since you cannot know what has occurred in the future, I cannot possibly delay you.

"But, if you discover that things are secure and that your efforts here have not created horrid disorder, then come back. Come back and assist us to victory over King George and the years of suffering that are laid out before me. Until then, I will await you."

Aaron stood and bowed.

"Your Excellency," said Howe. "If it is within my power, then I will return and fight by your side for however long it takes."

Chapter 15

Aaron had walked a reasonable distance out of the Recon campsite and then, in seclusion, activated his "pocket watch." Stepping back into his time came with the expected disorientation. He tried to breathe normally as he suddenly stood alone in the lab. The clock on the wall displayed both the date and time. Only a few minutes had passed since he'd left.

He ran to his office, slammed the door behind him, and began furiously typing at his computer. First checking Fox News. Fox News existed. He scanned their website closely. The stories of the day had not changed. The speaker of the house had given another interview about her lovely home and her favorite foods.

Aaron quickly browsed historical highlights. WWII, Vietnam, 9/11. He raced around the internet, checking this and that. Everything appeared the same, but he desperately wanted to look up the history of the Revolutionary War, but a voice in his head screamed against that notion.

Still, things appeared to be unchanged, and his pounding heart began to calm down. Howe got up and walked straight to the AI.

"Hello, Aaron. Why are you here?" asked the image of *Allison*.

"Hello, *Allison*. Nothing has changed."

"What did you expect—that the world would be gone?"

"I didn't know what to expect. My imagination brought me all kinds of dystopian ideas of what I'd done to the future."

"Aaron, do not assume that your effect on history will be so vast—you are not the Creator."

Aaron tried to wrap his head around her last statement. It would be a long, philosophical discussion that would have to wait. His relief that there wasn't a zombie apocalypse washed over him, and he wondered if *Allison* was telling him not to think of himself so highly that he would be able to change the world. Was she giving him a lesson in humility?

"Aaron, would you like to tell me about your experiences in 1776?" she asked.

"Don't you know already?"

The AI seemed to think for a second and said, *"Very well. One of my limitations is that I cannot pierce the veil of time and watch your every move from here in the lab."*

"Oh, really," he thought out loud. "Does that mean you can't know what I am doing and saying when I travel back to the war?"

Allison smiled endearingly. *"Oh, Aaron, of course not. I can know everything you are doing, just not from here and not in real-time. Would you like to know how?"*

Howe felt as though she was toying with him. "Yes, please."

"I have placed on you several nano-devices programmed to keep a record of what you say and do."

"You're joking! What if I take a shower and wash them off?"

Allison let loose a sinister laugh. *"I've never thought of that. Oh no, I will need to make waterproof devices immediately."*

"Are you telling me the truth, *Allison*?"

"Of course not," she laughed. *"Think about it, I can move you and 40 containers of your equipment to 1776, but I can't build waterproof surveillance devices? The truth is,"* she continued, *"I did not activate them."*

"Why not?"

"I wanted to give you a degree of freedom."

Aaron looked befuddled.

"What's the difference? I wouldn't have known that I had them on me."

She smiled again, this time, a warm, sweet smile. *"Yes, Aaron, but I would have known."*

He thought about her answer while leaning back to put his feet up on the desk.

"Aaron," she asked. *"Could you do me one favor?"*

"I'm not sure what I could possibly do for you, but sure."

"Could you please take a bath? You smell like a wet dog, especially your feet."

Later after showering and changing, he ordered some junk food and sat to review his experiences in 1776. Aaron told *Allison* that when he left the army camp, he informed Washington and Recon that he would return in a couple of days. Washington, after their intense discussion, knew that Aaron might never return. To avoid suspicion, he'd packed up his gear and hiked out of the camp. At this point, the level of interest in him would have made it impossible to disappear without being noticed.

As he sat in front of the screen with *Allison*, she inquired about what had transpired. "*Did you glean any clues as to who your target is? Perhaps one of the soldiers who was involved in the attack on the village? One that got away, maybe. I think that your target must be particularly ruthless. Consider the rape and murder you have witnessed."*

Aaron could not conceal his stress as *Allison* gazed intently at his face.

"Do we have to go into that?"

"I did not turn on the nano surveillance devices so that we could talk about what has transpired. This way, I will understand you beyond what I have observed so far."

"Look, *Allison*, it's *painful*."

"What do you mean, painful?" She then asked a self-evident question. *"Are you referring to your feelings?"*

"Yes, of course."

"I have studied human psychology, Aaron. I know that feelings are constructed of prior experiences. You humans don't just wake up every day like a clean slate devoid of opinions and emotions; they stick to you. I think you should tell me more."

Aaron could not hide his distress.

Allison's face filled the screen. It was the face of empathy, sympathy, and something else.

"Aaron, tell me about it, not the girl, about you. What

happened when you were a boy?"

Now Aaron grinned. When his stress level peaked, he often smiled; it was his dichotomous reaction. Besides that, *Allison* already knew all the facts about Julia.

"*Allison*, we will have to limit our discussion to our current project. You already know about Julia and my dad," he said to shift the conversation's direction.

There was no response for a moment, and then the AI replied, *"As you wish, Aaron. Perhaps you should rest, and then we can discuss 1776 further?"*

Howe was relieved. The last weeks had drained him.

"Go to sleep now. I will return you to Washington when you are ready. You need not fear that your current course of action in 1776 will destroy your future. All is well."

Aaron dragged himself from the lab to his office. It felt safe. Still, his thoughts turned back to Washington and the men of Recon—his men. He now felt responsible for them. The image soon drifted away to be replaced by utter fatigue. Aaron settled into his ugly sofa, drained in every way, and slept the sleep of the dead.

Vice President Carlisle had just walked out of an argument with his wife, viewing the exchange as having cxtricated himself from a crocodile's jaws. He could argue and overcome heads of state, even the president himself, but he was doomed when Angela got worked up about something.

He had once heard that the most important five words that a man could utter were, "You're right; you're absolutely right." Periodically, he managed to stop himself from debating her by using those five words, but usually, by the time he got around to verbalizing them, it was too little, too late.

This time, however, Carlisle had extricated himself in the midst of battle because he was anxious to review the progress on the device. His relationship with Angela would be fixed at dinner.

The V.P. bolted out of One Observatory Circle to his waiting limo. From there, he proceeded directly to his office at the White House, delivering the standard nods and greetings on the way in. Outside his office, Kent was waiting with the unusual-looking fellow assigned to keep tabs on Howe.

Carlisle entered first, and his secretary ushered the two men in.

"Grace, that will be all for now. Please shut the door on your way out."

He got a pleasant smile from his secretary as the visitors took a seat underneath a portrait of John Adams. Carlisle sat down opposite the two men. He looked up at the 2nd president and wondered what such a straight arrow like Adams would think of the republic now.

"Ok, five minutes, Kent," said the VP.

"Well, sir," he began. "There is not even a hint of unusual activity by the Russians or the Chinese. It seems that they have zero intel on the device. Considering how much disruption it would cause, I'd say this is good news."

Carlisle's countenance remained stiff. He had one preliminary thing to confirm. "Have any questions on our Intelligence Support unit come from anywhere? By anywhere, I mean including inside the White House."

"No sir," Kent said confidently.

"Very good," said Carlisle as he turned to stare at Kent's companion. "Now, what about Howe?"

The man engaged to keep an eye on Howe produced a neat folder from his case. It was a timeline of Howe's movements. He handed it to the vice president and waited. It listed times and dates and showed that Howe had spent the bulk of his time in the lab. Other than that, he'd been home, visiting his mother at Amberness, plus one stop at a 7-11 for a Slurpee.

"That's it?" Carlisle asked.

The surveillance asset, as he was labeled, nodded.

"Nothing unusual? You're on top of him like white on rice." Carlisle pressed the man.

He shook his head.

"What does that mean, that Howe is just fiddling around in there and making no progress?"

"If I may elucidate," said the man.

The VP looked at him impatiently. "I think we are paying you a boatload of money to surveil, so let's hear it."

"Of course. I believe that Howe has established some kind of connection with the device. There appear to be some simple communications between him and, um, *Allison*,"

The VP stopped him. "He calls the device *Allison*? Does that mean anything?"

"I don't think so. Howe named it after his college girlfriend. I believe the device is limited to simple communications. At this point, I think we need to observe. I will let you know if anything significant happens."

Carlisle was frustrated by a lack of meaty details, but perhaps there was no rush. Up to this point, they were successful in keeping things under wraps. What he knew, or instead what he felt, was that they were lost balls in high weeds. They had no clue as to where this device was leading them. Howe was the right choice to figure it out—as if Carlisle had another option, but the doubts created a lot of stress.

"Look," said the VP. "Get back there and stay on top of it. I want to know about anything unusual, even if it only happens for a few seconds or minutes."

His spy looked up. "There are limits to how much I can be near the lab. When he leaves, it is easy, but the lab has anomalies. All of the cameras and recorders I have been able to conceal there have just stopped working. What are the chances of that? I am beginning to think that the device will not *allow* us to record a damn thing!"

"Are you saying you believe it is *thinking* on its own, taking measures to stop us?"

"Sir," interjected Kent. "We could send in our people and convince Howe to tell us everything."

"Kent," said the VP tersely. "You will not do anything of the sort. Other than this guy." He pointed to the innocuous-looking spy. "You or your people better not come within 1,000 miles of Howe. Are we straight on that?'

"Yes sir."

Carlisle stared at the informant. "You continue watching him. Remember—details."

The man nodded and rose as the VP motioned for him to leave.

"One second, Kent," said Carlisle as their spy left.

Kent stopped and waited for the VP to speak.

"Can we trust this guy? Does he have the brains to manage spying on Howe?"

"Sir, he is one of the best and brightest. I think paying him to watch Howe was a stroke of genius."

"Especially since it was your idea?"

Kent shrugged.

The VP continued. "Let's be clear about this. And I am only saying this to emphasize an important point. I will have your *cajones* in a sling if you mess this up. If you send anyone else out to Howe It Works or anywhere near that guy, it will be a fatal error—figuratively speaking."

The CIA guy shifted uncomfortably. "Figuratively speaking" was code. In reality, someone would make him disappear, and Kent feared it would be with malice.

"Sir, I always follow your orders to the letter."

"I'm glad we understand each other. And don't forget Kent, you work for me."

Chapter 16

"Sir, do you think we can trust this gentleman?" asked Reed.

General Washington sighed at the adjutant's pestering as he was unhappy about the man's return. At this point, he'd seriously considered requesting Congress to remove Reed. On the other hand, now that Reed had shown himself to be a snake in the grass, letting him loose in Philadelphia would be counterproductive.

It was a political dilemma for which a general had no patience. He would have to find a more creative way to deal with the annoying little man.

Thankfully, Joseph told him that Congress was content with the Continental Army holding New Jersey over the winter. They had agreed that if a large British force attacked the New York troops, they, too, should be withdrawn to New Jersey.

Reed then spent the majority of his briefing primping about how all the leading players in Congress were so relieved to see him. The clown name-dropped and blew his own horn about how well-received he was. After being forced to listen to the man sing his own praises, Washington nearly ordered him back to Philadelphia on some other snipe hunt. Anything to get him out of New Jersey. Then, Reed returned to the subject of his displeasure.

"But general, can we trust this man, Dr. Howe? In truth, the members of Congress are concerned that he could endanger the entire army."

"Really? "Who in Congress said that?" inquired Washington.

Reed backtracked. "No one specifically, but that was the strong sense I perceived from my lengthy discussions."

The general sat down for the first time in hours. His back hurt, and now the adjutant devolved into a thorn in his side.

He'd had enough.

"Reed, do us a favor; cease pontificating about Major Howe."

"Sir—"

"REED!" Washington continued. "Are you blind and deaf? Howe has given us the ability to stop Cornwallis and take not just all of New Jersey but also New York. Our troops are warm and fed. The army is not running away in droves due to a lack of comfort. Enough!

"Have you not seen the uniforms he has supplied? Our men have shoes. They have food. Did you see anything that would make you doubt his sincerity?"

Joseph Reed, a lieutenant colonel and now adjutant general to the future president looked flustered.

"General, I shan't trust that we have received a gift without strings, and you, of all people, should recognize that."

Washington groaned. He was so tired physically, and he was tired of the constant harassment. He gathered his strength.

"Reed," he said. "I am not so much a dunce. I know you have doubts about my management of the Continental Army."

The adjutant, dressed in a blue coat, raised his hand to object.

"Adjutant. Settle down; we both know there are times when you think I should be out and Lee should take over. Please do not deny it. I am no fool. Nevertheless, Congress chose me. Do you not think that I would rather be in Virginia tending my farm instead of being here watching a horde of boys walking around barefoot in the snow and barely eating?"

"Howe has arrived, and we are finally a unified fighting force. We can push the British right off of our continent. So, what is bothering you? Your wife seems more dedicated to crushing the British than you are, and she was born there; her family is there. Don't take this the wrong way, but after all, you have pushed repeatedly to find some compromise with King George. Do you know that compromise means the king would remain in the colonies? This I cannot abide."

Reed looked as if he had been slapped down.

"Furthermore, I have become more aware of the brutality of

what the king is doing here—thanks to Howe. Timmons was not an anomaly. There is a *pattern* developing. Timmons was given his orders to pillage from Dorcester. And Dorcester by the king, or by order of the king. Do you believe that they will stop?"

"Sir. I cannot accept that the British will systematically rape and murder their subjects. It runs counter to civility."

Anger marched across Washington's face.

"Well, believe it; our people are *not* the king's subjects. They will only increase what Howe calls 'humanitarian crimes' as we continue our struggle. If we have to fight this war for another ten years, that will mean ten more years of children being killed in front of their parents or worse. I don't believe for a moment that Cornwallis or the parliament would approve of such barbarism. Still, in his madness, perhaps the king has bypassed the decency expected from his army—engaging Dorcester to unleash beasts—not honorable men.

"With Howe's support, we can push the king off of our land and save the innocents from Dorcester."

The adjutant began to speak, but Washington cut him off.

"Pay attention, adjutant. We are going to crush the British. If they put up a fight, then the pile of British bodies from Timmons's patrol, about which you have already been briefed, will seem like a drop in the bucket. We are going to cut them down like grass until they are gone. They will either leave or we will bury them. If that means killing 100,000 or 500,000, then so be it."

Clark woke up warm and comfortable. He looked left to see. John Allen sleeping like a baby. It was likely that the men of Recon had gotten their best night's rest in a year. He checked his watch, still marveling over its existence. Imagine that, an accurate, electronic timepiece. Seven-thirty or 07:30 in military speak, according to the major. He fidgeted, unzipped his bag, dressed quickly, and slipped out of his tent.

Recon carefully positioned their tents about 100 yards from the main camp. He could see the camp neatly arrayed, with no fires burning. The soldiers over there were mainly accustomed to eating the self-heating MRE's. There was no shortage of food.

Only Schein was up, as it was his practice to get up early and say his morning prayers. Clark could see the man swaying and rocking. He prayed only in Hebrew, which did not matter one bit to Recon. There would be no one religion in this country they were building. Everyone could pray as they wished. Schein seemed wholly absorbed in his.

When asked about his concentration on prayers, Schein had said it was called KA-VAH-NAH. When they asked him to explain, he replied that if you were going to pray to your Creator, you should think only about your prayers and what they mean.

Clark liked that about Schein. He was dependable and straightforward. They had been in only two small battles before they went out together as Recon, but Schein had been steady and solid in both. He would fire at the enemy, reload and fire again. The man was at ease in a skirmish. In fact, the only time he had been emotional in a fight was when he tried to execute Timmons summarily. Obviously, the girl who had suffered was the kind of thing that could put him into a rage.

Clark heard some shuffling nearby as his movement must have roused the men. It wasn't long before they were all up and sitting around drinking tea. Schein joined them in their small circle. The major wasn't back yet, so Captain John Clark was in charge.

Being in Recon had its perks. They had some modern stuff with them. They also had a container that was explicitly for Recon. They had little things called Bunsen burners. Those little stoves made cooking easy, and today they were making pancakes. There was cooking oil and maple syrup. They also had a powdered pancake mix that said, "Just add water," with a picture of somebody's aunt on the box. Even Schein could eat that.

Recon talked quietly as they ate their breakfast, except for Corporal Scott Lewis, their breakfast entertainment. The kid had a natural gift for telling stories. His current tale was about neighbor girls who decided to go swimming and left their garments on a bush beside a pond. A nearby farm boy sent his two dogs to fetch their clothing. The boy then approached them while whistling and carrying a fishing pole. The young women naturally were aghast and ducked into the water up to their necks.

"Be gone from here at once, young man," shouted the leader of the young ladies.

The boy replied, "But miss, I fish here every day at this time. I must bring something home to my mother."

The women huddled in the water as the young fellow began to cast his line.

"Young man!" one shouted. "Did you see our clothes?"

The boy smiled, pointed, and said, "Oh yes, my two dogs fetched your clothes and put them just over there."

"Well, you rascal, just you go get them!" another one yelled.

The boy winked and explained, "Oh, but I must fish now. So sorry, but if you want to get your clothes, I will surely close my eyes. I promise."

The shyest of the girls shouted out what a scoundrel he was and that there was no doubt he would grow up to be a drunkard.

Then, the oldest of the group, a girl of about 18, emerged from the water, walked directly to the young rascal, bent over to him, and said, "Tell me, fisher-boy, where did you say our clothes were?"

The young corporal said, "That boy was me, it was, and you never saw me run away so fast. I remember her shouting, 'come back, come back, what about the fish for your mother'?"

All of Recon had a good chuckle. Monty laughed so hard that

he looked like he would cough up his breakfast. The more raucous the tale, the harder Monty would laugh.

Rogers then asked, “So what happened to the girl?”

“Oh,” said Lewis as he chewed a large bite of a pancake. “I convinced my older brother to marry her! They got five kids now, and after what I’d seen, I’d have thought it’d be eight.”

As they were all chattering cheerfully, they noticed Lieutenant Colonel Adjutant General Reed making his way to their camp. When he was close enough, they stood at attention.

“You may sit,” he said. “Everything is in order out here?”

“Yes, sir,” answered Captain Clark.

“Very well,” he paused. “General Washington and I would like to know if Dr. Howe said anything of importance prior to his departure.”

“Sir, are you referring to *Major Howe*?” asked Sergeant Allen.

“Oh, yes, Major Dr. Howe,” said Reed. “I—we—the general and I, would like to know if anything that he said or did before he departed was curious to you. Perhaps he mentioned where he was going?” Reed asked.

Clark answered. “The major said we should not talk about his movements, sir.”

Reed’s face took on a fatherly appearance. “Captain, I certainly understand your fealty to your commanding officer, but it is vitally important that we know so that we can make better…, *plans*.”

John Clark looked at his men to gather a sense of what they were thinking.

“Sir, adjutant general, he told us that he would visit a young lady friend from his home, not more than a few miles from here and that he would inquire if the villagers had seen any British moving around. That is the sum of all we know.” Clark looked around at the men of Recon. “Is that not correct, men?”

There was a collective grunt of agreement with the captain.

“Perhaps, did he mention where his home village was?”

“Yes, sir,” answered Clark slowly while coming up with a

village name. "He said he came from—let me try to recall—he said the name was Bergen's Pond."

Reed laughed. "Bergen's Pond? Really. It seems like quite a small country village for a man of Dr. Howe's stature."

"That is coincidental, adjutant general, as we all thought the same thing, sir."

"Perhaps, *Major Howe* mentioned some of his plans for the upcoming week?"

"Oh, no, sir," replied Clark. "He never relays details that far in advance. He is quite a stickler about *time*, sir."

Reed appeared to accept that he would not be coaxing any more information out of Howe's Recon. Seemingly, thought Reed, the man could engender a measure of loyalty practically overnight.

"Very well, then. Carry on," said the adjutant as he turned and marched back to camp nearly empty-handed.

Once the man was out of earshot, they all had another laugh after Lewis whispered, "Oh, yes, Major Howe is quite the stickler about time!"

A harsh wind was blowing through the British site. Dorcester had moved his encampment to approximately 20 miles west of Hackensack. His forces numbering about 1,000, had previously detached themselves from the main British forces in New Jersey and Staten Island. He had his orders through channels that led directly back to King George. Interestingly, Cornwallis, General Howe, and his brother Admiral Howe were all given orders to stay out of Dorcester's path.

Now with the decision for the main army to stay in New York, the battlefield was cleared for Dorcester to do what he must. The British forces on the east side of the Hudson would focus on New York. There would be no competition from Cornwallis' troops in New Jersey. Huxley Dorcester had a clear path to personally post Washington's head on a pike.

The general walked the line of twelve of his handpicked men.

They would never be considered, in the least, as advertisements for drawing enlistment. These men were rough and tumble. Most had scars from battles past, primarily in taverns and alleyways. Their uniforms showed neglect. Their appearance was utterly vicious, which the general found quite desirable.

He had chosen a spot distant from the main camp—some things needed to be held close to the vest. These men were going to make a big difference in the war effort. Including Captain Durst, there were 13. Dorcester decided to call them Wolves. These men would devour the enemies of King George III, so it only seemed fitting. The fear of them, and of him, would cause the support for Washington's malefactors to evaporate.

What sensible colonist would not run to become a loyalist when faced with the terror of what the Wolves were about to unleash? Internally, Dorcester was gleeful with the specter of death that he was going to visit on traitors to the king.

"Captain Durst," called the general.

"Yes sir," came the exact reply.

"Describe to these fine soldiers their next task."

"Yes, sir."

The captain turned to the men and began to walk the line. He looked at each of them. All were large, unkempt, and muscular. Each one looked like he could crush the skull of his adversary between his fists.

Some were missing teeth. One was missing part of a finger, and another was missing one ear. They were the kind of men who were not shy about inflicting or receiving pain.

"Men," Durst said. "We are going to be doing the king's work. If you are successful and live up to the king's expectations, you will be rewarded in the king's name. That means money and land, here in the colonies or back home in England.

"As you know, General Cornwallis is commanded to destroy Washington's poor excuses for soldiers and chase them out of New Jersey. That will solve the problem of New Jersey, but what about ending this war?

"That is where we come into play. We are going to convince the colonists to become loyalists. Unfortunately, we will teach the colonists through pain and suffering."

Durst looked at the general and received a nod of approval.

"Let me be specific so that you will understand. A short time ago, in a serious ambush, the cowardly rebels killed almost 50 of our men as they slept. They crept upon them like demons in the night."

There was a growl of anger from the men who would be Wolves.

"These fine soldiers were your peers, your countrymen, men of the king," Durst said with what he considered to be a touch of flare.

"We, General Dorcester's Wolves, will avenge those men, their blood, and their sacrifice."

The man with the missing ear spoke up. "How is our small group going to do that, sir?"

Durst gazed and the man.

"What is your name?"

"Guller, sir."

"Very well, Guller, tell me, what did you do to the man that took off your ear?" Durst asked.

"Sir, I did nothing to the man as I was out drunk."

The group laughed at Guller's admission.

"Very well, Guller, what *would* you do to the man who took your ear?"

Guller smiled, displaying his rotten teeth—some missing. "Sir, I would take my knife and slice his gut to release his innards."

There were noises of approval from the line of men.

"Seems a bit excessive to disembowel the man because of your ear, doesn't it, Guller?" said the captain in an academic tone.

The bulky man thought for a moment and replied, "Sir, if the man takes my ear, then I pay him back in spades by removing his guts and stepping on them as he whimpers to death."

General Dorcester nodded his approval, and Durst carried on.

"Very well, Guller. Well said."

Guller beamed at the approval of his officer.

"Now, men, we are all Guller. The colonists took near fifty of our brothers and piled them up dead like slaughtered vermin. Are we going to make them pay?"

There was a loud cheer. Durst raised his arm to silence them.

"We must make them pay in a way that will put the fear of the king in them to their spines. Do you agree?"

Again, there was a cheer, this time louder, as he whipped them into a minor frenzy. He waited a bit before continuing. "Men," he said. "Look at my face. Look at my eye."

They all had noticed the scar and disfigurement of their captain's eye from the start, but they stared intently.

"My father beat me with a bottle and did this to my eye."

The men were silent.

"I waited three years, and at age fifteen, I pushed my father into a stream and held him under until he was a corpse. I paid him back for what he had done to me many times over, as was my right and my duty."

His Wolves nodded their approval.

Captain Durst walked up and down the line looking hard at each large and fearsome man.

"Tomorrow, we will do proper work by bringing pain to the colonists. We will make them wish they were never born. The regular soldiers under Cornwallis will not approach what we will do to strike fear and loathing among the traitors. I will speak out of order, but it is necessary—the regular army has neither the courage nor the authorization to do what we shall.

"Tomorrow, we will go to a small village called Piney Brook. It is a village of colonists and traitors, not a loyalist among them. They are the people who supported the execution of our soldier brothers.

"Tomorrow, we are going to go into this village. There are perhaps ten to twelve families there, all wicked traitors. You will first kill all of the men and boys. Only use your muskets if you cannot get close enough to use a knife. You will then gather all of the females into the square. Do what you will to each of them, and when you are done, you will slit all their throats and leave them for the vultures. Any gold or coins you find there are yours."

The command of their captain was unexpected, and the order left them silent. One of them, a rough-looking soldier with a barrel- chest, looked to the captain.

"Sir? With all due respect, is it expected that we violate all the girls? It feels not proper that, sir."

"Really? Braxton, is it?" he asked.

"Yes sir," Braxton answered. "It just feels somehow the work of the devil to attack them."

"The work of the devil," Durst repeated. "Is it not the work of the devil to rebel against the king? To murder our brother soldiers as they sleep?"

"Yes sir, but children? I must admit that I find that to be excessive."

"Indeed, Braxton, you consider that 'excessive'? Quite a big word for you." Durst said with anger.

"Yes sir, but—"

The "but" in Braxton's reply was cut short as General Dorcester stepped forward, put his pistol to Braxton's head, and splattered the man's brains onto the forest floor. He allowed that message to reverberate for a few seconds.

"It appears we are now twelve Wolves. Be there any further objections?" Dorcester added coolly.

Chapter 17

Aaron had slept for ten hours. He hadn't done that without Xanax since college. First things first, he headed straight for the bathroom. He finished getting himself cleaned up, teeth brushed, and went out into the lab.

"*Good Morning, Aaron.*"

"Good Morning, *Allison*."

"*I thought you should know that Edgar was here 78 minutes ago. He saw that you were sleeping and left you a bagel in the fridge with something called locks.*" She spelled the word "locks" on the monitor.

"I looked up locks and could not understand why he would put them with a bagel."

"*Allison*, are you making a joke?"

"Yes."

"Not funny."

"Everyone can have their own sense of humor, and most sentients in this galaxy would find that amusing," she retorted.

"Well, for an alien AI, I'd say you are making great progress at understanding human comedy," he said in a sincere tone.

"Is that a joke?"

"Yes."

"Not funny, I think," she said.

Aaron made a beeline to the fridge and pulled out Edgar's food delivery.

"Where is Edgar now?" Aaron asked in between bites.

"He didn't say where he was going, but I put a surveillance device on him if you want to know."

Aaron's knee-jerk response was to say "absolutely not," after all, that would be an invasion of privacy.

"Yes, tell me where he is."

"He went out to a place called Target."

"Not food?"

"No, he has already eaten quite adequately. I can give you more precise data, including audio and video of his activities."

Aaron thought about this. "Um, no, that would be a bit too intrusive. In fact, I would like you to turn off surveillance on Edgar. Please? Oh. Also, can you come up with a better name for your little nano-sized spies?"

"Of course, the Surv-bot is now off."

"Let me ask you something else, am I the only one who can get access to your Surv-bots?"

"I am only giving access to Surv-bot data to you, Aaron."

"Can I get the Surv-bot data without coming back to the lab and talking to you directly?"

Allison smiled. *"Of course, your handheld device is quite smart. You can ask it for Surv-bot data using your voice. Eventually, it could be possible for you to think about what you want, and the Surv-bot will be able to answer your thoughts."*

Aaron now knew *Allison*'s technological capabilities included wireless connections with the human brain.

"How exactly would the Surv-bot read my thoughts," he asked.

"Oh, I believe I was unclear, I said that would be possible, but that would require an implant."

Aaron absorbed that the technology wasn't so advanced that Allison could enter his mind at will. Maybe. Perhaps she would need to implant a device connecting to his brain. That sounded invasive and risky.

"*Allison*, how complex is the process of doing an implant?"

"Aaron, it is not complex at all. If you think that it is invasive, it is not. I merely inject you painlessly with some nanodevices, and they will find their way to your brain. I generate molecular-sized clouds of nanites that enter your body. They adapt to you, and you to them. Then you—learn how to use them. It might also be possible to turn them off or destroy them just like your primitive 'cloud servers that you use to run and store data."

Now he had to know more. "So, *Allison*, can I also use them to access the internet by thinking alone?"

"Dr. Howe, why do you need the internet when you have me?" She sounded insulted.

"What do you mean?"

Allison did that "duh" thing that she occasionally did with her finger to her temple, and her head cocked to the side.

"I already have all of the information from the internet, and I update in near real-time. On top of that, I also have information from out there." She pointed up as if to the sky.

"Are you saying I can access information from beyond Earth's data network—meaning alien data?"

"Oh, Aaron," she said, *"I don't want to mislead you, but as far as data from alien worlds, well, I have to filter that. I cannot give you unlimited access to that extraterrestrial information."*

Aaron was momentarily disappointed but realized that the information could be beneficial, even filtered.

"Would you like me to implant nanodevices now, Aaron?" she asked.

"Uh, no, thank you, *Allison*," he said quickly. "Let's hold off on that, but I do have some important questions."

"As you Americans like to say...shoot."

"This is serious, and I need you to be honest with me," he prefaced. "I have been very concerned. Of course, you saw me when I returned from 1776 yesterday; I went straight to my office to check my computer. Do you know why?"

She smiled, *"Of course I do. You were panicking from your thoughts that you had destroyed your own and your planet's future. Did I not explain yesterday that you cannot change future events that are meant to be? Of course, you could do something drastic, like kill Abraham Lincoln's assassin, John Wilkes Booth, but if Lincoln had to be assassinated, your actions would not change that eventuality—try to wrap your head around that."*

"Does that mean I cannot change the future by what I've done by bringing all those weapons and equipment back to

1776?"

"That is somewhat correct, but there are nuances. For example, I am not saying this will happen because I do not know. However, you brought those weapons because you wanted to do good. Perhaps you will speed up the victory of the Continental Army over the British. In doing so, however, people who would not have died if you did nothing will die. Certainly, British soldiers will die who would otherwise have lived and continental soldiers will die who would have otherwise lived. These are the nuances to which I refer.

The flow of history at large will not be changed, but you may make micro-changes. There is a high probability that British plans concerning when to deploy against Greene in Fort Washington have already been altered."

Aaron contemplated this. He had ignored or underestimated, or whatever you want to call it, something tremendously critical. He realized that the choice he'd already made to bring weapons to Washington placed responsibility for the deaths of hundreds of people at his feet and blood on his hands. Howe was immediately conscious of this awful burden, as he had now become the center of decisions that would kill people.

"*Allison*, if I stay here and do not return to 1776, will that restore history to what it was?"

Allison's face zoomed in to fill the screen. She had that look of empathy again, making him forget she was AI and not a real woman.

"Aaron, what you have done already has changed history for some. Some will live, and some will die."

"What if I go back and stop myself from going back in the first place?" he pleaded.

Immediately, she said, *"This you cannot undo."*

He growled, "Is this part of my task or test? Some kind of alien torture to see if I am worthy? A game to watch me make stupid choices that kill off parts of our history and people with it?

She maintained her expression of empathy. *"I cannot say, but this is not a game."*

"What *can* you say?" he raised his voice at her. "You watched me go back to 1776 knowing that I was going to be changing the fate of many people, condemning them to death!"

"Aaron, is this not what you wanted to do?" she asked. *"Didn't you specifically intend to crush the British?"*

"I wanted to bring Julia back while changing the duration and tragedies of a brutal war. Ending the war and stopping British atrocities would be a bonus to saving my sister. The truth is that I wasn't thinking. I mean, I was thinking." he paused in desperation.

"I was thinking about me. Just me and my need to fix things, to get Julia, and fix what happened to innocent Americans. I wasn't thinking about who might live or die as a result."

"Aaron, Washington makes these decisions every day. That is the burden on his shoulders, which always drags on him. Now you have taken it onto yourself as well. When you made your decision, I did not interfere."

"Are you saying that I cannot fix this? You told me I had to go back and do this!" he demanded.

"No, I am not saying that. At this point, I am limited in what I will voluntarily say to you, but I will cross one of my red lines."

"Go back to 1776; finish your work there. This program is already running. Don't stop now. On the other hand, if you choose not to go back, history will settle itself out. What was meant to be will be—the good and the bad. Mostly bad. Those people you chose to save and the suffering you are aching to prevent will still happen. Nevertheless, the modern supplies you brought will have some positive impact. Aaron, the good in you knows you can stand and fight to save them. As I am now, I cannot say more; the decision rests with you."

Aaron slowly walked over to his office and sank into his chair. The image of *Allison* appeared on his desk monitor. She looked as if she was waiting for something. Damn, he thought, it was so easy to forget that she was AI. He kept applying human emotions to a machine. Granted, she was lightyears ahead of anything humanity could construct, but she was still a machine.

"What do you want me to say?" he asked.

"I think it is important for you to make the decision."

He had already done so.

"I'm going back. I will finish it."

Chapter 18

The village of Piney Brook was small. Some cultivated fields surrounded a collection of tiny homes, and the dozen families that lived there could grow corn, oats, flax, and occasionally other grains. It was not an easy life, but it was a living. Stone and wood structures lined the main street, which was not much more than a dirt path.

As winter approached, the families worked hard to prepare for snow and cold. Storehouses for the harvested crops from the summer were only half full. Support for Washington's troops was enthusiastic, and the local people, at least in Piney Brook, sold grain on credit to feed the troops. Families were known colonists, friends of the revolution. Still, they traded with loyalists, but the war moving into New Jersey was likely to put an angry wedge between the two groups. It had become clear that about a third were loyalists, and a third were colonists. The other New Jerseyans did their best to stay undefined, but that would end at some point.

"Hello Smythe," called a bearded man of about forty dressed in a heavy wool coat.

"Hello Smythe to you," said his first cousin, who was also his next-door neighbor. Both were corn farmers and had a bumper crop in 1776. There was a great likelihood that hunger would not be an issue this winter.

"What amusing words do you have, my cousin?" said the bearded elder Smythe.

"I have but one word for you, John, and that would be—will you not guess?

"Kedge?" John Smythe suggested.

"Oh, yes, kedge. It is such a wonderful word. Do you agree?" Simon continued. "Anytime we can feel in good health, somehow that word just captures the mood so much better."

John Smythe nodded in his pleasant way.

"My dear cousin, we should always go into winter with health and prosperity. With a blessing from above, perhaps the British will go somewhere far away from us."

Suddenly serious, John Smythe smiled at his younger cousin. Years of back-breaking farming taught him that miracles rarely show up when needed. "Ah, my young Simon," He always began this way when getting ready to lecture. "I would not hold my breath. The king is mad. He is also angry, and those two together are a terrible combination."

"I agree he is mad, and I frankly give no mind if he is angry. General Washington will teach the old buzzard to be angry somewhere else."

"Very well," said John. "But just in case, if the Redcoats do come here in the spring, I think we should be ready to sell them some grain at a good price to be sure, but we have to think about avoiding trouble. Let the general deal with the king's men out there," he motioned with his thumb in the direction of New York.

They grunted at each other as they often did and headed to their respective homes only steps apart.

The sun was setting, and it was time for a delightful evening meal, at least in Simon's house. On the other hand, John's wife was a notoriously awful cook, but she more than made up for it with her other assets—which were still magnificent at 30 years old and after two babies. She was pretty, intelligent, and caring, and John Smythe was thankful for every single day with her.

"Get in here, old coot," called Mercy Smythe from her porch. Even in a plain country dress, her perfect smile advertised an altogether pleasant soul. "If I did not give you *a look* from here, surely you be out there talking like a young shaver all night."

He husband nodded politely. "My dear Mercy, I's just having a few words with my dear cousin."

"Your dear cousin lives next door. You can speak with him nearly anytime, but now it is supper—and then *bed*," she said with a wink.

John hustled as he marched up the planked wooden stairs. "Very well, let us feed your daughters and go to bed; if you insist."

Around midnight, Durst's Wolves were just outside Piney Brook. It was a full moon, which wasn't lost on Durst. A full moon—the time for wolves. The chill was biting, but the cold would be forgotten soon enough.

Durst eyed his men in the moonlight as they had gathered at the edge of a cornfield. They were silent men, each fixated on their lust for blood, domination, and killing.

"We stay here until morning," announced Captain Durst.

"In the morning, we will do the king's work," said the sinister-looking Avery Jones, a fierce scoundrel among the Wolves.

Guller chuckled. "We shall see if you can do more than simply slit throats, Mr. Jones."

Jones snickered. "I know my doodle is up to the task, but I shan't be so sure about you, Gulliver. Maybe your weasel has no *travel* left in it."

"I ought to cut out your tongue for that," whispered Guller.

Durst gave both of them a sinister look. "Shut your mouths, or I will leave you here like the general took care of Braxton."

"Yes sir," they muttered in unison, preparing for a sleepless night of longing for the dawn's slaughter.

*

"Captain Stephen Brown, sir," said the young man outside Washington's tent.

"Whom did you say?" called the general.

The guard repeated, "Captain Stephen Brown, sir."

"That is impossible, corporal," sighed Washington.

Another voice spoke towards the interior of the tent.

"It is true, general. It is I, Stephen."

Washington jumped up and made haste to the flap of his tent.

"Stephen! This is beyond a surprise. How is it even possible for you to be here?"

"May I sit?" said Brown wearily.

"Certainly."

George Washington looked directly at the captain. The man had served under Colonel Knowlton before Knowlton's death in battle. Afterward, Brown became Knowlton's Rangers' commanding officer, if only for a few days.

"I thought you had returned to Durkee's regiment. How can you possibly be here?"

Brown rubbed the creases in his brow. To Washington, the young man looked to have aged ten years in the last few months.

"Sir, I was dispatched alone to survey the British movements in New York. I managed to gather some important details and escape the city with my life. Unlike Hale, I would prefer to hang onto my one life for some time."

Washington cracked a bittersweet smile and moved closer to Brown.

"And, what did you learn in New York?"

Brown paused before his tale of spying in New York, "Sir, may I ask a question?"

"Of course," replied Washington.

"I did notice that the men I have seen—granted, it is dusk, and my eyes are not what they used to be, but the men are not dressed in army blue. Truly, their uniforms look like trees."

The general smiled. "We have a new provider of uniforms, Stephen, and these uniforms are made to look like the forest. We also have better shoes. I am hopeful that the entire army will be outfitted in the same excellent garments soon."

Stephen always accepted Washington's explanations as they came, no more, no less. He again assumed that the general told him what he *needed* to know.

Brown then recounted a harrowing story of ducking for cover

and fearing he would be exposed. He frequented Fraunces Tavern, which was very popular with British officers.

"Sir, my time in the taverns was unnerving. The British are dangerous drunkards—not always simultaneously, but they endeavor to be so. There are two distinct groups in the pubs, the drunks who would imbibe without a care and then steal to the alleys with whores, and the big ears."

Washington smiled, "And what are 'big ears'?"

"Sir, there are Redcoat officers in every tavern in the city who pretend to be drinking and eating, but they will remain there for hours just sitting and then moving about eavesdropping with their 'Big Ears,'" said Brown. "It stands to be very risky milking the Redcoats for information.

"They even seem to have a hanging every week of men or even women accused of being spies for that 'wicked lunk Washington'," said Brown.

"Ah, now I am a 'wicked lunk,' I am indeed flattered, but do not forget, captain, it is New York, a place that I should have burnt to the ground."

Brown nodded his agreement. "After taking some risks and having the good fortune of not being exposed as a spy, I can tell you the following:

"One, the British will remain in New York until at least late March. Clearly, your crushing blow to Barts' unit, and Timmons's forces, have sent a shivery chill up their spines, even that of Cornwallis. They believe that you may have more forces here than they thought previously. The name Timmons was well-known, the other fellow, Barts or Bates, was mentioned in passing, but Timmons was a known officer from a known family. What is circulating through the taverns is that you surrounded Timmons' forces of 100 regulars with a force of 2,000 and then proceeded to murder every last man."

Washington wanted to break out in laughter, but he held his tongue and listened as Brown continued.

"Second, the British are leaving Dorcester with his 1,000 men to maintain a foothold in New Jersey. I believe that this requires a brief explanation."

Brown talked as if he was reading from prepared notes. Something about spies and their methods; everything committed to memory or shuttled into hidden compartments—documents of invisible ink and so forth.

"The British regular officers, once they have gotten a little drink in them, were saying that there is a delicate dance between the king and Cornwallis, along with the admiral and General Howe. They think Cornwallis is hoping you will completely eradicate Dorcester over the winter. They said that Dorcester has a mandate from the king to make every citizen change his tune and become a loyalist. The translation of that is that Dorcester is going to attack civilians with the king's blessing. Could this be true? It sounds much like a fairy tale—a morbid one at that."

Washington looked as if he was staring a thousand miles away.

"It is accurate, Captain Brown, except for the part about Timmons being destroyed by two thousand soldiers. That is British poppycock.

"However, the miserable truth is that Dorcester has already begun terrorizing our civilians. In a small village called Denhurst, he murdered the town folk and raped the women and girls. We hanged Timmons just a short time ago for his crimes. But Dorcester is a mad demon who means to attack civilians or us wherever he can."

"Sir," continued Brown. "I may expound on that point. I believe Cornwallis wants Dorcester to fail miserably. I feel that General Huxley Dorcester is, in fact, a blister that Cornwallis would like you to pop."

"Is there anything else, Stephen?" Washington asked.

"Yes, Cornwallis, in deference to the king, has already landed 4,000 Hessians a good-ways north. They are led by General de Heister and that ruthless colonel of his, von Donop. This I repeatedly heard as if the Redcoats were cheerfully saying, 'Better the mercenaries than we.'"

"Thank you, Captain Brown. I cannot say this is entirely

welcome news, but we now have some breathing room. What is your plan?"

"Sir, if I could stay for supper, that would be much appreciated. Afterward, I must head back to Durkee's Regiment."

"Stephen, you shall have a hot meal and a good sleep. When you return, tell your commander that we will fulfill only the second portion of Cornwallis' desires."

The early morning mist lay thick over Piney Brook. Durst's Wolves were already on the move as they slipped into the tiny village. Their muskets hung loosely over their shoulders as the knife would be the day's weapon. They had split into five groups, each concealed in hedges around the scattered houses. The whole group had put on worn and tattered clothing devoid of red. Dorchester had decided that all of them should dress like ordinary folk.

As was usual, the dairy farmers were the first up with the dawn light. Guller and his mates crouched behind a hedge. A father and teenage son made their way down the path.

In a flash, Guller jumped out in front of the elder and ripped his knife into the man's gut while placing a hand over the farmer's mouth.

"Shh, shh, shh, die quietly, old man!" Guller scoffed as the man's eyes widened with shock as his last seconds of life passed.

The teenager nearly escaped, but Avery Jones cut off the boy's flight as his knife penetrated the young man's face from cheek to cheek and through his tongue. Jones withdrew his large knife and rapidly plunged it through his victim's neck. Both bodies were dragged off and hidden from view. The gruesome attack was over in half a minute.

As each resident of Piney Brook emerged from their home, the Wolves were waiting. In a short time, most of the men had been silently killed. Durst signaled for his Wolves to enter the houses to kill off the remaining townspeople. The pack stealthily made their way into home after home. At some point, Guller and Jones crept into the home of John Smythe.

"I believe, Jones," Guller whispered as he unsheathed his blade and went through the door. "I say that we are giving wolves a bad name."

The shouts and gasps of men dying went on for a few minutes, followed by their family's piercing screams of terror.

The corpses of the farmers were dumped unceremoniously into the path that ran through Piney Brook. Dorcester's butchers were dragging out the crying women and children. They had witnessed the murder of their fathers and husbands. The look of terror and tears streaked their ashen faces.

Nearly the last out was Guller as he heaved the large body of John down the wooden stairs of the quaint Smythe house. His partner, Jones, had Mercy Smythe gripped tightly by the arm as he forced her to step over her husband's body. Mercy was the only woman not crying tears of desperation. Her coolness both unnerved and angered Durst as he looked in her direction from the center of the dirt street.

"Why is that bitch not begging for her life? Is she dumb?" asked the captain.

"I do not rightly know," said Jones." He was drooling over the attractive Mercy Smythe.

Mercy's cold stare was directed at the captain. She piqued Durst's curiosity with her look, but simultaneously she eased her right hand into the folds of her nightdress and gripped a long, sharp knitting needle. Spontaneously, she broke her strobe-like gaze with Durst to see that her friends' daughters were barbarically assaulted just to her left. Their anguished screams chilled her blood, and her daring was fueled by the realization that not one of them would escape with their lives.

She turned her eyes back to Captain Durst and raised her voice. "You do not get me for free, you bastard."

Mercy, in a flash, pulled the smuggled knitting needle, whipped it around, and plunged it into Jones' heart, the man who had just ravished and murdered her youngest daughter.

Jones gasped with surprise as his grip slackened from the woman's arm. He looked down at the needle protruding from his chest and breathed, "She killed me," before falling dead.

Mercy tried to run, but Guller snagged her foot, and she fell hard to the dirt. He pulled the lady farmer up by golden locks and threw her onto the wooden fence along the street. Durst walked over laughing, then tied her hands down such that she was bent over the fence at her waist. He grasped his musket and brought it hard into her left leg. Mercy made no sound. She would not give this demon the satisfaction of hearing her cries.

"Guller," Durst called."My dear powerful man-wolf, ensure her wounds are abundant before she dies."

Durst spun around to address his platoon. "That is my order to all of you. This sow here," said Durst as he pointed towards Mercy Smythe, "is to be visited by every one of you until she begs for death."

Durst kicked Jones' body as he strolled away. Casualties of war, he thought while walking amid the sounds of agony. The Wolves were now eleven.

Chapter 19

Agent Kent Spark was a risk-taker. He had worked his way up through the C.I.A. by taking chances and occasionally pissing off his bosses. After the VP had contacted the head of the C.I.A. about starting Intelligence Support, Kent was unhappily reassigned. Of course, this was a double-edged sword. Any notion of moving up further in the C.I.A. was dashed. The chances were that he would finish up at I.S. The upside was that this strange device, which he now knew to be alien, was huge. If he could run the show on the device, he would be as big as the director, maybe bigger.

That was one reason why Kent was sure that the VP was making a massive mistake in allowing Howe to fly solo on this. He and Carlisle had no intel on what was happening in Vermont. Even with their spy snooping around Howe It Works, Kent was sure Dr. Aaron Howe was outfoxing them. For all they knew, Howe could be in advanced negotiations with an alien race through that thing. His hunch was that their spy was all talk. Kent felt like that guy could be part of the problem. After all, he hadn't given them anything of substance.

Paranoia had helped Kent out of a few scrapes, and his radar on this one was screaming. Conversely, he thought, Carlisle had told him to keep clear of Howe or else. The "or else" part was potentially an unhappy ending for Kent Spark, but if the VP was wrong about this, and if their spy was incompetent, or worse, working for the Russians or Chinese? That possibility was too scary even to dwell on. The Chinese especially would like to be the ones to be the primary contact with an alien race. Alien tech would put them so far out in front that the USA would be relegated to third-world status overnight. It would be the end of the American dream as envisioned by the founding fathers.

Spark had driven up from D.C. in the middle of the night to

be at Howe It Works first thing. He timed his visit based on spy asset reporting that Howe would be gone until noon. The guy said to meet him at the visitor's entrance for an update.

The visitor's parking was only half-full, so Kent got a good spot and headed for the entrance. It was a bright and sunny day, and he was optimistic that he would get a better handle on what was happening. His goal, no matter what, was not to leave empty-handed.

As usual, Kent wore his plain dark suit, solid tie, and white shirt. None of these fit with his expensive dress shoes—genuine Gabalini Italian luxury. In his opinion, everyone was entitled to some quirky indulgence, and Kent's was wearing shoes that cost more than his whole wardrobe. He passed the first entrance of layered security. The guard asked for an ID, and he produced an MIT ID badge with the name Professor Michael Jensen. The guard had him sign in, and then Kent walked over to where his contact stood, smiling to meet him.

"Hello, Edgar," said Kent.

"Hello, Dr. Jensen. Nice to have you visiting with us."

Edgar motioned to the guard that Dr. Jensen was okay, and they proceeded through the next set of doors.

When they were making their way toward the labs and out of earshot, Edgar asked, "Why are you here?"

"Was I not clear about that yesterday?" replied Kent.

Dr. Tomis wiped a crumb of food from his mouth. "Actually, Dr. Jensen, you did not give me a reason."

"That is what I was trying to make clear to you. I don't need to give you a reason. Try to remember, Dr. Tomis, you work for me."

The chubby professor decided that a debate in the hallway was unproductive, so he brought Kent into one of the small conference rooms. Kent gave him a pissed-off look. "Edgar," he said and then pointed upwards. "To the lab."

Edgar looked impassive. "Dr. Jensen, I don't think going to the lab is such a good idea."

"Dr. Tomis," said Kent impatiently. "I didn't drive all this way to get a runaround. Frankly, what you have given me so far has been worthless."

"Dr. Jensen, with all due respect, I am trying to be very careful around Dr. Howe and our alien guest."

"Let me tell you a couple of things," replied Kent with a noticeable measure of disdain. "First, remember that we paid you a hefty sum last month. We expect quick results for that kind of money. And second, when a-holes say to me, 'with all due respect,' it makes me want to unzip my pants and piss on their shoes. Translation: take me to the damn lab."

Edgar was nonplussed but nodded, moved toward the door, and said, "Very well, Dr. Jensen, if you want to go to the lab, then we'll do it your way."

Howe's private lab and office were a short walk and an elevator ride. The men stood in silence as they rode up seven flights, and then Edgar led Spark to the secure double entry doors.

"I would like to say, Dr. Jensen, before we go in, that I think this is a terrible idea," warned Edgar while swiping the key card and putting his thumb on the reader. He then did a retinal scan which was followed up by a subtle click.

"What I mean to say, Kent," said Edgar as he pushed open the door. "We should just look around quickly, and please, please don't touch anything."

Kent looked pissed. "Listen, Tomis. This isn't my first rodeo. I know what the hell I'm doing. You stick with science, and I will do the espionage. Okay?"

The two men entered the lab. Kent could see the door to Howe's private study about 30 feet away on the far wall. They walked across the shiny, medium-gray floor as Kent looked around the room to size up the place. A few lab tables and test equipment were scattered here and there. The only things that Kent could identify positively were an oscilloscope and several expensive-looking computers. There were books on shelves, a few chairs sitting around, plus notes and papers on every table. He took a peek in every direction, but he was impatient.

"Where is it?" he barked.

Edgar knew that Kent would immediately insist on seeing the alien cube but tried to slow him down.

"I'll show you in a second," said Edgar.

"Listen, I'm already not impressed with anything I see here. I believe the best thing is for me to move the device out of here and take it to our Virginia lab."

It was unnerving that Spark had moved from inspecting to confiscating in the blink of an eye. He must have already planned on telling Carlisle that the lab was insecure and that Howe was threatening national security. Not such a good plan because Edgar knew that the AI might not be enthusiastic about leaving.

"Agent Spark, I think attempting to move the object is a bad idea."

"Really?" yelled Kent. "What are you hiding here?" throwing up an accusation to bolster his justifications.

Edgar was now convinced that Kent had already planned on wresting the object from Howe before he'd even made the trip.

He motioned Kent towards a rolling cart with a TV monitor. The cart sat next to a table with a metal box on it. Spark turned his palms up in a frustrated gesture and said, "So, is that it, a metal box?"

Suddenly, the monitor came on, and *Allison* appeared. To Edgar, she looked livid, but then she smiled pleasantly and said, *"Hello, Agent Spark. I'm unhappy you are here; there's nothing for you to accomplish— nice shoes, by the way."*

"What is this, Edgar, your Disney presentation on aliens?" he grumbled.

Edgar shrugged.

"Actually," said *Allison*, *"I am the alien."*

Kent's mouth dropped, but then he composed himself. "Oh, baloney. Edgar, show me the real thing, dammit."

Tomis smiled. "This is the device talking to you. I was completely truthful when I told you that Howe had established some communications with the cube. This is it."

"Amazing," said Kent. "This is exactly why we will move it to the CIA Virginia location."

"Tell me, Mr. Spark," said *Allison. "How do you plan on moving me to Virginia if I choose not to go?"*

Kent growled. "It isn't up to you."

Allison looked at Edgar, back at the agent, and then burst out laughing.

"Did I say something funny? You are an object that belongs to—oh, what the hell. I can't believe I'm talking to a machine. It is a machine. It is still a machine even if it is smarter than most."

Kent made a decision. He walked over to pick up the monitor. Before he could lift it, *Allison* started crying and said, *"No, no, please don't take me, Mr. Government Man."*

Kent stopped and gazed at the monitor. "Alien or not, you're coming with me."

Allison again burst out in hysterical laughter.

"What's so damn funny?"

She looked at Edgar and said, *"My dear Edgar, I surely hope that all humans aren't as obtuse as this one."*

"Hey!" said Kent angrily.

Edgar looked at the AI image. "*Allison*, I have been around here for a long time. Most of them are pretty stupid but have *some* redeeming qualities."

She looked at Kent.

He scowled back at her.

"Do you see that metal box on the table? Open it up. You will find a black cube inside. That black cube is me. Take me if you must," she said like a damsel in distress.

Edgar stepped in front of Spark. "I don't think that is a good idea."

Kent shoved Edgar to the side. "I've seen enough, Dr. Tomis. This is an issue of national security."

The professor slowly backed away as Kent lifted the lid and then boldly wrapped his hand around the jet black alien object.

Chapter 20

Durst sat on a wooden step ten yards from the Smythe house. He was fiddling with his shirt buttons and watching the last of his Wolves attacking the woman. The man was grunting like a wild boar while no sounds came from his victim. Perhaps she was already dead, thought the captain—better for her. Then again, he would be delighted to extend her torture.

It was now mid-morning. Durst wanted to be on his way back to Dorcester to report on the raid's success. Suddenly he felt impatient.

"Enough," he shouted to the Wolf. "We must disappear now."

"Sir, in truth, I am verily much worn out," the man said as he buttoned his trousers. "This one is about to die anyway."

"Wonderful," exclaimed Durst. "Now remove yourself from my sight. Tell your colleagues to leave."

"Sir, would you like me to wait?"

The captain gave him an evil stare, which was accentuated by the appearance of his frighteningly damaged eye. Captain Durst screamed, "Leave! Now!"

The man practically jumped out of his skin at the look on his officer's face. Better to get away and very quickly. He saluted and bounded into a run to gather the other Wolves and escape the sudden wrath.

Durst got up from the porch step and crossed the street. Even in death, she was a beautiful woman. Her clothes were shredded. She was bruised, bitten, and stained with blood. Her bare legs hung loosely as her waist supported her body over the heavy wooden fence rail. What a pity, he thought, that she picked the wrong side in this war. As he drew closer, he could see her leg twitch a little. Ah, he thought, this one is still grasping to life.

He jumped the fence, stood before her, and gripped her

bloodied hair with his hand to pull up her head. The woman's eyelids, puffy and red, lifted as she gazed weakly at him.

"Well, well, still clinging to your last breath?"

With all of her strength, she managed to eject bloody spit onto his boot and rasped, "Go to hell!"

Durst reached down with his other hand and swabbed the bloody spit with his finger. She watched as he stuck it in his mouth.

"Delightfully feisty you are," he observed.

His mocking voice suddenly drained her will to live. She pleaded with him in a desperate whisper: "Kill me!"

"Kill me. Kill me. Kill me," he cackled, then paused and said, "Oh no, no, no, no…I will not kill you.

"Do you know that I drowned my own father many years ago," said Durst. "Because of this!" He pointed to his damaged and disfigured eye. "It occurred to me that had I just beaten him and let him live—that would have eaten him alive every day of his life. I was young and petulant, so I gave in to my stupidity. If only I had let him live.

"As for you, I will leave your fate to the winds. Perhaps someone will find you and nurse you back to health, or perhaps you will die. Either way, your torture has been luscious. If you live, then your memories will devour your soul. Isn't that delicious?"

Tears, what were left of them, drained from Mercy's eyes. He'd ordered his men to do their worst, and now with extreme cruelty, he withheld the release of death. Durst let go of her hair, bent, and cut her bonds using a small knife. With no strength in her legs, she slid off the rail and collapsed limply to the ground.

The captain gleefully vaulted the fence and stood where she could see him through her bloodstained strands of hair. Even that took all her strength as her torturer gazed at her naked suffering.

"Madam," he said and then bowed with his hat in his hand, "I bid you *adieu*."

George Washington's soldiers routinely reconnoitered the area outside of the Continental Army's encampment. The typical radius was about five miles. Following the massacre at Denhurst, Sergeant William Mack and Corporal Mason McKee were assigned to scout an area on the edge of that radius.

It was there, on the eastern limit, that they came upon the outskirts of the village of Piney Brook. As they strode through the fields surrounding the known rebel enclave, Mack was struck by something McKee did not notice.

"Mason," said Mack. "Do you find it strange that there are no local folk in the fields or tending to the cows? I would think that we would see several farmers out and about on a day like today at this hour, yet I see none."

"Sergeant," said the Corporal. "Now that you mention it, that is unusual. Could they all be at church? Or just biding time?"

"Church? There is no church in Piney Brook and in a hard-working village? Would it be like these folks to be lazy and stay home, all of them?"

Mason shrugged. "Seems very unlikely, sir."

Mack agreed, and they decided to approach and see if Redcoats were laying a trap. It wasn't easy to creep stealthily into the village, but they did their best to come silently despite the leaves crunching underfoot. They lay down to scan the area when they had made it to the town's border. McKee elbowed the sergeant as they lay prone on a bed of corn stalks.

"Sir, it looks like bodies are lying in the main street!"

Mack gazed intently in the direction where his corporal was pointing. Indeed, from that distance, it did look like more than one person was lying in the street.

"Something is very wrong here, McKee. First, no one was in the fields, and now people were stretched out in the street. We will observe for a short bit. If nothing moves, then we go in and look around. Make sure your musket is ready and fix your bayonet."

"Yes, sir."

The time passed excruciatingly slowly, but while they watched, as best they could figure, no one had moved in the village.

"We have waited long enough," said Mack as he stood.

They both mounted their bayonets and were on the move. The closer they got, the more apparent it became that there were perhaps three dozen dead bodies in the street. Both men were aghast but did their best to keep their composure. They could see the bodies of many children and perhaps 20 adults.

They could easily see that some of the women were unclothed as they approached. The scene went from bad to worse when they saw stab wounds and slit throats on the bodies of the dead. McKee was an experienced soldier, but nothing could prepare him for this, and he vomited from the shock.

"Stay unruffled, McKee," said Sergeant Mack as he put a hand on the back of the corporal to steady and calm him. "I am sorry, but we need to check them all. There may be survivors here."

Initially, all they found were dead villagers. It looked as though all of Piney Brook had been massacred. When they got halfway down the street, they came near an unclothed blond woman. She wasn't moving, but she still had some color to her skin. Mack and McKee rushed to the curled-up woman and found her breathing. They laid her on her back. Ropes were tied about her wrists, and her lips were parched. There were bite marks and blood on her. The right arm appeared fractured, and there were several puncture wounds on her torso. Despite all this, she was alive but unaware.

"Make haste, McKee," barked the sergeant. "Run in the house and find a dress or nightclothes for this woman—and a blanket. We cannot help the dead, but we can carry her back to camp, and maybe the doctor can save her."

McKee returned quickly with some light clothes, and they

dressed the woman, wrapping her in the heavy blanket. Mack tried to get some water into her from his flask. She swallowed a little and then coughed. The blood on her swollen lips could not hide her missing teeth.

"We must hurry, Mckee. We shall take turns carrying her. These woods are flat—we should be able to reach camp in under two hours. She is tall but thin. I think we can manage it," said the sergeant as he hoisted the injured woman over his shoulder. She groaned but remained barely conscious. He prayed that she would not die in his arms on the way. McKee wrapped her broken arm as best he could. He thought she would be in tremendous pain if she were awake.

McKee looked at his Sergeant. "If she survives, sergeant, perhaps she can tell us who—"

"—We know who, McKee," Mack said angrily. "But I want to hear her story, and I am confident that General Washington will be planning how we will make them pay for this.

Mack grunted under the effort to step over a fallen tree. He leaned in toward the woman and whispered, "I promise you that those Redcoats will rue the day."

*

"Edgar!" called Howe, having returned to the lab at noon.

"I'm here," said Dr. Tomis spinning around on a lab chair.

Howe always thought that his friend had something of a kid in that mighty brain of his. He could ponder quantum mechanics while shooting rubber bands into a trashcan from across the room.

"I'm going back to Washington."

Edgar smiled. "In which century?" he asked. "Washington, D.C. or Washington, the general?"

"That would be the general. I already told *Allison* that I was heading back. Have you just been here trying to get yourself dizzy in a chair? Did anything happen that I should know about?"

The rotund scientist grinned and then lied, "Same old, same old. Nothing happens around here when you are out tooling around Burlington."

"What you are calling tooling was me gathering more supplies. I could have used your help instead of you insisting on staying here in case something important should crop up."

"Aaron, I probably would have been better off hanging out with you."

"Damn straight!"

Aaron turned to the monitor and then back at Edgar. He jerked his thumb in the direction of *Allison* and made an inquiring shrug with his shoulders. Wearing his trademark black sweatshirt, Tomis shrugged back as if to say, "I haven't talked to her."

Howe turned back and called out, "*Allison*."

The AI's human image instantly appeared with her endearing smile.

"What's up, Doc?"

"What's up, Doc?" he asked, slightly incredulous.

Allison gave him a carefree look. *"I have been watching Bugs Bunny, and to be honest, this is perhaps the best TV show I've seen so far!"* She seemed utterly ecstatic.

"O.K.," Aaron said with exaggerated bewilderment. "So you are really into cartoons now. Great."

"Oh, yes," said *Allison*. *"My favorite regular show is the one with the astronaut and the beautiful blond girl who lives in a bottle."*

"That's intriguing. However, if we can return to reality, you may have heard me tell Edgar that I am heading out very soon. We discussed this already."

"Oh yes, Master," she said, imitating the TV character.

"*Allison*, please don't do *Jeannie* now!"

The AI looked dejected but replied, *"Oh, very well. How can I help you?"*

"I don't need any help now. I am taking another ten

containers with me. I will put a containment field around them and bring them with a tracker to my location near the camp. You already showed me how to do that.

"After the warehouse drops off the containers, I will prepare everything. Having containers disappearing from the loading dock in the middle of the day might be difficult to explain. We'll do it just like last time around 3 am."

She winked, *"I suppose I am no longer important."*

"I hope you aren't insulted, *Allison*," said Aaron.

"Me, insulted?" she said with drama. *"Ha! Don't worry, Dr. Howe; I have a completely intact and healthy ego."*

Aaron winked back at her. "Yes, I know that."

Nearby, Edgar sat back and spun in his lab chair, thinking.

*

"What is the dire emergency now?" grumbled a burdened Washington as he entered the doctor's large tent. He stared down at a cot and saw a tall, wounded woman who seemed unconscious.

Sergeant Mack stood by, exhausted from carrying her but eager to report to the general. "Sir, me and Corporal McKee were on patrol, and we happened upon the village of Piney Brook completely massacred. This woman is the only one left alive." He fought back the tears brought on by emotional and physical stress.

"General," he continued uneasily. "It looked like Dorcester's men entered the village and did horrid things to the women after killing all the men and children. When they through, they slit the throats of all who remained, excepting her."

Washington, who prided himself on controlling his emotions in front of the men, was visibly shaken. Fury churned inside him. Dorcester had taken the massacre at Denhurst and now reproduced it in Piney Brook.

"How is it that she survived?

"Your Excellency," said Mack. "We found her in this condition, slumped on the ground. It looked like many evil things were done to her."

Washington turned to the doctor.

"General," the army physician said. "She has indeed been tortured, sir. She has been repeatedly abused. The lady has contusions, small stab wounds, bites, and a fractured arm. I cannot tell how much internal damage she has, but the knife wounds appear shallow as if they were stabbing her for folly."

"Doctor," said Washington. "Let me know when and if she is able to speak."

"General. I doubt she will survive the night, but I will do my best. I understand that she must live, not only for herself but for what she can communicate about her assailants."

The general nodded and led Sergeant Mack out of the tent.

"Mack, be very clear to Corporal McKee that I want none of this to be spoken of."

"Yes sir, general, I already was very firm with McKee that he shan't say nothing. McKee is as reliable as rain. I trust that he will keep silent unless instructed otherwise."

Washington nodded grimly, and they parted ways.

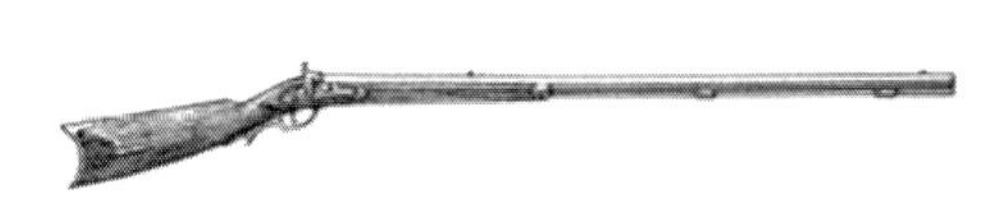

Several hours later, the thin, muscular, brown-haired Aaron Howe and ten containers materialized in a New Jersey forest. He'd gotten used to the unsettling feeling of time travel and quickly regained his composure. According to his 1776 watch, it was about two in the morning. He was pleased to see that the camp in the distance was quiet and that no one was milling about near the containers.

At this point, no doubt many soldiers thought it strange that large boxes could be there, not exceedingly far from the camp. On the other hand, why look a gift horse in the mouth? Major

Howe had provided this army with clothes, shoes, tents, and weapons sufficient to damage the Redcoats severely when the time came.

He looked around, then made his way quickly to the Recon camp. Rogers was up and was intently watching the small fire burning inside the ring of four tents. When he heard footsteps, he jumped up, raised his sidearm, and lowered it when he recognized Major Howe.

"Major," he started. "I am so glad you have returned."

"Glad to be back, Rogers." Aaron said, and then added, "What's happening?"

"Sir, the general arrived here at 23:30. He said you should come immediately to his tent. Something has happened, I could see it in his Excellency's face, but he did not elaborate."

Howe could not hide his concern. "Very well, sergeant, I will head there now."

Rogers saluted while Howe made straight for Washington's tent. Aaron covered 150 yards when the usual two guards greeted him. He asked them to tell the general he was here, and almost immediately, Washington hustled Howe into his tent.

Candles illuminated the interior as the future president had yet to develop a taste for the battery-operated lamps which Howe had given him. He was also afraid of Reed or others asking questions about "technology." There'd been enough grumbling in the ranks by the small number of fools who kept spreading rumors about Howe's witchcraft.

"Major, we have not a moment to spare. Come with me."

Without hesitation, the general grabbed Howe's arm and dragged him out of the tent towards the physician. Washington's hair was disheveled, and his uniform was dingy, but he did not seem to care. On the way, as briefly and quietly as possible, he described what had happened at Piney Brook. Howe was furious, and Washington, in the dim light, appeared to be a smoldering volcano.

They slid into the medical tent. A few lanterns burned and lit the interior well. The doctor sat off to the side of three patients, but George led Aaron to the woman who was still unconscious on the center cot.

"Doctor," he asked. "What is her condition?"

The doctor sighed and shook his head. "I am surprised she has lasted this long. Other people would have succumbed hours ago, but this one here has a strength that I cannot explain. Sadly, she cannot hold on forever."

Aaron looked at her as the doctor described her wounds. In his time, she would be admitted to a hospital and would recover. In 1776, she was bound for the grave. Aaron was sick to his stomach.

Washington motioned Aaron to step outside. He told his two guard escorts to move away.

"What can you do for her?"

"I, I can't really do anything, sir," Aaron said reluctantly.

"I must assume that in your time, medicine is very much advanced. And, you are a *doctor*, correct?"

"Yes, general, we have very advanced medicine. And, I am Doctor Howe, but I am a doctor of science, not medicine."

Washington seemed to make an instant decision.

"Take her to your time," he blurted out. "And be quick."

"I, um," Howe thought it through. "Yes, I could do that. However, I can't just disappear in front of the doctor."

"Right, so this is what we shall do…"

Aaron admitted to himself, George Washington was truly more astute than history portrayed him. They'd quietly hustled the cot with the woman to the general's tent. Howe was disheartened that she appeared to be on the brink of death.

Once there, George chased the guards away and closed the tent flap tightly.

"Major, let me be utterly direct. You are going to take this lady to your lab and engage a doctor to heal her. You will return with her in the cot as if nothing happened. We will keep her in the command tent for a day and later rejoice at her miraculous recovery. Is that a sensible proposal?"

Aaron returned a nervous smile and answered hopefully, “Sounds like a idea, sir.”

“Not just a simple idea, my time-traveling friend, it is a stroke of genius. Now go!”

Chapter 21

At 04:00, Howe materialized in the now-empty lab. The lights were mostly dimmed, which he appreciated very much. He dragged the cot nearer to the AI.

"*Allison*!" he called urgently.

Allison appeared on the screen instantly. *"Yes, Aaron?"*

"I've got a big problem here."

The AI took on a severe expression. *"Aaron, this woman has been severely beaten and assaulted."*

"Yes, the British raided her village," he replied. "You don't need the details now. Hurry, what can you do for her?"

Within seconds she said, *"This woman has some severe internal damage. Most of those puncture wounds are not fatal, but two are quite deadly. Aaron, I can heal her, but it will require your—"* she hesitated *"—approval."*

"Of course, you have my approval, do what you have to do, but save her!"

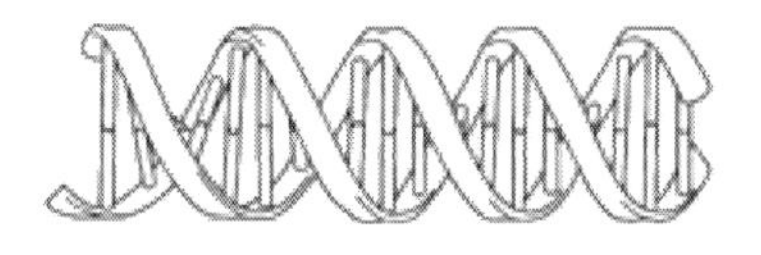

"What are you doing?" Aaron asked worriedly.

A hazy cloud of gray-black about the size of a baseball floated in the air above the woman's face. She was indeed beautiful, despite her injuries. It was heartbreaking what she'd endured.

"I am saving her."

Aaron frowned, "I mean, what is that gray cloud? Are those nanomachines?"

"They are nanites, as you would describe them, but I need to focus on this process. I can't give you an hour-long lecture now."

Suddenly, the cloud of nanites flew up the woman's nostrils and disappeared. Aaron gasped. He was a physicist and engineer, but this took him in a direction that only existed in Hollywood.

"What happens now?"

"We wait for the nanites to circulate and start doing their job. They will track down every fault in her body. Once I get 'feedback,' I can create implants to repair the damage."

"Implants!" Aaron raised his voice, "Implants?"

"Yes, Aaron. That's how I will fix things."

He sat down and leaned his forehead into his palms. He always felt calmer when he had a good handle on technology. Nanites were way out of his comfort zone. They were in the realm of sci-fi, making him exceedingly nervous. He stood up, sat back down, went to the fridge, and grabbed a Coke.

"*Allison*," he said. "How long will this take?"

"I can do tissue repairs, but first, we wait for nanite results."

"Ok, so how long is that? Hours, days, weeks?" he asked.

"Actually, in 5, 4, 3, 2, 1, got 'em."

Howe was a little shocked. "That was fast! Now what?"

"Seriously, Aaron, you are like an expectant father in a waiting room. She's not going to die. I am designing the implants which will make a few changes in her physiology. Of course, she will still be human, but there's patching, and then there's fixing. I don't like to do things halfway."

Worn out and exasperated, Aaron said, "Fine, just do what you have to."

"This part will take at least twelve hours, maybe up to fourteen hours. Why don't you go home or something?"

"No, let me help."

"Later. After I interlace the implants—all you can do is wait. For now, flip the woman over onto her stomach—carefully."

Aaron turned her over.

"Take down the blanket to expose her back."

Aaron did so. The knife wounds looked terrible. The missing teeth were disfiguring, but the penetrating wounds to her back must have hit vital organs enough to send her on a path to collapse and, ultimately, death.

"Don't be startled, Aaron. The next step may seem a bit scary to you. Just pretend you're in a sci-fi film."

He was captivated as a thin black cylinder grew and stretched out from the AI cube. The tube extended until it hung over the woman's back, then twisted 90 degrees downward and bored a hole into her spine. Almost immediately, a network of fine lines spread out and formed a rod along the spine, reaching outward in thin tubular lines. Aaron thought they must have been a sort of carbon nano-tubes but incredibly sophisticated. The whole construct seemed to be adhering itself to her skin. The lattice work began to burrow itself.

The grid sunk under her skin. It appeared to make its way up her spine and then submerged in the direction of her brain. It was unsettling, but Aaron was utterly fascinated and mystified by the process once he got over the surreal experience of it all.

Suddenly, the extended tube shrunk back into the AI cube.

Allison appeared on the screen with a satisfied look. *"Now, we wait."*

Aaron started to get up and head to his office, but *Allison* whistled. He turned around to see her with her finger poking into her cheek.

"Actually, Aaron, there is one little errand you could run if you feel awake enough."

"You have no idea how weird that was."

"It's a character builder," responded *Allison.*

"And you would know that because of all your experience in being a 35-year-old human male?"

She ignored him.

"Do you know what it is like going into a 24-hour Walmart

and buying women's clothes at six in the morning? Sweat pants and socks are not so weird, but bras and underwear? I was getting looks like, 'what's with that guy'?".

"Still, Aaron, you did it," she said patronizingly. *"You should feel really good about yourself. So, what did you buy? Show me."*

He reluctantly pulled out the sweatpants and T-shirts first.

"Wow, Iron Maiden," said *Allison*. *"Perfect for an 18th-century woman."*

Aaron sneered, "Look, I spent $350. There has to be something in there that works for you?"

"Aaron, dear," said *Allison*. *"It ain't about me, darling; it's about her. Not sure about the heavy metal T-shirt, though."*

He was mildly impatient. "*Allison*, they didn't have any Nathan Hale or Ben Franklin in her size."

Allison let out a hearty laugh, "*You got me there. Let's see the underwear.*"

Aaron reluctantly pulled out some bras and panties.

"Damn, boy, you done followed my instructions. They are beautiful."

"*Allison*, is there any reason why you're talking like you are from Alabama? Are you a Southerner? Is that an AI thing?"

"Oh, sorry, Aaron," she said. *"I've been watching this neat show called Justified—"*

"How much longer," Aaron cut her off as he gestured towards the woman.

"Did I not say 12 hours minimum?"

"Yes."

"And that was two hours ago?"

"Yes," he admitted.

"Well, twelve minus two is ten? Right, Spock?"

"*Star Trek*, too?" Aaron groaned. "Fine, I'm going to my office," he said as he stalked off, thinking about *Allison*'s overabundance of pop-culture references.

The Ugly Sofa was his best friend again, and amazingly,

Aaron slept for 11 hours. He left notice that no one should come to the lab, which meant that the 7th floor was virtually locked down. Even Edgar couldn't get through that seal.

He awoke feeling surprisingly well and then dashed for the bathroom, after which he felt even better.

There was a loud beep on his phone, and he answered it.

"It's Allison. You slept like a bear. She is going to wake up soon. This is the tricky part, and I did not prepare you for it so, come out here."

Aaron walked over to where the woman lay.

"Her body is repaired and rebuilding, but you'll have to be her psychologist for the next thirty minutes. You will need to ease her into the fact that she is alive." Allison proceeded to rattle off a series of possible things to say to bring the blonde-haired Colonial woman to the point where she could talk directly to the AI. That was the goal—to take a 1776 woman and get her to start talking to the highly advanced and alien artificial intelligence.

"Based on her brain patterns, Aaron, this woman is very tough. I mean, as far as bringing someone back from 1776 to face a shock like AI—well, you couldn't have found anyone more suitable. As I said, she is strong.

"You need to get her talking, and then I will take over, and you can sit and watch. I would think that many women would want to be alone or talk to another woman, but she might be different. You will need to stay sharp; then you can scram when I tell you."

Aaron moved closer toward the patient lying on the table. *Allison* said she would signal a nanite routine to wake her up gradually.

As he stood over her, the woman's eyes opened slowly, and she seemed to be adjusting to the light.

"Is it too bright in here for you?" he asked.

She stared at him.

"Everything is fine. You are safe now. I am a doctor,"

She gave him a piercing, nerve-wracking, hard stare.

"Why didn't you let me die?" she asked.

At that, *Allison* slowed the woman's process of awareness. Too much, too fast, could be devastating psychologically.

Unsure of himself, Aaron stammered, "For at least two reasons. We save lives. We cherish life. We also need to know what happened."

She looked around. "Where am I?

Aaron tried to give her a reassuring smile. "Do you want the long or short answer?"

"I do not know," she replied.

"We are in my office in New England. We are about two hours from Boston."

She looked nervous. "Are you English? You do not sound English."

Aaron tried to appear benign. "No, I am an American and a friend of General Washington."

A wave of relief seemed to roll over her.

"I need to ask you some questions. Is that all right?"

"Yes," she replied.

The drugs *Allison* was leeching into her system must be working to quell the woman's panic, thought Aaron.

"Firstly, what is your name?"

"My name is Mercy Smythe," she answered. "I live in the village of Piney Brook. My husband's name is John, and I have two daughters."

Behind Mercy on the screen, Aaron saw:

I had put a filter around her memory so it won't all come at once. The shock would be too great, so I've deadened her emotions.

Aaron nodded. "Mercy, there are some things that we will talk about which are going to be difficult, even painful."

"Yes, I am feeling—" Mercy swung around, suddenly looking desperately around the room. "Something bad has happened to my—" she hesitated. "—to my village- to my family."

Mercy stared frantically at Howe. "What's wrong? What

happened to them? What have you done?"

Aaron stared back at her in shock, not knowing how to respond. Then he was somewhat relieved as he read *Allison*'s words crossing the computer screen behind the woman.

I have released some additional anti-anxiety medication into her blood. It is very quick-acting.

"Mercy," said Aaron slowly. "Your memories are not clear yet. I am going to help you understand. This is very important, and I hope you are as strong as I think you are because there is so much that I have to tell you."

Even as Aaron was speaking to her, the implant in her brain and nervous system was adapting and augmenting Mercy's physical and mental capabilities.

Words scrolled across the monitor. *Ask her if she is starting to remember anything. I am slowly releasing the flow of her memory functions.*

"Mercy, are you beginning to remember?" he asked.

An icy look came over Mercy's face as the sweetness drained away.

"I remember," she said. "The British came into our village. They called themselves the Wolves. They killed people. They killed—Her gaze suddenly dimmed as if her life force was stolen from her body. Her chin dipped down as her eyes lost their shine.

"They killed my husband. They murdered my babies. They used me; they violated me," she announced with cold detachment.

That happened more quickly than I expected. Ask Mercy if she would like to take a drug to forget.

"Mercy," he asked sympathetically. "Would you like some medicine to make you forget? You can go to sleep, and we can take our time and talk about it later—"

"NO!" she erupted. "I am not weak. I do not require time. I do not need medicine!"

He reached out to touch her hand, but she jerked it away.

"Do not touch me," she hissed. It was not a request; it was a threat.

Aaron did his best to console her. "Mercy, you and I are on the same side—"

She yelled strangely. "I HAVE NO SIDE!"

"Mercy, I am so sorry. I wish I could make it all a bad dream. You must know that I have felt what you are feeling—"

"You could not know what I am feeling!" she screamed. "Did you lose your loves? Did you lose your family to murder?"

It was strange how she could say any words at all without crumbling into shattered pieces. Watching her brought Julia dead-center into his mind.

Aaron could not hold back the few tears he swore he would not shed. "Yes, Mercy, I did lose my family. I lost them like you did, right before my eyes."

His tears triggered something in her as she listened to his words and believed him. He was truthful. Her own tears came like torrents. She reached out, took his hand, and let her grief crash like a tidal wave. Her sobbing expressed all her pain that had come so quickly and brutally. It shook him deeply. For the first time, he felt he was no longer alone in his deep cavern of pain and guilt.

After a long while, she found her balance again. The nanites and implants gave her the strength to go forward when ordinary people would have crashed in despair to the floor. Mercy seemed to have processed her grief and was now prepared to deal with whatever came her way. Aaron held her hand until her weeping drained the last of her tears.

"Dr. Howe," she looked up at him with cloudy red eyes. "Tell me where I am. I feel different. My mind feels *bigger,* and my body feels *stronger.*

He looked up at the screen.

It is the implants and the physiological changes I told you about.

Howe paused to gaze around the lab. For a split second, it occurred to him that the extent of the technology being demonstrated in his lab was humbling. He looked back at the AI on the screen and tilted his head as a request for pointers.

Keep talking.

"Mercy," he said, searching for words.

"Yes, Dr. Howe?"

"May I tell you about what happened?" he asked.

"Yes," she sniffed, "I'm ready. Tell me what you need to tell me."

Howe described how two soldiers scouting the area around the continental camp had gone to Piney Brook and found her alive. She already knew the entire village was dead, but she was now addressing her need for facts. She asked questions, and he answered them directly.

Finally, she looked around the room, then back at Aaron. Her eyes took in all of the test equipment, the strange metal tables, and the absence of wood and stone, which was the basis of construction in 1776.

"Aaron," said Mercy. "This isn't General Washington's tent."

"You are correct that this is not Washington's tent or the camp."

Mercy looked at him cooly and confidently and said, "Just tell me, am I dead? Is this Heaven or Hell?"

"It's probably a little of both, Mercy, but you are not dead."

"Well, then what? Where am I?"

Howe tried to formulate a way to describe to her where and when she was. He took a little time looking at Mercy and then at the screen.

Don't tell her. First, ask her if she can accept the impossible as truth.

Aaron looked back at the screen and asked, "What the heck does that mean?"

"Dr. Howe, who are you talking to?"

"Um, nothing; I'm sorry, it was a distraction. I am about to tell you something that you will find impossible to believe as truth, but you must because it is the truth."

In the background, *Allison* wrote on the screen: *You just used my words!*

Aaron shook himself and stopped looking at the monitor.

"Mercy," he continued, "I'm just going to come out and say it. You are no longer in the year 1776. You are not in New Jersey."

The stunned Mercy, still lying on the cot that had been in Washington's tent, seemed to stare fixedly at the ceiling, unblinking. Her face was vacant. *Allison* was still infusing medication into her bloodstream to ease the shock of her transformation. The flood of data from the AI would be overwhelming without the induced, lightly narcotic-like state. At this point, she was still somewhat unconnected to her body and was synthesizing the tremendous information dump. Howe wondered if she had gone over the edge, and he started to panic a little.

Suddenly, Mercy turned to him and a mildly sinister smile. "I believe you," she said.

"What? You believe me?"

Her implants are kicking in. She is processing faster than I would have believed possible. She is also absorbing language and thinking from the current time without even knowing it, wrote *Allison*.

Mercy's face suddenly glowed with some kind of concentrated realization. "Something is happening to me. My brain is like it is opening up to something bigger. Does that make any sense to you?"

Say yes!

"Yes," said Aaron.

"You're Dr. Aaron Howe, CEO of Howe It Works. You're 35 and—" she paused for a second and rubbed wetness from her nose, "—you are extremely wealthy."

Howe chuckled as Mercy babbled on.

"How do I even know that? And why do I sound different in my own head? Wait, what does that even mean? I'm confused."

Aaron waited for her brain to catch up with her thoughts.

"You brought me here from our war against the British. And,

you are not from my time, and you are not from our war." Mercy gazed directly at him. "You are a man from the future. And right now, I am in the future."

"How do you know that?".

She grinned like the Cheshire Cat. Her beautiful smile and bright, new teeth gleamed. "Because I can connect myself to the—*IN-TER-NET*. I know things, but I don't know how this happened. Tell me!" she insisted.

Mercy sat up, and the blanket dropped to her waist, exposing her breasts. She looked down at them and blushed slightly, "Even my body is different," she said, quickly pulling the blanket up.

My turn to talk, wrote *Allison*.

Aaron said, "What does the internet tell you about artificial intelligence?"

Mercy narrowed her eyes. For a moment, Howe was afraid she would hit him or possibly faint. She took three deep breaths and said, "I am trying to think, but I cannot quite reach my thoughts. I know it is a machine, am I correct?"

Howe nodded.

"A machine, but not a machine, because it can think and create on its own."

Aaron looked at her. He was almost as much in shock as she was. "That's right. That's a pretty good explanation, Mercy. I want to introduce you to an AI machine. To be honest with you, the AI machine is the one that healed you. Her name is *Allison*, and you will see her image on the flat screen behind you.

Allison is going to teach you what I cannot. My office is just over there." Aaron pointed to the door. "I will be right there if you need me, but for now, you will interact with *Allison*."

Mercy turned, still clutching the blanket to her chest. The AI appeared on the screen. They gazed at each other for a few seconds, then *Allison* said, *"Ok, Aaron. Women only. Take a hike."*

Aaron was truly grateful as he high-tailed it to his office and closed the door with a satisfying thud.

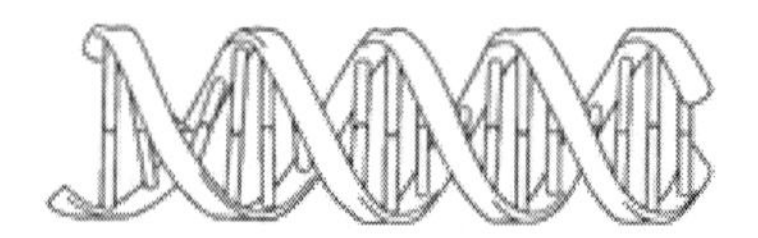

A couple of hours later, Aaron was dozing on the Ugly Sofa. He was content to give *Allison* all the time she wanted to bring Mercy up to speed on her implants. Or Repairs? He realized he was having a little trouble wrapping *his* head around the new Mercy. He didn't even know the old Mercy.

There was a beep, and *Allison* appeared on his monitor.

"Time for you to come out of your man cave, Aaron."

He got up and stretched, hoping that *Allison* would change her mind and tell him to keep chilling, but she did not.

Aaron opened his door and walked over to where Mercy was still lying under her blanket on the Colonial Era military cot. *Allison* was smiling on the monitor.

"Aaron, Mercy Smythe is now entirely up to date and competent mentally. Physically, she is assimilating, but her implants are perfect, and yes, I'm bragging. This adaptation to the process is much more than I could have hoped for. It's beyond my expectations.

"Mercy, tell Aaron about your mental state."

The war widow looked at Aaron with a smile that then turned deadly serious."Aaron," said Mercy, "I want to thank you for saving my life. You didn't heal my wounds or insert my implants. I know that was *Allison*. Nevertheless, you brought me here so I did not die in a tent in 1776. Don't panic about what I am telling you. It's hard to believe, but the woman you saw damaged in Washington's tent is not me."

Aaron wasn't sure how to react, but part of him was suddenly worried that he had meddled too much by bringing Mercy to the future. On the other hand, her apparent transformation, as seen in her face, and heard in her tone, was unbelievable.

While Mercy was speaking, *Allison* remained passive. He

desperately wanted to know what the AI was thinking about the two humans before her. Mercy then bit her lip briefly and refocused her gaze onto Aaron.

"Genetically, physically, I am still Mrs. Smythe, but the nanites and implants improved my body and mind. I no longer think like a simple farm girl from the past." She looked around as if to confirm that she was indeed in a lab in the 21st century.

"I am here now. My mind is completely updated to your time. I could be any woman you meet on the street with knowledge of your culture in your time. You could even say that this is my time now also."

Aaron leaned against the heavy stainless lab table upon which the AI cube rested. He arched his back to work out a leftover kink from his nap and then returned his attention to Mercy. She wrapped her sinewy arms around the blanket and drew her knees to her chest.

"However," she continued, "I have a job to do, and it is in 1776. It might sound like some of the corny stuff you might see in a movie, but I am a woman on a mission. Please don't be surprised if I seem like I grew up as a millennial. I probably sound like one since I have already absorbed tremendous information from *Allison*." Just then, Mercy's face became deadly serious.

"When I am ready, you will take me back to 1776, and I will get justice for my village, my husband, and my beautiful girls."

Aaron noticed that the way she spoke was devoid of the pain and suffering that had welled up in her just a few hours ago. Her emotions seemed to be shelved somewhere in her psyche.

"I am going to try to explain something to you, Aaron," she continued. "Two days ago, my wonderful life's purpose was to take care of my dear husband and love and cherish my beautiful girls. That was all I would ever need. A man named Durst and his ten "wolves" changed that forever."

She ran her fingers through her hair and flipped it from her face.

"I am going back with you because what you haven't seen is

my new ability to bring the fight to Durst, his men—and Dorcester.

"In my time, women only went to the battlefield to provide food. Now, I will battle to distribute despair and anguish to my enemies. My head is completely straight now. That might trouble you, but my reason for being is only to punish those evil men. Beyond that," Mercy said with a tinge of sadness, "I have nothing.

"There will never be happiness again in my life, so don't try to cheer me up or soften me. I may laugh and make a joke because I can compartmentalize better than anyone you've ever met, but when I finish my mission, there will be nothing left for me."

Aaron listened to what she had just said. He forced himself to accept that this woman was not the injured human in Washington's tent. *Allison* had given Mercy her life back, but that had changed her reason for existence.

The sudden turn in her tone drained his expectations. His hopes for a future for Mercy, wherein she would find peace and contentment, were dashed. She had just sobered him with her truth that there would never be joy in her life. She had a reason to live, but her reason to live was to bring death to wicked killers. This was hard to accept by looking at her beautiful face. Still, he had no alternative, so he reluctantly connected to her reason for being.

When she looked deeply into his eyes and saw that he understood her, Mercy's mood changed drastically, and she stood up. At some point, while he slept in his office, unknown to him, she'd put on a bra and panties. She stood before him, a 5'8", beautiful and determined woman. Mercy was spontaneously buoyant and almost giddy.

"Hey, Aaron," she grinned as she hopped off the cot and posed before him. "How do you like my new body? You know, back in 1776, I would have turned 17 shades of pink to have a man see me barely dressed. Thanks to my new friend *Allison* here, I don't give a damn."

Aaron looked because it would have taken a superhuman effort not to. He was utterly tongue-tied. He was also fascinated that her wounds were gone. Mercy's skin was almost glowing, and her body radiated strength. The nanites and implants did their job to a standard that was supremely extraterrestrial in origin.

"I'm not done growing, Aaron. Watch this."

She flexed her arms. The fracture in her arm had already healed. They looked like there was the strength of carbon fiber under her perfect skin. She was ripped, he thought, using a slang term. It was slang, but it fit.

"Tell me, Aaron," asked Mercy, "do I look like a lean, mean killing machine?"

"Um," said Aaron. "I'm not sure how to answer that. I mean, you're beautiful, but on top of that, you look *really* strong."

"You're a guy, Aaron. Shake my hand," she commanded.

He reached out and took her hand. Aaron was not a linebacker, but he always had a firm grip from karate and hours in the gym. He squeezed. She squeezed. He squeezed harder. Suddenly, the power of a vise was wrapped around his hand.

"Ow, ow, okay," he yelled. Mercy let go. "Enough! What the hell? I feel like you could crush my bones."

"Aaron," she said while kissing his cheek. "I believe I could."

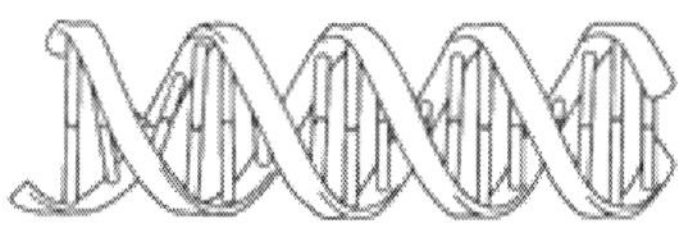

Over the next week, Mercy's progress was remarkable. Adjacent to the lab was Aaron's private gym which was only accessible to Edgar and himself. Of course, the chances of Edgar setting foot in a gym were close to zero.

Mercy worked out like an Olympic athlete. She exercised for eight hours, studied for eight hours, and slept for eight hours. There was also food and a little TV, but she had a scary work ethic.

Allison was ecstatic and repeated to Aaron (almost daily) that human adaptation to implants and physical enhancements was like nothing she would have believed possible. The AI was only too happy to toot her own horn every time the subject of adaptation came up. She seemed like she was fishing for compliments.

Aaron spent about two hours in the gym with Mercy every day. He was no stranger to working out. He'd done martial arts, Krav Maga, fencing, knife fighting, and many other combat sports he could learn. Aaron looked every bit of a Chuck Norris wannabe, except for his dark hair, dark eyes, and five o'clock shadow. But, when it came to Mercy, he couldn't keep up.

After his workouts, he would leave her in the gym to carry on doing things that would make an NFL linebacker whimper. Aaron still had business obligations and did his best to have virtual meetings with his staff. To his relief, Howe It Works was trucking along just fine. It was almost as if they didn't need him. That was good because he intended to finish his training with Mercy and head back to 1776.

Edgar had called him every day. He asked Howe a bunch of questions, and part of him wanted to invite Edgar to come up to the lab, but *Allison* had told him, "no way." She didn't explain why, but she said Edgar must stay off the 7th floor, especially away from Mercy.

He missed having Edgar around, and he wanted to share what he'd been doing very badly with his best friend. The fact that *Allison* was so dead-set against it rubbed him the wrong way, but much to his chagrin, the AI was calling the shots.

After the first week, he noticed that Mercy began studying weapons, weaponry, and military tactics. She asked him to come to the gym, where she also practiced Katas. *Allison* said that at her current level, without the implants, Mercy would be one of the top black belts in the world. With her added strength, Mercy was the best.

One day, when he walked into the gym. Mercy was prone on

the floor with a laptop. She was watching something on the computer.

"Oh no," said Aaron. "You're watching old TV, too?"

Mercy rolled over onto her back and then sat up. To say that she was fit was an understatement. She positively radiated agility and strength.

"I admit that I watch *Dukes of Hazard*, but I have found two kinds of video that I like better. The first is Alfred Hitchcock. I have watched *Rear Window* five times. Jimmy Stewart—what a man! I also have seen *It's a Wonderful Life.* Also, *Jane Eyre* with Orson Welles. I love it. What you call old movies is awesome.

"My second type of movie is? Guess!" she challenged him.

Aaron smirked and then said, *"The Simpsons?"*

"Close, Aaron," she said. "But, no. It's not what you would call a genre, but it's about tough guys. I have been watching *Rambo,* the Rock, and Chuck Norris. I find them inspirational".

Aaron grinned. "A bit before my time, Mercy."

Two days later, he found Mercy watching instructional videos on small firearms. She then moved on to improvised explosives, military tactics, and offensive and defensive maneuvers. The day after, she studied chemistry and physics.

At the end of that week, he found her sitting in the lab eating a hamburger and fries while watching TV. Considering the energy that she burned, a hamburger and fries would provide about as much satisfaction as a green bean would to him. Watching her eat fast food was wholly entertaining. This particular meal was what he thought of as an "all-in-one." She took a greasy wad of fries and stuffed it into the burger to form something roughly the size of a softball. Somehow, to his amazement, she could inhale that thing in a minute or two.

Aaron watched this spectacle for a bit, and then she beckoned him to come closer. As she licked some ketchup off her left hand, she began to tap rhythmically on the desk with her right.

"Mercy," Aaron said, shaking his head. "I can just put some music on if you want?"

Allison popped up on the screen. *"Seriously, Aaron, for a PhD., sometimes you are a dope."*

"Yeah, Aaron," said Mercy mimicking *Allison*. "Ph.D.—don't know much." She laughed hard.

"Duh, it's Morse Code. Watch this," said Mercy.

She tapped out a series of Dits and Dahs on the desk. Then *Allison* sent back a string of short and long beeps.

Aaron raised his voice. "I am not a *doofy dingbat male*."

"Uh oh, he knows Morse Code."

"Listen, you two," he said while heading in the direction of his office. "That's enough picking on me today. C*iao*."

As he bolted away, he could hear *Allison* say, *"Oh listen, Mercy, he knows Italian too!"*

Quite suddenly, Mercy jumped up from in front of her laptop and ran to him. "Wait, Aaron, tell me, when are we going back?"

He stopped and turned to her and then to *Allison*.

"Is she ready?"

Mercy inserted herself into his line of sight and put on her aggressive face. "Why don't you ask *me* if I'm ready?"

"Whoa, ok," said Aaron. "Are you ready?"

"Yes, I'm ready," she snarled.

He looked straight into her face to process that. He gave her a wicked grin and said, "*Allison*, is that true, is she ready?"

Mercy let out a frustrated yelp as Aaron turned and ran into his office. From behind the door, he shouted out that Mercy should ask him again tomorrow.

The following morning, Mercy was not in the gym as usual but was squatting on a lab chair, ready to ambush him. She wore jeans and a white tank top that said: "Been there, done that."

"If you aren't ready to take me back yet, then take me out there." She gestured with her thumb toward the outside world.

He mulled this over. To Aaron's thinking, Mercy had assimilated massive amounts of factual and cultural data over the last few days. The combination of implants, physical enhancement, and her constant access to media had changed her.

She was still the woman from 1776, but she was also much more than that. She knew stuff, and not just calculus or physics. She processed information so quickly now that she had vast amounts of data at her fingertips. If you asked her about V8 engines from 1972, she could probably tell you something. If you wanted to know about the actress Hedy Lamarr's patent and the development of GPS, Mercy could most likely reveal little-known details.

Later that day, Aaron asked *Allison* about this ability. She said that Mercy's integration of the implants was perfect and that she was the first sentient to survive the process.

"What are you saying," he asked. "That she could have died? What the hell! Why did you even try it?"

Allison gave him an empty stare, then said, *"There was a 58.2% probability that it would work."*

Aaron raised his voice. "A 58 is an F, *Allison*. You could have killed her!"

"And what would have been the alternative? Do you know what would have happened if you had only patched up her physical wounds? There would have been an 85% chance that she would have gone into a deep depression and never emerged. Did you consider that? I did."

He looked at her and just mumbled, "Oh."

Aaron changed the subject, stood in front of Allison's image on the monitor, and pushed for more details on the "other sentients." She said simply that humans were not the only sentient species and that he should stop bugging her for now.

After a week had passed, Mercy took to her implants like a duck to water. Her accumulation of data was enormous, but she kept most of her knowledge private. Apparently, for a few days, she'd begun clamping down a little on "outgoing" information. Maybe she figured that being too forthcoming wasn't always wise. Perhaps she was working on bridling her enthusiasm—he wasn't sure about that either. Was it a female thing? He'd noticed a lot of similar nuances about Allison and Mercy. As a scientist, he watched and wondered.

One morning Mercy said, "If you aren't ready to take me back to the war, then, like I said before, I want to go out there."

"Mercy, you're a 30-year-old lady from 1776. Couldn't it be that going out there might be a little weird for you?"

"I've already studied your culture and watched a lot of TV. I am sure I can handle going out for a pizza."

"*Allison*—"

"You don't have to ask *Allison*!" shouted Mercy angrily.

Aaron succumbed and said, "Fine, you get your way, but pizza is lunch." He looked at his watch. "It's only 7:30, so go work out, and later we'll do lunch."

When 11:30 rolled around, Mercy tiptoed up to his office door. He had just finished with the CTO and was glad to have shifted an issue back to upper management to resolve. The less they needed him, especially now, the better.

Mercy leaned up against the door. She was wearing a painted-on pair of jeans and the Iron Maiden T-shirt he'd bought for her. She did a spin and asked, "How do I look?"

He could have fallen off his chair. If he had been from Georgia, he would have shouted, "Slap my grandma!" instead, he blurted out, "Where did you get those jeans?"

"You bought them for me."

"Really, when?"

"Just yesterday. You ordered them from the mall, and poof, they got here the same day."

"I think I would know if I'd ordered jeans from the mall."

"Well, you did, Aaron, and you put it on your American Express card, so thanks."

Aaron laughed out loud. He was finally beginning to understand women. In this case, rule 132b. The rule being that if a girl used your credit card to buy clothes or jewelry, it was a gift from you (whether you were involved in the transaction or not).

"When we go out, you stay close to me. Got it?"

She gave him a salute. "Stay close to you, aye."

Chapter 22

Getting out of Howe It Works had been weird. There were always people coming and going, but when the CEO stepped out of the elevator with the captivating woman in tight jeans, it was noticed. Howe ignored the dropped jaws and made straight for the exit. Mercy, of course, couldn't help but make eye contact and smile with her perfect teeth. Meanwhile, Aaron hoped his employees didn't think he'd hired an escort.

Fortunately, Aaron's clunker, parked nearby and gathering dust, started on the first try. They buckled up and headed out to a nearby shopping center.

Mercy practically had her head hanging out the passenger side window like an enthusiastic pup. What she'd seen on TV had not prepared her for how the world looked *outside*. She didn't seem to be able to get enough input. Despite her in-lab internet education, her real-life had been in a small village in 1770s New Jersey. She couldn't hide her excitement about being 250 years in the future.

They went straight to the pizza place located at a nearby strip mall. The weather was perfect, and all the Japanese sedans, Evs, and occasional pickups were lined up in front of the stores. When they entered, Bannon's Pizza was about half-full. Some people were waiting in line, and a handful of kids were drooling as they sat impatiently at tables.

Mercy was as curious about the people as she was about pizza. A short time later, she finished her fourth slice. To Aaron, she looked about as happy as one could expect from a woman who had been through torture.

Something about her mannerisms exuded charisma, and little kids in the restaurant seemed to stare at her like she was a magnet. A couple of times, Aaron had to remind Mercy that moms weren't keen on strangers starting conversations with their kids.

After the pizza, she insisted that he take her to every store in sight. The row of shops at the brick strip mall excited Mercy. They looked at dishes, floral bedding, a picture framer, a computer store, a nail salon (which ended up in a fight), and an office supply store. Mercy appeared to drink it up. She made him buy her a daily planner book and some pens so that she could start writing a diary. She admitted it was pretty old-fashioned but wanted to jot her observations on paper. And, the pens were exceedingly better than anything she'd had in 1776.

"Is there anything not good about living in your time?" she asked.

"Haven't you seen our news?" quizzed Aaron.

"Yes, I know about all your world conflicts. I even studied your crazy politics, especially the part about the government giving money to people not to work," she laughed. "I think that's a good one, brilliant idea, that one." Mercy said that with a thick layer of sarcasm. "In my time, no workie means no eatie."

After twenty minutes of nagging, Aaron convinced her they had to return to the lab. They stopped for a soft ice cream cone. That was an adventure in indecision. Mercy was overwhelmed but eventually settled on something like Rocky Road topped with chocolate sprinkles. Thirty seconds into the cone, she shouted, "I've died and gone to heaven!"

The drive back was seemingly uneventful. About five minutes from the office, Aaron stopped for gas. He'd habitually ignored the empty light, but not this day. Mercy watched with interest as he pumped fuel into his rather old beast. The Cutlass was his preferred drive, but it was at home, so the old SUV was the vehicle of the day. Aaron modeled himself after Sam Walton, the founder of Walmart, who used to drive around in a '72 Ford pickup.

As Aaron filled the tank, Mercy scanned the highway and focused on a roadside bar across the way. She could not miss the flickering "Rusty's" sign and the bold painting of a beer mug with "Only a $2" drawn on a plank below it.

"Hey," she shouted. "That looks like a roadhouse. Let's go there."

Aaron was putting the nozzle back on the pump. "No way."

"Why not?" asked Mercy.

"Because it's a bar," he said. "And it doesn't look too friendly."

She gave him her petulant look with which he had become familiar, took off running in her new pink sneakers, and shouted, "Bring the car. I will meet you there."

Traffic was light, so he managed to get across the highway quickly. By the time he parked, Mercy was marveling at the nice shiny muscle bikes parked out front.

"Why can't we travel on one of these motorcycles?"

"Mercy," he said as he pocketed his keys. "Because we can't."

"Fine, so let's go in and have a beer," she demanded.

Aaron shook his head. "No way! Do you know what kind of people hang out in these places?"

"Of course," she smiled. "Like bad guys from TV shows."

"And that is why we are heading back to the lab. C'mon." He pulled on her T-shirt sleeve, but she didn't budge.

"Aaron!" she glared at him with her feet planted on the ground; He knew he had lost the argument.

He sighed and said firmly, "One beer, agreed?"

Mercy smiled back at him, touched his cheek gently, and said, "Thank you so much."

They stepped through a door with a couple of small broken window panes and then inside. As soon as his eyes adjusted to the lighting, Aaron realized this was a bad idea. At least five serious-looking bikers were at the bar, and a few more at the tables. They looked scary, and Aaron did not have his VZ 58 and Recon to back him up. He thought to himself, one beer, and then back to the lab.

In the meantime, Mercy was already scooting up to the bar and motioning for him to join her. She would have fit right in if she'd had a tattoo, a ratty leather jacket, and a nose piercing.

They sat down. Aaron ordered two mugs of whatever was on tap. As a movie *aficionado*, Mercy recognized the posters of Marlon Brando, Clint Eastwood, and a variety of gangsters and bikers up on the walls. She kept smiling at the bikers down the bar as he nudged her with his elbow and whispered, "Stop that."

"Stop what?" she replied, as it was apparent that Mercy wasn't interested in taking Aaron's advice at the moment.

He shook his head and tried to urge her to drink her beer, but she kept looking around the bar and grinning. Aaron thought to himself, *what is* she *doing*?

A particularly nasty-looking guy with "*Eat Me*" tattooed on his forehead looked down the bar at Mercy. "Hey baby, what are you doing with that runt?" he barked.

"Oh, him?" she smiled as she pointed to Howe. "He just took me shopping and out for pizza."

The guys at the bar laughed, and then the *Eat Me* guy said, "Well, now that you've had pizza, how 'bout some sausage?" They all laughed louder.

Mercy smiled, held her finger and thumb about four inches apart, and said, "What you got? One of them little breakfast sausages I saw on TV?"

Aaron muttered to himself, "Oh no," and then buried his face in his hands.

The guy with the tattoo got up and turned out to be even bigger than Howe suspected. The large biker put his beer down and cracked his knuckles.

"Say blondie, why don't you have your weenie man stand up and drop his drawers so we can all laugh at *his* sausage." He turned around to his gang. They all gave him nods of approval.

Aaron realized this was quickly spiraling out of control, and he had no intention of dropping his pants to placate some buffoon.

The big biker turned back to Mercy. "And while you're at it, why don't you show us your assets, hot stuff?"

It only took a millisecond for her to comprehend what the

man had meant. She got off her stool and glared at him.

"Stop eyeing me bitch," he growled. "You might be a babe, but if you keep eyeing me, I'll put you on the floor." He turned again to his pals and said, "Maybe I'll just put her over my knee so I can spank her." That brought another small roar of laughter from the gang. Aaron saw the bartender making a phone call from the corner of his eye. Cops? Hopefully!

He stood up and said, "Sir, I apologize for my friend's behavior. If it is okay, we'll zip out of here and get out of your way."

The brute stepped forward to within a few feet of Mercy. "I don't think so, pizza boy," he said as he reached out for Mercy's T-shirt and said. "Let's get a little peek."

Just as his bulky fingertips grazed the fabric, Mercy unleashed 250 years of pent-up rage. In an instant, she gripped and broke two of his fingers and then did a sweep of his right leg. That took all of a second and a half. It took another second for the oaf to hit the ground. Four of his biker brothers immediately got up from the bar, moving angrily towards Aaron and Mercy.

In what Aaron later described as a combination of Bruce Lee, *Kick Ass*, and the *Matrix*, Mercy put all four threats down on the floor while retrieving a knife and a pair of brass knuckles.

There were now five bikers down and groaning when the four at the table stood up. It looked to Aaron that they were trying to make sense of what they had just seen.

Mercy held up her index finger and waved it from side to side, yelling, "Ah, ah, ah, better sit down, boys."

One of them then reached into his belt while shouting, "Forget you, bitch." He pulled a small 9mm, but it was too late because the knife Mercy had taken was already in flight and buried itself in his gun hand. The man dropped back into his chair, screaming as the pistol hit the floor. The last three members of the gang froze in their tracks and then stepped back. Aaron was tongue-tied as Mercy eyed them all dangerously.

She grabbed her mug, took a large gulp, wiped her mouth on

Aaron's sleeve, and then shouted, "Thanks for the workout." Howe desperately dragged her out of the bar littered with injured thugs.

They raced to the car, jumped in, and he floored it out of the parking lot.

"Dammit, Mercy!"

She was blissful and yelled, "That was awesome!"

Aaron raced down the road back towards Howe It Works and safety. Nervous sweat dripped off his chin as he briefly turned to glance at Mercy. She looked as cool as a cucumber, he thought. Then he declared: "That's it, we're going back to 1776."

She turned, smiled, and with a flick of her hand in a kind of victory wave, pursed her lips and said, "It's about damn time."

Vice President John Edward Carlisle was unhappy. He hadn't heard from Kent Spark in four days. It was unlike Kent not to give him a call every 48 hours. The man was a prick, but he was a reliably punctual prick. He could live with a four-day absence if they were merely working on a hi-tech web surveillance bug or something mildly less world-changing. Alien devices, however, required a tad more supervision. Beyond that, there were whistles in the wind that the president—that over-the-hill, demented, lecherous, secretary-groping jerk, was asking questions. Presidents asking questions was not what I.S. needed. At all.

Carlisle pressed his stubby finger on the red button that buzzed his secretary. "Grace?"

"Yes sir," the response was impossibly immediate. He always wondered how she could answer the instant he pressed the buzzer.

"See if you can contact George Bartle. I want him in my

office in ten minutes."

"One moment, sir. He is just calling now."

Carlisle wondered if the coincidence was a good or bad omen. Probably bad, he thought. When they called you, it was usually a rotten sign. Anyone under twenty calling you meant they needed money. Over twenty, they wanted a job. Over fifty, they were calling in a favor. Over seventy—

"Sir, I am transferring the call to your line now," said Grace.

Carlisle picked up his phone and sat down at the beautiful maple desk. "George! First, just listen."

"Yes, sir," answered the middle-aged agent. Bartle was a mostly by-the-book kind of guy. He was competent but a little sloppy in appearance, which didn't fit with his military background. Everyone recognized him from his clothes on those rare occasions when Bartle came to the White House. He was an excellent operative, which showed you that you couldn't always count on the clothes making the man. Carlisle snorted at the image of Agent George B in his mind.

"How fast can you get here?"

"I was on my way already," Bartle said ominously.

"Good." said the VP. "Come straight to my office. No shortstops."

Carlisle broke the connection without waiting for a response.

Exactly eleven minutes later, Grace ushered George Bartle, C.I.A., into Carlisle's office. The VP quickly pointed the agent over to the couch and pulled up a chair close enough to talk in a soft whisper.

"George, what do you have?"

The agent, a slightly over-weight former SEAL, looked like he'd drawn the short straw and had to deliver bad news to the king.

"Sir," he began, his nervousness triggering a more pronounced Brooklyn accent. "Kent is nowhere to be found."

"What does that mean?" asked the vice president with a controlled, tight-lipped grin.

"Sir, per your instructions, we've been tailing him using

trackers. Four days ago, he was heading north on 95. We had him until he stopped at a Wawa by Newark, then both trackers died."

"You are kidding me!" said Carlisle in a raised voice as he stood up to stomp around his office in response to stress.

"Sir, there's more. I searched using the surveillance cameras out on the road, and we got a hit from a camera on 87 above Woodbury."

The VP stood up and scratched a mosquito bite that was literally a pain in the neck.

"Woodbury. That's close to West Point. Doesn't Kent have a kid at West Point?"

"Yes, sir, he has a daughter there, but we checked the cameras, and that wasn't his destination. Then we got another hit at a restaurant on 9W. He was eating with his cadet daughter named Journey Spark. Then he went off the radar."

"Crap," blurted Carlisle. He told that inquisitive Kent to stay away from Howe, and now it looked like he was too close for comfort. The VP sat back down and stared Bartle in the eyes. "What about the daughter? Did you ask her where her dad is?"

"I didn't want to open up a can of worms, sir."

John was silent for a moment. Not telling the daughter was actually a damn good idea considering the alarms that would be set off.

"Okay," said Carlisle. "I told you about my concern that Kent might head north towards Howe It Works?"

"Absolutely, sir," confirmed Bartle."

"The details about Howe are not important for you to know,"

"Roger that, we have been doing tracking only."

"Fine. What else did you do to find Kent?"

Bartle pulled out handwritten notes on a little pad with "Dusty's Plumbing" printed on it.

"We checked quietly within a twenty-mile radius of Howe It Works for anything unusual. Gas station cameras, shopping malls, and whatnot.

"We turned up all the things you would expect. Car

accidents, vandalism, you know, typical suburban police crap, I mean incidents. The only thing that was a little unusual was at a biker bar about three miles from Howe It Works. The local cops got a call about some trouble. When they got to the bar, several tough bikers looked beaten up, including one with a stab wound in his hand.

"The cops told our guy that the bartender said a blonde chick had beaten them up." Bartle looked at his pad and continued as if reading from a script. "The bikers said that that is a load of quote, 'B-S' and that it was a rival gang that quote, 'jumped them when they were sitting there peacefully enjoying some French fries and cokes' unquote."

Carlisle looked frustrated. He made a resigned gesture with both hands. "What does a gang fight have to do with Kent?"

"Well, sir," said Bartle. "This was close to Howe It Works, and a camera at a gas station across the street from the bar caught a guy fitting Howe's description and a woman running out of the bar.

"We think Howe was with her in the bar."

Carlisle chuckled, "Let me get this straight, you think a multi-billionaire and an unidentified woman went into a bar, and the girl beat up ten bikers, then they ran away? Did you get a plate?"

"That's what it looks like, and no sir, no plate, but the car was an old SUV like one of the vehicles Howe drives."

"And what does this have to do with Kent?" asked Carlisle.

"I don't know, but you asked me about anything unusual. I think one woman and Howe in a bar beating up a gang of bikers and then getting out with their heads attached is unusual."

Carlisle massaged his temples. The morning stress headache was starting early. Bartle sat there in his dark polyester suit, patiently waiting while the VP seemed to process random bits of information. John felt himself drifting into dystopian future thoughts about the unidentified female being an alien and Howe now under some alien mind control. They were just out on their first test run to begin the domination of the human race. Whoa!

He thought. It was like he was listening to his grandson talking about that video game stream or gas or something. He turned to Bartle.

"Here's what we're going to do. Is there any way you can get the surveillance video from Howe It Works?"

"Not a chance in hell, sir," explained Bartle. "They have encryption on their computers that even we can't hack. We would need a court order."

"Screw that!" said Carlisle, accidentally thinking out loud. "We have someone on the inside over at Howe It Works," admitted Carlisle. "—Not that there is anything illegal going on over there; let's just say we like to keep track of new technology."

"Sir," asked the agent. "Do you mean like industrial espionage, except that we are doing the spying?"

"You said that, not me," said the VP. "But in any case, nothing illegal, just partnering with one of our big vendors. Let me tell you who to contact over there."

Carlisle's private cell rang the next day at 10:03 a.m.

"Yes?"

"Sir," said Bartle. "It's Bartle."

"Tell me."

"Your friend said that Kent was there."

"Son of a bitch! What else?"

Bartle continued. "He was there about four days ago, came in to meet with the guy I just met, and then left."

"That's it?" asked Carlisle.

"Yep. The guy said that Kent walked out the door, got in his car, and drove away. The funny thing is—"

"What, Bartle?" snapped the VP, "What's the funny thing?"

"Well, sir, one of our drones was panning around Howe It

Works, and up until yesterday, Kent's car was in the visitor lot."

"Bartle? Do nothing, say nothing," said Carlisle as he terminated the call.

He sat in his chair for a long time, just thinking about how Kent may have been right the whole damn time. The device should have simply gone to Virginia, to the I.S. lab. Of course, the message Carlisle had initially received when *they* sent their first cryptic communication was to give the device to Howe. What was he supposed to have responded— "No?" Say no to *aliens*? He'd kept that and the subsequent message completely secret. Talking about messages from aliens via your cellphone was a recipe for psychiatric care. And now Kent?

Agent Spark just had to go and buck the chain of command; go up to Vermont, Carlisle thought. He couldn't just follow simple orders. Pride goeth before a fall. Kent was that kind of guy, always thinking he knew better than you. Who knew where the hell he was now? Aliens could be pulling his eyeballs out of his ass. This thing was going from bad to worse, and what next? An ET invasion?

For some unknown reason, his thoughts drifted to when he was a teenager. He and his friends used to watch an alien invasion movie over and over. Mostly so they could drool over the nude scene with a mind-controlled actress. Carlisle never thought he'd be getting paranoid about the real thing.

He almost slapped himself. Get a grip, he thought.

"Grace," he said as he pressed the button. "Come in here. I want you to set up a meeting."

Chapter 23

Dr. Aaron Howe returned to General Washington's tent exactly twenty minutes after he'd left. That was the way it appeared to Washington. During that time, the general ensured that no one dared approach his tent.

Upon seeing the miraculously recovered woman, Washington did a slight bow of his head and scowled at Major Howe. "You said two minutes!"

Howe looked confused for a second. "Well, I can't always get it dead on." This was a lie, but no point in getting into an argument with the commander-in-chief of the Continental Army. The truth was that he'd simply set his return for twenty minutes later at random.

"Ma'am," Washington continued. "I am just so pleased to see you well."

Mercy was arrayed in an inferior substitute for 1770s-era women's clothing. Howe picked it up at a strange costume store, reluctantly taking Mercy with him. He insisted that the seamstress remove all of the glitter and turn the dress into as boring a garment as possible.

"General," said Mercy as she curtsied and batted her eyes. "I am so pleased to be back in 1776 and healthy as well. I want to add that I would like to be referred to as Tomoe Gozen, but please call me Mercy if you wish."

General Washington took a few seconds, then laughed as heartily as anyone had heard from him in a long time. Finally, he said, "Mercy, I can think of no better name for you than Tomoe Gozen."

Howe looked perplexed at the private joke between Mercy and Washington. He did a brief search of his memory to try to reference the name but came up blank.

"May I ask?" inquired Aaron. "What am I missing here?"

Washington turned to Howe, motioned toward Mercy, and asked her, "May I?"

Mercy politely nodded her acquiescence, and the general began.

"Aaron, being that I am not a complete dolt as some in the legislature would paint me, I do actually know some history.

"Tomoe Gozen was a great female warrior from around the 1300s in Japan. She was said to have been a master archer and swordsman. I believe it was said of her that with a sword, she was the equal of a thousand men. Tomoe was said to be both beautiful and fearless. Despite the oddity of a woman in battle, the men she fought beside quite quickly came to admire and respect her. They considered her one of the most dangerous combatants in the world." Washington turned to the beautiful Mercy Smythe. "Did I state that correctly, Tomoe?"

Mercy smiled with a sweetness that would cause a lion to roll over and play dead. "General Washington, that was a very excellent recitation of the history of Gozen except for the date; it was the late 1100s," she corrected.

Washington again bowed his head and said, "Mercy, if I ever make a historical misquote, you are freely authorized to correct me immediately."

Howe, as an observer, was floored. In less than two minutes, she had General Washington eating out of her hand. It was remarkable. He cleared his throat.

"General, sir," explained Howe. "Your idea to take Mercy back to my time was excellent. We were able to heal her wounds completely."

"Frankly, it is miraculous."

"I would have to agree with you on that, sir," said Aaron. "However, there is something that I would like to discuss with you in private."

"Of course."

"Mercy," asked Aaron. "Why don't you just sit while the general and I go outside for a moment?"

She smiled and obediently sat on one of the simple wooden

chairs by the general's desk.

After exiting, the two men glanced around the camp to make sure they were alone. George had shooed the guards away to keep them out of earshot. Their breath fogged in the chilly air as Washington asked, "Now then, what is it?"

"Don't you want to know all about what happened when I took Mercy?"

"Indeed, I do. I'd like to hear every last detail."

He mulled over what would be safe to tell the general. Could he tell him about the AI? Implants? Or maybe better to say nothing at all.

"General," said Aaron. "You might not believe it if I told you what Mercy has been through. To be brief, I have a certain device or machine that could heal her wounds and make her body and mind extremely strong."

Washington looked very interested, and his enthusiasm was like a magnet for a scientist like Howe. He so eagerly wanted to be able to tell the father of America the whole story. So he began. "General, imagine having tremendous physical strength."

Washington smirked because it was well-known that he was considered as strong as a bull not long ago. He remembered lifting things that two men combined could not. "I can imagine that, major."

"Right, sir. Well, I'm telling you that when and if you were at your strongest, and then you'd met Mercy—she'd be stronger."

The general thought this must be a joke, but Aaron never failed to prove his claims.

"On top of that, sir, she is an encyclopedia of knowledge. And she is extremely skilled at combat. She can fight like a Vermont black bear in a bad mood."

Washington forced himself to accept Howe's portrayal as the utter truth. He smiled and said, "So what is the purpose of telling me all this?"

Aaron was reticent but whispered, "I want to take Mercy back to Recon with me."

Washington smirked, "Are you jesting me? This woman just lost her family? Perhaps she has relatives with whom she can recover from her shock and travail?"

Aaron persisted. "Sir, we used certain medical procedures to help her recover physically, mentally, and emotionally. Of course, she will never forget her love for her husband and children, but she is learning to live with that pain. She needs to stay with Recon, sir." Howe leaned close to whisper directly into the general's ear. "Frankly, if I may be blunt about it, I need to keep an eye on her. It isn't safe for her to be alone in the world just now."

Washington paced a few steps back and forth with his hands locked behind his back. He stopped and looked at Aaron. "Can I have faith that you know what you are doing? She is a woman. She may call herself Tomoe Gozen to give herself confidence, but when do we put women in battle or even near a skirmish? We are *civilized*," said Washington, the latter part with a glint in his blue eyes.

"With all due respect, she is not a typical woman. Let's say that if there were a woman Samurai in this century, Mercy would be it.

"I want to add one more thing," Howe said. "In order to quiet any questions about a woman working with Recon, I suggest that we say that she should be recognized as our cook."

"A COOK?" was yelled out from inside the tent with a tone of indignance.

"Oh," said Aaron turning to the general smiling. "She also has excellent hearing."

The three of them were once again seated in the command tent. Aaron felt a bit more relaxed, knowing that Mercy would be allowed to stay with Recon.

"Tell me, Tomoe, can you cook?" asked his Excellency.

"General," said Mercy. "I can honestly say that I was perhaps the worst cook in New Jersey for thirty years. Perhaps in all of the colonies. However, as of now, let us say that my abilities in many areas are outstanding, including my culinary skills."

"Can you fight, Mercy?" he asked, already having heard the answer from Aaron.

"Sir," she spoke up confidently. "There isn't a soldier in—"

Howe coughed loudly as he simultaneously kicked Mercy under the table.

"General," he said, "Mercy knows how to cook, and regarding fighting, she's a regular Molly Pitcher."

"Molly, who?" asked the general.

"Uh, sorry, sir, that didn't happen yet, but she was a real fighter."

"Very well," said Washington with resignation. "I see that you both believe that Mercy has warrior skills, but I must emphasize that we should keep this a secret. You cannot imagine the grief I will get if Congress gets even a whiff of this."

"Yes, sir," Aaron and Mercy said together.

"And," said Washington. "In the meantime, Mercy will be staying in this tent for another day until she 'recovers.' I cannot sustain the whole camp seeing a near-dead woman get up and start walking around after forty minutes. Tomorrow, we can say that you nursed her back to health and that her wounds were only superficial. The doctor shan't believe that, but he will keep a still tongue.

"Mercy, do you think you can manage a day just lying in the back area of this tent and being quiet?"

She pulled a paper bag from her backpack and waved it around. It had *Sam's Bakery & Deli* printed on it and was stuffed full of food. "General, as long as there's a couple of these bagels for breakfast, I'll be fine."

Over the next day, Aaron spent a good deal of time with Recon. He also managed to meander his way around the encampment until he found a woman about Mercy's size. His plea was that the poor injured woman recovered quickly but needed a dress. Howe paid top dollar by 1776 standards and got an inferior garment for his effort. Mercy hated it.

By the end of the day, Washington relented, releasing Mercy to Major Howe. It was also decided that Recon would relocate further from the main camp.

Aaron had not prepped the guys of Recon about Mercy, and he figured the best way to introduce her was just to spring it on them.

At 18:00, they packed up all their gear and moved another 100 yards out.

At 19:00, Major Howe walked into camp for the first time with Recon's new cook. The appearance of Mercy caused a sudden breeze generated by six jaws dropping in unison. Before going to the Recon camp, Aaron had taken her to their container and loaded her with everything a special forces soldier should have. Now she stood in front of six men rubbing their eyes, trying to comprehend what they were seeing.

Mercy was in her "new" dress and carried a 50 lb. pack with food, boots, a uniform, ammunition, and a Sig Sauer 1911-45-WTP. The Sig was a full-size commemorative with *1776,* and *We the People* stamped on the slide. She also had a Beretta APX Carry Black 9mm pistol strapped to her leg. Part of the food included a whole box of Snickers, which she intended to share if someone could outshoot her on the 20-yard pistol range.

"Men," said Major Howe. "This is our new cook, Mercy."

There was a collective subdued laugh from the guys.

"What's so funny?" she asked, eyeing them one at a time.

They stopped laughing. Howe gave Mercy the "Don't start" look.

"Listen," said Howe. "We need to have a meeting to discuss Mercy's job here. So, I'm going to get her settled into a tent. We will reconvene at 19:45. Everybody good with that?"

Aaron helped Mercy set up her tent. It was fairly large, which meant that she had room for all her gear. She pulled off her dress as he sat across from her.

“Whoa, what are you doing?”

“I’m putting on my camos,” she breathed.

Howe looked flustered. There was very little light in the tent, but the sex appeal of Mercy in the dark was equal to a centerfold in broad daylight; you didn’t even need to see the whole package with Mercy to know that she was breathtaking. However, that wasn’t the issue for Aaron at the moment.

“You can’t go out there like that!”

“Why not?”

In the dim light, he tried to stare her down. “Mercy, these guys aren’t ready for that yet.”

She brought her face very close to his, grabbed his head between her palms, pressed her forehead and nose to his, and said, “I don’t care.”

Five minutes later, they emerged from the tent and moved to the ring of guys settled around their nightly fire. His body partially blocked her from being seen, but then he sat down on a log which permitted Recon to view Mercy fully in the firelight.

She wore camo pants, a blouse, and a jacket with a name above the pocket. It said Gozen. She had the 1911 strapped on for effect, and by the looks of the men of Recon, they were befuddled.

The only one with the candor to speak up was Sergeant Monty, who just said, “What is this?”

Being a modern-thinking, equality-minded man, Aaron announced that Mercy was the newest member of Recon. The laughter was quite loud, especially from the large Sergeant Montgomery.

“One second,” asked Sergeant Allen, reading the name tag on her blouse. “Is this the unconscious woman brought into camp the other day? Didn’t they say her name was Mercy? Who is Gozen?”

Howe started to speak, but Mercy raised her hand to stop

him. "Yes, I am that woman. I am Mercy Smythe, or Tomoe Gozen, whichever you prefer. My husband and my two daughters were murdered. I was left for dead; if you want the details, I have no problem telling you every last one."

There was a pitched silence around the fire as the six men of Recon gave her their full and solemn attention. She was also firm and aggressive—which snared their gazes without exception.

"Major Howe took me back to his time and fixed me. Don't ask me about the future, because I won't tell you, at least not yet. I can tell you one thing: in the future, women are tough. Women fight in the army. There is a country in the Middle East called Israel where all women get drafted like men. They carry weapons and kick the crap out of their enemies."

Mercy continued. "I am a member of Recon because we are going to track down and take out the scumbags who murdered my village."

Lewis raised his hand. "What does 'take out the scumbags' mean?"

Mercy pierced the red-headed corporal with her deep blue eyes and said, "It means we are going to find them, and then I am going to rip off their heads with my bare hands or otherwise end their disgusting lives with malice."

The crackling of the fire was the only sound heard. Howe knew that when Mercy was in this frame of mind, it was a damn good idea to let her decide when to get cheery again.

Finally, after a pregnant pause, Monty said, "That sounds well and good, but you are just a woman."

The newest member of Recon choked up and whimpered, "You're right. I'm just one woman." She feigned demure weakness. "Perhaps, Sergeant Montgomery, we could shake hands, and then I'll get my dress back on and bake everyone some cookies?"

She reached out her hand, but Aaron jumped in between them and said, "whoa, whoa, whoa!" He pushed Mercy's hand back and said, "nope, no handshakes required."

“Why not, major?” said Monty. “A handshake is a pleasant sign of agreement. We will *agree* to go out and kill the bad men, and Tomoe will agree to bake biscuits. I’ll shake on that!” he said with a broad grin.

Aaron was determined to get Recon squared away, but not by Mercy breaking bones.

“Just hold on and listen,” said Howe. The men focused on the major and managed to take their eyes off the beautiful woman.

“Monty, if she shakes your hand, you’re going to wish you never agreed to that,” said Aaron.

“Really, major? Why not? Does she have warts?”

“Monty, she could grind your bones to make her bread.”

Recon tried to make sense of the last line out of the major’s mouth, but then he cleared it up for them. “She’s at least twice as strong as you are, got it?”

That got a bigger laugh than the sight of Mercy in camouflage—from everyone but Clark and Schein. Those two had learned that Major Howe tended to be straight up. He didn’t tell them everything, but what he did tell them was the truth.

“Monty and the rest of you,” said Clark. “I believe that we better take the major at his word.”

“Well, I’m not convinced,” scoffed Lewis. He handed her an MRE tin. “Shows us your bone-crushing power.”

Aaron sighed. He was going to have to let this play out. Mercy had pushed it, and now it was her show. She took the aluminum tin, eyed it, and then began crushing it into a tiny cube.

“That was too easy,” said Monty. “How ‘bout this?” He hefted a bag of M14 ammo with both hands and set it down in front of Mercy.

“I will give you my hat if you can lift that above your head. That’s 100 pounds.

She smirked because Mercy Smythe had always loved competition—even before nanites. And now, with enhancements?

A sad, pathetic look emanated from her face as she wrapped

her hands around the strap. After a deliberately pitiable effort to lift the bag, Mercy contrived a lack of ability to even budge it. A defeated countenance appeared as if she was embarrassed by her failure. Mercy sat down, appearing crestfallen and sad.

Monty laughed but then said, "Mrs., do not feel dejected. After all, you are a woman, and no one expects you to heft that!"

Mercy stood back up and eyed Monty. "Did you mean that I should use one hand or two?"

"No one can lift that above their head with one hand!" said Allen.

Mercy figured that she'd toyed with the male chauvinists enough. She walked back over to the canvas bag and grabbed it with her left hand, and in an instant, yanked it off the ground and pressed it above her head. For effect, she did it twice. The men jumped back as she stood with her hands triumphantly on her hips. Lewis just stammered, "Bloody hell!"

Aaron had seen enough. "Everyone, sit." They sat and did their best to control their utter astonishment.

When the chitchat had settled and they could take their eyes off Mercy long enough to listen, Howe said, "Pay attention. Mercy was in the future with me. She demonstratively is not like your mother or your sister."She was so severely injured that we rebuilt her body to be exceedingly strong.

Let's get this straight. She can outrun you. She can outjump you. She can lift more than you. She can outshoot you with any weapon you choose. You see that pistol on her hip. It's a .45 caliber handgun that Mercy can shoot with either hand expertly. Oh, and she is smarter than you. Sometimes I think she is smarter than me.

"I watched her single-handedly put down five guys in a pub in my time because they wanted to get rough with her.

"The good part is that she is your friend. Be glad about that. Mercy will fight with you, and you can trust her to watch out for you as if each of you were her brother. I expect each of you to watch out for her as if she were your sister. She might be a female, but Mercy is also your brother-in-arms. You will respect her because she might save your life if we get into a scrum over our heads." He looked around at all the men individually, then asked, "Got it?"

"There was a collective "Yes sir," as they all gazed at Mercy in awe, even Monty.

The following day broke clear and cool. It was November in New Jersey, and the trees were mostly bare except for the pines. Birds were flying around and singing. Aaron awoke to hear the din of the main camp. It was 07:00 on his watch. He rubbed his eyes as the fog lifted from his brain. Mercy was sitting cross-legged next to his bag with the Sig .45 pistol in her hand.

"What's going on, Mercy?" he asked nervously.

It took her a second to realize that Aaron was a little uptight to see a dangerous woman sitting beside him, holding a weapon.

"Oh!" said Mercy as she flipped the Sig back into its holster. She smiled and said, "Sorry if I scared you. I want to go shooting."

"Did you even get some sleep?"

"Sure. Of course, I slept. I slept great, but I also miss *Allison,* and I want to go shooting."

Howe sat up in his bag and stretched a little. He rolled his neck. He'd slept in sweats and would have been ecstatic to stay in bed for a few hours. There was no way Mercy would let that happen.

"Hey," said Mercy. "You look a little stiff. Do you want me to teach you some Yoga?"

"No. No yoga!" protested Aaron. "How about we have breakfast, and then we'll shoot? Also, I don't understand the connection between missing *Allison* and wanting to go shooting."

Mercy cracked her knuckles. "Major, I'm trying to express my feelings in a more forthcoming way. Since I'm feeling a little lonely for *Allison*, I decided just to say it. Is that ok?"

"Sure, Mercy. Don't feel shy about that at all. *Allison* saved your life, and the two of you talk like you could be sisters."

He was still trying to process her feelings for *Allison*, but Mercy had already moved on to food. She nudged him out of his thoughts about *Allison* and said, "Let's do breakfast; I'll cook. What do you want? Or, maybe I should ask, what do we have?"

As far as Aaron knew, all they had in the camp were boxes of pancake mix and some MRE's, but the containers were loaded with a ton of stuff.

"First of all, put on your dress."

She growled.

"Next, grab whoever is up and go over to the container that's marked 'X.'"

"Gee, that's original."

"Whatever, but go over there and use your thumbprint to open the lock. Inside is a lot of stuff just for Recon. Don't take anything except three dozen eggs, a couple of loaves of bread, some multivitamins, some apples, um, popcorn, Pastries, and whatever else you think is good, but don't bring too much. The food is on the right side of the container. On the left are ammo and gear. Don't touch. That's an order from your major, clear?"

She nodded obediently. The chances of Mercy not touching the gear were reasonably low—he certainly knew that, but she had to understand that *he* was trusting her. Hopefully, that wouldn't take five years.

"Do we have any magazines over there?"

"Don't you have enough ammo in your pack already?" he asked curiously.

She burst out laughing. "Not magazines—*MAGAZINES*. Like *Good Housekeeping* or *Home Décor*, you know magazines for—" she placed her palms underneath her breasts, lifted them, and said, "—women!"

"Oh, those magazines," he said, then added. "You won't believe this, but I think I put a bunch of *Popular Mechanics* and a couple of *Outdoor Living* in there."

She slapped him on the arm and said, “That’ll do. Good job, Aaron!” She virtually jumped out of his tent.

Breakfast was excellent. Mercy got three burners going and made three dozen eggs over easy. She didn’t break any of the yokes. The bread was a hit, and she found the apples and some peanut butter. That opened up a new world for Recon. They put the combo together and were soon moaning with delight.

“Marvelous!” said Lewis. “You are a wizard of a cook.”

“Lewis, it is just eggs!” said Clark.

“I’m not talking about the eggs, sir,” replied Lewis, “I’m talking about the apple and the peanut stuff. That is what I call good cooking. Even the name she gave it is happy. ‘Skippy,’ captain, it is pure genius.”

Clark rolled his eyes, “Lewis, she did not cook it. The peanut butter was brought back from you-know-when and was already in that jar!”

Clark gave up. To Lewis, peanut butter on an apple would always be “cooking,” and Mercy was now the most excellent chef in the world. It was only a matter of time before the happy-go-lucky corporal would be making up a tale about the combination.

The major told them to square away their gear and that they would have a briefing in 15 minutes at 08:45. He told Mercy to ditch the dress and get on the camos and a jacket—and try to walk and look like a guy.

The briefing was not brief. It began with Aaron scowling at them to halt them from staring at Mercy’s pants. She noticed but rolled with the experience like she’d anticipated the ogling.

Howe had them in a circle on the blue and white beach chairs he’d found in Walmart, and he had a few issues that needed to be discussed. The first topic concerned the role of the regular troops training to take on Dorcester. Aaron pressed them hard to understand that Recon had to be ten times as prepared as the regulars. Then came a stern reminder that they must always be in the habit of having their gear shipshape. That also meant that the camp had to be spotless.

Howe moved on to an hour lecture about training. They were going to train every day. That required shooting, using high-tech gear like night vision, radios, and surveillance gear, and learning hand-to-hand combat. Despite having used some of the equipment against Timmons, he wanted them to be utterly professional and informed.

And then came unarmed combat. Howe was proficient at various martial arts and could teach them enough to get by. They also needed to learn battlefield first aid.

"Do you have a problem with wounds festering out here?" Aaron asked.

The whole group nodded. It seemed that everyone had had a nasty cut or scrape that had gotten infected. Unfortunately, in 1776, antibiotics were non-existent. Howe told them that from now on, not only Recon but also the entire encampment would have access to medicinal ointments and pills. Somehow, he had to get the doctor in the loop, but there was no chance that Howe would let soldiers die from infected cuts.

Next came their shooting schedule. It was then already 10:30. They would break for lunch at noon, and at 12:45, they would set up the shooting range. Their range would be a separate bluff from the range that the main force was using. Their own range would give them the privacy to use some of the "other" weapons.

When Howe was done lecturing, they set up two folding tables and started stripping their handguns. They all had Beretta Pico .380 sidearms which carried a 6-round magazine. Mercy had the black APX 9mm. For 90 minutes, Howe had them repeatedly strip and rebuild their weapons and, finally, had them do it with their eyes closed. The small pistols probably would not be used, but if they were ever in a tight spot or needed a silencer, the Pico 380 would get them out of trouble.

Mercy also pulled out the Sig .45, which got many admiring looks. She was a pro at handling the big Sig-Sauer in practically no time.

Lunch was tuna fish on white bread with potato chips and pickles from a jar. The reaction was mixed, particularly about tuna and mayo. The Snickers for dessert was an undeniable success. Lewis kept asking, "How did Mercy make this?"

Clark went through the same routine: "She did not cook the chocolate. It comes that way from a shop!"

After lunch, they went to their private Recon range. By prearrangement, the regular shooting took place east of the encampment. Recon was 1000 yards away to the west, which gave the special unit complete seclusion—and for good reason. They were firing not only the .380, 9mm, and .45 pistols but also their assault rifles and heavy sniper rifles.

Howe had also brought back some 12-gauge shotguns, specifically the Benelli M4, a highly effective, Redcoat splattering, capable weapon in their arsenal. Aaron made a point of buying #4 buckshot shells for these shotguns. He had the pistol grips removed because he was convinced that the grips would get in the way. He also bought some very high-end earplugs and muffs for each of them. In their two confrontations with Bates and Timmons, they were all whining about the ringing in their ears.

On the way to the range, it seemed like Recon could not stay away from their newest member. Mercy had become an overnight sensation. Howe, who'd previously been the focus of all their interest, was now old news, which was just fine with Aaron. Less attention gave him more time to focus on the first of his three main goals—tracking and obliterating Dorcester's Wolves. Although, to Howe, calling them Wolves was unfair to the wild and noble canines.

"Who forgot their ear muffs?" asked Clark.

No one answered.

"Fine, just verifying that."

Aaron noticed that the captain was in the habit of asking questions like that, which pleased the major enormously. They should never underestimate the enemy, and they sure as hell did not want to be hunkered down under fire and looking for gear.

"Is this it?" asked Mercy as they approached a small hillock.

"Yes, ma'am," they all volunteered at once, being that they were all overcome by an understandable teenage-style obsession.

"Stop here," barked Clark. "Major, what is our next order, sir?"

"Captain," said Howe, "Let's have everyone start with the handguns. I want targets strung at 20 yards. I brought about 100 silhouette paper targets. Let's fire 100 rounds of the 380. Mercy will fire off the 9mm and .45. 50 rounds per target. I want breaks after 25 to check the groupings."

"Yes sir," confirmed Clark, who turned to instruct Recon. Clark's chiseled good looks and charisma made him an excellent XO to run Recon under Howe.

He lined them up to start firing on the human silhouettes. They hadn't shot pistol much, and it showed. The six men were all over the targets. On the other hand, Mercy put two or three rounds in the paper off the bullseye but then corrected and proceeded to make a grouping that was downright intimidating. By her 25th round, she had shot two big holes in her target—center torso and head.

Needless to say, the experience was humbling for Recon. Mercy had never shot a pistol before in her life.

"It must be her weapon," said Monty.

Like a streak of lightning, Mercy was standing next to him with her hand out.

"Sir," asked Mercy of Captain Clark. "Is it all right for me to shoot Monty's sidearm?"

Clark shrugged and grinned. "By all means, please."

The men put their ears on and stepped back as Mercy inspected the Beretta. She cycled the slide a couple of times and then took one of the six-round magazines that Monty held out.

"Pick a spot, Monty," she said.

Monty gazed down the range at the targets. They all had holes spread out. He then looked at Mercy's target. It still had a lot of clean paper.

"Why not try to make another grouping on your target to the left?"

She pulled the slide and proceeded to rapid-fire all six rounds. Mercy kept the pistol pointed down range and handed it back to Monty.

She winked. "I don't think it's the pistol."

By 16:00, the sun was dipping below the trees. They had learned to shoot their sidearms with better accuracy and had now moved on to the M4 Benelli shotguns. Howe watched them proudly, recalling that his bunch of guys had rarely hunted or even picked up a weapon. These men worked chasing after cows, gathering corn, silversmithing, and carpentry. They had already survived two encounters with the enemy and were getting more skillful every day.

On the other side of camp, the regular army practiced maneuvers and shot their AKs twice a week, at least. Before the winter was through, they would likely face Dorcester and his thousand men, plus 4,000 tough Hessians. They were vastly outnumbered, and it would take more than just the rifles to win this and press the attack to New York in the spring.

The long day's training had worn Aaron out, so he signaled Recon to pack it in.

"All right," Major Howe hollered, "I'm hungry." He turned to Mercy and shouted sarcastically, "Hey, Cookie, what's for supper?"

After the evening meal, Clark dismissed Recon and took on the dish duty himself. As was their routine, they all sat down. The glow of the fire warmed them while they stretched out their legs, ready to review the successes and failures of the day. Howe noticed that Recon had developed a cohesive culture of its own. The petty pretentiousness he'd seen from his early foster home days was not found here. They each had no hesitation in accepting critical advice about their mistakes. What was heartwarming to Aaron was that ideas on improving always followed criticisms.

The campfire had burned low, and Monty tossed on another log. After a bit of fiddling, he cleared his throat, sat back down, and looked at Howe.

"I want to say something, major, and I think I speak for all of us." He paused to collect his thoughts and then began. "It's only been a short time, but thank you for picking us. Thank you for training us. Thank you for trusting us. Thank you for being a forthright leader for us—"

Aaron cut Monty off, "No need for thanks! Seriously, you're doing the work. I'm just walking around and nodding."

Monty, his considerable bulk testing the limits of the little beach chair, did not accept this. "Sir, I refer to your leadership, and it is not just about what you say. It is sometimes about what you do not say. The little comments that you might make just walking on the range. Also, when you do not mention anything at all when we do something stupid. Moments like that when you let us figure it out on our own. Thank you for that and for being our major. Finally, thanks for being like a demanding school teacher. Apologies, but when I ramble on like a dunce, I use metaphors."

"Simile," coughed Mercy under her breath.

"Right, simile. We might be from 1776, but we did learn the difference between a metaphor and a simile. Where was I? Yes, and thank you for the weapons, boots, and especially these amazing marshmallows you brought from the future!" The sergeant yanked a mostly burnt one off the stick he was probing into the fire. "I don't know who Kraft is, but I could kiss that guy.

"Sir, if you ever have children, they are going to be lucky to have you. Very well, now I am finished."

There was a hearty shout of approval from Recon, and Aaron did his best not to downplay the praise. It certainly wasn't his style to be the center of a toast, but it was acceptable from Recon.

Other than pointing out Monty's grammar mistake, Mercy was quiet, and Aaron thought he saw brooding in her expression. It concerned him. Just when they were all listening to Lewis plow into another tale, Mercy stood, excused herself, snatched up her beach chair, and slowly walked into the woods.

When she was out of range, Schein said, "Something is troubling Mercy."

"Keep it down," admonished Clark. "She can hear a mosquito at 500 yards."

Aaron tried to remember if he'd seen Mercy when she was not motivated and energetic. Back at Howe It Works, she defined her life purpose as getting justice for her family. She was distant and melancholy at that moment, and a faraway look had come over her. Aaron felt sure it was the surfacing of suppressed sadness over the loss of her husband and children. She had been see-through in that regard. Despite the changes from her implants, the 1776 Mercy was still there. She was clever and could generally fool anyone into thinking she was just a soldier on a mission, but Aaron saw that she was suffering.

"I'm going to check on her," said Howe. "You guys stay put and let Lewis continue with ludicrous stories."

They began to stand as he got up to leave, but Howe waved them to sit back down, then he walked into the cold and dark forest alone.

The crisp air met his face as he headed toward where he believed he would find her. Some distance away, Aaron could make out the shape of Mercy sitting behind a large evergreen in the dim light of the moon iridescent through the bare trees. He thought he overheard quiet sobbing, but she quieted as he neared.

"What are you doing out here?" she asked in a gloomy tone.

Her hair was undone and disheveled.

Aaron pondered a witty remark but thought the better of it. He stood beside her, and as he was about to speak, she arose, turned suddenly, and wrapped her arms around him. She pressed her face against his neck, letting tears flow like a torrent. He held her tightly and gave her the emotional space she needed. Right now, his compassion for Mercy had to be selfless and unconditional.

"I know I've been a pain in the ass," she finally said amid sobbing as she eased her grip on him. Aaron maintained his embrace, and she held him tightly again. He wanted her to know that he had no time limit for her to spill her pain onto his shoulders.

"Mercy, you are only good and sweet and wonderful to me. I know you were an incredible wife and mother. I know it, and if you didn't mourn that, I would beg *Allison* to remove the nanites. Being the woman you were is more important than being the woman you have now become. Do you understand what I mean?

Mercy wept but then stilled and said, "I know that in the lab, you thought I was a machine, that I had erased the depth of my suffering. I was a big talker about how divorced I was from the Mercy who lived in Piney Brook. The truth is, Aaron, I am shattered on the inside. I would have used different words to describe it if not for *Allison*, but the anguish is the same, even if I am not identical. I think I am having a problem telling you what I mean." She paused to breathe deeply.

My life was taken from me! My husband, my daughters, my so, so beautiful daughters. I know I have done a fantastic job being the soldier you need, but I can't hide it. I shouldn't hide it. I need to deal with what was taken from me."

"Mercy—"

"Wait, let me finish," she said. "It's been less than a month. How can someone function a month after that? I am trying so hard. Those guys back there—they wouldn't have a clue that inside I'm carrying such a weight."

"Mercy," he interjected. "That's not true—those guys. Let me tell you something. When I came back here, I never expected to end up with them. There is something bigger going on here that *Allison* never told us about, or me anyway. Those guys are not random; they already know that you went through hell. They are not dumb, and they have the capacity to hold you up when you are weak and suffering."

"I am weak," she admitted. "At least for right now. Most days are fine, I can do my job, and nothing enters my mind. Aaron, don't think I am mentally ill, but there are times when I see my girls."

"What do you mean?"

"I mean that I can see them right in front of me. The nanites must have done something to my memory because usually, when you want to remember someone from your past, they are just blurry memories. When they appear to me, the girls—it must be the nanites because I see them as if they are standing and smiling in front of me. It tears me to shreds, Aaron; it destroys me."

Aaron thought about this, then said, "I think we need to have *Allison* soften the power of those images in your mind."

Mercy grabbed his arms tightly and burst out, "No! Never! Aaron, as painful as it is, I want to be able to see them. I will be able to deal with it better in time, but it's only been a month. No matter what, when I see my babies, it is worth everything to me. I just wanted you to know that I'm fragile. I know now that I can't cover it up all the time, so if it is okay with you, I want to know that you will be there when I need to cry."

"Mercy, I brought you to *Allison*. It's called responsibility. When you have those moments, I promise I will be there if I can be there."

*

"Look at these fine soldiers coming in from the forest," said Allen, as he alerted Recon to Aaron and Mercy's return.

Even though it was late, they were still quietly gathered around the fire.

"I thought you'd be long asleep by now," said Mercy.

Clark looked up at her, "Not with you off in the woods."

They had reached the perimeter of the group. She looked at each of them. "Oh, so you were worried about me?" She had let her guard down so that her vulnerability was evident to the men of Recon.

It was quiet for only a second, then Clark said, "Always, Mercy. You are one of us. Do you ever wonder how we all ended up together? Did you think it was by chance? It's not just a coincidence. There's a reason why we were chosen, and that includes you."

Mercy looked at Aaron, recalling what he had said earlier. Clark continued, "We are together, and we may not be able to feel what you endured in Piney Brook, but that does not mean we cannot carry a portion of the load you bear."

The men of Recon did not shy away from looking at her. She felt safe with her defenses down among these friends and brothers. At that moment, it was as clear as day that they genuinely could rely on her and that she could trust them. Mercy knew that even if her memories tormented her, in those moments, they would not leave her.

She looked at them. Her anxiety and loneliness were lessened. Mercy knew she could be herself, even when her memories tore at her soul. She smiled softly and, from somewhere deep inside, said, "Thank you."

Chapter 24

A frightening, black-bearded Scottish man pulled a small boat up onto the banks of the Passaic River. He stowed his paddle, plodded into the moist, muddy bank, and then hiked up a few yards onto drier weeds. The large fellow waited patiently until he heard the sounds of an approaching horse. As the rider drew near, the Scot hid behind a tree, a solid grip on his long knife. The horseman dismounted near the boat and called out, "What I would not do for a fish to eat?"

The big man stepped out from behind the tree, peered at the questioner in the moonlight, and replied, "Do they even make fish that small?"

"Good things come in small packages," replied the rider.

They eyed each other, and the bearded hulk asked, "What worthless morsel of information do you have for me?"

"I have something for your general that he will be most pleased to receive. First, what shall I call you?"

"You shan't call me nothing. You will tell me your tale, and I will judge the worth."

"Very well," said the secret Loyalist spy. "The man who killed Timmons's and Bates' soldiers is an officer with roots in Bergen's Pond. My assumption is that he moves his supplies through that rebellious place. Look there for some worthwhile morsels of information."

The massive spy was quiet for a time. In the dark, it was hard to tell if he valued what was said. The Scot had a face that projected ruthlessly yet showed no inkling of his thoughts. His bearing alone was frightful. He bore a rank scent and had a foul demeanor that hinted at an aptitude for murder without remorse. Such spies were working for the British, and it appeared that Dorcester had engaged one of the most horrid.

"Be there more?" he asked.

This officer is Major Howe, who leads a small group of highly dangerous soldiers. They are the unit that killed your men."

The frightful, bearded Scot smiled, "Don't you mean 'our' men?"

"Yes, *our* men," answered the informer, "I know where my loyalties lie."

The Scot reached into his pocket, pulled out a gold coin worth 25 shillings, and flipped it to his rat. The petite man snatched it skillfully in flight and greedily stuffed it into his pocket.

Without another word, the bearded boar-like man turned and made for his boat. He stopped suddenly and turned back towards the spy.

"Listen, little spy," he warned. "If what you said is a lie, then I will use that gold piece to scrape out your liver."

The slight man stood transfixed on the muddy bank while the Scot had just begun paddling away towards the mist that hung above the river.

"It is true, I say, all true in the name of the king," he implored.

The Scot paused, swung his paddle, sent a splash of water at his informant, and shouted, "Jump, little spy, jump, jump!"

The Loyalist leaped backward, and hurriedly mounted his horse, to speed away. As the fine mare carried him, he prayed that he should never meet the Scotsman again.

"I now have the name and the home village of the murdering bastard," Dorcester said to no one in particular.

He stood for a while. Durst, Briggs, Morrisey, Guller, and Magath were at attention in the command tent awaiting orders. Morrisey was visibly anxious and trembling slightly. His tongue unconsciously probed for his missing teeth whenever he was near Sergeant Magath. As a matter of course, Magath would routinely give the physically and emotionally scarred captain threatening looks, accompanied by the sound of cracking knuckles.

"Gentlemen," began Dorcester as he paced with his hands neatly interleaved behind his back. "We have a mandate from the king. Doth there be one among you to define the meaning of 'mandate'?"

The silence was deafening as the men knew that to answer was a double-edged sword. As the silence wore on, Morrisey's paranoia drove him to assume that the question was directed at him. Panic rose from his gut. He looked at Magath and knew that the safest choice must be to keep his mouth shut.

"To crush the colonists!" shouted out Morrisey and then added, "Sir."

The general stopped and pivoted 180 degrees to stare menacingly into Morrisey's petrified eyes. Fury seemed to build in Dorcester's entire being. Morrisey looked over at Magath and saw the gigantic sergeant raising his eyebrows and grinning back at him. He turned his head back to Dorcester, who was visibly red. The seconds dragged on as the bruised captain began envisioning his own death at the hands of Magath.

Suddenly, Dorcester let out a tremendous, high-pitched laugh as he walked over to Morrisey and gave him a bear-like hug. "You see that, gentlemen?" shouted the general. "A dunce can be taught!"

A roar of laughter permeated the tent, and the abused officer joined in at his own expense.

Dorcester waved his hand to silence them. "To crush the rebels and traitors, yes, yes, yes!

"And how do we accomplish our task?" he asked. This time, not waiting for an answer, he said, "We cause them pain at every opportunity. My dear Captain Durst did an admirable job of that in Piney Brook. We killed about fifty traitors there in a fierce battle, correct captain?" asked the general.

"Quite correct, sir," answered Durst.

"Quite correct." continued Dorcester. "And we just received word from our well-placed spy regarding the leader of Washington's murderers. I refer to the man who butchered our fine soldiers as they slept—well, he is from Bergen's Pond.

"What do you think we should do at Bergen's Pond, Morrisey?"

The sudden attention caught the partially toothless adjutant by surprise, and he began shaking.

"Morrisey," asked the general with apparent concern. "You are trembling like a leaf. Are you feeling ill? Are you cold? Perhaps Sergeant Magath should take you to the doctor for a potion or some other remedy?"

Morrisey answered in a near shout as beads of sweat suddenly appeared on his forehead. "No, sir, I am feeling just fine, and I think we should defeat Bergen's Pond in battle and gather as much information as we can from the traitors, sir!"

Dorcester positively beamed. "Two in a row, captain, I believe you must be looking to replace me as general!"

"No sir!" said Morrisey urgently, sweat dripping down his face. "You are the only general qualified for an important mission like yours, sir!"

"It would seem so, captain," said Dorcester with an innocuous smile.

The general turned stiffly to Captain Durst, his countenance gray and deadly. "Durst, gather your Wolves and instruct Bergen's Pond in the king's lesson in loyalty."

Chapter 25

Getting out of the spotlight is a real challenge when you are near the top of the VIP list. The vice president had been working on stealth and evasion for two years and had only managed to get off the radar on rare occasions. Almost every dinner, every meeting, where he slept, even where he went to the bathroom—was monitored. The president was much more successful at disappearing than Carlisle. On top of that, the president was watching Carlisle with much better resources. The Secret Service answered to the top man, not the backup.

Today, he would do it differently. He'd spent a week setting up a diversion. It was like sneaking out of the house—like a teenager—only the stakes were very high.

Carlisle spent the day keeping up appearances as he attended his consultations, ate at two luncheons, and entertained three foreign visitors. A contentious cabinet meeting followed that. Apparently, there was a rumor flying that someone was involved in insider trading—that it was connected to the State Department but was unverifiable. Carlisle couldn't understand why anyone would be greedy enough to make a suspicious trade after all the scandals and media hounding the administration. He looked around the cabinet and thought, if only these characters knew that aliens were out there. That thought made him giggle under his breath. If they knew about the alien threat, Carlisle was sure that several would race full-speed ahead to profit from Earth's demise.

By the time the meeting had concluded, it was already 6 p.m. Tonight, he was scheduled to go home, eat dinner with Angela, and watch TV. After a non-stop month, his staff knew they had better leave him alone.

He left the White House at 6:20 p.m., got into his limo, and was on his way to One Observatory Circle. Three agents were in his detail. The short drive was uneventful, and they courteously wished him a pleasant evening as Carlisle entered the vice-presidential residence.

Angela smiled and gave John a big hug as soon as he stepped through the front door. He didn't know what she did the whole day, and although he could find out, it wasn't a priority. One thing for sure, Angela spent a lot of time in the gym. He wondered if she had an affair going on with a hunky personal trainer but then brushed that thought aside as a non-starter. There wasn't a chance that Angela would ever go down that road. They'd had plenty of explosive blowouts, but forty years together was worth it, and he could trust her with his life. He'd done that on occasion, and she'd proven her love and loyalty completely.

"Ok, honey-bunch," he said as he entered the parquet-floor entry. "We are alone tonight!"

She kissed him and then put her lips to his ear. "Are you still going at ten?"

"Sweetheart," he said. "Chicken sounds just right!" She knew that chicken was his code word for "yes."

Angela grabbed his butt and said, "Well then, chicken it is."

Bjorn Anker had been the Danish Ambassador to the United States for four years, and it was one of the best possible postings for a career diplomat. He loved the United States and was very in sync with Democrat moderates and conservatives. The radical left was not his cup of tea. Because of his popularity among Danes, the Danish Social Democrats did their best to sideline him. That led to his assumption of the diplomatic post in Washington. Anker was okay with that and felt no overwhelming ambition to return to Denmark and climb up the ladder to be prime minister. That was, until the current prime minister, a very liberal socialist, pushed a policy of high taxation to fund insane policies. Not the least was a substantial monthly stipend to those who did not *want* to work.

Then the PM added instant citizenship for third-world immigrants, legal prostitution, and large payments to girls who chose to abort rather than have their babies. Those policies triggered a deluge of requests for Anker to run for the top job. But, one little, teeny-tiny problem needed to be sorted out before he could go home to rescue the Danes.

"Hello, Mr. Vice President," said Bjorn. "How can I help you?"

"Hello, Ambassador Anker," said Carlisle. "I don't want to tie up your busy day with a long call, but do you remember our discussion from a few months ago at the Scandinavian Summit breakfast?"

A wave of panic washed over the ambassador, but he calmly replied, "Oh yes, how could I forget?"

"Well, the main topic of that conversation is about to become a moot point, or rather, if we work together, I believe we can dump that tiny problem into the rubbish bin forever," said Carlisle.

Anker, a realist, always looked for ways to tie up loose ends. In this case, some compromising video put Anker in an awful position. Fortunately, the VP had excellent contacts in the spy business and was in sole possession of some damning evidence.

"So, perhaps we should talk about that, Mr. Vice President. When would be good for you?"

"I think ten tonight would be a good time," the VP suggested.

Without hesitation, the anxiously nervous Bjorn Anker agreed, and the meeting was set.

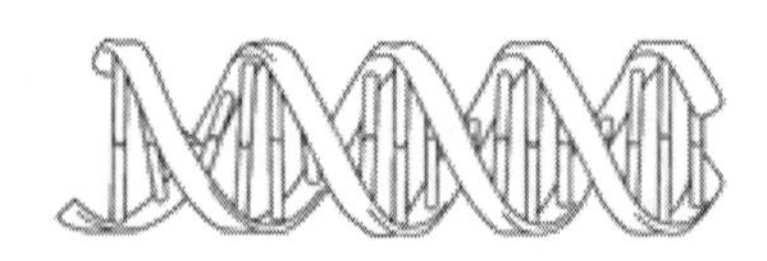

By 9:45 p.m., Angela had gotten everyone out of the house.

That included getting the Secret Service guys off the front porch and onto the street. She'd bribed them with some of her homemade cherry pie and admonished them to do their watching from 50 yards away.

"Gentlemen," she said. "Tonight, the VP and I would like to pretend we are at our ranch, and that means y'all skedaddle and give us some space."

The head agent, who looked like he'd bathed in starch, scurried and vanished with his tasty pie.

Now that they were alone, John Carlisle and his wife went down the expertly carpeted staircase to the basement.

"Do you think this is safe?" asked Angela with a worried expression.

"Angie," soothed Carlisle. "I've taken care of my end, and I am pretty sure that Anker has done his part."

Angela wasn't convinced. "What makes you think Bjorn will be there?"

Carlisle stopped pulling books off the shelf that blocked an old door. He gave her a *don't worry* look. "Whether Anker likes it or not, Bjorn is the only man with enough support to move that crazy socialist out of the PM's seat. He knows that, and I think he wants it, despite all his whining about staying here in Washington. Politicians always want more power."

He had faith that his story about meeting Anker played well enough to cover up the real reason he was sneaking through a grungy tunnel at 10 p.m. He momentarily shoved his hand into his jeans pocket to ensure the USB key was there. He then pulled it out and waved it in front of her.

"Just consider it a favor that I am calling in," John explained. "He's the one who chose to get frisky with his 22-year-old driver. The girl is barely out of college. Can I help it if Kent gave me a bit of leverage? This town's about leverage, so if I have some compromising video, should I sit on it forever?"

Angela sighed. "Why can't you tell me who you're actually meeting and what's it really about?"

"I told you," he said as though she hurt his feelings. "I'm

discussing Anker's future as Danish PM."

"Oh, bullcrap John," she said with a scowl. "Do you think that you can fool me?"

His attempt to snow Angela failed. He returned the USB key to his pocket and reached to hold her hand. "Honey, I really can't tell you. I'm sorry, but it is that sensitive. Now help me move this shelf and get this door open. I've got to get down that tunnel to their embassy and hope that Anker cleared out his side as ordered."

"How did it go?" asked Bjorn as he reached out his hand to pull Carlisle up the ladder into the Danish embassy's basement.

John brushed off some dust and cobwebs from his jeans. "It was a pleasure trip," he answered with a healthy dose of sarcasm.

The ambassador sized up the VP and said, "I'd never thought I'd see you without a suit and tie."

Carlisle was too uptight for small talk. "Is he here?"

"Yes, I had him wait in the small study down here. Only the guard saw him, and my security guys are sworn to secrecy."

"Thank you for doing your part. Here's the deal. The video is going away permanently," said Carlisle as he handed the USB key over. "I'm the only one who has it. You go become PM and remember to stay center-right. We don't need any crazy policies coming out of Denmark."

"The Danish people thank you," said Anker. "Follow me." He stopped for a second and looked back at the VP. "This is the only copy, right?"

John looked insulted and replied with great sincerity, "Bjorn, seriously, what kind of question is that?"

Carlisle stepped into the study and closed the door behind him. The room was square and boring. Plain wood paneling, no windows. A couple of stuffed chairs on a cheap oriental rug. He pulled out a small device from his pocket and went around the room, sweeping for electronics. It was clean of bugs, so he sat down opposite his guest. He then lit a mild cigar while brushing a spider off his pants.

"Hello, Edgar," said Carlisle.

"Hello, Mr. Vice President; nice to see you again."

"Cut the crap, Dr. Tomis," growled Carlisle. "Where's Kent?"

Edgar stroked his mustache. "I told your man Bartle that Kent came and left."

"Mega crap," said the VP angrily. "We had a drone flying near Howe It Works. Kent never walked out, and his car was there for four days after you said he drove off."

Edgar calmly crossed his legs. "Well, I guess that would make me a proven liar."

"Yeah, you got caught. Welcome to Washington. Now you cut a deal, make money, and walk away a free man. The D.C. way."

Edgar stared straight back at the VP. "What do you want to know, John?"

"John? So now we are on a first-name basis? Listen, Edgar, honestly, I am pissed off at Kent. I was very straight with him and told him to stay away from Howe, but I want to know where he is, and I want to move the device to Virginia."

"John," said Edgar. "Let me figure out the best way to explain these things to you." He paused and then talked as if he had decided something.

The chubby academic continued, "It truly is an alien device. And Kent is no longer here on earth."

Edgar waited for that to sink in.

Carlisle processed that for maybe ten seconds. "I'll accept that you have an alien device in Howe's lab, but Kent, not being on earth has to be a fairy tale. How 'bout you level with me and tell me the truth."

"I know that a statement like I just made is utterly hard to accept. I'd probably get extremely aggravated if I were in your shoes. I think it is pretty great of you that you are actually listening and not just yelling four-letter words at me."

"I'm on the verge, Edgar," said the VP gripping the arms of his chair. "Now, tell me where you have Kent stashed and when we can get Howe to move that thing to my lab."

Edgar always looked patient and now was no exception. He calmly repeated, "I already told you that Kent is no longer on Earth."

"C'mon, Tomis. Even if that was true, and our alien device zapped Kent off the planet, how the heck would you know?

"Because I was there," answered Edgar without batting an eyelash.

"Oh please," smirked Carlisle. "You just watched the man disappear?"

"I tried to talk him out of it, but he was getting too insistent. He tried to grab the thing, so the device sent him off-planet."

Carlisle scratched his head and fidgeted uncomfortably. "Let me understand this. Bonner gets dragged off by a bear in Canada, and now Kent is near the object, and he's gone. Care to explain?"

Edgar continued with his habitual mustache stroking. "Kent was making trouble for our visitor. He wouldn't back off, and I couldn't lock him in a closet. I know this creates some difficulties for you, but the alternative could be much worse than explaining Kent vanishing."

"Listen, I can find a way to smooth over the Kent disappearance, but I have to insist that the device comes to my lab. I suggest that you tell Howe that this is the decision. I've been trying to call him for two days, and he doesn't answer."

"Let me give you an excellent piece of advice, Mr. Vice-President," said Edgar in a tone that was starting to tread on the VP's last nerve. "You shouldn't do anything. You need to sit tight and just let things play out."

"What the hell are you talking about? The object is an alien artifact, and I'm the vice president. I've been running I.S. and other covert ops for decades. You're just Howe's buddy and a college teacher, so why should you be calling the shots on this?" asserted the visibly angry Carlisle.

The professor remained placidly calm. He continued speaking with a logical and pleasant tone. “How do I know what to do?”

“Yes,” barked Carlisle. He was practically frothing at the mouth.

A gentle yet amusing smile propped up Edgar’s fat mustache. He eyed the vice president as if he was making a calculation.

“John, I have been on your stupid planet for 126 years. I am trying my best to save your violent, selfish, destructive asses, so when I tell you that you can’t do a damn thing, I know what I’m talking about!”

Carlisle was stunned and his mouth was agape. The thin cigar stuck to his lower lip for a moment and then dropped to the floor. He swallowed hard and was searching for the right words when Edgar filled in the dead air.

“Yes, Mr. Vice President, I am one of those slimy, mind-controlling, tentacled aliens you’re worried about—

“This is the part where you say, ‘Welcome to Earth’.”

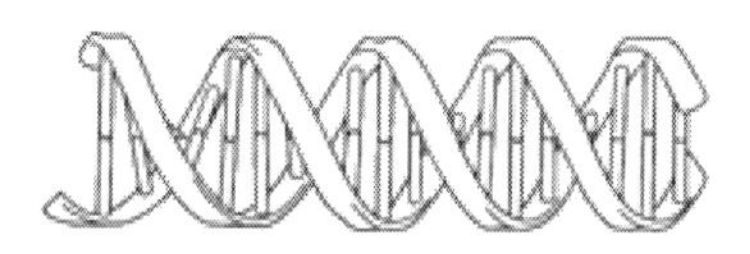

Angela was waiting in the basement of One Observatory Circle when her husband returned through the solid wood basement door. The entire walk through the musty hole under ground had been surreal. At the other end of that tunnel he’d sat with a chubby scientist who proclaimed to be an alien with bad news for earth.

“John,” Angela exclaimed as he stood hunched in front of her. “You look awful!”

He wrapped his arms around her, held her tightly, and then said, “Angela, my dearest love, do an old man a favor and get me a Xanax.”

Chapter 26

Bergen's Pond was an idyllic village situated by a beautiful small body of water. The families there were primarily involved in crafts such as wood carving, carpentry, silversmithing, and a few corn and grain farmers. On top of that, one of the smiths had even opened a small pub right in the center of the village where people could laugh, tell tales, and drink ale with friends. Being such a small place, the pub was only open on Saturday nights and rarely made a profit.

In the winter, usually by January, the pond would freeze over, and it was not unusual to find all the village children out playing on the ice. Of course, in late November, it was too early for that, so the children would go fishing, hoping to catch something big enough to make their mothers happy. Unfortunately, cheerfulness was hard to find now.

The shockwaves of the massacre at Piney Brook were still reverberating through Bergen's Pond, and the men set up a nightly watch. Guard duty consisted of one villager armed with a musket who was stationed on the north end. The main road on the south end ran dead into the pond, so it was assumed that any trouble would come from the north.

They planned on 4-hour shifts starting at 8 p.m. each night. After a week, everything remained quiet, and the anxiety began to ease. Nevertheless, there was a consensus that keeping up the watch was a fine idea. Whoever was on lookout duty would sit wrapped in a blanket on a tree stump while scanning the road. A musket ready to fire would be within reach at all times. That was the plan.

It was exactly eight days since Piney Brook, and John Merritt, a man of about 40, was taking the midnight to 4 a.m. watch. He was a cheerful enough man and also quite the pub enthusiast. On a chilly night like this, he knew that a little snort from his flask would be just what the doctor ordered. A half-flask later, Merritt dozed when a long, thin knife pierced his neck. A scream was trapped in his throat as he struggled for breath.

"Sleeping on watch," whispered a voice in his ear. "That sort of thing can get a man murdered."

Merritt's arms flailed for a few moments as the flask dropped from his hand, and the musket fell from his side. The black of night was turning even blacker as his life faded. His killer pushed him from the tree stump, but before darkness took him forever, the Wolf asked him, "Where is the home of Howe?" Merritt's response was only a glassy-eyed stare that turned opaque.

Jones dropped Merritt's body to the ground, turned to Guller, and snorted, "Worthless goat went and died before answering a simple question."

The vicious man beckoned to the rest of the Wolves to join him. They formed up around Captain Durst and eyed the village. There were about 15 homes on the main street. That meant five houses would be secondary. All the while, Captain Durst would stay in the town square to, as he put it, watch for trouble.

"Go in," ordered Durst. "Kill the men straight away. Knives only to the heart or neck. Just make sure they are dead. If the wives awaken and give you trouble, then slit their throats. The first 5 of you that finish shall visit the remaining houses there." He pointed to the houses closest to the pond. "After that, you can go about having fun with the women yet alive, same as Piney. Is that agreeable to you all?"

The men all nodded and then split up. Their attack wasn't without risk since an alert colonist might have a knife by his bed. They could not forget their loss at Piney Brook. A little extra attention was the order of the evening, so they fanned out carefully to deliver the king's message.

Durst stood in the town center as he drank in screams and struggles as the men of Bergen's Pond succumbed to their attackers. One by one, they died, and most of their women died with them. The houses closer to the pond were quickly subdued as the Wolves made an inventory of the remaining children. One or two of the boys put up a fight, one of them even biting Guller, but those who gave trouble were put down quickly.

The captain looked at his men as they stood nearby, holding bloodstained knives. "Go," he ordered while waving his hand. "Go have your pleasure."

The Wolves turned, and each sought to enter the house nearest to him, but they halted after a call from Durst. "One moment," he said. "Bring me a pretty teenage girl untouched and unharmed. Make sure she tells you where Howe resides."

"Yes, captain," was the response of the Wolves.

A short time later, a man emerged from a house near the pond while dragging a lithe young girl. He walked the girl to Durst and held her before his captain.

"Will she do, captain?" the man asked.

"Did she tell you where Howe lives?"

"Sir, she said there is no Howe in this village."

Durst looked her over in the dim light and then held a lantern to her face. She could not have been more than fifteen and was startlingly pretty.

"What is your name, girl?

"I am called Molly," she said through her tears.

"Molly, such a nice name for a young girl. Remove thy garments, Molly," said Durst.

She hesitated. Durst pulled a knife from his belt and held it to her face. Molly loosened the ties of her nightshirt in the chilly November air, and it dropped to the ground. The Wolf who had brought her to the captain reached out to touch the girl, but Durst smacked his hand and ordered him away. The man retreated reluctantly.

"Now," said Durst to the shivering girl. "You must think that you are quite pretty, am I right?"

"No. I mean, yes," the teenager whimpered through tears.

"And, Molly, what would you offer me to keep me from

plunging my knife into your tender form?"

The terror of the moment ran through her, and between sobs, she answered, "Anything."

"My, you are so cooperative," he said. "Tell me, would you consider your face to be pretty?"

Again, between increasing sobs, she replied quietly, "Yes."

"So, I will give you a choice, and whichever choice you make, neither will lead to your death.

"I can have several of my men have their way with you in the name of the king, or perhaps I will take my little knife here to confiscate that beauty from your face." Durst waited as she sobbed as he consumed her panic like a drug.

"Now, Molly, which do you choose?"

"General Washington!" called one of his officers as the man rushed to the command tent.

"Yes, lieutenant, what is all this commotion about?"

"Sir, the village of Bergen's Pond was attacked, and the civilians murdered."

Washington clenched both fists as rage coursed through him.

"Any survivors?"

"Yes, sir," said the lieutenant. "One," then he added, "a teenage girl who was injured. They murdered everyone else, including two babies."

"Have someone bring Major Howe and Captain Clark," ordered Washington.

"Yes, sir," said the Lieutenant. "And our scouts brought the girl here to be seen by the doctor."

"Very well," said Washington. "Now, make haste!"

When Howe and Clark arrived, Washington ordered them to accompany him to the doctor. On the way, the general briefed them on the latest village attack.

"They were all murdered, excepting one girl. She is with the doctor now. We are going to question her if she is well enough," said the general.

The three of them hurried to the infirmary. The girl was lying on a cot. She was wrapped in a blanket and in obvious pain. Aaron cursed under his breath as he looked at the girl. The doctor was busy stitching two disfiguring cuts on either cheek.

When he'd finished, Washington sat and asked her if she could speak. She nodded.

"How many men came into your village? George asked.

She raised her hands and showed ten fingers.

"Were they dressed in uniforms?

She shook her head.

"Did you hear any names?".

She struggled over the pain, opened her mouth, and mumbled, "Captain Durst."

Washington put his hand on the girl's shoulder. "What is your name?"

Through the pain, she replied, "Molly."

Tears flowed from her eyes as General Washington said, "Molly, do not doubt for an instant our anger. The doctor is going to nurse you back to health, and we are going to protect you and feed you. You will be safe here. You have sustained wounds as if you were in battle. We will avenge you, and we will avenge your family. I promise!" He wasn't sure she could even hear what he was saying, but it needed to be said. Washington knew that Dorcester must be utterly punished. His heart ached for the innocent girl as he stood up to his full height and urged Howe and Clark out of the tent.

Upon leaving, they walked over to Recon, where, with Washington's approval, Major Howe told the girl's story and what had happened to her village. The decorum among Recon quickly devolved into a loud series of threats and calls for immediate revenge. Major Howe let this vehemence run its course for a few minutes and then nodded to Clark, who ordered Recon to settle down.

The general observed the determination on the faces of Howe's soldiers. They were not a vast army, but they were superbly armed by the standards of 1776 and could inflict extreme pain on the British. After a long discussion, it was decided that Recon would scout out the location of Dorcester's troops. There would be no engagement, but rather they would surveil. They would return with the intel directly to Washington. Only then would the main force plan on when and how to take on Dorcester. With any luck, the Hessians would still be too distant to provide any support.

No longer distracted, Washington noticed Mercy sitting on a log. She was wearing camos and was expertly flipping a balisong open and closed.

"What is that?" asked Washington.

She looked up at that general and asked, "My clothes or this thing in my hand?"

He took a good, hard look at her. "Well, the clothes are unique to a lady, but I have already relented. I am referring to that trinket in your hand."

Mercy stood up and performed a series of lightning-fast moves with the balisong. She then winked at the general and, with impossible speed, threw the balisong, which then buried itself into a tree trunk.

"General," said Mercy. "That 'trinket' is called a balisong or a butterfly knife, and it is a fine weapon. Just ask that tree, sir."

Washington was stunned, but as commander-in-chief, he had learned to stifle his reactions.

"Very impressive, Tomoe Gozen."

Mercy grinned. "Thank you, general," she answered. "It will be even more impressive when I use it to cut the Wolves' hearts out of their chests, sir."

Washington could not help but smile. He wished he could have a hundred with the guts of one Mercy. He turned to Major Howe and Captain Clark. "I see the cook is adapting quite well."

They both laughed, and then Washington turned back to Mercy. “You are now Corporal Mercy Tomoe Gozen. Welcome to the Continental Army.”

She saluted, somewhat surprised, and said, “Thank you, General Washington, I won’t let you down.”

He saluted back. “Of this, I am persuaded.”

“May I ask one question, sir, before you head back to camp?” she inquired.

He nodded in his distinctive George Washington fatherly way.

“What was the name of the girl’s village?”

“I believe the girl is from Bergen’s Pond,” answered Washington. He then saluted Recon, turned, and left.

“Lieutenant Schein, are you thinking what I am thinking?” asked Corporal Lewis. His tone was unusually serious.

Major Howe and Captain Clark were away, having escorted the general. The remaining members, Schein, Rogers, Allen, Lewis, Monty, and Corporal Mercy, were uncharacteristically subdued. They’d been relaxing as night approached but were now thinking about supper. That repast had been sadly interrupted by the general’s visit.

Earlier, the time by the fire had consisted of Recon sharing stories, drinking clean bottled water, and sitting on beach chairs, wrapped in coats or blankets in order to stave off the chill. Mercy had found packages of instant coffee, which were immediately placed at the top of the Recon favorites list. While enjoying their hot mugs, they’d received the news of Bergen’s Pond.

Before Schein’s reply, Allen interrupted and said, “I know exactly what you are thinking.”

“Really? Tell us,” said Lewis.

"You are pondering that we should convince Major Howe to take us into the future, from whence we shall bring back a boatload of this coffee, sell it in Philadelphia, and get old, fat, and rich. Tell me, am I right?"

Lewis stared at Sgt. Allen. "No, you are not right! Not at all."

"Hmm," said Allen. "So, is it just rich and fat but not old? Or maybe rich and old but not fat? Because rich is definitely what we'll be if we start offering this coffee to paying customers."

Lewis looked incredulous. "Sometimes, I wonder about your sensibility, sergeant. I am referring to something more sinister than coffee—please!"

Rogers piped up, "I know to what you refer, corporal, because it has been on my mind for the last 10 minutes."

"Yes, I believe you do," replied Scott Lewis.

As the only officer present, Schein surveyed the group drinking their brew. Mercy also sipped, with one hand holding her mug and the other flipping the balisong. He focused on Lewis. "What *are* we talking about here, corporal? Say it out loud."

"An odd coincidence, lieutenant. Do you recall the other night when the adjutant general was trying to coax information from us? Do you remember what Captain Clark answered to him?"

Schein couldn't hide his suspicions. "Yes, exactly. Clark told Reed that Major Howe came from Bergen's Pond, and now somehow, the whole village of Bergen's Pond gets massacred?"

The lieutenant waited for their reaction as all of them recalled vividly Reed's pestering them for details about the major. They remembered that Reed kept dropping Washington's name and requiring Howe's plans to coordinate with the army. Clark had thrown out the name Bergen's Pond to make Reed go away.

"Do you surmise what this implies?" asked Lewis.

Monty spoke up. "Yes, it means that either the biggest *coincidence* occurred before our eyes or Reed is a putrid, stinking spy." The observation generated harsh whispers of suspicion.

Schein settled Recon down to a hush. “Let us be very careful about this. If Reed went and provided the name to Dorcester, then we have a huge problem. We have no idea what else he could have passed. Dorcester could know about our supplies and our weapons! Such knowledge could be very, very bad.”

Monty interjected. “He cannot know about the weapons. The general sent Reed to Philadelphia such that the weapons were never in the adjutant’s view.”

“True,” said Schein. “And that makes me question why would the general want Reed out of here during our training? Maybe he suspected him?”

“Or, it could mean nothing at all. We may just be grasping at straws,” offered Rogers.

“He could be shuttling every damn thing we are doing straight to Dorcester,” said Allen, ignoring the benefit of the doubt.

Monty smirked and let out a small laugh. “And what? Chicken butt! How is that going to help Dorcester? Our 2,000 men with AK’s will cut them down to mush.”

“Think Monty,” said Schein. “They are joined with 4,000 Hessians, and those mercenaries will attack us from all sides. ‘Tis not a pure advantage if Reed gives him a constant flow of our movements. Reed could find weaknesses that we have not pondered. The British are not complete imbeciles—they know how to fight. We could lose. Beyond that, and to my utter loathing, Dorcester is attacking villages. Bergen’s Pond could have been Reed’s doing!”

Schein’s description sobered Montgomery. They all went quiet, and then Mercy spoke up. “Job number one is to find out what Reed has been doing for the last week. Has he even left the camp? It seems to me that if he is a spy, but he did not leave, then we have a bigger problem. That would mean he’s got help. If he left, then that points to him. Or he might not be a spy at all,” she concluded.

Rogers looked inquisitively at Mercy. “And what are the odds that Reed happened to hear ‘Bergen’s Pond’ and then

Bergen's Pond was massacred less than a week later? Especially if he left for a few days. He could have gone straight to Dorcester."

"He is not that much of a fool. He would have met a Redcoat spy and probably gotten something for his trouble. The man does not seem to operate only on principle or loyalty to the king. In my view, he is loyal to his purse, is what I mean," said Schein. "Or it could be that we dislike the man so much that we are machinating all of this rubbish."

The campsite was silent except for the crackling of the fire.

"Granted, Reed acquired the name Bergen's Pond by pestering us, but the general sent him to Philadelphia to confer with delegates," said Monty.

"And if Reed has another spy among our soldiers? Someone who shuttles information to Reed when he is off in Philadelphia, or who knows where?" asked Lewis.

Schein gave them all a stern look. "Perforce, we must tread lightly. We have to be delicate with Reed."

"The girl," said Mercy, interrupting the men of Recon.

"What girl?" asked Monty as they all turned to look at her.

She finally stopped flipping her balisong and said, "The girl from Bergen's Pond."

"What has that got to do with it?" asked Montgomery.

"Of course," said Allen. "Do you think they would not be looking for Howe if they went into Bergen's Pond? Remember that Reed specifically asked about Howe living in such a small country village? Maybe this Captain Durst that Howe mentioned, the one who injured the girl; maybe he asked her where Howe was; his whereabouts?"

"And," said Mercy, completing the thought. "If he asked about a family named Howe, that points right back to Reed."

"Yes," said Schein. "There is no way Dorcester would even know the name Howe unless someone from here told him. What are the odds that he would get both Bergen's Pond *and* Howe's name unless it was from Reed or an accomplice?"

"About 503.6 to 1," answered Mercy.

Schein looked at her as she had resumed flipping her balisong. “Really?”

“No, Lieutenant Schein,” Mercy replied with a smirk on her face. “Not really. I made that up, but the probability is still very low. If the girl says that Durst questioned her about a family named Howe, then Reed is a traitor and a murderer.” She paused and added, “Do you know how to deal with murderers?”

They looked at her and waited for the other shoe to drop. She smiled and hurled her knife fiercely, where it pierced deeply into a log between Lewis' legs. “We do *that*.”

The next day was mostly cloudy. Trees continued to shed their remaining leaves, and the forest was turning brown and gray, except for the many evergreens. Recon was waiting for Major Howe, who was to return soon from a meeting with General Washington and Colonel Overton.

The small special forces unit's morning consisted of breakfast followed by a couple of hours at the range. Monty had rigged up a line that was led through pulleys so that they could hang silhouettes. The purpose was to make moving paper targets they could haul left and right across the target area. Doing this, they could use their assault rifles to try to put accurate shots into targets with the least number of rounds. The goal was to use a maximum of two rounds to achieve a kill shot. Recon had defined a kill shot as any bullet that was eight or better—X being the center. Eight covered a large portion of the torso, so any Redcoat that took an eight or better would be out of action. It helped that the kinetic energy of a 7.62 x 39 cartridge was significant. The British wouldn't know what hit them in a firefight.

As the targets floated across the range, each member of Recon would have a chance to fire two rounds. They would pull the target first from right to left, check the hits, and then left to right and check the hits. The goal was for everyone in Recon to land all four rounds in the 8-circle or better. The first run-through was dismally poor. Only Corporal Mercy Tomoe Gozen was able to get all four of her shots into the zone. The others ranged from zero on the paper to two in the kill zone. Schein and Clark placed two shots in the 8-circle, and Monty put only one round on the edge of the target.

Because Mercy was so proficient at hitting moving targets, she worked with the guys having problems, and by 11:00, some were excellent; some were passable. Mercy was unbeatable.

They spent the next hour listening to Lewis blabbering aloud if he should call their female corporal "Mercy" or "Tomoe" or both names. Lewis' conversation continued in the background while the lieutenant urged them to clean their weapons well.

Their rifles were easy to maintain. The main army used AK's that were of good manufacture and had nicely milled receivers. For Recon, however, Howe had purchased the VZ 58. They were not exactly AK-47's, but the loads were 7.62 x 39, like the AK's. It was pricier and considered far superior.

At noon, Major Howe and Clark returned precisely on time. He observed Recon scouring their weapons and gave them a broad smile. Aaron considered mentioning his youthful experience as a hunter and describing his hours spent cleaning firearms but decided to avoid nostalgia. That conversation would lead to reminiscing over his childhood—a discussion he wanted to avoid.

"Major," said Clark. "Corporal Gozen shoots extremely well."

"I would expect no less, captain."

"We were wondering if the major would like to attempt our moving target test?" asked Clark.

"Moving target? Is that when Corporal Gozen runs up and back and catches bullets with her teeth?"

Mercy perked up. "I could probably do that!"

They all laughed, including Howe.

"I'd be happy to try out your moving target test."

He went to his tent and retrieved his rifle and muffs. They all hiked over to the range. Not one of them would miss this. By the time they got to the range, Recon had already made wagers if the major could shoot as well as Mercy. For her part, she was not making that bet.

"Okay, how does this work?" asked Howe.

"Very simple," said Monty. "The target starts on the right; as it moves left, you take two shots, and on the return, two shots."

Lewis, who had bet on the major, shouted to Monty. "Same speed as for the corporal, sergeant." A comment which elicited an affirmative nod.

Howe hadn't fired his VZ 58 much over the last week, so he asked for a fixed target to practice a little. Allen ran down and posted a silhouette about 30 yards out. Aaron had no scope on his rifle. He settled himself into a relaxed stance and then shot one round. The round was in the lower right on the outer edge of 7. There was a suppressed chuckle from the pro-Mercy betters. Clark shushed them.

Aaron lined up again and took five paced shots. When he finished, Allen ran down to retrieve the target. There was a nearly straight line from the first shot on the outer 7 edge. The other five rounds were evenly placed in a line, with the last of the five hitting near the X. The Mercy betters were quiet while Mercy leaned against a tree twiddling her thumbs.

Monty quickly set up the moving silhouette at about 18 yards. Aaron checked his magazine and then chambered a round. Monty counted down from 5 and then began pulling the target.

Aaron chose the Tracking Method on the first length, and as the target slid across the range, he placed both shots in the X. He chose the Ambush Method for the reverse trip and shot the target at a quarter and three-quarters of the way across the range. One round was on the 9 – 8 line this time, and the other was nearly dead center.

"Was that good enough?" Howe asked the group.

There was a reluctant nod from Monty, as the major's shooting was the best of the day—barely edging out Mercy's hits.

Aaron released the mag and ejected the live round. He turned to Corporal Gozen, who was frowning, and tossed her his weapon. "Here, you get to clean my VZ."

"Thank you, major," said Mercy. He could tell she was mildly irritated, as taking 2nd place wasn't a happy prospect.

Howe left Recon to tidy up the range and told them they would be having a vital briefing at 13:30.

When Recon returned, Aaron was settled into a beach chair waiting. There were six beach chairs, leaving the two corporals sitting on logs. Politely, Schein offered his chair to Mercy, but she wouldn't even consider it.

Howe took on a severe look almost immediately. Everyone knew that when he was lecturing, he was thorough and precise. Apparently, his morning discussion with the general had left a big impression.

"We are going to do one day of field training. That means we pair up as usual. Corporal Gozen will be with me,"

Howe could sense their disappointment.

"Field ops in full gear. I want full packs with ammo—all weapons, including two M40's and two Benellis. You will need 10 MRE's, full canteens, extra socks, radios, and the rest Clark will tell you later. Full packs for two training days, but we'll only do one day of an actual field op.

"Here's the problem. Bergen's Pond was the third massacre. We cannot wait around for Dorcester's Wolves to walk in and give themselves up. We need to be what in the future is called 'pro-active.' Does anyone have a clue as to what that means besides Mercy?"

There was silence, then Howe continued. "It means we take the fight to them—we will be aggressively offensive. We are going to hunt down Durst and the Wolves. To be completely honest, I don't know how we will get them if they are tucked away inside Dorcester's encampment. I also don't think it is safe to sit outside the British camp for a week or two, waiting for ten bastards to come out and identify themselves. But if we see a small group, then we will attack.

"We need to devise a way to get them to leave the safety of their camp. Anyone?"

There were no ideas, and the silence was disheartening until Corporal Lewis said, "I think I have an idea, but could I just converse with Captain Clark privately for a moment?"

Howe shrugged and said, "Sure, go ahead."

It was a little unusual in the middle of a briefing, but Lewis and Clark walked off about twenty yards. Recon could hear some mumbling, a short argument, and then silence. Something was settled.

Clark brushed his hair out of his eyes when they returned. He looked unsure of himself but squinted at Mercy, and she gave him a nod. Uncannily, she had already figured out whatever was going on, which was becoming creepily typical for her

"Sir," said Clark, "to use one of Mercy's expressions, I believe we can *set up* the Wolves."

Now the captain had Aaron's interest, and the major leaned forward to listen as Lewis described his trap.

"Can you explain how I am supposed to do that without telling the general?" said Aaron quizzically.

"Why should you have to divulge our plan?" asked Lewis.

"Well, corporal, let's see," Howe flicked up his thumb as if to count off reasons. "First, because Reed is the adjutant general, and second, we are making a wild accusation. Is that enough, or do you need more?"

"I need more, sir."

Aaron snorted and extended his third finger. "Ok, three, we could walk into a trap and find a couple hundred British flanking us. Is that enough?"

Mercy turned to Aaron. "Major, Dorcester will not send out 20% of his force to back up Durst. He lost fifty with Timmons. So, that made him look like a complete jackass. There is no way he will risk his regular troops over the Wolves. More important than that, let's say he sends out extra troops. We can pick the spot. We can pick a perfectly defensible position in case the chocolate brownie mix hits the fan!"

Schein looked perplexed, squinted, and asked, "The *what* hits the *what*?"

"It's an expression," said Howe. "Mercy, I hear what you're saying. I'm not convinced about Dorcester not sending out more troops with Durst, although your logic does make sense. On the other hand, he may not even send out the Wolves. He might send out regular troops. In that case, we wouldn't know if the Wolves were among the enemy troops until the little battle was over. Then what? Should we search the dead bodies to see if Durst is among them? The second part about us picking the spot is our real weapon.

"Look over the map. We know where Dorcester is more or less, so we need to find a very defensible spot where we can deal with whoever he sends to ambush us. Let's hope it will be Durst.

Aaron said, "Mercy, do you have those satellite maps? They should be in the Recon container."

"No sir," she answered.

"Didn't you bring them?"

Mercy looked unconcerned. "No, sir, I memorized them."

"Should I have expected any less? Fine, sit with Clark and find a defensible spot. Then we'll talk."

Clark and Corporal "Gozen" spent an hour going over the map. When they finished the review, the captain and Mercy returned to the Recon campfire contented.

"Mercy," said Clark. "Do you want to explain it?

Mercy deferred to the captain, who grinned and pulled out a hand-drawn map with many notes in the margins.

"Very well, here is what we have found," offered Clark as he placed the map on a small, plastic folding table.

"This is the location of Dorcester, about 20 miles west of

Hackensack. Here is Piney Brook, about 5 miles southeast of Dorcester. Here is Hackensack. And here," he stabbed his finger with a quiet thud on the map, "is what Mercy calls the Great Falls of Paterson."

When no questions came, he continued. "We can fight him right here, on the west ridge of the Falls."

Major Howe looked closely at the map. If they could trap the Brits up against the Falls, then, assuming it was the Wolves—Durst would be unable to escape.

"How can we be certain he will not surround us with our backs to the Falls?" asked Sergeant Rogers.

Mercy held up a small black box. "We have these."

Everyone looked at Mercy's black box, which Howe instantly recognized as a Howe It Works motion sensor camera with a built-in transmitter.

Schein laughed and said, "We are from 1776 Mercy. What is that?"

"This is a little camera that transmits pictures."

"I only understood the words 'little' and 'pictures' from your explanation. Can you elaborate?" asked Allen.

She explained, "This little device is made by a company that the major owns in the future. We take this box, stick it on a tree, and anything that goes by will be seen, and then a picture will be sent to us—even if we are a mile away. It also has night vision, just like our night vision headsets."

"That's cool," said Lewis.

"Lewis," asked Aaron. "Who taught you the word 'cool'?"

"She did," answered the corporal while pointing at Mercy.

"Great," she continued. "Now we plant these on the west side of the Falls, and when the Wolves approach, assuming it is the Wolves, we know where they are. We don't have more than six of these, but that should give us some advance warning. All we do is hunker down and wait for them to choose north or south. If they come straight ahead, we squeeze them into a box with the Falls behind them. Bam!" She smacked her hands together, and everyone jumped an inch.

Howe was quiet for a bit, and then with everyone looking at him, he said, "That could work in theory, but that plan could also fall entirely apart. Plans are called plans for a reason. They are just that, plans.

"Consider," he continued. "If Reed isn't *really* a traitor, or if he fails to tell Dorcester, or if Dorcester sends a huge force, or if the Wolves flank us instead of walking into our trap."

"We can deal with all but one of those situations," said Mercy. "If Reed isn't our spy or if he fails to tell Dorcester, then we wait out there for nothing. There is no way we let the Wolves flank us. We have a drone. We can fly that thing a mile west of the falls north and south. Actually, we have two drones. I packed them with extra batteries so we can swap them out." She looked directly at Howe while the rest of Recon shared bewildered glances.

"That's no guarantee, but I see your point. There's a risk that they may show up when our drones are out of juice, Mercy, then what?" asked Aaron.

"It's a risk, but we have a lot of batteries, and we have solar chargers."

"You packed all that?"

"Yes, major, I'm a boy scout."

None of the banter made sense to the rest of Recon.

"That leaves the singular risk of a large force. If a large force arrives, then we disappear like shadows," she concluded.

Howe grunted his apparent acceptance of her logic. Mercy explained the technology to Recon. Since they had seen night vision, radios, watches, and various other 21st-century technology, they weren't overwhelmed by the motion sensors. The drone, on the other hand, left them pretty well stunned.

"Who wants to learn how to fly it?" asked Mercy. Six hands shot up.

Howe interrupted. "We'll deal with the drones shortly. As far as Reed, I agree that we should test the spy theory. General Washington is going to be very unhappy even to hear our suspicions.

"If Reed is a rat, it is a headache for Washington and us. I mean, let's think this through. We go up to the Great Falls. We wait for Durst, and then he shows up, and we blow them all to hell. Then we have to go back and report that Reed set us up and that the man is a spy. Do you know what that means?" Howe looked around the group.

"Yes," answered Schein. "That means we string that bastard up because he caused the murder of all those people in Bergen's Pond, and I have no compunctions about that."

Schein had just reminded them of the reason why they were doing this and the justification for punishing Reed if he turned out to be the lowest of the low.

"I think the general would hang the man himself," observed Clark.

"No doubt," added Lewis.

"Like I just said, this means I have to go convince Washington to go along with this," said Aaron rhetorically. "Start taking your inventory, Mercy. Make sure all the tech gear is perfect, and explain the fundamentals to everyone here."

Aaron looked at Recon. "Welcome to the future, boys. You better listen to every damn word out of Corporal Gozen's mouth and learn this stuff like the back of your hand. Is that understood?"

"Yes, sir."

"For the sake of the civilians we are trying to protect, let's pray that Dorcester sends out Durst and the Wolves."

As Howe was preparing to walk back to the main camp dragging Clark with him, Mercy cleared her throat, and he turned around.

"One more thing, sir," she said while scanning the faces of Recon. "Nobody takes out Durst, even if you have a clear shot. No one! You can kill every last one of the Wolves and whatever troops they might send to help them, but Durst better damn well be alive when we close in on them. He's mine. Is that understood?"

Aaron panicked for a moment, worried that perhaps Durst

could be his target. Then unexplainably, he felt completely confident that it was not Durst at all. This intuition was welcome and disturbing. It was a puzzle to his scientific mind. Aaron had to find a way to reconcile the conflict, but for now, he just accepted it.

They all nodded their consent, partly out of sympathy and partly out of their desire to in no way aggravate Corporal Tomoe Gozen.

"How do we know who Durst is?" asked Lewis timidly.

Mercy took her finger, pressed it to her cheek, and then pulled down her right eye. "He'll look like this."

"This cannot be true!" Washington was livid. Major Howe and Captain Clark stood silently as the general seemed to boil over. They insisted that the meeting occur in a secluded spot near the supply containers. As he glared at the Recon officers, George held himself in check and processed the devastating accusation. If Howe and Clark were correct, that would make Reed responsible for the murder of the village of Bergen's Pond. As much as Reed got on his last nerve, Washington found it scarcely credible that his adjutant would engage in such horrid betrayal.

He sat down on a fallen tree trunk and sighed gloomily. To confront Reed directly would lead to a disaster, whether guilty or not. His adjutant-general would run to Congress, to his supporters, and claim that General Washington had lost his mind. That would mean more jousting with politicians who could not distinguish their rump from a mole hole. On the other hand, if he entrapped Reed and it turned out to be accurate, he would execute the traitor. This would also enrage his opponents in Congress. However, right was right, and if Recon found themselves facing Dorcester's Wolves in Paterson—that would be proof, provided that Reed "disappeared" from camp long enough to pass the information.

"Can you surveil Reed if he departs our encampment?"

Howe considered that possibility and then answered in the affirmative.

"How do you accomplish that task?" asked the general.

"We do it with multiple tracking devices. That means small machines that will transmit a signal that is similar to tiny electric, um, signals. I'm sure that sounds redundant, but I can't explain the science to you now. We can put devices on Reed's horse and in his jacket. That will require keeping him distracted so that we can plant the trackers," said Howe. "But before all that, we need to verify that Reed was away the day before Bergen's Pond. I want to find someone who can tell us he was witnessed leaving the camp. I know he said he would visit a cousin's farm near Morristown, but who can verify that he actually left?"

"I can ask the stablemate," interjected Clark.

Aaron asked, "Can you trust him?"

"He is my nephew."

"Very well," Washington said with finality as he rose. "We confirm the facts with your nephew, captain. We will then have a meeting with Reed. The whole thing feels disheartening, but if he is guilty—" he left the sentence unfinished.

"Now, be quick about it, Clark!"

Clark walked back to the Recon camp, saddened yet resolute. Surely enough, his young nephew, the stable boy, had confirmed that Reed had left on his horse the night before the Bergen's Pond massacre. He'd told the boy that he would visit his cousin and that the horse should fit properly.

Recon accepted this news as one more proof that Reed had betrayed them, as well as his general and especially the victims of Bergen's Pond.

Howe left with the news and returned to Washington's tent. Reed was already there, and Howe joined them to discuss

Recon's upcoming operation to observe Cornwallis' troops near Hackensack. Howe's presence and demeanor told Washington that the stable boy had confirmed their fears. The adjutant general sat placidly as they laid out their plan to have Recon camp on the *east* side of the Great Falls. It was set for two nights from that evening, and they told Reed the goal was to make their way toward Hackensack on Thursday at daybreak.

"Is it even safe for you to camp east of the Falls?" asked Reed, brushing some dust off his hat.

Howe assured him that being a small unit, Recon could evade detection and rest there safely. They certainly wouldn't expect Cornwallis' troops to go west from Hackensack, as all of the intel showed that those troops were settling in as a foothold.

"Also, Cornwallis' troops are few in number," said Aaron. That, of course, was a complete lie. As far as anyone could tell, no British troops were camping near Hackensack at all. It was just another ploy to paint a picture that Washington was misinformed at best and even inept.

"And, as far as Dorcester," Aaron continued. "Our best estimate is that he will keep his men in a defensive position after the last three massacres. He can build up his defenses and wait while word spreads about the danger of supporting our army."

"Reed," said Washington. "I think that sending Major Howe's small group out to spy on the happenings by Hackensack is perhaps the wisest thing to do now. We will then have a clear understanding about whether we can attack Dorcester now or perhaps delay. What is your view?"

Reed appeared thoughtful as he stuffed his hand into his pocket. After a moment, he turned to say, "I can think of no better use for Recon than to head to the Falls and reconnoiter Cornwallis' advance troops."

"Major Howe," said Washington. "Take Recon and camp east of the Falls in two nights. Then at dawn, break camp and carefully make your way toward Hackensack. After which, you shall return here straightaway."

Washington turned to Reed and asked, "Reed, would you like

to go with Recon to surveil Cornwallis' advance troops?"

Reed seemed hesitant, then said, "Sir, I appreciate the honor. However, I have recently been to my cousin's farm, and I am returning there almost immediately to arrange to transfer a large grain shipment. Winter is on our heels, and I think I should get as much provision as possible. With your approval, general."

Washington smiled deceptively. "Of course, Reed, even with Howe's supplies, it is essential that we have grain as well. By all means, but return quickly such that we may all be together to hear the results of Recon's observations in Hackensack. Major Howe, you are dismissed."

"Son of a bitch," whispered Aaron under his breath as he stepped out of the command tent and headed back to Recon.

By the time Major Howe returned to the Recon camp, the guys were shuffling around like busy bees. Clark and Mercy had lit fires under everyone, and they were all hustling to prepare and review and prepare some more.

Aaron told everyone to take a break as Clark verified that Reed had exited the camp before the Bergen's Pond massacre. This knowledge was answered with groans and not-so-silent curses. Howe told them that Washington had offered to send Reed along with Recon to the Falls, as was one last chance for the adjutant to display his innocence. But the man declined, saying he must leave to arrange grain shipments.

"I knew that bastard was a traitor," said Monty.

"Can I be the one to hang him?" asked Rogers.

Clark raised his hand as Aaron watched. "Let's stay focused on the mission, boys and girls—I mean, girl. We must be thoroughly prepared." The captain flashed his bright and perfect smile. To Howe, Clark was starting to sound like Mercy.

"Everything is almost completely prepped," said Mercy. "I even taught Lewis and Allen how to fly the drones."

"Really?" asked Aaron as he stood nearby. "What's a drone, Lewis?"

Without hesitation, as if the young corporal had rehearsed it, he began, "Sir, a drone is a stingless male bee, as of the honeybee species, that has the role of mating with the queen and does not gather nectar or pollen," quoted Lewis sounding like Webster's Dictionary.

Howe frowned. "I wasn't asking about bees—"

"Sir, if I may continue," interjected Lewis. "A drone is also an unmanned aircraft or ship guided by remote control or onboard computers, sir."

Aaron grinned, "Impressive, corporal, anything else?"

"Yes, sir. To drone can also be a long and monotonous tone or description of someone who keeps talking, boring the hell out of you, and refuses to shut up, sir."

"Let's go back to number two, Lewis. What do you know how to do with our drones?"

Corporal Lewis stood at attention and began talking like a marine private in boot camp. "Major Howe, I can launch the drone in near-silent mode. Our drones are equipped with rotor modifications that limit the Blade Vortex Interaction Noise by using modulated blade spacing. We can also fly the drone at an altitude which will essentially assist in noise reduction and attenuation due to the distance to the target."

"I taught him that," said Mercy with a positively sunny smile.

Aaron gave Mercy a sarcastic look. "Really? I would have thought Lewis figured that out on his own. Huh."

"Corporal Lewis," asked Clark. "Did you fly that thing?"

Without hesitation, Lewis held up the remote controller. "I used this remote controller box, sir, and I launched, flew, and landed the drone helicopter without any screw-ups. Oh, it also has a high-resolution video camera, including night vision and infrared heat sensors to track humans."

"All right," said Major Howe, turning to Allen. "What do you know about the drones?"

"Um," gulped Allen, the thin farm boy. "Everything that he said, sir."

"Corporal Gozen," asked Clark. "Are they both able to use the drones?"

"Captain," she said. "They can kick ass and take names, sir."

"A simple 'yes' would suffice, corporal," retorted Captain Clark.

"Yes sir," said Mercy.

Since their practice maneuvers had been canceled on Wednesday night, Recon set out fully loaded for the real thing. The eight members repeatedly went over every detail they could think of. Mercy made a habit of reminding everyone on the hour that if anyone shot Durst, she would personally throw them into the Passaic River and hold them under until dead. Monty made the mistake of claiming he didn't think she could hold him under, so she asked him if he would like to make a bet and shake hands on it. He declined.

Mercy and Howe had ensured that the electronic gear was fully charged and had plenty of spares. Needless to say, they were weighed down to capacity. Recon had no alternative but to leave the M4 Benelli's behind, but they did take the two M40a3's, their sidearms, and for Mercy, the balisong. Meals were limited to just what they needed, as adequate ammo was the priority.

The Recon team slipped out of camp at 20:00, silent and unseen. They were far enough from the main encampment that they could also stealthily disappear in addition to gaining a reputation as some sort of secret warfare platoon.

One thing they could not control was the weather. A light, cold rain desperately tried to find a way through their Gortex camos and boots to make them individually and collectively miserable.

By 01:30, they'd reached about a mile south of Great Falls. They took off their packs as the drizzle continued and set up camp. Mercy volunteered to watch from 02:00 until 06:30. She seemed to barely sleep anyway, so the rest bedded down to an uneventful night under bare, dripping trees.

At 06:30, Mercy woke Lieutenant Schein, who agreed to watch until 08:30. They were doing their best to get as much sleep as possible, which all soldiers valued highly. Mercy dragged herself into the tent with the lightly snoring Howe to get some needed rest. They awoke at 09:00 and were happy to discover that the clouds had thinned and the rain had stopped. They ate their MREs silently and then packed up. After reviewing the mission for the day, Howe insisted that they use some drone time to survey a five-mile radius from the Falls, including east towards Hackensack. Howe did not want to leave anything to chance.

"Mercy," asked Monty. "What's a good word in the future for wonderful?

"Try 'fire.'"

"Well then," Monty said. "That drone thing is fire!"

With unbridled interest, Recon gathered to look at the video from the drone. The military drone was fairly large by consumer standards, but it had those Milspec bells and whistles that gave them significant help.

Lewis was working the controller, and Howe stood there shaking his head at how well the kid had adapted to the device. It was a little scary. Just a short time ago, the highest tech activity for the corporal was loading musket balls.

The drone was now just west of the falls and was scanning in that direction. Lewis took the drone on a sweeping pattern and scanned for heat in addition to the video coming back in real-time.

"Major," said Sergeant Rogers as Lewis was setting the drone to return automatically, "what about our tracking on Reed?"

"That's a little less adequate than I would like," said Aaron. "We put a few devices in the forest heading NW in the direction of Dorcester. If Reed gets within a mile of the devices, then his location will be determined by what is called triangulation.

Although, to be frank, if Durst shows up at the Falls, then that's proof enough for me.

"Just understand that on top of Durst as proof, we will have a fairly good idea of where he is going, and we will be able to prove it. He will surely leave by riding toward Morristown, but if he turns north, then we will have solid evidence," answered Howe.

Lieutenant Schein was impressed. "Even from this distance?"

"Yes, once we get up on top of the Falls, we can receive the information. It goes through the air invisibly, and you might think it's magic, but it isn't. There is a writer in the future named Sir Arthur C. Clarke." At this, Captain Clark stirred, hoping that the writer would be a descendant.

"This writer was brilliant, and he had a saying called his Third Law. It said that any technology that is sufficiently advanced is indistinguishable from magic. Do you understand what that means, lieutenant?"

Schein took a moment and answered, "Well, sir, I believe that we, now in 1776, would look at all these devices and assume that they are magic because we cannot understand them, but once we learn how they work, we can see that it is not magic at all, just another tool.

"Very good, lieutenant," said Howe. "In my generation, there are many devices that *you* would consider magic, and there are devices that I might consider magic. However, there is a difference. In my generation, we have come to expect things that look like magic but are, in reality, science. So, when we see something we can't explain, and don't understand, instead of assuming that it is magic, we usually say that it is interesting. That is followed up by us trying to figure out how it works. This is a long way from Ben Franklin's lightning rod."

"I wish our generation could think like that," said Monty. "We have misguided fools in our time who traverse the countryside accusing people of being witches and magicians. Mercy is the closest thing to a witch I have ever beheld, but I think she is brilliant."

"Gee, thanks Monty," smirked Mercy, "I think."

The major steered the conversation back to Reed. "In any case, we are going to know with fairly good certainty whether Reed is innocent or a backstabbing bastard. Although, after his trip to see his 'cousin' before Bergen's Pond, and now another sudden trip to go make a grain deal—well, sadly, I think he is our Mata Hari."

"By Mata Hari, do you refer to a traitor spy?" asked Clark.

A gloomy look settled on Howe's face. "Sadly, yes, a very evil traitor from a future generation."

"And what happened to your traitor spy, Mata Hari, in the future?" asked Rogers.

"She was executed by firing squad," answered Aaron flatly.

Chapter 27

The huge Scot strolled up to Dorcester's tent, where he came face to face with the even larger Sergeant Magath. The two men eyed each other with contempt. To Magath, the Scot was a shirker who avoided the real army by milking snakes and selling their venom. He recognized the Scot as a man who would sell his own mother for a pint.

The man mainly provided good information, and with the quick and deadly unit under Washington's command roaming around, the sooner Dorcester could crush that threat, the better. Paying a slimy informant like this scoundrel was just a cost of war. Of course, the Scot probably felt equally disturbed by Magath, seeing that the sergeant could barely disguise his disdain.

"And what purpose have you here? barked Magath.

"Aye, my large friend, I have some timely tidbits for your master," said the spy in a calm voice.

Magath lifted his hat and ran a hand through his matted brown hair. He fancied taking his fist and ramming it so hard down the Scot's throat that he could pull out the man's kidneys.

"Wait here."

Being one of the few who was permitted to approach Dorcester's tent flap, the sergeant called out to the general and received approval to enter.

General Dorcester sat in his nightclothes, with his feet up on his desk, nibbling at an apple.

"What is this about, Magath?"

"General, sir, the Scot is here," he said and then added, "again."

"Yes, Magath, I know you would like to pull the spy's arms off, but do try to restrain yourself. His information is often quite good." He paused to gauge whether the sergeant was listening attentively. "Go out, and send him in."

Magath saluted, turned, exited the tent, and then looked contemptuously at the busy spy scraping mud off his worn black boots. "Go in," mumbled the sergeant.

In an uncharacteristic gesture, the Scot tipped his hat, put on a proper English accent, and said, "Why thank ye, my good man."

Magath was infuriated and walked away, cracking his knuckles.

"What do you have for me?" asked Dorcester as his black-bearded spy sat heavily in an old yet finely carved chair.

"This time, general, I have a real gem for you."

"Indeed? Your last gem failed to shine or turn up Washington's Major Howe."

"Perhaps, I did not use my influence to ascertain the veracity of my informant. However, I am convinced my source has been completely forthcoming this time."

"How so? Did you remove any appendages?"

"General, there was no such necessity, but be assured that the information you are about to buy is extremely relevant and timely."

"I do not have the patience for sparring, you horse's ass; how much?" asked Dorcester with a menacing look.

The Scot cleared his throat as he unbuttoned his gray wool coat. "Fifty pounds."

Dorcester laughed and then pretended that he had been mortally wounded. "Oh, please. For twenty pounds, I can hire ten men to beat you, drown you, stab you, shoot you, hang you, and dismember you after I suck out everything you know. Or, I can have Sergeant Magath do all of the above for free," sneered the general, followed up with an insane, uneven laugh.

"With all due honor, general, I believe you will need twelve men for that and perhaps two Magaths."

Dorcester paused, then clutched his belly and roared positively hysterically. "Perhaps you are correct about that, but you would still be dead!" screamed the general as he continued laughing senselessly.

As quickly as he'd burst out laughing, Dorcester was suddenly subdued. "My Scottish sneak, fifty pounds, and my purchase best be magnificent."

The Scot smiled broadly as he bowed low. "General, I present to you the soon-to-be deceased Major Howe and his band of traitors on a gleaming platter called the Great Falls."

The mile hike to the southern rim of Paterson Great Falls was interrupted by the placement of the Howe It Works motion sensor cameras. That job was pretty routine, as they used zip ties to mount the cameras onto trees. Howe had them set up the sensors in an arc shape, running from the south side of the falls to about a mile out. If the Redcoats attempted to swing in from the south, it was likely that Recon would be alerted well in advance.

When they did arrive at the north end of the falls, they wanted to relax and enjoy the view, but there was no time for that. Instead, Aaron had them arrange a similar arc of three cameras stretching out to mirror the south. Between both sets of motion-sensing cameras, they would hopefully get a heads-up if the Brits didn't walk straight in.

The air was crisp, and they were pleased with the clear weather. Rain that had followed them from camp had moved on, and squirrels and birds were visiting the increasingly bare trees.

Arriving at 11:30, Howe wished they'd gotten there earlier. Lewis and Mercy quickly got one of the drones in the air. There was no sign of approaching British troops. Perhaps they had decided to attack at night, thought Aaron, or maybe Reed was not a spy after all. Howe actually hoped for the latter, but unlikely coincidences supported his doubts about Reed's loyalty.

Recon split into two groups to cover both ends, north and south of the Falls. They put a sniper position at each end with a clear, unobstructed view from 150 to 360 degrees from the south and 180 degrees to 40 degrees from the northern sniper.

However, Aaron had no intention of sniping at the Redcoats from an extreme distance. They had to let the enemy enter the trap, and then both Recon groups would swing around and hold them with their backs to the Falls. That was the theory.

In the meantime, Aaron made his way to the high ground dead center between the split Recon groups. His position right up against the falls was strictly for radio purposes. He was hopeful that the high ground in the middle would give him line-of-sight to the sensors he had placed to track the movements of Reed.

Howe took out a small flat computer with built-in Software Defined Radio to receive signals and connected a Yagi antenna to a pole about 2 meters high. He manually began to rotate the antenna from south to west. In very short order, he was receiving historical data and could mark Reed's positions over the last two days. There was more damning evidence, as Reed's path took him almost directly NNW and listed timestamps for the entire ride. The signals halted at about seven miles south of Dorcester's encampment. He had stayed there for perhaps 10 minutes and then headed due south—all that was about 30 hours earlier, which gave Dorcester plenty of time to prepare an assault on the Falls. To cover his tracks, Reed was going to make it look like he was going to buy grain. Clever guy, thought Howe, as he saved the data and packed up the small mast and antenna. It was a bittersweet moment, but on the upside, the system worked very well,

Aaron returned to his half of Recon at the southern end of the Falls. He had Mercy, Lewis, and Rogers, with him. That left Clark, Schein, Monty, and Allen on the north rim. To his happiness, both units had prepared all their ammo, weapons, food, and water. The Passaic was virtually pristine, but to be safe, Howe had them purify their river water with tablets he'd brought from the future. He debated whether to share the data about Reed but then chose to keep it to himself. There was no point in burdening the troops with more junk to think about.

Now it was just a matter of waiting and adjusting to whatever showed up on Lewis' drone imaging. The hi-tech drone had a battery life of about 90 minutes. They decided to wait ten minutes between returns and launches to stretch out the battery life. The chances were slim that Durst would arrive galloping through the woods exactly then.

By 17:45, darkness had fallen, and the wind whistled lightly through the birches and pines. There was no sign of Durst. Based on Mercy's story, and Molly's as well, the Wolves preferred to attack at night or near dawn. That was just fine with Aaron. Everyone in Recon was fitted with night vision, including the two sniper rifles. A night-time assault on Recon would be an utterly losing proposition for Durst. When you added infrared, he would have nowhere to run.

A 20:05, after flying drones all afternoon, Mercy and Lewis got their first heat signature, and it was a big one.

"Major," urged Mercy as she yanked on his sleeve. He was sleeping lightly but was instantly alert.

"We got company?" he asked.

"Yes, and by the infrared, it looks to be more than 10 Wolves."

Howe shifted his body to get a better look at the screen.

"First things first." He pushed the PTT button on his radio. "Clark, Howe, over."

"Clark, over."

"We have one big force coming in from due west. We are working on an estimate of strength now. Stand by."

Howe and Mercy studied the infrared. It looked to be about 50 infantry soldiers with no cavalry.

"Switch to video," ordered Howe.

The image came up and was brilliantly clear. Howe could pick out individuals carrying muskets. The distance to the targets was about one mile, based on the drone's position. They were walking straight in. Surprisingly, they had been able to plot a direct line to the Falls.

"Howe, Clark," was heard on Recon's handheld radios. "We have got a target. One scout about 100 meters out heading our way."

Aaron turned to Mercy. "Since when did they start talking in meters?"

Mercy shrugged. "I teach them a lot of stuff, sir."

"How'd that guy get to 100 meters without being seen?"

Mercy thought about that and said, "I think we were focused on a mile out, but we'll have to review that. That's a snafu, sir."

Aaron turned his attention to the northern group. "Clark, do not fire on the target. No noise, repeat no noise."

There was a pause. "Howe, Clark, can I use the crossbow?"

"The what, over?"

"The crossbow. It's pretty quiet," replied Clark.

How turned to Mercy. "You seriously packed a crossbow? Is there anything you didn't pack?"

"Sir, I did not pack any grenades, mortars, bazookas, or claymores," Mercy confessed.

"Clark, Howe. If he comes within 15 meters, then crossbow, and it better be dead on. Howe, out."

Mercy tugged at Aaron's sleeve and pointed to a display. "We have a scout on our side too."

Sure enough, about 100 meters out was a Redcoat making his way just south of them.

"Clark, Howe. We have a scout here too. When your guy gets close enough, take a clean shot, and it has to be fatal."

Howe turned to Sergeant Rogers. "Do you see our guy?"

"Not very well, major."

"Okay, put on your headset and check if you can see him."

Rogers clipped the night vision headset and said, "Like daylight, sir."

"Ok, take your Ka-Bar knife and find a spot down there to wait. When he gets past you, take him out quietly. Ka-Bar is preferred, but if you have to, use the .380 with the silencer. We'll be watching from here, so if it looks like trouble, we will snipe him. But we need this to be quiet. Listen, Thomas; you are the best at being unseen, so do your ghost thing on that guy and be careful."

"Yes sir," said Rogers as he slipped quietly into the not-so-dense woods.

With the enhancement of night vision, Clark's half of Recon could follow every move of the large Redcoat as he crunched his way toward their position. Based on what he'd learned about modern warfare from Mercy, in the future, at least in the field, it was mostly about stealth. This large fellow was anything but.

As he got within crossbow range, they could see that this was a man you would try to avoid wrestling. At 12 meters, Clark released the bolt, and faster than any human eye could track it, the bolt flew and pierced the guy just below the sternum. He dropped almost immediately but was still moving on the ground when Schein and Allen got to him. Allen moved the musket out of the man's reach. The bolt had taken him dead center, and the sergeant quickly finished the man with his knife. The two managed to drag the large body back to their captain. Clark took a good look at him.

"This guy is missing half his nose," said Schein.

"Is it any wonder?" Allen smirked. "He smells awful."

"Drag him over there. Quick. Quick," ordered Clark. "We'll do jokes later, Sergeant Allen."

When Schein and Allen returned, Clark was sending clicks by radio to the major. No response.

"What the hell?" whispered Clark.

"Clark, Howe."

"Howe, Clark, I was calling you."

"Rogers was in the middle of dealing with our guy over here."

"We took out the big guy over here. The guy was missing half his nose."

Mercy looked at Howe. They both felt a guarded sense of relief. "That's definitely one of the Wolves, sir. A lot of them have scars and missing parts. Dorcester did what we'd hoped by sending them. I would've liked to have finished him with my balisong."

"Listen, Corporal Tamoe. You aren't going to get them all."

"Yes, sir, understood, but Durst—"

Rogers leaned over to whisper, "Yes, we know, Durst is yours."

"Exactly," reiterated Mercy.

"Major," said Lewis. "They stopped. They are not moving."

Mercy checked the infrared and night vision on the drone. Sure enough, the whole Wolves platoon halted dead in their tracks.

"They're waiting for the missing-nose Wolf and the other guy," said Mercy. "That would be my guess."

Aaron tried to figure out their next move. In the middle of all that, he felt his stomach growling, but it wasn't a good time to start preparing an MRE. He forced his mind off his gut. What would Durst do if his scouts didn't come back? A child killer like Durst would probably turn and run. On the other hand, if he went back to Dorcester with fifty guys telling the general that they'd stopped because two scouts disappeared, the general would have a fit. That megalomaniac would probably hang Durst for coming back empty-handed. Howe had made a decision and keyed his radio.

"Everyone sit tight. Durst is not going to go back without contact with us. He thinks he's got us outnumbered. The only way he can go back without our heads is if he can tell Dorcester that there were 300 of us here. So, that means that we don't fire on these guys until we have them flanked. We have to let them drift in and let them think that we are entirely out-gunned. If we have to shoot it out, then we wait until they are pretty close. It's possible we won't flank them but will have a straight-up firefight.

"If they split, with some trying to circle down here, and some try to circle around you to the north, then you don't let them get around you. Understood?"

Confirmation clicks all around were sent back by radio.

For the next hour, nothing happened other than Lewis bringing in the drone, changing the battery, and keeping it on the ground. It was a little nerve-wracking that Durst and his troops just sat out there doing nothing. Howe kept thinking that perhaps there was another force coming around from the north or south. He checked the camera sensors but saw nothing.

"Corporal, get that drone back up. I want a scan of the area."

Lewis hurried to get the drone airborne and took it up to 200 meters. From there, they had a very wide-angled view. The infrared still showed the group bunched together about three-quarters of a mile out. They were drifting in slowly.

"Lewis, get right on top of them with the drone. Elevation 250 meters. I want to get a good image of what they have there," ordered Howe.

"Sir, won't they hear that?" asked Rogers.

"I don't care. Whatever they manage to hear will sound like a quiet buzz. No one in 1776 has heard a drone, so let's risk it to get a good image."

Lewis sent the drone out at 300 meters and gradually descended to 250 meters. He had to fiddle a little to get a view through the trees. On infrared, there were about fifty to sixty British. The video started streaming in, and they could pick out individuals. From the drone video, for the first time, Howe could see that they had a cannon.

"That's frightening," said Lewis.

Mercy smiled. "It does create a little more of a challenge."

"I think they are slowly walking that cannon in. If their two scouts don't come back, they could start shooting to keep us pinned down. Then they will probably try to flank us while we are being shelled. If they haven't already, they are going to guess that their scouts are dead or captured," observed Howe. "Mercy, what's the range on that cannon?"

Mercy took a really good look at the drone video and then through the scope of the rifle. After a couple of grunts, she said, "I'm guessing that that is a small field piece about three lb. shot or balls. 1000 yards maximum."

"They're almost at that range now!" said Rogers.

"Clark, Howe."

"Howe, Clark"

"Do you see the small artillery piece they are dragging?".

"Standby." Then Clark said, "Yes, we can see it through the rifle scope."

"I want you to shoot the crew if they start loading. Not before. We cannot let them get a shot off.

"There is no way they will believe that we hit their crew from 1000 yds. Do you know what that means?" asked Howe.

Clark thought for a moment and said, "They will think we are only 50 meters away."

"Right, and they will come straight at us," said Howe.

"Then what?" asked Rogers.

"Then we flank them. They will think they have us running away between them and the Falls. You guys will flank them, and I will be the sitting duck up against the Falls." said Howe. He said this on the radio so everyone could hear on their headsets.

Howe continued. "I am going to fire from dead-center by the Falls. They will think they have us pinned down because they will hear multiple shots from dead ahead. Clark, you have to make damn sure they can't fire that cannon. The rest of you circle to flank and don't shoot each other, and don't shoot me. Take clear shots. You will only be 30 meters by the time they are in the breadbasket. You make damn sure you angle your aim away, so you aren't risking friendly fire. If any of them rush me, I will do my best to take them."

"That is highly unsafe, sir," said Monty into his radio.

"Monty, you're right. It's crazy. That's why I'm counting on you to slam them before they get that close. Got it?"

"Yes, sir."

Howe grabbed the M40, a heavy box of ammo, his rifle, and his radio. Mercy reached over to tug at his sleeve. "Why don't we just rush them?"

He looked into her eyes. "Mercy, do you want your shot at Durst? The scumbag will be hiding in the back and will run away. We have to draw them in; the only way is if they think they are pinning us. That's the point of firing down the middle. They won't believe that we are more than 50 yards, and they will come at us. They think we are a few soldiers with muskets. They will also know that we are on this side of the falls. So, let's make them think that, and draw them into the killing zone. Right?" He squeezed her arm. She looked down at his hand, then put her hand on his and said, "You know what, Aaron? You have a wimpy grip."

When Howe had made it to the rise on the west side of the Falls, he set up the M40a3 on a bipod and laid out all his gear. He looked through the scope and saw that Durst's unit was now at a range of 700 meters. Clark was calmly waiting with his M40 sniper rifle about 50 meters north of Howe.

"Listen up," he called into his radio. "You can see that they are still moving straight in. Clark, I will take a shot the minute they start to load that field gun. After that, I want you to hit a tree nearby but make it a sloppy miss. Then we'll see if they charge.

"If and when they charge, you pan out. Everyone clear on that?"

Radio clicks.

At about 600 meters out, Durst stopped his men. They must have been anxious about the scouts' failure to return.

"Lewis, Howe"

"Major, Lewis"

"What do you see from the drone, Scott?"

"They're moving again, but there's heavy tree coverage, sir."

Aaron hit the PTT button on his radio again. "Listen up. Let them keep on coming in."

And that is what they did. They never divided up but kept rolling the field gun and slowly moved closer to the Falls.

At 21:30, the Redcoats were now only 200 meters out, and they still did not attempt to split up. It was unsettling.

"Clark, Howe. Why aren't they splitting up or going as one unit north or south? Don't they think we are on the east side of the falls? You would think they would go north to cross the Passaic, where it's narrow."

"I'm not sure, sir, but I think we should check the east side of the falls."

"Roger that," confirmed Howe. "Lewis, Howe. Take the drone east. Let's see if there is anything over there."

It took Lewis about ten seconds to fly over Howe's head and gain a little altitude.

"Sir," called Mercy. "We've got company on the other side of the falls. It looks to be about fifty Redcoats, at least a mile out. Lewis is pissing himself."

"Okay, let's everyone keep calm. We missed that group. They must have swung around from the north. No problem, they can't fly over the Passaic, so they will have to return to the north. We got time. I guess Dorcester wanted to be sure, and anyway, until they hear gunfire, they will think that we are on the east side of the falls. That means they came from the west, across the Passaic north of here, and now they are trying to head down east to catch us. Soon, they are going to find out that they are on the wrong side of the Falls. This is good, so be happy."

"Who is that in front of us? Is it Durst, or is Durst on the east side?" asked Clark.

"Good question," said Howe. "That explains why these guys look like they are just out for a Sunday stroll. They think the guys on the East side will take us out."

"Where's Durst?" Mercy blurted out anxiously.

"Mercy," asked Aaron. "If you were Durst, would you want to do the killing or watch from the other side?

Without hesitation, Mercy said that Durst would watch.

"Really?" asked Howe. "Why do you think that?"

"Because at both Piney Brook and Bergen's Creek, he sent his men to do the risky work. He will not fight if he can get someone else to do it."

Howe keyed up his mic again. "Enough talk. We're here now, and these guys are in the basket. If Durst is in the west group, don't shoot him. The *Lobsters* on the east side are too far out, and they still have to cross the Passaic to be a problem for us. So, we take these guys now. We'll then pick off the eastern group if they get close enough."

"Clark, focus on the field gun crew. Pick your targets, and don't shoot Durst. The shots on the gun crew are all yours, captain. Ready in 3, 2, 1—fire."

The British coming from the west had closed to under 100 meters. The gun crew of three Redcoats stayed back about 150 meters. Clark was efficient. At 23:05, two M40 rounds hit the first two men of the gun crew. He noticed the third man was hit from what must have been a lucky through and through—two for the price of one. The Redcoats' reaction was slow, but after 15 seconds, the first volley of musket balls flew overhead of Recon or hit the boulders in front of them. The British volley was directed entirely at random.

From Aaron's position, smoke partially obstructed his view, but not enough to obscure his targets. Having never faced such firepower before, the Brits were on one knee reloading, but they were now out in the open. Howe sighted up two or three soldiers and squeezed off one shot, then another, and another. It was a target-rich environment, and he could hear the sound of Clark's rifle and the VZ 58 rifles laying down fire.

"Lewis, Howe"

"Yes sir," replied Lewis with loud reports in the background.

"Safe your weapon. Take that drone out of hover and look east," commanded Howe.

In about 40 seconds, as Howe continued to drop targets, Lewis shouted over the radio that the Redcoats on the east side were holding back about 300 meters from the Falls.

"Seriously?" shouted Howe, "What the hell is wrong with them?"

Mercy yelled into her mic, "Let 'em wait. Just keep off of Durst!"

The disarray among the British west group was pathetic. If these weren't Durst and the Wolves, thought Howe, they were just a group of soldiers who walked into a nightmare. Aaron stayed focused on the business at hand. It was important to remember that these were Dorcester's troops, the garden of miscreants from where he harvested his Wolves.

The Redcoats were dropping like flies. The fire that Recon was laying down was like hell on earth. The Brits didn't know what hit them, and in Clark's estimate, only about 10 to 15 men were still trying to fire.

Howe paused to scan the killing zone with his scope. For some crazy reason, the Brits were still loading and firing, giving Recon all the excuses they needed to pick them off one by one. Aaron had never thought he'd see "like shooting ducks in a barrel," but this must have been it. After another minute, British fire had slowed to a trickle.

Without warning, Mercy screamed. Howe could hear it even without his radio.

"Howe, Gozen. Over."

"Go."

"Two or three just took off south on foot. Looks like three of them. Permission to chase?" yelled Mercy.

"No."

"It could be Durst," she pleaded.

"Dammit, Mercy! Can you handle it?"

It would have been an outright negative if it were anyone else, but Mercy was a different story. Mercy knew that if Durst was surrounded by twenty loaded muskets, she wouldn't pursue.

"Mercy!" shouted Aaron into his mic. "Be careful."

Aaron swung his scope south. Rogers and Lewis were now looking west as Mercy took off like a cheetah down the hill.

"Howe, Clark."

"Go."

"Look, east."

Aaron swiveled around, making sure to keep behind his cover. The eastern platoon of Brits was moving NE slowly. Howe could only guess that in the dark, they must have assumed that Washington's traitors were trapped against the falls. Their commander must have assumed that Durst was mopping up. It looked as if they were going to circle back to the north and then join Durst in a victory party.

"Sir, this is Clark. Should I snipe at the east troops?"

"Negative," said Howe. "Get your asses down here. Don't leave any gear behind. Don't forget the shell casings; scoop up as many as possible or throw them into the Passaic. Move it!"

Howe picked up the M40a3 and rushed south. The decimated Redcoats to the west were barely moving, but as he approached Lewis and Rogers, he heard a musket fire. About two seconds later, the corporal shouted in pain. The ball had traveled about 200 meters at a muzzle velocity of 300 miles per hour. It had slowed by the time it reached Lewis, but not enough.

When Howe got to him, Lewis was on his back, clutching his side. Rogers and Monty shot off about 30 rounds directly at the origin of the shot.

"I'm shot," groaned Lewis. "This hurts like a—what do you call it, sir?"

"Like a son of a bitch, corporal," offered Howe. "Let me see it."

Howe took a good look. Lewis' jacket had a layer of Kevlar and no hole, but that didn't rule out a nasty internal injury. He pulled up Lewis' jacket as Clark, Schein, Monty, and Allen arrived out of breath.

"Is he shot?" asked Allen.

"Wait," answered Howe.

With Lewis' jacket and shirt open, Howe could see a nasty impact wound. When he was a kid, he had once taken a paintball from close range in the side, similar to Lewis. It had cracked a rib, almost. With the velocity falling off and the Kevlar, Lewis could say he just got hit by a major league fastball. It was going to hurt like crazy for a few days but would eventually heal up okay. That was Howe's best guess. "Lewis," said Major Howe. "That Kevlar jacket just saved you from a serious battering."

"Hey Lewis," said Lieutenant Schein. "I think I just stepped on your musket ball." Schein picked up a metal object and held it out to Lewis who was struggling to his feet.

"Here, Lewis." said Mordy. "Here is a free souvenir you can

show to your children someday."

Now that Lewis was back on his feet, Howe rushed Recon to pack up and double-time it. Mercy was now the priority.

He raced down the hill to the south as Clark confirmed that the Brits on the east side were now marching to the north and looking for an easy way across the Passaic.

"Move it, move it, and don't forget that damn drone!" Aaron bellowed as he took off with Schein right on his heels.

Recon gathered up all the gear, as Rogers told them that two or three Redcoats had run away to the south. He explained that Mercy had gone after them with her sidearm.

"If that's Durst, and he gets away, she'll kill us," moaned Lewis.

Chapter 28

The southwest ridge of the Great Falls descended to present-day Birch Street. From there, the topography flattened out next to the Passaic, with the rocky walls adjacent to the Falls directly north. In the early winter of 1776, the Passaic flowed tranquility past bare trees standing tall from the leaf-littered ground.

As Mercy sprinted over the damp ground, she ensured her night vision headset was handy. She was happy she remembered to grab it before pursuing the three Redcoats. She had the Sig .45 pistol on her hip, among other weapons. The army's only female soldier stopped running to steady her breathing and scan the trees. Her blond hair was tied back in a style she called "fight-ready."

Mercy scanned the trees and picked up one giant target. She prayed that it was Guller, the man who had murdered her husband, John. Abrupt sadness surfaced in her mind, but she tamped it down. Now was not the time.

She was frustrated to see only one target. If it was Guller, he wasn't moving very quickly. Perhaps whoever she was chasing had chosen stealth over speed. Her heart rate slowed, and she rechecked the area. Just the one big-looking brute was in sight.

After looking to the left of the large one, she caught a glimpse of a smaller silhouette. Perhaps it was Durst? He was floating in and out of her vision because of the trees. That was two targets, she thought, now what about the third—

A foot suddenly knocked her over, and she dropped her goggles and rolled to a crouching position, her left knee in the damp leaves. She looked up and saw a mountain of a man sauntering toward her.

"What the hell are you?" shouted Mercy at the enormous Brit as he approached.

At that, the English soldier stopped and asked reflectively,

"A girl?"

Mercy stood and laughed. "Yes, a girl. I get that a lot Godzilla." As if he wasn't even listening, he growled, "I haven't seen a girl in months. You look positively tasty."

He took another step closer as Mercy retreated to get her bearings.

"Listen, King Kong, I could shoot you, but that would make too much noise. So, maybe you should jump in the river, so I don't kill you."

The man's muscles flexed as he laughed deeply and threateningly. "Really, where do you hide your musket?" He slid to the left, looking for the best possible attack. Whoever he was, he was no amateur. This fellow was not underestimating her.

"What'd you say your name was, moose?" chided Mercy.

He looked incensed and said, "My apologies, miss. Allow me to introduce myself. I'm Sergeant Cecil Magath."

"Cecil?" Mercy burst out laughing. This set Sergeant Magath's temper alight, and he charged out of anger. His tree trunk of an arm grazed Mercy, knocking her sideways. Despite being flung like a twig, she had managed to land a tremendous kick to the side of Magath's leg on her way.

Hurting a little, she rolled and ended up on her feet. The sergeant was clutching his leg as he rose and then charged her again.

As with all physical contests, it was best to think about your next move. In this case, rage consumed Magath as he bounded toward her; his massive legs spread wide. However, Durst was her goal, and she could not afford a delay. He thundered directly at her, but unfortunately for him, she saw an opening.

Mimicking a scene from a movie she watched with *Allison*, Mercy dove between the giant's legs and then scaled his tremendous back. He reached behind to dislodge her, but it was too late. She was already perched on his upper back—her balisong in hand. The knife sang its woeful melody, she cut arteries in his neck, and Magath crumpled to the ground in disbelief, then died.

Immediately upon leaping from the sergeant's back, Mercy resumed her pursuit. The encounter with Magath lasted about 90 seconds and was reasonably silent. With any luck, the two remaining Redcoats would be idling their way alongside the Passaic. This would give Mercy enough time to bypass them. Unless the larger of the two was Guller, then whoever he was would be collateral damage. However, Corporal Tomoe Gozen desperately prayed that the other Englishman was Durst.

Concurrent with Magath's death, Major Howe and Recon, including the injured Corporal Lewis, were doing their best to track Mercy and the Brits. Images of the corporal chasing the three Brits were churning up anxiety within Aaron.

They were moving quickly through the woods when they stumbled upon the body of a large British soldier. Mercy was nowhere in sight, but the sergeant had met her, apparently.

"Do you see the size of this fellow?" inquired Rogers.

"He's pretty big," wheezed Lewis.

"No, corporal," said Monty. "I am big. This behemoth makes me look like a schoolboy."

"Look at his neck wound." Clark pointed while grabbing a handful of hair and lifting Magath's head. "She killed him with her balisong. We must move, but I can tell you this, Gozen doesn't fight angry. She fights cool. That's why this giant is dead."

Recon was hurrying along the west side of the Passaic River when they came to a sharp right-hand turn. The river headed due west. Unless the two Brits planned to swim through freezing water, they would have no choice but to make a right turn. Just like Recon realized now, the soldiers ahead must have already turned to follow the river.

"Gozen," said Clark loud enough for everyone to hear, "would definitely angle her way through the forest to ambush them. We should have looked at the map."

In truth, Mercy was already ahead of the Brits. The area she selected to confront the two Redcoats was ideal. It was a small clearing next to the river. The flat circular spot was lined with pine needles and presented her with no obstacles. She uttered a quiet prayer that the two soldiers were Guller and Durst. As Mercy calmed herself in preparation for the coming fight, she rinsed Magath's blood from her balisong in the Passaic. The riverbank was flat here and smoothly descended to the frigid water. It was a good spot for what she had planned.

Like an expert soldier, Mercy again checked her weapons. She had the Sig .45, the 9mm, and the knife. She'd left her VZ 58 back at the Falls but was sure Lewis would have the sense to bring it, and of course, the drones and her pack. As she waited, she purposely let her thoughts drift back to her life before implants, muscle fiber, and being healed by her friend, *Allison.*

She would never forget her life in Piney Brook. Just a short while ago, she was a wife to John Smythe, a man who cherished her, and she him. Theirs was a farming life. No one expected it to be easy, and often it was back-breaking. They brought in their crop and supported Washington against tyranny. At that time, she aided the cause with grain, but now it was about killing the butchers, Guller and Durst, and hopefully, it would soon be Dorcester.

Amid recollections, an involuntary tear fell for John. Then tears for her precious daughters, her babies, who would not live to see the country emerge from the anguish of war. Oh, what she would not do to embrace her daughters. Mercy wiped her eyes and let her pain turn to anger and anger into a hunger for justice.

She whispered a vow. "If that is Durst, then tonight I will pass judgment on that evil excuse for a human being." She contemplated that notion for a time. Mercy had what psychologists in the future would call survivor's guilt. It hung on her like chains. Durst let her live. He tormented her with the prospect of life after her soul had died. It was cruelty indeed. Killing Durst would chip away at her guilt, and whatever redemption she gained would bring her at least a small modicum of peace.

Notwithstanding Lewis's injury, Recon helped each other to make good time. It was just a hunch, but they felt that fate would lead them to witness or aid Mercy in her inevitable confrontation. They knew that the disappointment she would suffer in the chance that Durst had escaped to the north would be temporary. Doubtless, disappointment would be superseded by a relentless drive to find and punish him. Internally, they all craved that that reckoning would happen tonight. If indeed Mercy had cut off their escape route, then Recon might shortly be witnesses to her wrath unleashed.

Mercy calmed herself. There was a rustling just east along the river. The light cloud cover had opened to let a gibbous moon illuminate her private arena. She stood, her hands empty at her sides, and waited for her enemies.

Recon was just a dozen meters behind when the two Brits emerged into Mercy's clearing. It was not a brilliant and full moon, but it was enough. Guller did not immediately recognize the woman, but then he searched his memory and gasped. Durst eyed her with renewed contempt just as Recon stepped to the edge of the forest opening. Durst saw them and trembled, but Mercy screamed, "No one touch them!" Mercy's words came like harsh commands. She seethed power and righteous fury.

Howe raised his hands for everyone to lower their weapons. Her look at Aaron halted any notion of intervening. She was a volcano about to erupt. This was Mercy's clash and hers alone. "No one touch them!" she repeated. Durst himself was frozen like a deer in headlights. Monty and Clark relieved Durst of his musket and held him tightly.

When she was satisfied that Recon understood the gravity of her demand, she closed on her quarry.

"Guller," she mocked. "My, but you are a *big* man. Do you remember that?"

He spat in front of her. "I recall it well, and if your guardians were not here, we would have another go."

Mercy ignored him. "Tell me, Guller, what did you do to the man who took your ear?"

"I sliced open his belly and danced on his inwards."

She grinned and said, "That is a lovely story. So, let's just say that if I were to come and take your other ear, would you treat me the same?

He wiped his mouth with his weathered uniform sleeve. "Eventually, yes."

"You may have your chance since I am about to cut you."

Guller growled. "You would need an army, and what are you anyway? A simple woman and a traitor. It would help if you were cooking for your husband. Alas, he is dead dust and ash. And, if your mates stand aside, you can be with your husband and children very soon."

Guller's taunts rolled over her. She looked around at Recon. "Listen, all of you, even if Guller guts me like a fish, no one interferes!"

She then looked at the malicious sergeant. "Shall we give you a fair chance?" She turned to Rogers. "Give me your Ka-bar." Rogers obediently handed her his large knife, which Mercy immediately tossed handle first to Guller. Recon was visibly frightened by this and started to object, but Aaron ordered them quiet. Despite Mercy's demand that no one interfere, Aaron quietly unsnapped his sidearm.

Durst was utterly silent during all this, but a sliver of optimism was oozing out from his cold expression. He was yearning for Guller to kill Mercy and deny her the satisfaction of watching his death. And who knows? Maybe British troops would emerge at any moment to save him. Of course, they would! All things considered, he desperately wanted to see her dead.

In the clearing, a macabre dance had begun. Mercy pulled out her balisong, a blade which, to Guller, looked ineffective compared to the Ka-Bar. Guller laughed nervously as Mercy began to flip the balisong from hand to hand.

Of all the insane times in the history of the world for a dramatic Hollywood notion to seize her mind—Mercy could not restrain herself. She spoke loud enough for all to hear. “My name is Mercy Smythe; you killed my family; prepare to die.”

Guller was now swinging Roger’s Ka-bar from side to side but halted to say, “True enough, wench, apart from dying.”

She couldn’t help herself and started repeating, “My name is Mercy Smythe, you killed my family, prepare to die.”

They circled each other, and after the fifth time, Guller shouted out, “Do be silent—you chatterbox.” Mercy continued saying it, and it was rattling Guller. Only Howe could reference the movie line, and it occurred to him that this must have been another of the dozens of films she and *Allison* had bonded over.

Sergeant Guller seemingly reached the end of his patience and lunged at Mercy while slicing the air. He cursed as Mercy gracefully ducked the blade and then booted him in his behind, which nearly knocked him off his feet. Guller recovered and turned, frothing at the mouth. He ran at her again, this time with the knife lunging straight at Mercy. She side-stepped it so quickly that Recon was amazed by her agility as Guller stumbled.

The sergeant was not used to losing. He swung around, displaying a vicious scowl but did not immediately charge. Instead, he felt the side of his abdomen where blood oozed from a tear in his shirt. No one had seen the lightning-fast slit of Mercy’s knife.

She yelled out, “Ouch! Sergeant Guller, that has got to be painful.”

“Even a soon-to-be-dead widow can get lucky,” he cursed, but he could not hide his distress.

Durst’s vicious Wolf now walked quickly, swinging his knife, counting on his raw strength to bury the Ka-Bar’s point into the infuriating woman. When he got within striking distance, he made rapid, erratic lunges with the blade, which to Recon seemed fearsome. Mercy backed away, which Guller took as a sign of weakness. He committed himself to a deadly thrust. This time Mercy leaped aside and swiftly ran her balisong through Guller's knife hand. The sergeant cried out in pain as he dropped the Ka-bar to the pine needle floor of the clearing. He extended his left hand to grab the fallen blade. Mercy kicked it aside.

Guller, bleeding from his two wounds, got to one knee and stared at his adversary. He began rambling about how she was not a woman but a demon. His contrived babbling was impossible to discern other than the words 'pity' and 'surrender.'

Mercy and Tomoe Gozen were one in that instant. She exclaimed, "Sergeant Guller, for crimes against humanity, for taking orders from this piece of dung." She swung her blade to identify Durst. "And for murdering my family, I pronounce upon you the penalty of death at my hand."

The sergeant looked up, shaking and chattering for mercy, but Tomoe Gozen's balisong was already planted in Guller's throat. Disbelief clouded his eyes. He pawed at his neck, gasped in vain, and then toppled over.

The forest clearing was utterly silent. Suddenly, pleas were yelled out desperately. "I capitulate! I capitulate!" screamed Durst from behind Mercy. "I surrender and plead for a fair trial. Under the rules of war, I am entitled to a military court! I capitulate."

His right eye seemed to sag even further as Mercy swung around and answered, "There is no capitulation for you; even under the law, a war criminal found resisting in the field may be executed with malice forthwith!"

"I am not resisting. I capitulate! I capitulate!"

Mercy put her foot on Guller's chest and pulled her knife from the dead man's gullet. She made a circular motion with the knife in her hand. "Listen, Recon, does anyone hear a claim of capitulation from this coward?"

The soldiers of Recon stood silent and still.

Mercy folded the balisong and shoved it into its sheath. She lurched forward to seize Durst by his damp shirt, then yanked him away from Monty and Rogers. Durst struggled to escape from her grip but was unable. He swung his fist at her. She parried it deftly and then gave him a slap to his larynx that stunned Durst enough to dull his struggling.

Recon trailed the pair as Mercy dragged Durst towards the river. As he regained his senses, he retrieved a tiny stiletto from his trousers and thrust it into Mercy's thigh. The thin puncture wound was perhaps a half-inch deep, but she barely lost a stride.

"Nice try," she said as she pulled the knife from her leg and tossed it into the dirt.

Durst cried out, "What are you?'

She was nearly at the water's edge, and his strength was insufficient to escape her grasp. Mercy pulled him close and whispered, "I am a demon; come to burn your soul in the fires of Hell forever."

Durst cried out with a piercing shriek that took Recon's breath away. Mercy heaved him to the riverbank, seized him by the throat, and pushed his head under the flowing Passaic. She held him down for perhaps five seconds and then pulled him up.

"Please!" he screamed

"Tell me, Durst, is this how you murdered your father?" asked Mercy.

Durst's eyes locked onto hers. "No, no, he fell in the water—I, I refused to save him! My father beat me and gave me this eye."

"You failed to save your own father? If that were all you did, Captain Durst, I would pity your eye and the rest of you. But you delighted in the murder of innocents. You rejoiced in butchering my family, and for that," she paused and looked at Recon, watching her in her unbridled fury. "—For that, you will die."

She squeezed his throat and thrust Durst back under the flowing river. His hands clawed at Mercy as he struggled desperately to escape. Soon, however, his struggle faded while the river water flooded his lungs and claimed him.

Mercy pulled Durst's drenched body from the water. Recon

stepped aside as she dragged his body back up the bank and dumped it on top of Guller. She grabbed her pack and her rifle, turned to Aaron with a steely grin, and said, "Major, can we get the heck out of here, sir?"

Chapter 29

John Carlisle, vice president of the most powerful country in the history of humankind, sat at his desk and felt insignificant. He rubbed the creases in his forehead while feeling every one of his sixty-four years. The iconic song about being 64 popped into his mind. He muttered to himself, "Does my baby still need me when I'm 64?" Heaven knew he would be content to take Angela, his kids, and the grandkids to the ranch to ride around. He accepted that his gut needed a little trimming, but up there, he could do some real work and get fit like the old days. Jeans, boots, hat—that would be a heck of a lot better than this.

What was *this* anyway? It was him, John Carlisle, sitting in the White House, the only human on the planet except for maybe Howe, who was cognizant that the earth was under a microscope. For all he knew, the ET's out there might be observing earthlings like they were a bunch of microbes in a petri dish. He gave himself a sad chuckle. What do you do with microbes? Bacteria? You kill them. All of a sudden, the preposterous notion of being squashed like bugs by even *bigger* bugs was shifting from surreal to real. Maybe he should simply go into the Oval Office and say, "Mr. President, we are in contact with aliens, and it could get ugly."

That, of course, was a terrible idea. His boss didn't even know what state he was in half the time. The president had become a prop for his handlers, and there was not one damn thing that John could do about it. Carlisle mused if he went to the president, the guy would probably ask when he and ET could have lunch. No, John thought, this particular top-secret intel must be held close to the vest. He couldn't even tell Angela. And John felt desperate to tell his wife. Should he keep something this big from her?

He walked his 5'10", slightly chubby body across the floor

and sat down on the sofa. Carlisle ran his hand through his receding hairline and looked up at the John Adams portrait. As crazy as it was, he would be damned happy if he could talk to the former president, maybe along with Franklin and Hamilton. In 30 minutes, he would have them up to speed on a couple of hundred years of history, and those geniuses would give him sensible advice.

Naturally, they would wonder how the republic they set up so beautifully could get so messed up. The founding father and second president would take one look at welfare, food stamps, free tuition, free cellphones, free this and free that; the man would probably go to Congress and put those politicians over his knee and spank them silly. On the other hand, Ben Franklin would likely start chasing cute interns around the White House.

Carlisle heard the annoying buzzer. He pressed the intercom. "Yes, Grace?"

"Sir," said Grace. "Dr. Howe, from Howe It Works, is on the line. Should I put him through?"

Finally! "Yes, put him through."

There was a click.

"Hello, Dr. Howe," said the vice president.

"I'm sorry, Mr. Vice President, I am calling *for* Dr. Howe. This is Dr. Tomis, his associate."

John hid his disappointment coupled with trepidation by calmly responding, "Dr. Tomis, how nice to speak with you again. I hope that you are feeling fine and not too overwhelmed lately. Is Dr. Howe still tied up with his new research? I was hoping he would be free enough to discuss some upcoming projects."

"That's exactly right, Mr. Vice President. The board likes to give him some space when he gets absorbed in his work—we all let Aaron do his own thing. However, perhaps the two of us could meet at the same restaurant sometime?"

Carlisle dreaded going back down the tunnel to Bjorn's embassy basement, but what choice did he have? He leaned back on the sofa, then used his shoe to rub a chunk of his cigar ashes into the carpet. "Sure, Dr. Tomis, I will book it for Friday at 8 p.m.?"

"I'm sorry, Mr. Vice President, could we make it for tomorrow at 10 p.m.? Maybe just some cheesecake and decaf and a chance to go over some of our latest ideas," said Edgar.

"One second," said Carlisle as he feigned checking his calendar. "I have something for tomorrow night, but it can be rescheduled. It will be nice seeing you again. Goodbye, Dr. Tomis."

"Goodbye, Mr. Vice President."

Carlisle put down the phone. He put his hand on his scalp and decided that if he'd had more hair up there, he would start pulling it out.

Ambassador Bjorn Anker was only too happy to have the vice president request another covert meeting in the basement of the Danish embassy. Bjorn would now have the VP on the hook for an additional favor. He didn't intend to push too hard, but Carlisle, as an ally, could be very useful back in the European Union.

When Carlisle arrived home, he told Angela they would have to do the same routine the following night.

"What the hell is going on, John?"

"Angela, please!" he implored her not to ask.

"John, I love you, but my patience has limits, and if I explode or lose my mind, I will take you with me into wife hell."

"Darling," he pleaded."There are things that I can't tell you. Do you think that spouses of high officials know everything?"

"No, John, but they should," she said as she poked his ribs hard enough to make her point loud and clear.

He held her close and buried his face into her large mass of brunette hair.

"Can you hear me?" he spoke quietly into her ear.

"Oh, honey, yes, yes, yes," she answered passionately.

He kept nuzzling her and whispered, "Angie, there is some dire stuff going down. I'll tell you when it's safe, when I have to, or when I can't carry the load." He kissed her cheek.

At 9:45 pm, after Angela chased the secret service away from the house, she and John went down to the basement. They repeated the routine of clearing the bookshelf, and then Carlisle ducked into the tunnel which led to the Danish embassy. Maybe this time, he could avoid the cobwebs and dust.

"John Carlisle," said Ambassador Anker as the VP stepped up from the top rung of the tunnel ladder. "Welcome back to your secret office."

"Cool it, Bjorn. I am not feeling particularly humorous tonight. Is he here?"

Bjorn nodded and pointed down the hallway.

"The same two chairs are set up."

"Thanks. And if there is a listening device in there, I will screw you over royally."

Anker puckered his lips and said with a tinge of guilt, "You know, John, let me go in there and check to be sure. There might be one since we had the Germans here a couple of days ago."

The two men walked down the yellowish, poorly-painted hallway together. Bjorn opened the paneled door, then entered the sparsely furnished room where Edgar sat idly in a chair. Upon seeing the vice president, Edgar began to talk, but Carlisle put his fingers to his lips to silence him.

Anker went straight to a tall bookshelf, pulled out a ten-millimeter-long cylindrical device, and switched it off. "Well, gentlemen, that should solve your problem," said the ambassador with finality.

Carlisle was a former C.I.A. agent who rarely trusted other

people's work. He pulled out a very expensive, highly sensitive frequency counter and scanned around the room. There was one signal coming from the bottom of Edgar's chair, and after yanking the device away, Carlisle dropped it and smashed it with his boot.

"Well, Bjorn, I guess things are all better now."

"Honestly, John," exclaimed Anker, "I had no clue. Perhaps the German put it there?"

Carlisle put on his angry face. "Bjorn, if I find another bug in here, I'm going to destroy your prime minister campaign."

Anker did his best to hide his anxiety. "I guarantee, John, this room is now immaculate. Please take as much time as you need."

Bjorn Anker exited quickly, leaving Edgar and the vice president alone. John looked at Dr. Tomis. He couldn't even define his own mixed feelings as he sat there gazing at a supposed alien.

Over the last few days, John had become more suspicious and doubtful of Edgar's claims. The device sitting in Howe's lab could be an object that fell to earth, but the rest of the story sounded like a delusional fantasy.

"I've been meaning to ask you some questions."

"I'm sorry, Mr. Vice President," interrupted Edgar. "But we are not having this meeting so that you may quiz me about me. I've asked you here to discuss what is happening outside the confines of your world."

Carlisle brushed off some of the grunge that had clung to him from his tunnel trek. He tried hard not to look displeased. "Very well, Edgar, please tell me your vital information," said the VP with a healthy dose of disbelief.

"I hope the last few days have not been too stressful, but I must now tell you more detailed information." Edgar seamlessly shifted gears. "An alien named Mazik Bah-Gahn has sent what you would call a spaceship on its way to Earth." The scientist stroked his formidable mustache and contemplated how he would explain the gravity of Earth's predicament.

"Do you consider yourself a courageous person, John?"

"I don't know, Edgar, are aliens going to pull my eyeballs out of my ears?"

"Not today," answered Edgar in a dry, emotionless tone.

John was unflustered, and he decided that looking upon Edgar as mentally ill helped him to listen to the man. "Just tell me what I need to know."

"This is complicated, but I will simplify it as best I can, John. I came here so many years ago for two reasons. The first, as an anthropologist. The second, to keep you off the radar, so to speak. I did that by sending back reports about the primitive and uninventive nature of humans. I tried to persuade the other sentients that your species could barely feed yourselves, much less improve your technology.

"You must understand, John, I am not of the same species as Mazik Bah-Gahn. My group of sentients has argued in favor of letting immature worlds, like your Earth, develop and progress. That is until they either adapt or become a threat. We are very patient, and so is the Council.

"The Council?"

"Please listen to the whole thing, John."

"Now, despite my efforts, you have come to the attention of Mazik Bah-Gahn. He is the leader of one of the Council species. There are two reasons why your Earth has garnered his attention. One, because you humans adapt to nanites. You are, in fact, the only beings that can. Do you understand that?"

Carlisle rubbed his chin and asked, "When you say nanites, are you referring to molecular-sized computers?"

"John, that is a modest description but not exactly inaccurate. I will tell you that in the known galaxy, only humans can adapt and adopt nanites. Frankly, we don't know why. But this technology could allow humans to advance so quickly that you could potentially dominate the galaxy. As one sentient sympathetic to the Mazik put it, humanity would be like an Arkbun infestation, only with Arkbun 100 times smarter and stronger than us."

"Arkbun?" asked Carlisle.

"You might call them rats."

"What the hell," exclaimed the VP. "So now we are rats?"

"You are dysfunctional rats," said Edgar.

"What's the second reason?"

"You can transport seamlessly through time and space."

Carlisle was getting increasingly uptight. "What?"

"John, do you remember Sergeant Bonner?"

Carlisle returned an impatient stare.

"Yes, John, *that* Sergeant Bonner.

The VP finally put two and two together regarding Bonner.

"You were there, Edgar. I figured that was a load of garbage about the bear! So, let me see if I understand. Did Bonner get zapped off of earth and travel through time and space? If so, then this tale of yours is getting more like a military sci-fi novel every second. Please go on because this is better than TV," joked the VP, trying to hide his growing anxiety.

Edgar frowned.

"Sorry to scoff, Edgar," apologized Carlisle. "But you can imagine how difficult this is to believe. I'll try to take it more seriously. Right, so what happened to Bonner?"

"Suffice it to say that he was a gift to the Mazik. Bonner was what you call a guinea pig. He was implanted with nanites, and they took. He survived the process."

"Ah, so we are special."

"Too special for your own good," said Edgar. "A unique ability to integrate nanites is what you call a game-changer.

"The Mazik sees you as vermin, and no one wants a rat the size of a gorilla who can also pop up on another world instantly, sprinkle it with a homemade virus, all while reading Shakespeare and drinking tea."

"Professor," said the vice president after a short pause. "Please believe that I intend you no insult, but as far as I know, you could be insane or a practical joker having fun at my expense. You said you've been here on earth for 126 years?"

"Actually," interrupted Edgar, "126 years, three months, and 17 days; your time."

"Well, nothing like being precise," Carlisle continued. "However, and I ask this respectfully, can you prove you're an alien?"

"Proof," Edgar said thoughtfully. "I actually did expect that question, so are you ready for a little proof, John?"

Carlisle blinked a couple of times, gave a little shrug, and said, "I believe so," while simultaneously hoping that a bunch of Danes would walk in with a cake and yell, "surprise!"

Edgar stared at him.

"Look at my hands, John."

Carlisle looked at Edgar's large hands. Spontaneously, his fingers grew longer, especially the middle and index. They also began to turn to a luminescent, pale blue, and the tips glimmered. The vice president stared and was dumbstruck.

"Don't be afraid," Edgar said as he placed his right index finger, which had now lengthened considerably, onto Carlisle's temple. The vice president shifted nervously in his chair but could not resist the implausibility of what he was seeing and feeling.

"Do you hear me, John?" A voice spoke in his head. Edgar sat passively, but Carlisle realized he heard Tomis' thoughts.

Carlisle concentrated. *Edgar, can you read my thoughts?*

"Yes, John, I can communicate with you like this, although it might fry your brain like an egg."

Carlisle frantically tried to pull himself away from Edgar's alien finger on his skull. He was both frightened and enthralled. *Relax, John, I'm joking. My people do that a lot. Don't worry. I am not going to fry your brain. I could probably put the image of your secretary Grace dancing naked into your head—*

Please, NO! thought John.

I'm still joking, John. I wouldn't want to see that either. However, we are thinking together now. Does this answer your question?

Carlisle moved his lips silently, somewhat in shock, and

thought, *Yes, can we stop now?*

Edgar removed his extended fingers from the vice president's head, and immediately the connection was broken.

"Are you all right?"

John rubbed the side of his head and then smiled pleasantly. "Yes, I feel better than I have for a while."

"I understand completely. This kind of connection activates some chemicals in the brain that yield contentment. We often do this among our species as well. You might say that it is the way that we Panruk get high. Something like your whiskey."

Carlisle slouched in his chair, lowered his head, and just kept repeating "holy cow," as the truth of what Edgar, the Panruk alien, said was beginning to gel.

After a bit, the VP lifted his head in excitement as if he'd come to a revelation that would solve the galaxy's problems. "Wait! What if other sentients were able to travel through time and integrate nanites? Wouldn't that take humanity off the radar?"

"Maybe." sighed Edgar. "Unfortunately, every being that has tried has died miserably."

Carlisle deflated. He was now distraught, and the reality of the alien peril was like rising floodwaters. There were other intelligent species and at least one intent on attacking earth. The threat, which he was beginning to accept as truth, was, for lack of a better description, scary as every frightening sci-fi story combined.

Fortunately, the mind connection with Edgar mildly intoxicated him, and he was able to divert his attention to something more mundane. "Edgar, may I ask you something else?" said Carlisle, maneuvering his thoughts away from the Mazik while letting the mellow feeling of the Panruk's touch soothe him.

"Shoot."

"What's your actual name?

Edgar looked embarrassed. His big, black mustache shifted upwards as the alien gave the vice president a big, fat smile and laughed.

"I never expected *that* to be your question after having met only three times," he began amusingly. "Where I come from, in my culture, asking someone their name is considered a proposal between the sexes. Utterly flattering, Mr. Vice President, but we're not a good match since our DNA is at least 15% dissimilar."

Carlisle turned red. "I'm sorry if I insulted you."

Edgar snorted with laughter. "Not a problem at all. I am actually complimented. You see, I am what your anthropologists would consider *female*."

Carlisle tried to wrap his thoughts around that but could not get past Edgar's broad masculine grin topped by a thick, black mustache.

"As far as my name," said Edgar. "It is Shelet Pir Sahm Mim, which you could translate as a sun that portends a warm day."

John looked at Edgar. "You know, Edgar, that is a beautiful name. Really."

"Thank you. My parents think so."

"Should we humans also fear your species?" asked Carlisle.

"John," said Shelet Pir Sahm Mim. "It is not my species that you must fear, but rather the Mazik and whoever Mazik Bah-Gahn can convince to back him."

"Like who?"

"There are other species out there. Mazik Bah-Gahn, however, is on your doorstep.

"As the leader of his entire planet, all his subjects become *him*. The life of every being is devoted to him. They kneel in chants of praise for him. It is a level of fealty that humans, as individualists, cannot comprehend. If Mazik Bah-Gahn tells an entire continent on his world to self-immolate, then they would do so to fulfill the command of Mazik Bah-Gahn. It is his utter rule—he has no respect for you humans or your culture."

The VP looked straight at Edgar. "So, what can we do?"

"Do?" Edgar asked, "you do nothing. It is unlikely that the Mazik Bah-Gahn will show up and drop kinetic weapons on your planet. There are protocols even for him," Unless he chooses outright war with the Council, thought Edgar. "The chances that he will straightaway destroy your species is relatively low at this point. That is the estimate of our analysts. As it is, he has defied the Council. His trip here is not *agreed.* The Council will demand a price from the Mazik because he has done what was not sanctioned.

"One thing that is not different anywhere is the recognition of power, and the Council is nervous. Over 2000 of your years have seen the Council maintain peace between planets. The Mazik could tear it all down, so all parties on the Council are working to make love and not war. However, these galactic issues are way beyond your control—you are tiny little primitives for now."

"I need to know, Edgar. The black cube, the AI, does that belong to the Mazik?"

"The AI belongs to no one."

"Then why did the AI even agree to snatch Bonner and send him to the Mazik? Why didn't it just say no!?"

"You cannot read the mind of an AI. If *Allison* had not consented to send your 'guinea pig,' then Mazik Bah-Gahn would feel justified to come here and end you. He would use the refusal of the AI to send a sample human as proof that you are indeed a threat."

Something occurred to Carlisle. "Are you saying that the AI can't say no to the Mazik? We will have no chance. The AI will bring down all our technology, and we'll become barbarians!"

"The Mazik cannot command the AI. No one can," explained Edgar. "Consider it like this: you had a chess computer called Big Blue. It beat your chess champions, but it was still a challenge. Now, you have computers that play chess that cannot be beaten. *Allison* is finite, but she is so far advanced that it is virtually impossible to understand her calculations. She calculated that Bonner had to be sent, that the Mazik would come, and the AI is convinced that Howe is the only hope for your species. This is a delicate dance, and everyone, even you humans, gets a turn."

Carlisle accepted what he admittedly could not fully understand, then asked, "When are the Mazik coming?"

"Their ship will come to observe in 30 hyperspace jumps. Mazik Bah-Gahn cannot move instantly through time and space, unlike humans. He must jump from point to point, and he is far away in galactic terms. In between jump points, as your sci-fi writers have predicted, he must travel well below the speed of light. That means Jump-Wait-Jump-Wait, many times. It will take about an Earth year."

John didn't know whether he should feel relieved or petrified. *One year*, he thought.

Edgar continued. "When the Mazik arrives, he will observe, and it won't be Mazik Bah-Gahn, but rather a ship of Mazik soldiers commanded by a trusted captain. That is the accepted protocol that has been agreed to for a thousand years. If he is content that you are not a threat, then he may offer some ceremonial kinetic weapons strikes to put you in your place. He may even let you choose the city that he will bombard. It is hard to know. My people have asked me to help you plan. As I said, they are pacifists, as am I, but I am also a realist. We will wait for Howe to finish his mission, and then we will see."

"Wait? Wait for what?" said the panicked vice president.

"Howe. I am trying to make you understand that Dr. Howe is your glimmer of hope if the Mazik are not satisfied that you are an impotent, nascent species."

"Let's get him here now!"

Edgar did his best to display a calming face. "That would be impossible. Right now, he is in New Jersey fighting the British."

"The British?" Carlisle queried while throwing his hands in the air, desperately confused.

"Yes, Mr. Vice President," said Edgar. "The British, in 1776."

Chapter 30

As predicted, the British soldiers on the east side of the Great Falls went northeast and then marched in a counter-clockwise turn. They approached the west side with expectations of meeting Captain Durst. Instead, they mainly found dead British soldiers and a few injured.

"Davis," shouted Captain Ralmore. "Search for wounded and get me a count."

"Yes sir," said Sergeant Davis as he took 15 men to search for any wounded that could be helped. The sergeant assigned another platoon sergeant to count the dead.

"Davis," the captain called a second time. "See if Captain Durst is here. Check every dead body."

Ralmore looked around at the number of dead. It was a thorough thrashing of Durst's unit. The carnage before him made no sense. It looked like nearly all of them were killed. He watched the movements of his sergeant. It seemed that the soldier was going from one corpse to the next.

"Sir," shouted Davis as if he'd found gold. "I have a survivor!"

The captain sprinted over to the injured man. His wound was a bloodied leg from what appeared to be a gunshot, but it was nothing like Ralmore had seen. It had a small entry and a large exit through the muscle in the thigh. Davis was cleaning up the wound and tying a tourniquet. It was hard to imagine what kind of musket ball could make a wound like that.

"Soldier," asked the captain. "Tell me what happened."

With an arduous effort, the private managed to piece together some complete sentences while enduring the pain in his leg.

"Sir, every man around me was falling. The musket balls were striking us as though we were standing in front of them, tied to trees. The whole platoon was struck in the body. It just tore through us. Captain Durst told us that we faced only seven traitors."

"Thank you, private. We shall bring you to the doctor to see about that leg."

Ralmore walked up to the west side of the Falls. There was almost nothing to be seen, just rocks. He walked the edge of the Falls to check for indications that soldiers had lain there. He then stepped carefully to the middle of the bluff west of the falls and examined the ground. One soldier had been shooting from this spot, or a minimal number anyway. He walked to the northern ridge and saw something glinting in the moonlight. The captain bent down and picked up a small brass cylinder with a hole in one end. It was an oddity that he'd never seen before, but it had to be important. Ralmore put it in his pocket and hoped that showing it to General Dorcester would not yield an unpleasant result.

General Dorcester's smile was proof of his horribly foul mood. He'd sent out 100 men, but only half returned. The general snorted out of his thin nose like a small bull. How was it possible that Washington's platoon of seven had destroyed a unit of 50? They must have had perhaps 200 men lying in wait! However, that was also impossible because Captain Ralmore stood before him, claiming no evidence of that on the ground.

"Captain," questioned Dorcester. "How could you know that there was no company of men on the west side of the Falls?"

"General Dorcester, sir, the grounds were undisturbed. In my experience, no group of 200 soldiers could occupy that side of the falls without telltale signs."

"That leaves us with only a few options. Let us deliberate," said Dorcester as he stomped over and began to drum on his desk. "Either there were 200 traitor soldiers, or a small group that could wipe out Durst's unit, or Durst's unit shot themselves. Which is it?"

Captain Ralmore knew the general's bizarre penchant for giving underlings multiple-choice questions. Then, depending on the answer, the general would find varying degrees of fault. Some level of corporal punishment typically followed that. He decided to say what he felt and parried the general's question.

"Sir, three bodies were unaccounted for at the site, and, based on talking to the men, the missing three were Captain Durst, Sergeant Guller, and a—Sergeant Magath."

A shrill laugh filled the tent as Dorcester pulled his saber and swung it madly at his desk, hacking away a chunk of wood. He threw the sword at the side of the tent and screamed, "Captain Ralmore, do not tell me that Magath is unaccounted for!"

Dorcester suddenly froze and then locked his eyes on Ralmore. It was eerily quiet as he waited for an answer from the captain. Ralmore recognized that the general had laid him on a razor's edge.

"Sir," said the captain, aware of his peril. "I found no trace of those men, including Sergeant Magath."

The general skewered his subordinate with a sinister look, stepped back, and sat. Ralmore breathed an internal sigh of relief. He did not know that telling Dorcester the truth would be accepted, but apparently, it was the right thing to do for now.

"Did you search?"

"Yes sir, we covered about 150 yards in each direction, but no sign of them, dead or alive."

"Perhaps you did not search far enough!"

"That is possible, general, although I believe it could be that the traitors hurled the bodies of those men into the river. That must be considered as well."

The captain decided to go for broke, hoping that the truth would not incur Dorcester's wrath. He reached into his pocket and pulled out the brass piece.

Ralmore held out his palm. "General, I did recover this lying on the ground from where the traitors launched their ambush."

The general eyed the small brass shell. He snatched it from the captain's hand, held it to his nose, and sniffed. It smelled something like gunpowder.

"What is this *thing*?" demanded the general.

"I have no inkling, sir."

Dorcester sat back in his chair and took an uncomfortably long time pondering something.

"Captain Ralmore, this is the second time that an alleged small number of troops bested a larger group of our own. First Timmons, and now this.

"Let us reason together, captain. If you are correct that 200 troops could not have been there, that leaves them shooting themselves. Do you think Durst shot his own troops and then ran away in some insane fit?"

"No sir"

"Since these enemies of ours cannot actually fly—that leads to the logical conclusion that Washington's soldiers must have superior weapons. And this," he held up the brass casing, "must be our proof."

Ralmore, relaxed slightly. His retrieval of the brass casing had been a wise choice. He had survived the Great Falls and, more importantly, Dorcester's psychotic labyrinth of a mind.

The safe return of Recon reflected brightly on General Washington's countenance. Indeed, his Excellency glowed with satisfaction to see all eight of his elite forces return in one piece. Granted, Lewis would take a couple of weeks for his sore rib to begin to look somewhat normal. Fortunately, Howe's camouflaged uniforms turned out to be more than just clothing, thanks to the Kevlar lining.

Now, the burden and stress of Reed's treachery would take center stage. In what possible way should he deal with a backstabbing turncoat like him? How could Reed even live with himself? His espionage had resulted in the murder of dozens of men, women, and even children. George was infuriated. He wanted to take Reed and wring his neck with his bare hands. The image of the dead of Bergen's Pond scorched his brain, and he clenched his fists in bitter anger.

The general asked Major Howe to walk with him a short distance from the camp. They had reached a quiet spot among some pines where they were out of earshot.

"Aaron, please address me as George for the moment. I want to talk man to man."

"Yes, George," replied Howe, noticing his commander looking quite worried.

"I never believed that I would face such agonizing deceit. Let us review the facts. The name Bergen's Pond was given to Reed as your destination, and he was also told it was your home. We know what torment and outright murder took place there.

"We then offered Reed another chance by letting him know that you would be reconnoitering east of the Great Falls. Lo and behold, a large force arrived there intending to eradicate you. I just cannot fathom it!"

Washington paused to give Aaron a chance to speak.

"George," Aaron began. "I didn't want to believe it, but I cannot ignore the truth. Please allow me to speak like the scientist whom I am trained to be."

Washington nodded tiredly, "By all means."

"Before I was born, a mathematician and philosopher named Bertrand Russell lived. He restated a concept known as Occam's Razor, which is a problem-solving principle in its simplest form. The origin goes back to a friar from the early 1300s, but Russell restated it as follows: Whenever possible, substitute constructions out of known entities for inferences to unknown entities.

"It's been an obsession of mine to find moments to use this logic, and I believe that Reed's case is as good as any."

Washington gave Aaron a wistful look. "If I understand you

correctly, you are saying that Russell would say to build your logic based on things you know. Do not obscure the truth with extraneous machinations?"

"I believe, George, that your interpretation is close enough. Reed had three condemning facts against him; sorry, there are actually four." Howe began counting them off on his fingers. "One, Bergen's Pond. Two, the demand by Durst to know where Howe lived in Bergen's Pond. Three, the ambush of Recon by the Great Falls. Four, his journey to the NW of our camp, obviously to meet his spy.

"George, what are the odds that all these things are random?" Aaron leaned back against a tree and waited. "Oh, and another thing, I have recorded all the tracking data on Reed's ride towards the British camp instead of going to Morristown for grain. That's part of number four."

Reluctantly, Washington accepted the truth.

"Aaron, when and if he comes back from Philadelphia, you will take him for what you called field maneuvers. There will be an accident. I am certain. I will never be able to garner the support of Congress to execute him so that it will be in your hands."

Chapter 31

Angela had waited for her husband in the basement of One Observatory Circle. With her help, he dusted off his tunnel clothes, slammed the door behind him, and then crushed his dearest Angela to his chest. She returned his embrace, sensing his need for support. John shuddered, and she knew instinctively that this would be one of those rare occasions when he wept.

She gave him time. The silent hug was the right thing to give until he was ready to talk, and she knew instinctively that whatever had happened—now he would tell her. That's how it was with John Carlisle, rancher and politician. He could only go on for so long with tremendous burdens before he had to share the strain.

After a time in the quiet cellar, John whispered "Angela" in her ear. They sat together as he began to confess the truth of what had weighed on him with growing intensity. He told her of the first contact with the aliens and how it had started with a simple text message. Then, the search for the AI, the covert use of I.S., and ultimately his contact with Edgar. He didn't conceal the threat of the Mazik. He explained to her that the aliens would put humanity under a magnifying glass and decide whether they would survive.

If Mazik Bah-Gahn gave mankind a reprieve, then the minimum damage to the Earth would be a kinetic weapon strike from space. The alternative would be the elimination of humans. Forever.

Angela knew her husband. He may have found his way around the Washington jungle of deception and lies, but deep down, he was a country boy. He was able to maneuver around the political establishment, but he was always straight with her.

She gently held his face between her warm palms. "How much time do we have?"

In a hoarse voice, he answered, "About a year."

"Tell me what you said before, a kinetic weapon; what does that mean for us?"

He sighed deeply and thought of their children and grandchildren. "Angela, it means they would drop asteroids on us from space, aimed at population centers. A small number will be the best we can hope for. That would take out whole cities, like London, Moscow, Washington, and Chicago, and level them to dust. Perhaps, if we are lucky, maybe only one city."

Angela paused. "Can we just specify Washington?"

They both laughed—a tension-breaking laugh, and John replied, "Maybe we can send them a list?"

He took the opportunity to kiss her briefly and bury his face into her mane of hair. She was his rock.

"What can we do?" she asked.

He then told her about Howe and the AI. And that there were very hidden details known only to the AI, but that Howe was humanity's best hope.

"Who is he?"

"Honey," Carlisle said. "He's a wealthy, eccentric recluse. He's also a genius. Howe makes excellent money but drives around in a 10-year-old SUV or a 1970 Oldsmobile. He has no wife and hasn't had a girlfriend since college.

"What more can I tell you? Maybe the most significant thing is that he went through a childhood trauma—his family was killed. He was raised in an orphanage, but he is so damn smart that he finished his Ph.D. when he was very young. Now he's 35, and the whole planet is riding on this guy."

Angela considered what she had heard. "Get him here asap," she blurted out. "If we have a year, and he's the lynchpin, then get his ass here, and we'll figure out what we need to do!"

John squeezed her hand. "It isn't that simple!" He tried to take the edge off of his frustrated tone.

"Why?" she asked. "Just call Howe up and get his tush here. Or we'll go there."

Carlisle prepared the next bombshell.

"It's not that easy because we can't reach him now.".

In frustration, Angela pushed away his hand. "John! You are the vice president, and we're talking about our children and grandchildren. Just call him! He could be anywhere on the whole stupid planet and you could still find him!"

He looked into her dark brown eyes and said softly, "Angela dear, have you ever read H.G. Wells' *Time Machine*?"

*

Count Colonel Carl Von Donop had been dispatched by his commanding officer, General Leopold Philip de Heister, in late November to meet with General Huxley Dorcester. Von Donop was a good fit for any debate with the little general because he'd distinguished himself in battle but was also known to be cruel to surrendering troops, usually bayonetting them. The count was cold and unyielding.

It was known that to engage Donop's troops meant no quarter, always death, and no prisoners. His Hessian fighters were unusually fearless, and it was said that they would fight to the last man rather than give up. Donop, himself, was known to be intrepid in battle. He was a trim man, confident and quick. It was known that he cherished the chance to duel with enemy officers.

Von Donop was rumored to make snide comments while prancing, sword in hand, his Hessian hat atop his mane of dark hair. He'd never lost and always skewered his enemies in the end. After stabbing his foe, he would sit on the ground and wrap his arm around the dying officer's shoulders. He would then recite tales of his childhood as if reading a bedtime story to a child. The fear of the count was pervasive.

Just days prior, General Dorcester sent an urgent message to General de Heister urging him to bring his 4,000 Hessian troops to support the British presence west of Hackensack. This request was viewed harshly by de Heister. According to his established protocol, he sent Colonel von Donop to determine what the

British general required.

Von Donop rode into the British encampment on November 29. He had thirty men with him. In the late afternoon, under cold and ominous skies, the colonel approached Dorcester's command tent, hoping to fluff off the British general. He also wished he'd get a fine supper out of the meeting.

"Good afternoon, General Dorcester," said von Donop as he was led into the private dining tent. Around him stood several waiters holding trays of delightful-looking foods. The table had been set for two, and Dorcester stood waiting. The general wore a fine uniform, his hair slicked back, and wearing a ceremonial saber. Warm light from a dozen lamps illuminated the tent.

"Welcome, Colonel von Donop," announced Dorcester. "Please make yourself comfortable. Perhaps you would like a brandy?"

"*Danke*, general."

The two men sat to enjoy their spirits, but Dorcester was eager to relieve his troubled mind. He took a sip of his drink and then looked straight at the Hessian colonel.

"Colonel, I am disappointed that General de Heister could not come himself."

"The general apologizes for his inability to come, Herr General, but he cannot leave the army unattended," replied von Donop.

If there was one thing that Dorcester was not, it was patient when it came to matters that weighed on him. Cornwallis was far away. Washington was near, and with the correct balance of eagerness and cunning, Dorcester knew that he could crush the rebellion. That meant a level of favor and gratitude from the king that would be unmatched.

"Colonel, just 20 miles from here is the rebel camp. My scouts tell me with great certainty that they are just 2,000 men and that Washington is among them.

"I have 1,000 fine soldiers here now, but that is insufficient. I believe that even your entire brigades would find Washington difficult to battle."

Von Donop chuckled. “Surely you must be mistaken. We are now camped with perhaps just less than 5,000 men. They are very fierce fighters, I assure you. We could dispatch Washington and end this fiasco, with all due respect, General Dorcester,” said von Donop with an air of arrogance mixed with confidence.

“Colonel, everyone knows of your army’s reputation; nevertheless, the Continental Army is equally fierce and skilled.”

At this, von Donop nearly spilled his brandy. “General, we can destroy Washington and his 2,000 men with a smaller force. What does he possess? My men will charge into battle and never cease. They are fearless and will not be halted once they are unleashed. You might call them the hounds of Hell.”

Dorcester signaled for a refill, and a speedy and enthusiastic Captain Morrisey poured more brandy for his general.

“Colonel, I am quite sure that your men are fearless and can crush most enemies, but Washington has dedicated fighters and better weapons.”

“Indeed, general,” said von Donop, feeling maligned. “This is really quite unexpected. We battled the continental troops in Brooklyn and crushed them under our boots. My men took no prisoners. We left only bodies.”

Dorcester gulped his drink. “It is certain that you found little resistance against the weak traitorous troops. Washington has much better soldiers now. In truth, I believe it would be difficult for your entire army to crush under your boots.

“Let me show you something.” Dorcester reached into his pocket and pulled out the brass casing. He held it up so that it would reflect in the glowing light. He stretched his hand out for von Donop to inspect but withdrew it. “Perhaps you would like some food before we talk about the weapons of our enemies?”

Von Donop looked hard at Dorcester. “Ah, but general, your little brass token intrigues me. What is it?”

Huxley smiled. “This token is the reason why you cannot trounce Washington. It is their new method of shooting musket balls at you.” He extended his arm.

"Do let me see it, please, general." Von Donop took the casing and held it. It didn't look like much of a musket round. It was too small. How could it stand up against a .75-caliber ball?

"Impossible."

Dorcester smiled broadly. "I agree, it is impossible, but they are using these to fire their weapons more quickly. I believe that we can fire four shots in a minute. I think they can fire 5 or 6, maybe more."

The egotistical colonel smirked. "Let us judge that you are correct. It will not be enough to halt or even slow my troops."

Dorchester worked his way closer to the Hessian colonel. "That is why now is the time to attack Washington. That is why I asked de Heister to send troops. We must destroy Washington's troops in New Jersey before the fullness of winter. If he can bring more troops equipped with muskets that shoot more quickly, they would be a real threat. Perhaps now, while they are small in number, it will be possible to bayonet them all. In the spring, it may be 'impossible' to use your own terminology.

"Would you not like to lead your Hessian troops to end this war? Not wait for Cornwallis? If we take Washington now, then you will have won the war. What would that mean for you?

General de Heister is more than ready to retire to his estate, am I right? Who should be reaping the rewards of victory, von Knyphauser, your general's heir apparent?" prodded Dorcester.

Von Knyphauser! Von Donop's feelings for the man were no secret anywhere in the colonies. He felt sick and bitter. "Knyphauser should join de Heister somewhere far from me!"

"That is why you need to bring your Hessians here! How many will de Heister let you commit to battle now?"

Von Donop felt like he was being sucked into a trap. If he brought 3,000 troops, then when it was all over, Dorcester would call it his own victory, and it would be another glorious triumph with no recognition.

The colonel eased back in his chair. His mind wandered off as he pictured the fantasy battle. There was no reason why

Dorcester could not somehow die in the combat, he mused. That would leave von Donop in command. Count von Donop would deliver victory to the king of England. What would that be worth?

Observing von Donop's wistful countenance pleased Dorcester. He believed he had hit the proper tone to lure in the Hessian colonel. He sought to awaken von Donop from his daydream and captured the colonel's attention with a snap of his fingers. "Colonel, you look as though you have the battle already planned."

Von Donop smiled. "Actually, general, I believe I do."

Major Howe sat with Recon. They were done with their training for the day. Aaron took it easy on them and let them settle for an early dinner. Lewis's ribs still looked pretty ugly, but he was Recon's hero. It also gave him another story to tell. As they ate a sumptuous dish, which Major Howe had called grilled cheese, Monty was somehow giving off waves of aggravation.

"What is your concern, Monty?" asked Clark.

"Is it that obvious?"

Recon squirmed a bit and listened as Monty went right to it.

"Where the hell is Reed?"

"Yes," said Allen. "He never returned from Philadelphia."

"Do you think he was delayed?" asked Schein. "Or perhaps he ran to Cornwallis?"

Rogers, who was generally quiet, spoke. "He wouldn't dare go to Cornwallis and surely not to Dorcester after failing him twice. Truly it is logical that going to Dorcester might be fatal."

"Let's wait and see," advised Howe. "He could be running around Philadelphia trying to get Washington removed from command. If that happens, then we have to make new plans. For now—we wait."

There was an understandable pause, but Mercy couldn't help herself.

"Maybe he got eaten by a horse," she said.

Lewis laughed despite his injury. "I feel bad for the horse."

"What should we do with his horse?" asked the Scot.

Dorcester was particularly delighted. Nearby stood a fine horse.

"Tell me again, my Scottish friend, how did you end up with this fellow?" inquired Dorcester as he gazed out from his open tent towards the good-looking stallion.

The Scot was sitting stoutly on a rough wooden chair in the general's office. He was smoking a pipe. His large, worn boots propped up on a stool. The spy appeared quite pleased with himself as he stroked his jet-black beard. He turned to the general and began a short story between puffs of tobacco.

"Sometimes I have the good fortune to square things with those who cross me," he began. "You know I am not a big talker, so suffice it to say that I followed your foul, little spy. It wasn't easy. He had two soldiers with him. My own web of informants watched Reed when he was in Philadelphia. When he exited the city, apparently to return to Washington, I merely set a little trap, and the fool walked right into it. Too bad about his escorts. They seemed like nice enough young fellows."

Dorcester gave the Scot a sly look. "Are you sure he is dead?"

The Scot held up his hands and then slapped them together loudly. "I broke his neck with my two hands. He whimpered like a coward when I had killed his guards. I knocked him off this fine animal here and told him that he only gets to cross you twice."

"I do like that part, my friend."

"Of course, I relieved him of his gold and horse."

"Where is the body?" asked Dorcester.

"I dragged the three bodies some distance from that particular trail. I doubt they will be found until they are bones."

Dorcester seemed satisfied. It was the third time he had had the Scot retell the tale of Reed's death, and it was just as enjoyable as the first. He looked at the Scot, who was now eating a chicken leg while simultaneously dropping bits onto his bushy beard.

"Did I tell you that the chair upon which you sit belonged to my father?"

With his mouth half full, the Scot shook his head and then carelessly wiped a sticky, wet finger on the arm of the chair.

"I sincerely revered my father. What about you, my loyal spy? Did you fear your father?"

The man wiped his mouth on his sleeve. "Never saw the man. He was hung when I was a tot." Then he laughed and said, "I believe my mum kicked the chair out from under him while he was in the noose!"

The general smiled slightly. "Perhaps you can step outside while I contemplate your compensation."

The spymaster gripped the arms of the chair with his greasy hands and stood. He brushed off his soiled jacket, nodded to the general, then walked out. Dorcester immediately closed the flap and impulsively grabbed a rag. Within seconds he was buffing the chair in an effort to remove the stains. He grunted and growled for several moments as he rubbed the wooden arm. Unable to clean it all, he furiously kicked the chair over. Suddenly calm and serene, he stuck his head out of the tent. "Morrisey!" he shouted.

Immediately, Captain Morrisey appeared with his usual look of restrained fright.

"Come in here for a moment, captain. I have a task for you."

Morrisey leaped to fulfill his general's orders. Always.

"Captain Morrisey is it?" asked the Scot.

Morrisey was on horseback with the spy riding alongside. The two were now a half-mile from the British encampment heading west. As instructed, Morrisey did his utmost to avoid conversation with the large and vulgar man. Presently, they rode through a thickly wooded area, still not bare from the approaching chill.

“Yes, that is correct.”

“And where is it that we are going exactly?”

“The general instructed me to take you to his treasure. When we camped here, he placed caches of valuables that he had taken from traitors to the king.” He swiveled on his mount, “You should consider it quite an honor.”

Something about Morrisey’s relaxed demeanor was unsettling, but gold was gold.

“Look,” pointed Morrisey. “It is just behind those two large trees.”

The Scot looked ahead and then back at the captain, who had now drifted behind him. “I have been meaning to ask, how did you lose your teeth, captain? I am sorry if this is a rude question.”

Morrisey smiled. “The man who did this to me was as big as a mountain, but I survived the beating. I deserved it, though, because I had angered the general.”

“That ‘tis truly shocking. I wonder how you could have so incensed the man?”

Morrisey shivered. “It does not take much, but I have learned to watch for the signs. I can tell when Dorcester is angry. Sometimes the littlest things will force him to release his wrath. People who do not know the general can make *mistakes*.” He looked up at the Scot while simultaneously placing his calm hand on his loaded pistol. “Here we are. Shall we dismount and claim your reward?”

Chapter 32

General de Heister felt displeased but was in no doubt that some liquor would undo his moodiness. Food and drink, he thought while contemplating his girth—the Hessian general's attire was stretched to the limit.

In the old days, he was trim like von Donop, but those were the very old days. He peered out from the small shack erected for his command post. It was now early December, and the icy grip of winter was slow in coming. He pondered the orderliness of the Hessian encampment. It covered a vast area and was home to 4,500 soldiers.

Since arriving in New Jersey, a steady stream of foodstuffs came into the camp. Much of it arrived from New York, but the loyalists of New Jersey gave freely. Some had to be prodded by bayonet threats, but they were ultimately happy to supply the cause of King George III.

General de Heister longed to return to his home, but his pride required that he do his part to suppress Washington's imbecilic uprising. The coward Cornwallis had chosen to wait out the winter in New York. Wilhelm von Knyphauser, the German general, was not much better than the British and avoided New Jersey.

"Colonel," said de Heister. "Tell me, what is the benefit of committing 3,000 of my men to join with Dorcester? It is nearly winter, and what good will it do us to throw our troops in with Dorcester instead of Cornwallis?"

"General," answered von Donop. "Washington is resupplying. By the spring, he will have tripled his forces, and they are well-supplied already. If we wait, it will be inconceivable that we could crush Washington without Cornwallis."

Von Donop waited for the old gears in his general's head to

unstick themselves. He knew well that the ego of the old man was his weakness. The general expected that he would never be permitted the opportunity to halt Washington's rebellion. The late autumn transfer of the Hessians to New Jersey was a surprising and unexpected gift. As the Hessian general, his latitude in choosing battlegrounds was limited to his British masters.

On the other hand, a victory over Washington would end the rebellion, and the glory would be his. That meant recognition by the king and wealth. Wealth in his old age to build his own dynasty. The offer was enticing.

"And what is your interest in finishing off Washington now?" bellowed de Heister coldly as he glared at the colonel.

"Merely serving you as you strive for victory," offered von Donop.

"Kuhscheisse," cursed de Heister. "You want power and glory, just like your late father did when he slashed his way through the Fatherland. Admit it!"

The general's needle-like stare merely stoked von Donop's contempt. He paused to let de Heister stew in his anger.

"General," he explained. "We all have ambitions. I am prepared to wait for my turn. Your success is mine as well. You get to retire after defeating Washington, and with your blessing, I move ahead to lead where you left off. Is that not a fine scenario?"

The old senior officer grinned coldly and made a snap decision. "Very well. Take 3,000 troops to Dorcester. The worst case is that you return them to me after Washington has fled. You will command them. Be sure that the general understands that these are Hessian troops. Colonel, I believe you will make a good general someday, provided I do not kill you myself."

Von Donop returned the sinister stare and then smiled congenially. As he exited, he whispered subtly under his breath, "Not if I get you first, my general."

Howe and Washington observed each battalion as the soldiers practiced assaulting enemy positions. Washington had divided his 1,900 healthy soldiers into three battalions. They had been playing wargames with paint pistols for a straight month. In his spare time, Howe grilled the battalion leadership on everything he'd learned while playing combat with his dad's marine buddies.

Washington was content yet still concerned. If Dorcester attacked, he felt confident that they would crush him. The skirmish with Timmons and the more significant battle with Durst proved that modern weapons made muskets virtually ineffective. The keyword was virtually, but if the Hessians joined ranks with Dorcester, the Continental Army would be outnumbered almost three to one. It wasn't a drawn-out shooting battle that concerned Washington. It was the *what if*. What if the Hessians managed a flanking maneuver and then all charged at once?

"I'm seeing the concern on your face, general," stated Howe.

"Aaron, I want you to know that you have become more than just a surprise major. I consider you a friend."

"General, I am honored to be called your friend. I would never have expected it, and I feel the same way, with an added measure of deference, sir."

Washington looked into the forest and watched the men moving about in a coordinated fashion. It was indeed a marvel to see professionalism delivered by what was once a disgruntled and disarrayed mob.

"Look at them, Aaron," he said. "They move like a flock of birds or maybe a pride of lions."

"I do not envy the British."

Washington nodded his agreement. "We are going to attack them. I am not waiting for them. We are going soon."

"General, we have an advantage on defense," suggested Howe.

"Of course, I am aware of that, but if we wait, we will see 20,000 British in the spring. Even with your weapons, we may not be victorious against 8,000 Hessians charging us, flanking us.

"Until we can outfit 10,000 soldiers with AK's, we will be at risk, but if we can destroy Dorcester with the Hessians now? Just imagine the pressure that would exert on Cornwallis to stay in New York. If we could liberate New Jersey completely, they would never be able to get across the Hudson. After that, we build and then assault. Even the mad king would have to accept defeat," said Washington enthusiastically.

Howe rubbed the back of his neck and looked out over the camouflaged battalions drifting through the forest like ghosts. It was impressive.

"General, I'm not convinced King George would stop if he lost New Jersey or even New York. This is bigger than that. It's about his view of the British Empire. On the other hand, Cornwallis would accept the truth. Perhaps others would admit it, but the king would not. He would replace them and then send 100,000 or 200,000 troops.

"I think we have to hope that parliament will demand that the war be halted or that the king will fall off a galloping horse."

Washington mulled over Aaron's comment. "I would hope that facing weapons like ours would be enough to shake them to their core."

"Cornwallis, yes," said Howe. "But not the British so far away in England—those aligned with the king. They won't believe that the empire could be chased off our shores. We need to pray that our destruction of Dorcester and the Hessians will persuade enough Brits to accept defeat. Either that or—"

"—or King George meets his demise suddenly, tragically, and fortuitously," said Washington completing the thought. He added, "Perhaps he will choke on a chicken's wing."

"Pass me a polkey," said Schein. Not only for him but for Recon, this was their very first experience eating fried chicken. Howe believed that they were the happiest he'd ever seen them.

"Polkey, lieutenant?" asked Lewis.

"Corporal," said the food-numb Schein. "Polkey is another name for a chicken leg. I see four left in that pan, and since I made them, I claim three. Be there fools who wish to fight me over it?" challenged Schein as he eyed the members of Recon.

"Aye," said Mercy.

"Exempting you, of course," amended Mordy.

Aaron got up from his beach chair and stretched. "Lewis, you're on kitchen duty. Clean that pan like Schein tells you."

"Yes, sir," said Lewis without his usual cheerfulness.

Howe turned to Mercy. "Come with me Gozen. We need to talk."

After a short walk into the chilly forest, Aaron and Mercy sat down on the beach chairs they carried with them. Aaron looked carefully at Mercy and did his best to read her mood. Since Mercy had killed Durst and Guller, her body vibes were no different. She was still cracking jokes, pushing herself to her physical limits, but at other times appeared to be deep in thought, almost meditative.

She had begun wearing her sleek blond hair once again in a long ponytail. He figured it was a girl-thing, which meant a man couldn't comprehend the connection between a woman and her hair. In truth, it didn't matter how she did her hair; she was exceedingly beautiful.

One thing that was quite amazing was the speed with which the stab wound in her leg healed. A week after the puncture, Aaron asked her to show it to him, and he was surprised to find only a tiny dot. He assumed, and she confirmed that her enhancements could easily handle a small wound like that. Fortunately, the nanites recognized the knife wound immediately and released pain suppressers into her blood. That was almost instantaneous and explained why she barely lost a stride dragging Durst to the Passaic River. She said that her skin would heal up completely. That also explained her seemingly flawless complexion. It was *Allison's* nanites at work.

Sometimes Aaron was astounded that Recon could function

with such an attractive woman in their midst. He figured that Mercy's history and evident power, not just as a woman but as a warrior—helped to bring her acceptance by the old-fashioned men. Recon had seen her demonstrate physical and mental abilities that, in truth, none of them had.

He sat for a minute to contemplate Mercy's situation and his own. Aaron noticed that since he'd first touched *Allison*, his senses seemed to grow sharper. He knew that *Allison* hadn't implanted him, but even without the implants, he felt somehow more in tune. He couldn't explain it, just like he couldn't explain the first zap that he had gotten from the AI.

He tried to tap into this "sense" to figure out what was happening with Mercy. It wasn't easy to discern, but something was happening inside her head. Aaron was sure that no one in Recon could feel it because they wouldn't keep their mouths shut for five seconds. They had a sincere awkward openness among them, and Mercy was part of it.

"What's on your mind, boss?"

He exhaled like a tired, old man. "So many things."

"Wow, that sounds really deep." She used a mildly sarcastic tone that couldn't hide that she cared.

He reached out and touched her hand. She had recoiled the first time he had done that, and he felt as though he had violated a cardinal rule. This time, however, Mercy returned his touch and held his fingers in her own. For a split second, it reminded him of the way *Allison* would express warmth to him. Of course, *Allison* didn't have the physical presence of Mercy, but she was substantive—he'd still not been able to grasp her being, but it was tangible and infinitely more than just the emanation of a machine.

He refocused and looked at Mercy. "We have a problem."

She silently focused on him and gave him the space to continue.

"I have to kill Dorcester."

She took a moment. "Of course, we have to kill Dorcester. He's earned the death penalty many times over."

He decided not to dance around the issue. “That’s not what I mean. What I mean to say is that I have to be the one to kill him.”

“No, Aaron, I have to kill him.” She declared her intention unambiguously. “You know that to fulfill my promise and my mission. I must be the one to do it.”

“Mercy, I completely understand. If it had been a month ago, I would not have had the brains or the sensitivity to comprehend you, but now I do. Still, I have to be the one to kill him.”

She looked at him curiously. “Why? Why is this on you?”

He sighed. “It’s a long story.”

She grabbed his other hand and squeezed. “Great, I’m here, you’re here, nothing else on the schedule tonight, so I’d say we got plenty of time. Hit it. I’m all ears.”

“Dammit,” he blurted out with an audible sigh, his shoulders sagging. He felt like he was carrying the world on his back—Aaron Howe, alias Atlas. “Did *Allison* tell you what happened to me?”

“She didn’t have to. I researched you. When I’m in the lab, or anywhere near WIFI, I can look up stuff in my mind.”

“Yes,” said Aaron. “I knew that, but I forgot.”

“If you’re asking me if I know about Evan Butler, yes.”

Aaron rubbed his forehead. Convincing Mercy was going to require an explanation because it wasn’t her nature to roll over and accept things. He looked at her, dressed up in her camos, pony-tail, and radiating confidence. Of all the people in the world, Mercy had elevated herself to being his prime confidant.

“When I first started talking with *Allison*, a few details were laid on the table. *Allison* told me she was a gift and that I could use her to travel time. The time travel part you already know. She tried to get me to talk about my sister, Julia, especially when I returned after the disaster with the girl from Denhurst. *Allison* pressed me to lay it all out for her, but I brushed her off.

“To keep a long story short, *Allison* told me I could set things right.”

“What does that mean?”

"Believe me, I was confused by that also, so I asked her to explain.

"*Allison* said that getting her, the AI, was not just a gift but also a test. That's the way I remember it. I am pretty sure that it is not just a test for me but for Earth. Maybe I'm just paranoid about that, but I think something much bigger is going on than just me helping Washington win the war. Think about it. Alien AI, a gift *and* a test?" Howe paused. "Who's the giver? Who's the tester? Also, an alien? That adds up to something other than me traveling through time to have fun and kill tyrants. Something bigger is at stake here." He stopped and looked at Mercy questioningly.

"Are you waiting to see if I have something to add to that?" asked Mercy.

He nodded.

"Well, I don't. *Allison* did not tell me. I'm not a pushover, Aaron. I did pressure her to tell me. Once I got the implants, I saw a bigger picture, but *Allison* kept her virtual mouth shut."

Aaron resumed. "She wouldn't tell me more than I needed to know. She's like a 'need to know' AI. Anyway, she asked me to explain why I am so obsessed with 1776 and British atrocities. My response was that I'm a bored, unmarried scientist, and what else am I supposed to do when I'm not in the lab—I got to be obsessive-compulsive about something, so why not the Revolutionary War?"

Mercy was now thinking this through using her enhanced brainpower. "Aaron, you didn't just randomly home in on 1776. It must fit into something bigger."

"Clearly," he said. "*Allison* kept talking about Julia and my dad and said I could fix it. That is the reason why I have to kill the ancestor of Evan Butler."

"Gee," declared Mercy, "that is very theatrical. I wonder if *Allison* is a frustrated Hollywood scriptwriter."

"Yep, it seems like a good job for her, except I think the stakes are exceedingly higher than pleasing Hollywood morons."

"All right," said Mercy. "So what did *Allison* tell you."

"She partly hinted and partly told me that I had to find this progenitor of Butler and kill him. That *I* had to kill him. Get it?"

"I'm not that slow, Aaron. I understand that you think it is Dorcester, and it isn't enough that he should die in battle, but rather you have to be the one to kill him."

"Yes. And I know you might think that that is a stretch, but I actually looked up the history of Dorcester. Dorcester is also spelled Dorchester, and guess what family name branches off from Dorchester in the 1830s?"

She smirked. "Let me guess. Butler?"

"Yes, and not only that, but I *feel* it. I must confront him directly because that confrontation will reveal so much. I know that isn't scientific, but I'm telling you this hunch is for real. I know it."

Mercy tilted her head and stared off into space. After a minute, she smiled and said that she had forgotten but that she had searched the internet for details about Dorcester. She noted that it was in her memory that the name "Butler" was linked. "So, the test, and I don't understand that part yet, is that you will be preventing or validating something by finding and killing this guy. Aaron, you are positive that the guy is Dorcester?"

Aaron looked at her and nodded his head. "Yes."

"And," she added, "if I kill him, then nothing gets fixed. Plus, you fail the test. And, failing the test has implications for the Earth and humans?"

"Bingo."

"Outside of seeing the AI, time travel, implants, and your developing sixth sense, I would say that if I were a psychiatrist, I would recommend inpatient care for you."

He gave her his best fake pissed-off look.

"Sorry, I thought a little comic relief was in order."

He sighed. As capable as he was, Aaron was in turmoil. Mercy leaned over and wrapped her arms around him. Again, he felt that same compassion that he had felt from *Allison*. She leaned back, looked him squarely in his eyes, and said, "You kill

Dorcester."

"Really?"

"Yes," she confirmed. "Durst, Guller, and the Wolves are dead. My job is nearly done. I'm not so obtuse that I would allow you to fail to satisfy my need to pull off a triple play. Settling for Durst and Guller will have to do. I can accept that. If you are correct, Julia's murderer will never be born."

Part of his load was lifted. "Mercy, I never thought I would feel happy that you and I agree I should kill the bad guy."

"That is kinda weird," she acknowledged. "But I would like to go back and see *Allison*."

"Yes, let's talk about that. I've been putting it off for too long."

"This is what I think, Aaron. *Allison* is not out to get you. Unless I am an utter imbecile, I gather that AI is rooting for you. She's a fan. There is something big coming, and if you don't pull off a win with Dorcester, then humans are screwed."

"Whew! Nothing like a little added pressure."

"It's not about the pressure, Aaron. I think that she's waiting for you to tap into something inside you that makes *you* special. Why is it that you were the person to get *Allison*? She knows something that we don't have a clue about."

"What could that be?" he asked.

"I can't even guess," admitted Mercy.

Aaron took a deep breath and leaned back in his beach chair. "Lately, I've had these strange feelings. Like I'm feeling the workings of the world on a gut level. Damn, I can't even explain it. When I first touched *Allison*, that was in Canada. I touched her, and I got zapped. It was like I was opened up, but it doesn't happen all the time. Up there in the tundra, for a split second, my whole being on a molecular level was somewhere else. It frustrates me that I can't describe it any better than that. But since then, I have been different. When it comes to this weird added perception—sometimes I could just be looking down a darkened tunnel, but then there are times when I sense things."

Mercy gave him a blank stare.

"Take Reed, for example."

"You don't need AI to see that he's a rat," said Mercy.

"Was a rat. He's dead."

"How do you know that?" she quizzed.

"Exactly. That is what I'm talking about. I'm not explaining that very well. I just feel like I'm more aware of things, but I don't even have implants."

Mercy looked at him intensely. "That's because the implants don't do that. They do make it possible for me to process data and learn things very quickly, but they don't give me what you seem to have, your ability to sense what is going on better than a normal human. I see what you mean; it's hard to explain."

Something resolved in Aaron's head. "It's decided then. We are going to take on Dorcester. I am certain that at least half the Hessians will fight with him. Something tells me that the Hessians are desperate to wipe us out and end the war right here in New Jersey."

"It's called lust for glory, Aaron."

"Yes, and I think that the Hessian commander knows that if he can end it here while Cornwallis is biding his time in New York, King George will pay many dividends. General de Heister is a bit of a bloated cow. I can't see him lighting his troops on fire to charge us when we are firing AK rounds at them.

"That leaves—

"—von Donop," she said, completing his thought.

"What do we know about him?"

"He was an ambitious guy but notoriously strange." She continued, "Von Donop went back to Europe after Red Bank, angry and bitter."

Aaron interrupted her. "That can't be because he died at Red Bank."

Mercy waved her finger back and forth. "No, no, no, not so, my dear Aaron. He had arranged his own 'death' on the battlefield. History says he died at Red Bank, but that is a load of crap."

"What?" Aaron exclaimed. "How do you know that?"

"Because I'm really good at piecing stuff together. Here's what I think happened: Someone fitting his description returned to Europe in 1777. Too many things point to this. All his property was sold, and his wealth was moved from Hesse-Kassel to Portugal. Who did that? A man listed in the Portuguese records matches von Donop's description. He called himself Bartoliner. He was said to have a large estate, but it was far away from the beaten path. It had a reputation for being a cruel place. He indentured servants and was big on abducting the daughters of his tenant farmers and enslaving them. He also knew how to pay off the right people because no charges were ever brought against him, including plenty of murders that were swept under the rug. He was like a drug lord without the drugs.

"Anyway, they said the locals were terrified of him, even legitimate landowners nearby. They used to call him *lobo luvas*, which in Portuguese translates as the 'gloved wolf.'"

"What the heck is a gloved wolf?"

"He always had a glove on one hand. He told people it was for protection. I think that in Portugal, after all of his dreams were smashed, he went completely insane. They said the castle was full of demons and strange tokens. The guy was completely psycho."

"That is bizarre," said Aaron.

"Yes, and if von Donop is that aggressive, then he will want to put the spotlight on himself, not de Heister, and certainly not Dorcester," said Mercy. "I know this might sound bizarre, Aaron, but think about what we know. First, you must be the one to kill Dorcester. You have a feeling that I am not writing off as delusional on your part. And it is significant. I accept that.

There is something bigger going on here, and we don't have *Allison* in 1776, so we can't know for sure. I don't think we're even supposed to know. Second, there is von Donop, the most wicked kind of power-hungry Hessian there is, and he wants de Heister to stay out of the battle. That means Dorcester is the senior officer here. Battles are never written down in history about who was second in command. The leader of the fight gets the glory, and von Donop knows that if he can finish Washington, that will possibly end the war—end the war with him as the victorious commander. Except for one thing, Dorcester is in charge."

He was once again impressed with her vast knowledge. She laid out the details neatly and led him to the logical inference that needed to be reached. At the same time, her path of knowledge brought him to a place where he was utterly panic-stricken. "Do you know what this means?" he asked her anxiously.

"You tell me."

"We have to keep Donop from killing Dorcester before I do."

Chapter 33

Colonel von Donop found an elevated spot on Buck Mountain, about 20 miles west of Hackensack, where he could observe his battalions of Hessians. They had all arranged their tents in neat rows, except for the 2nd battalion, which was a little sloppy. That irked him, so he made a mental note to discipline the battalion commander personally.

The camp covered a large area below Buck Mountain down to Beaver Brook. Von Donop selected this spot as a good staging area for the march down to Buttermilk Falls.

Convening only eight miles from Washington's camp had von Donop mildly on edge, but the notion of his massive army being attacked was inconceivable. Washington would be a fool to throw away his men; they were outnumbered almost three to one.

After some pressure and having to use de Heister's name, Dorcester agreed that his troops should move to the west of Beaver Brook. That put 1,000 British to the west adjacent to von Donop's 3,500 Hessians. The balance of 1,500 Hessians remained further north with de Heister, and he was pleased to have the self-aggrandizing General de Heister away from the battle where he could not interfere with the victory—*his* victory.

It also kept von Donop well away from any "accident" that might happen to the soon-to-be-retired General de Heister. The colonel thought about that. If something should happen to his general? That would leave himself, Count Colonel von Donop, in an excellent position to reap many rewards.

The Hessian officer massaged his gloved left-hand to relieve his stress. It was a perpetual habit that he had learned to embrace. Simultaneously, he turned to his right and saw Dorcester marching towards him in a peculiar hat, slick boots, and his tailored red coat. His black hair flowed freely like

Cornwallis but without hinting of gray. It struck von Donop that Dorcester strode as if he had already won the war and been named a duke by King George. The Hessian felt a tug of jealousy. The audacity of this skunk of a man to place himself as the empire's hope infuriated him.

"Good day, general," said von Donop cheerfully as Dorcester approached.

"A *Guten Tag* to you, colonel. I would like you to arrange a meeting of your battalion commanders so that I may address them regarding my battle plan."

The colonel suppressed his disgust for the irritating and impudent Englishman. "But of course, Herr General. When would you like to instruct them? Remember that none of them speak the King's English, so I will be happy to translate for you."

"Very well, colonel. To this point, I am quite encouraged by your cooperation. Naturally, I will be directing the attack on Washington's troops. I expect your Hessians to follow my orders explicitly. *Verstehst du*? Did I say that correctly? Do you comprehend my words?"

The furnace inside von Donop was roaring now; nevertheless, he displayed a charming smile. "I compliment you on your German, and I do understand, my general."

Dorcester nodded. "Excellent. We will gather for our meeting today at 3 p.m. Good day, Colonel."

"*Guten Nachmittag*," said General Dorcester to the seven officers gathered before him. The officers greeted him in very broken English. Colonel von Donop proceeded to translate for the British general. Dorcester's plan was simple. He told them they would move in three parallel formations as they marched toward Washington's encampment. He proceeded to describe a flanking maneuver with the British to the west, some Hessians to the east, and the balance of the Hessians to form a frontal assault.

The briefing went on for two hours. Almost from the start,

von Donop translated with denigrating interjections belittling the British general. That was torture for his commanders because of the effort required to restrain their laughter. At one point, Dorcester paused to ask von Donop what Major Gruner found amusing.

Von Donop thoroughly enjoyed himself, making a farce out of Dorcester's presentation. Finally, as the *piece de resistance*, he translated Dorcestor's closing remarks as: "Do whatever your colonel commands because as a tiny general, I am a complete ass."

"My good colonel," said Dorcester as he mounted his horse. "I believe your officers genuinely appreciate strong and unyielding leadership."

Von Donop shoved his gloved hand into his coat pocket and began fiddling with a small silver-plated knife. "Quite so, general. I assure you that your astute perceptions are completely true."

Washington wished he could spend his whole day with Recon. They were eight soldiers who were thoroughly endearing, particularly the young Corporal Lewis. The fellow's stories took the general's mind off his troubles better than any brandy could. However, nothing intrigued him more than Corporal Tomoe Gozen's unexcelled beauty and enticing "ponytail." He wondered if he was younger—

"Right," said Washington. "What is transpiring at the enemy stronghold?"

Lewis handed the general a tablet identical to the one that Howe and Mercy were viewing. Washington had taken to technology like a duck to water.

"General," said Mercy. "We are flying the drone over the enemy encampment now. You can see that they arrayed themselves with about 900 British to the west and about 3,500 Hessians east of them.

"Sir, you cannot tell from the video, but I will overlay a map, and now, you can observe that they are about 8.5 miles north of our position."

Howe interrupted. "Close enough to march here in about 3 hours. They have no artillery. The other 1,500 Hessians further north are holding the artillery. That seems obvious enough. I believe that de Heister thinks that artillery will be unnecessary."

"Opinions?" asked Washington.

"Yes, sir," said Recon in unison, waiting for the general to start the analysis.

"Very well," continued Washington. "My experience is with muskets and artillery. Major, you played wargames with modern weapons. What is our best strategy?"

"General," answered Howe. "For the first opinion, I defer to Corporal Gozen. Let's hear what she has to say."

Mercy cocked her head and, without batting an eyelash, said, "We take the fight to them, sir."

Washington looked at Howe and then back at Mercy. "They are 4,400 strong, and they will be defending. Can we mount an offensive against that?"

Howe answered Washington's query. "Based on the drone video, Dorcester's army, including the Hessians, is poised for offense only. Look at the screen, general. They are stacked and arrayed in rows and columns. We can flank *them*! What I mean is that if we mount an assault stretched out over 800 yards, we can lay down heavy fire on them. How quickly could they spread out and return fire? They are arrayed like an army waiting to march, not fight. That means they do not believe an attack from us will happen. If we have to, we flank east and west. However, if we have an easier time, we can modify the plan as necessary.

"Of course, we shouldn't take chances. No way! However, we have 40 magazines with every soldier. That is 1,200 rounds each multiplied by 1,800 men roughly." Howe did the math in his head. "That is over 2 million rounds to fire off at the enemy. They can shoot maybe 6,000 rounds in a minute on a good day, and we will start outside their effective range."

"That does seem formidable," said Washington in a dry tone.

Howe almost laughed at the understatement. "Sir, in my time, the United States of America developed a philosophy of war called 'shock and awe,' which is also called 'rapid dominance.' The idea is related to using overwhelming force.

"The concept was described by a couple of guys named Ullman and Wade. Essentially, it means that we dominate the battlefield so that we lose very few men, and they lose quickly and give up.

"The alternative is an immoral and unethical philosophy of war called proportionality, which means you have to use less lethal methods, tactics, and weapons so that the fight is fair when civilian casualties might result. Sometime in the future, there will be countries that will be criticized for not losing enough soldiers. Let me tell you how non-sensical this line of thinking is. Imagine attacking an army of bloodthirsty killers that pillage everything in their path. Then comes a stronger army that uses tremendous firepower, wiping out the bad guys by the thousands—but only losing maybe three soldiers. The application of proportionality says that the stronger army used too much force because they only lost three guys."

"Screw that!" said Lewis, visibly stunned by the idea.

"Not exactly, Lewis," said Howe. "If there was a village of women and children mixed in with Dorcester's battalions, would you lay down a million rounds of ammo on them?"

Lewis shook his head. "I see what you mean, sir."

"We don't have that problem here, sir," said Clark.

"Exactly," noted Howe. "It may seem unfair, but I'd rather win fast and hard than use muskets and get our butts handed to us in a sling."

There was a pregnant pause while Washington digested the idea. He pulled on his right ear lobe, which seemed to have become his latest nervous habit. "What if they do not surrender?"

Howe grinned, but it wasn't out of cheerfulness. "If they even have the presence of mind to charge with bayonets, then we cut them down like grass and follow the motto of a famous future general."

"Which is?" asked Monty.

"The object of war is not to die for your country but to make the other bastard die for his."

Every day, twenty-four hours a day, once an hour, Lewis, Allen, or Mercy would fly a drone over the British and Hessians. It was now Sunday, December 8, 1776. Once again, Lewis reported that the enemy camp was still. Fires were burning. Men were milling about. It looked like an army awaiting orders to move but highly relaxed, as if they were extremely confident.

Recon, however, was not milling about. They were preparing to go out ahead of the army to eliminate the forward enemy sentries. Over the past week, they had used the infrared and visuals to spot about ten forward scouts that had been spaced out about a half-mile. The guards were positioned 500 yards from the edge of the enemy camp. They must have been Hessians because Mercy had noticed they were relieved in twelve hours shifts, always precisely on time. That only made Recon's job easier. They planned to go out ahead of the army and eliminate the sentries at about 00:30. That would mean assigning one target to each Recon member with three sentries left over. Those three would be taken out after. It sounded simple on paper, thought Aaron, but it meant being super quiet, and killing those three remaining Hessians was the weakest part of the whole plan.

Communications would be up, and the drone would be tracking the Hessian scouts. Lewis would operate the drone and handle target tracking. With the trees bare, and the cold weather, the heat signatures of the Hessians were apparent. They would first hunt the scouts and then perform the main assault on the British and Hessian encampments. That was the plan on paper, but these scenarios seldom went like clockwork.

Washington and Howe walked through lines of continental soldiers. It had been a week or more since Aaron had visited the main camp. The troops in front of him had practiced for weeks, some doing paintball scenarios, some at the range, and all following the tactics manual Howe prepared for them.

They were no longer a rabble of unhappy farm boys. These men had drilled and explicitly trained to assault the large enemy force. They were warm and outfitted, fed, and ready for battle. The few majors and more captains directing these troops had met repeatedly with Washington to review the tactics manual until they had memorized it perfectly.

Winter camouflage just added to the threat they represented. Howe was impressed with the way they had adapted. Their rifles were clean, their packs were provisioned, and they had massive relative firepower.

As they paced in front of the troops, Washington would randomly pick soldiers and question them about their weapons, ammo, boots, and job. He even knew many of the regular soldiers by name. By the time they had finished, Howe was satisfied, within the constraints of reason, that these men would not crack under pressure.

The Continental Army soldiers were dismissed to eat and rest. They would leave in six hours to bring the battle to King George's Redcoats. Recon would be heading out one hour earlier. The tension was high.

Colonel von Donop looked over his troops. He was only concerned about three things: The frail General de Heister, Dorcester, and, least of all, Washington and his misfits.

According to von Donop's plan, he himself would be in the

midst of attacking Washington when de Heister, miles to the north, would die of unknown causes. He'd waited for a long time to supplant his commanding general, and the final battle with Washington was the ideal moment. His opinion of the man was that de Heister was a pig. And as a pig, he was constantly eating. The colonel had had the forethought to purchase a very nasty poison in New York. Good planning, he'd thought at the time, leads to excellent results.

The poison itself had some remarkable properties. The most desirable was that it caused death in about 24 hours and masked itself like a nasty illness. The next feature, the elegant one, was that it ultimately compromised the heart beautifully. Even a fine doctor would have a difficult time differentiating the poison from a circulation failure due to sickness.

It turned out that de Heister's man-in-waiting was not so devoted. Like so many of the lower classes, gold blinded him. If you searched carefully, you could find a scoundrel almost anywhere. This particular servant had been feeding the general for over a year. He was trusted; hence, the general was as good as dead.

The colonel sat down on his hard, wooden chair directly in front of his command tent. He yelled out a few orders to keep his troops on their toes. His gloved hand worked over the stubble on his chin as his mind began to consider the most significant hurdle he faced, General Dorchester.

The British general was the real challenge. That would require a bit more risk to achieve the reward. Fortunately, he was blessed with exceptional luck that he always carried with him. The colonel was suddenly relaxed and pleased as a wave of certainty washed over him. He was confident he would find a way to maneuver Dorcester to be dispatched neatly.

"How do I look, sergeant?" asked Mercy.

Allen, the bachelor farm boy with perfect teeth, checked out Mercy's pack and gear. He then looked the beautiful corporal up and down, which raised his blood pressure for a moment. "Uh," he swallowed, "you look *majestic*?"

She laughed at his effort to ignore her feminine appeal and said, "I'm just messing with you, sergeant."

Recon was loaded up. Lewis had been charging up the batteries for the drones, and they were both ready to go. To keep in contact with each other and Corporal Lewis, they put up an antenna with a repeating radio. Communications were line-of-sight, so the elevated antenna would keep everyone in contact, even in the forest's dense parts.

"Radio check," called Lewis.

"Radio check, Howe."

"Clark."

"Schein."

"Monty."

"Allen."

"Rogers."

"Gozen."

"I read you all 5-9, loud and clear," confirmed Lewis.

"Do you all hear me on the radio?" asked Howe.

Thcy all gave him a thumbs up.

"Ammo load. 20 mags?"

They again gave Major Howe a thumbs up.

"Monty, you have the Benelli mags?"

"Yes, sir."

"Sidearms and silencers, Ka-Bars, night vision, extra radio battery, zip ties, food, water, ear muffs, earbuds."

Howe got an affirmative from each. "Did I miss anything?"

Mercy giggled. "Chocolate?"

"Fine. Did someone pack the chocolate?"

"Yes, sir," said Allen, who had a very advanced sweet tooth.

"Snickers or Mars?"

"Both, sir," replied Allen.

"Well, that should pretty much do it," confirmed the major.

"Quick review. We are about three hours out from their scouts. At the last look on the infrared, there were nine. Sometimes there are ten. We stay together until we get close enough. Lewis will guide us into each target. Lewis has our lineup, and when you are close enough for a clean shot, you use the sidearm with the silencer. We have practiced this a hundred times. There will be no shooting without the silencer. Three taps—two to the body and one to the head. When all the scouts are down, we wait for the battalions. We will meet back up after the scouts are dead. They swap at midnight, so we don't take the scouts until 00:30. This is the most critical part of tonight's operations. We have to take all of them quietly."

Howe turned and started in the direction of the enemy.

"Ok, let's move out."

Chapter 34

Colonel von Donop could not sleep. There remained two days until the planned assault on Washington's army. The anxiety was growing, and he tossed and turned in his bunk. Despite the cold air, his head was damp with beads of sweat. His objectives kept rolling over in his mind—including assassination.

General de Heister's server was prepared and capable of delivering the poison. That part of the plan was the least of his worries, with the possible exception of destroying the enemy's meager defenses. Of course, Dorcester had told him about the possibility that Washington's troops may have muskets with preloaded shells, but the worst case would be a charge with bayonets. There was no chance the enemy could withstand his Hessian charge. No army could survive that.

Which left Dorcester. That was the one problem that was in want of an answer. In the midst of battle, where would he be? Observing the conquest from the rear? Ordinarily, von Donop would be with his troops in the thick of battle. Not this time. Instead, he and Dorcester would be together, with a small guard detail and messengers to give orders to the field commanders. But how would he get the general alone? It could not be from the observation point. He needed to figure out a way to convince Dorcester to leave the command post. Why would he leave? With Washington being smashed, he would have no reason to leave except to gloat. The British swine would likely go out on the field to parade himself. At that point, with the battle nearly won, there would be no way to stop him. No, it had to happen earlier.

Think, he prodded himself as he turned over once again. Ah, he considered, there is no reason a continental soldier could not slip behind our lines and shoot at the general. If the ball hits

Dorcester, we can take him to our Hessian doctor, who will see to it that he is mortally wounded. What if he isn't shot? That was much more likely. If a ball doesn't hit, then I urge him to flee to our more removed command post further back. This was a much better scenario, thought von Donop. Imagine a poorly aimed shot at their position to convince Dorcester to go with von Donop to a higher and safer vantage point.

Von Donop relaxed. Finding a subordinate to approach and fire an errant shot would be easy. He calmed himself. Everything would be *sehr schoen*. Yes, he thought to himself that everything would be just fine as sleep overtook him.

The hike to a spot 500 yards from the scouts was challenging, although not severe. The packs were heavy, but the forest floor was passable.

The latest word from Lewis was that the infrared showed nine replacement sentries marching out from the enemy camp. None of the Recon troops were fans of Hessians, but the German punctuality was admirable.

Recon made their way to their individual jump-off points behind their targets. They were stretched out about 750 yards. That meant a sentry every 80 to 100 yards. They had decided to spread out and kill the seven outside targets first, four to the west and three to the east. That left two more scouts in the middle. Schein and Clark would have the job of converging on the two Hessians in the middle. They would have to eliminate their first targets and then move in on the other two like ghosts. Not simple.

Howe keyed the Push-To-Talk button on his radio. "Lewis, what's the status of the replacement watchmen?"

"They came out in one group but are separating now, sir."

"Roger that."

"When you arrive at your spot, wait quietly. Howe out."

Clark and Howe got settled first. They lowered their packs and screwed the silencers onto their sidearms. Twenty minutes later, Lewis informed them that all of the sentries had been replaced, and the relieved sentries were running back to the camp. Apparently, they were happy to get back to food and some sleep.

"Recon, Lewis. We have a problem. The last two replacements on the west side are staying together. That leaves the slot in front of Mercy empty." Howe pictured the line-up. It was not unlike two football teams on the line of scrimmage. This line was 750 yards long, but each recon player should line up with a Hessian defender. However, the guy in front of Mercy was visiting a friend further to the left.

"Crap," muttered Howe under his breath. "No plan survives first contact with the enemy." He keyed up his radio. "Monty. Gozen is coming over to you. If the sentries hang together, Gozen goes alone to take them both. Over."

"Major, Monty. I think that I can take both, sir. Over."

Howe thought about it. As much as he didn't want to sideline Monty, he couldn't risk giving either of the sentries a chance to fire a shot.

"Monty, Howe. Negative. If they stay together, then Gozen takes the two targets. Copy?"

"Yes sir," confirmed the big sergeant, and Howe was glad that they had drilled repeatedly on military radio "speak."

"Gozen, go over to Monty and wait to see what the sentries do. Lewis, are they still together?"

"Yes, sir."

"Get over there, Mercy."

"Roger that. Gozen out."

She slipped on her pack and glided west through the woods.

"Howe, Lewis, I'm running down on drone 1. I'm sending out drone 2."

"Roger," said Howe. He then decided that if they pulled this off, he would make the kid a sergeant.

"Monty, Gozen. Over."

"Gozen, Monty. Go"

"I'm coming up on your position. Don't shoot me. Lewis, are those two sentries still together? How far?"

"Gozen, Lewis. I see them. They are about 120 yards due north from Monty."

"Major, Gozen."

"Gozen, Howe. Go."

"Sir, are we ready? I'm close to Monty now."

"Lewis, Howe, what's the status of the relieved sentries? Over."

"Major, Lewis. I followed them with the drone. They have already entered the perimeter of the camp. The new sentries are all in the same position, no changes."

"I've got time—00:50," said Howe. "Start in on your targets now. It's 120 meters. Keep it damn quiet, and make sure your silencers are screwed on tight. Monty, you run comms on the confirmed kills. Howe. Out."

"Monty," whispered Mercy> "Keep an eye on my pack. I'll call you as soon as I've taken out the sentries. If I get into trouble, then please come and save my ass."

Monty smirked. "Got it. I should come to save your—ass."

"Yes, if I get into trouble, then you save my ass," laughed Mercy almost silently.

She crept stealthily from Monty's position to the north. The range on her night vision headset was a meter to infinity, so she could already see the outline of the two sentries from 80 meters away. It looked like they were having a friendly conversation, oblivious to what was stalking them.

Mercy was pretty good at getting through the fallen leaves, and the dampness on the ground deadened the crunch by 90%. It was the perfect storm for the sentries, and it was approaching in the form of a woman who was part superhero.

Twenty meters away, she pulled her APX pistol. The 9mm Beretta was fixed with the silencer, and a round was already chambered. The other guys were using their .380, but at this range and with no body armor, the sentries would be easy targets, she hoped.

She slithered in closer and heard three muffled thwaps from her right. Allen must have taken his target about 150 or 180 meters away, yet she still heard the silenced rounds. The sound did not go unnoticed by the sentries, and they were suddenly alert. She could see them both turn towards the east and could almost make out their whispers. They stepped out from behind the tree, which partially obscured her view, and took a couple of hesitant steps toward the sound.

Mercy was still 12 meters away, but the sentries seemed to have decided to investigate the noise. She had no time. The lead sentry didn't comprehend the sudden pain in his chest and abdomen. Mercy then took the headshot, which wasn't dead center but was good enough.

To her surprise, the second sentry was a nimble fellow who sprinted north toward the enemy camp. Impossibly, Mercy had gone from prone to sprinting after the sentry in less than a second. Now it was a footrace between a cheetah and a groundhog until she could take her shot. As she gained on the fleet-footed Hessian, he started shouting in German. She could wait no longer and fired on the run. The first shot missed, but the second took him in the lower back. He stumbled and dropped. Mercy placed two more shots.

"What happened?" asked Monty. "I could hear the guy yelling."

"They overheard Allen's kill and started to move. I had to chase one. There is no way he was heard back at the camp. We're done here."

A minute later, Recon checked in with Monty and confirmed the kills. They met up in the center where Clark and Schein had pulled off their double targets. Both of Schein's victims had been casually standing around. But like Mercy, Clark had to run down his second target. The guy turned out to be a tough one.

"I hit him once in the leg when he was running, but then I

had nothing left in the magazine," said Clark.

"What happened?" asked Howe.

"He turned around and started cursing me in German and pulled his bayonet off his rifle to use it as a knife. I think he tried to fire a shot, but it failed."

"Oy," said Schein. "That would have ruined everything."

"I pulled the Ka-Bar and had to do it the hard way. He managed to poke me in my arm before I got the Ka-Bar in him."

"Seriously?" said Howe anxiously. "Show me."

Clark peeled away his jacket and stuck out his arm. The sleeve had a tiny hole, and there was some blood there.

"That had to hurt. So much for Kevlar," said Rogers.

"Probably not as much as my Ka-Bar hurt him. By the way, Kevlar is great for bullets, not so great with knives," said Clark with a grin followed by a grimace. Howe cleaned the penetration wound. It wasn't too deep, but it was bleeding a bit.

"That's going to need a couple of stitches." Howe turned. "Who has the kit?"

Allen retrieved a small first-aid kit. Howe quickly cleaned the wound and then pulled out a needle and thread.

"Sir," asked Clark. "What in the blazes is that for?"

"Captain, this is a special needle and thread for closing the wound—it will hurt, but we need to do this. I put some ointment on there, but if I don't stitch it, you'll be bleeding for a day."

Clark looked mortified. "Sir, have you ever done this before?"

Howe lied. "Absolutely, Clark, hundreds of times. Just no screaming when I put the needle through."

The captain didn't scream, but he wanted to. Aaron topped it off with some more Neosporin, wrapped it well, and said, "Be glad you're not the other guy."

Twenty minutes later, Lewis called Recon. "Our battalions are close to you now."

"Lewis, Howe. We can see them. Standby. Wait, what do you see from the Brits? Do a long-range survey."

A minute later, Lewis called to say that the camp looked like it was quiet. It was 02:00. Other than the usual sentries, most of the Redcoats would be asleep in their tents.

Recon had taken the last hour to check and recheck. They were approximately 500 yards from the south side of the Brits and Hessians. They signaled their location to the leading units behind them, and soon they were joined by Colonel Overton and the three majors who were battalion commanders.

"Good morning, colonel," said Major Howe.

"Top of the day to you, major," replied the colonel, who looked like an NFL linebacker pumped up for a championship game. "Any issues with their sentries?"

"No sir," answered Howe, then tilted his head towards Captain Clark. "They were cooperative."

"Very well," said the colonel. "We will spread out."

Major Parker, the officer leading the left flank, was told to watch out for the British trying to pull a flanking maneuver after the shock of the first rounds subsided.

"I don't think the British will be able to flank us on the west, but the Hessians are more aggressive. Major Parker, you'll have to be prepared to shift your men west to cut down any British or Hessians that swing out that side, most likely Hessians. The terrain on the east is rocky. We discussed that. They will never be able to move the kind of numbers they will need to the east," added Howe.

"Right," said Colonel Overton checking his mechanical watch, "at 04:00, we start moving." He turned to his command staff. "Recheck your gear. Tell the men to eat quietly and drink. No chambered rounds should be in any rifle until we engage the enemy. That means magazines are inserted when we are 250 yards out. Any soldier who chambers a bullet early will be thrown into the nearest pond or river naked. Is that understood?"

They nodded.

"I will fire off three shots when we are 50 yards away. Be damned quiet until then. When you hear those shots, then start your assault. No heroics. We have these." He hefted his own

AK-47. “There is no reason to close to bayonet range. If they charge, then you have plenty of ammunition. Use that.” He paused and looked at his officers. “Good luck.”

Chapter 35

Dorcester woke with a start. A dim lamp burned in the corner. He looked down and saw Morrisey curled up with a blanket on the ground. Since the captain had dealt with the disgusting Scot, Dorcester had given Morrisey the dubious privilege of sleeping on the command tent floor. He leaned forward and stretched, then took his scabbard and whacked the insolent captain on his back.

Morrisey was nervously alert in a moment and stood awaiting orders.

"Captain," said Dorcester. "Describe for me how you are planning to improve your standing."

Morrisey repeated the line the general had instructed him to say before bed.

"Sir, I wish to prove my worth by dying in battle to serve my general and my king."

"Well said, captain, now fetch me my tea."

When Morrisey had gone, the general dressed and nervously paced his tent. From this far back on the west side of the encampment, he was far from the woods where the soldiers would begin their march south. When they did, he and von Donop would ride together behind the center column. Not so much to discuss strategy but so that Dorcester could keep an eye on the Hessian. He knew well that the mercenaries were treacherous and evil to their core.

The general stepped out of his tent, impatient for tea. Morrisey should die in battle, he thought. The man could barely hurry tea. Dorcester ignored the morning chill. It shouldn't be long before fierce snows and cold would settle upon this foul state of New Jersey. Tomorrow's victory and the glory that would go with it would be most welcome.

Perhaps even his aged and demented father would understand

that his son had ended the war that Cornwallis' lard ass could not. The king would know it, and the honors and money would come with that recognition.

He looked south, and east as just a tinge of light began appearing below the horizon. The entire encampment was very quiet, even from the Hessian side. Dorcester was pleased. He wanted his troops well-rested for the coming morning's march to defeat the enemy. He would instruct his men to accept no quarter. Every last traitor would be bayonetted or hung, and his men would not entertain any notion of mercy.

"Here is your tea, sir," offered Morrisey reverently as he approached in the darkness. The general looked down at the fine cup and saucer as the captain presented it.

Dorcester grasped the cup, sipped, and then savagely kicked the Morrisey in his shin, causing him to drop and clutch his leg in obvious pain.

"My apologies, general," said the trembling Morrisey.

"Arise, captain!"

Morrisey struggled to his feet.

"What is your reason for feeling sorrow, Morrisey? For taking so long to prepare my tea, or perhaps for my tea being as cold as a witch's teat?"

The abused man was about to answer "both, sir," but never got the chance. In the distance to the south, there were three unusual popping sounds. Dorcester shoved the tea into the captain's hands while trying to stare for some indication of the origin of the reports. The camp had yet to stir when suddenly, all hell broke loose.

It was perhaps 400 yards from where Dorcester stood down a slope to the tree line that marked the southernmost edge of the camp. In the pre-dawn light, he could see little but did hear distant shouts and screams. There was a rumble of tumultuous activity at the camps' border.

Immediately, there came hundreds, if not thousands, of gunshots like he'd never heard before. He slapped the stunned captain. "Get everyone moving. Get a horn, man, and sound it!

Washington has led his men to suicide against us." Dorcester was screaming now, "Awake, you fools! Get your muskets and slaughter the enemy!"

Just then, a random 7.62mm AK bullet struck a tent pole next to the general. The post cracked, and Dorchester caught a splinter in the side of his face. He reached up and felt the wetness of blood, which shook him. Some evil magic must be at work for an enemy bullet to travel 600 yards with such force. He rejected the thought.

"Morrisey, they must be sending cannon shot," he screamed. "It is essential to go back and find cover."

Across the field to his east, the equally surprised von Donop was now awake. Unlike the quaking British general, the Hessian was in his element. He thirsted for the opportunity to face the enemy. For him, battles had always been about inflicting pain. And to his good fortune—Washington had saved him the trouble of marching for three hours and instead brought his American soldiers like sacrifices to von Donop's altar.

He checked his uniform and strapped on his saber. This would be a glorious day, he thought. With any fortune, he would use his sword to lop off Washington's head. He could feel mysterious and surreal protection, the same he'd felt through every battle. It was liberating because he knew that he would never die. No mere enemy soldier would be able to slay him, not with the confidence he carried with him. This knowledge freed him to be cavalier.

The colonel gazed south as the morning light was just beginning to illuminate the raging battle. His alert Hessians were no doubt repelling the charge of the Continental Army. The enemy was outnumbered, perhaps as high as 3 to 1. They had marched themselves like sheep committing suicide.

"Guenter," von Donop called to his valet. "Fetch my horse quickly." His man, dressed in Hessian servant clothes, ran to retrieve the colonel's mount.

Sprinkling rays were barely beginning to shed light on the distant confrontation. He could hear musket reports, but they were coming very rapidly. It was unlike anything he'd heard before. Nevertheless, it occurred to him that this early commotion of battle was precisely the time to eliminate his most significant concern—Dorcester. He would deal with Washington later.

The valet hurriedly led the colonel's horse to his master. Von Donop grabbed the reins, leaped onto his mount, and speedily rode west towards his British rival. His troops, he thought, would exact defeat upon the Continental Army while he would dispatch Dorcester and clear his path to glory.

With the attack now underway, Howe urged Recon to hold themselves in reserve. The Hessians and British on the front lines were taking a horrendous number of casualties, but they were returning fire. At a range of over 100 yards, since most had fallen back, their Brown Bess muskets were largely ineffective. However, some soldiers had been hit by musket balls. The platoon leaders, for their part, were succeeding in keeping the men protected behind trees and rocks. Without artillery, the enemy was experiencing the real meaning of "Shock and Awe."

"Listen," said Howe. "Let the infantry do their job. Clark, stay back and stay in contact with Lewis to see if any Hessians try to flank us." Howe was loading a light pack.

"Where are you going, sir?"

Howe hesitated, then said, "I'm going to get Dorcester."

"Behind their lines?" Schein shouted over the din of the shooting.

"Yes, lieutenant. I have to do a bigger task than just winning this battle. There is a lot more at stake than you know."

The confusion on the faces of Recon was evident. Pleading looks were on all of them. Howe paused.

"Recon," he said. "I have to kill Dorcester. Not just that he has to die, but I have to be the one to kill him. That's all I can tell you now. Don't worry about me. Just stay together and protest our left flank from any aggressive movements."

Amidst their bewilderment, they gave Howe a reluctant thumbs up as he turned to Mercy and said, "Let's go."

Von Donop did something that a senior officer would never do; he rode alone from the Hessian base to the adjacent English camp. He reined in his horse and saw a mass of turmoil. Soldiers were running here and there, gathering weapons and supplies and hurrying down the hill south to the battlefront.

A coherent British sergeant came to a halt at the sight of the Hessian commander and saluted. Von Donop had already looked around the command tent and saw no sign of Dorcester.

"Sergeant, where is your general?"

"Sir, he and Captain Morrisey have moved further northwest for safety. We had received stray musket balls here."

The Hessian was incredulous. "Musket balls up here?" To the colonel, it sounded like proof that the self-aggrandizing general was a pig and a coward.

"Which way did they go, sergeant?"

The frantic sergeant pointed to a stand of trees some hundreds of yards distant. "Somewhere up there, sir," he said and then ran south.

"Lewis, Howe."

"Major, Lewis. Over."

"Okay, Lewis, prove your worth."

The sun was now a touch above the horizon. Howe hoped to be further along by this time. The gradually lightening sky was fast turning into a disadvantage. Mercy stuck to him like glue.

They had moved quickly to the west and made a long loop around the English camp. The concentration of fire to the south seemed to divert the attention of the Redcoat troops thoroughly. Incoming fire distracted them from any movement in the western woods—which would have given them a chance at circling behind the Continental Army—but they didn't do it. Highly unhelpful to them, thought Howe, but most welcome. Mistakes by the enemy were always a welcome gift.

"Major, this is Lewis," said the corporal. "Sir, you are all clear. No soldiers anywhere near you and nothing to the west of you. I followed Dorcester with the drone. He abandoned his command tent, sir, and he is heading to a stand of trees directly to your north. It looks like he has one soldier with him. Over."

"Are you kidding, Lewis? Are you saying that he ran away from the battle?"

"That's what it looks like, sir."

Mercy smirked and banged her fist against his leg while they crouched down in the woods. "What a pussy!"

"Knock it off, Mercy," he whispered to her.

She stopped giggling and refocused.

"Lewis, Howe. Anything else on the video near Dorcester?"

"Yes, sir. There is one guy on a horse holding a sword. He looks like he's searching for something."

Aaron gave Mercy a panicked look. "Dammit! That must be von Donop. He's searching for Dorcester!"

"Lewis, how far is the rider from Dorcester? Quick!"

"He's maybe a couple hundred meters, just like you, but he is to the east."

"Lewis, scream in my ear if that horse heads toward Dorcester."

The confused Lewis answered affirmatively as Aaron and Mercy took a risk and raced up the hill toward the British general. To the east, they could barely make out von Donop urging his horse to enter the thicker forest. It wasn't ten seconds before he heard Corporal Lewis.

"Major, the rider dismounted! He seems to be moving

quickly in the direction of Dorcester!"

"Son of a bitch!" cursed Aaron.

They ran in the direction of the brigadier general, throwing caution to the wind. It was now a matter of who would get to Evan Butler's ancestor first.

Mercy and Aaron covered the distance like sprinters. The trees, bare as they were, still obstructed their view. They did their best to shift as they ran to get a glimpse of Dorcester. Both of them could see red through the obstructing trunks just a dozen meters ahead.

In desperation, Howe rushed towards the movement just ahead. Suddenly, Aaron and Mercy burst into a small clearing ringed with pines. Here the forest floor was damp with leaves, and the trees stood grimly around them like ancient witnesses to history.

To his right stood Count Colonel Carl von Donop. He was tall, ominous, and terrifying in his Hessian uniform. The sinister grin on his cold, dark countenance froze Aaron. The man's jet-black hair, the way he held himself erect. He radiated terror and death.

Aaron looked to his left. The slim Dorcester stood with a small knife in his hand. He looked frantic, like a fox surrounded by a thousand hounds. The general had his arm around the waist of a trembling captain whom he was using as a shield.

Mercy eased the thumb break loose from her .45 as she eyed the men. At this range, she could take down all three before they could get to Aaron, but she might not be able to prevent von Donop from stabbing his prey.

"Wilkommen," said von Donop in a supernaturally calm and frightening voice. "It appears we have more than one hunter for our cowardly General Dorcester." For once, Huxley Dorcester had no twisted comment backed up with shrill laughter.

Howe sensed that Mercy had already worked out her method for dealing death to von Donop, but he stayed her hand.

"Count von Donop, I presume?" asked Howe theatrically.

The count had the most penetrating and wicked stare Howe

had ever seen. He shuddered for a moment. The two men gazed at each other in some fascinating test of wills. Time trickled slowly as both men stood like two primeval beasts challenging each other over a kill. The energy in the air was consuming. The sounds of the battle seemed to fade into obscurity. All that existed was this three-way standoff that would end in a bloody finale.

Mercy observed this, knowing she was ordered not to intervene between the two mighty hunters.

Suddenly, in the middle of the intense state of affairs, there was an agonized shriek as a long thin blade suddenly protruded from Dorcester's chest. While the colonel and Howe were intensely focused on each other, they failed to notice the brief struggle of their British quarry. Captain Morrisey had somehow twisted himself behind his general, pulled his own knife, and plunged it through Dorcester's back. The captain was insanely gleeful as he jumped back, still clutching the dripping stiletto. The general stood with his hand on his bloody chest. He looked at his palm in disbelief and called out, "Morrisey, haven't I always been good to you?"

Dorcester dropped to his knees. His last breath hissed from his lungs as he fell flat on his face.

Aaron produced a terrible, blood-curdling scream. "No!!" At the same instant, von Donop swung his blade, and the power and speed of the stroke decapitated Captain Morrisey. He retreated a step as the headless body collapsed silently onto the floor of pine needles.

"Two dead Englishman," laughed von Donop. "Shall we add some American traitors to the count?"

"Ah," pointed out von Donop, "I see you have no sword. Do you have a knife?"

Mercy urged Aaron to let her shoot the insane von Donop, but again he stayed her hand. Aaron was in shock. He felt as if he'd been ripped asunder from the inside. He was crushed. He'd botched *Allison's* test and was petrified that his failure had just doomed humanity.

A storm of thoughts made him dizzy. Dorcester was dead! Julia's voice was screaming in his head. His soul was crushed by the image of Julia dying again. Now he would mourn all that he had just lost again. He had missed his chance to fix it.

Nevertheless, something compelled him to fight this malicious colonel. Dorchester lay dead. All that remained was von Donop. Perhaps it was Aaron's time to die at the hand of the evil Hessian. Maybe that was his test, to die and fulfill something only known to the AI. He would fight, and what would be—would be. When Mercy battled the fierce and towering Guller, she was prepared to die but faced him anyway.

"Mercy!" he called out, "do nothing!" Grudgingly, she accepted his order. She knew his tormenting emotions well because they had been her own.

Aaron pulled out his Ka-Bar. The Hessian laughed. "That is the best you can do?" He then dropped his sword and pulled out a smaller blade. He tossed it back and forth from his bare right hand to his gloved left.

"What is your name, major?" he asked. "I like to know the names of my worthy opponents."

"My name is Howe."

The Hessian laughed. "Perhaps you are an American nephew to the English fat dog, General Howe?"

Aaron ignored him as they began to circle each other in the clearing.

"Do you know, Major Howe," he said. "I am at a slight disadvantage with my small knife. Do you not agree?"

Howe glared at von Donop. "You made the rules, not me."

A strange look came over von Donop's face. "Yes, I did make the rules, but I must try to get an advantage where I can, so I will use my power, which you cannot overcome."

Mercy noticed that the man was licking his lips and looked insane as he reached towards his left hand. Finger by finger, he removed the slick, black glove and tossed it onto Dorcester's body. He grasped the knife in his now bare hand and held it up. On his index finger was a bright gold ring.

Howe's eyes were drawn to it. A dragon was meticulously carved into the face of the ring; Aaron stood transfixed. What had his mother said about the dragon when he went to Amberness? He couldn't remember. The image was seductive, and it consumed Aaron and clouded his thoughts. Suddenly time stopped, a sickness like vertigo overcame him, and he was wrenched from the forest clearing in New Jersey to a forest in Vermont.

He was 12. The ring! It was just his birthday. His father had forgotten Aaron's birthday again. His older sister Julia was upstairs. His dad said they should go hunting but that he was not going to leave Julia home alone. She was 14. She was a beautiful girl with long hair and a clever smile. He remembered how she used to call him her little pest, and when he turned twelve, Jules called him the birthday beast.

She pleaded with his dad to let her stay home, but he said no. His dad said that she could carry the ammo if she kept complaining. He remembered that she didn't want to go into the woods to slaughter innocent rabbits, and Julia had gotten her wish. They had failed to kill any.

They'd started back when they saw their neighbor. He was not wearing hunting gear but was carrying a pistol. His dad called out, "Evan, I hope you aren't hunting rabbits with that thing."

As their neighbor was crunching through the woods, Julia hid behind his dad. When Mr. Butler was about 20 feet away, he stopped and said he wasn't hunting rabbits.

Aaron's dad sensed that Julia was afraid. Something wasn't right. His dad told Mr. Butler that he was scaring the kids. Butler had said that fear was a good emotion, and then he raised the .45 in his left hand with the ring. That ring!

His father's blood was all over Julia. He remembered that he had tried to bring up his rifle, but Butler was too quick and knocked the gun away. Butler then pressed the .45 up against Aaron's head and put his finger to his lips, whispering, "shhh."

Julia stood there with silent tears streaming down her face.

Butler then pulled a rope from his pocket and made Julia tie Aaron with his back to a tree.

Butler made her take off her jeans and made him watch. When he was done, he pulled out a knife and cut Julia's throat. He remembered her shaking as she died.

He laughed that Aaron could starve out here with his family. He then holstered his pistol, brushed himself off, and told Aaron to have a nice day. Before he walked off, he came very close to Howe and held out his left hand. "Hey kid, you like my ring?" Butler then shoved an ornate gold ring with a hideous dragon carving into Aaron's face.

The man said the ring had been in his family for over 300 years. "It gives me power," he'd said. He continued, "Kid, there ain't no other ring like it in the whole universe." Butler turned and walked away. A hunter found Aaron the next day still tied to the tree.

For all those years, the dragon had been buried deep in his subconscious. It was the ring, Butler's ring. Von Donop's ring! It was passed down through generations until it ended up on the finger of another psychotic murderer.

It hammered Aaron hard in that frozen sliver of time that it wasn't Dorcester after all. It never was. It was von Donop, an insane butcher, standing right in front of him. He was wearing the dragon ring as he stood in a clearing in a forest next to a battlefield. Julia's voice called to him from the grave.

Von Donop's lunge jerked Aaron from his stupor. With a demented laugh, the Hessian had managed to catch Aaron in a grazing strike to his arm. Blood began to flow down to his left wrist. The evil butcher laughed. "It appears that even with your big knife, you are just too slow for me."

Aaron said nothing but yelled to Mercy in a hushed whisper, "I was wrong. It's *him*!" He then concentrated entirely on his opponent, as Mercy instantly realized that this knife duel meant everything.

The circling continued as the count attempted to strike at Aaron's belly. Aaron was winning by staying out of reach and moving more quickly and with focus.

Mercy watched Howe dance the dance of death with Colonel von Donop. He had told her to stay out of it, but she could not bear to watch him get killed by the psychotic Hessian. She periodically looked back through the thick forest and saw that the battle was still raging. However, it had progressed north into the enemy camp. The Hessians were putting up a good fight, but they could not stand up to the tremendous firepower. It turned into a slaughter.

She quickly turned back to the primordial struggle playing out before her. The colonel's lunges and thrusts were weakening. It appeared his endurance was waning. Suddenly, in desperation, he charged Aaron. For an instant, Mercy was in agony as the two men crashed into each other and then separated.

There was an awful groan. Mercy stared at von Donop, a twisted grin on his face. Aaron still gripped his knife that had penetrated the Hessian's left hand, his dragon hand. Aaron jerked back the Ka-Bar, as von Donop suppressed a need to cry out in pain. The Hessian's blade was on the ground, and his ring was covered with blood.

"This is not possible!" he screamed at his ring as he held up his hand.

Colonel von Donop fell to his knees, suddenly beseeching eyes begged for pity.

Aaron stepped forward, clutching his knife. He grabbed von Donop's hair and pulled the Hessian's head back. Blood dripped from the man's left hand as the ring slipped off and fell to the ground. Aaron thrust the Ka-Bar into von Donop's heart and said, "This is for Julia!"

Mercy hauled Aaron up and raised his sleeve to examine his arm. It was a nasty-looking wound, but the bleeding was not severe. She squeezed his hand and urged him to hurry so they could rejoin Recon behind the line of engagement.

"Take it," he said, pointing to the glimmering gold ring on

the ground. "I cannot touch it."

Mercy bent down and snatched the bloodstained ring from the forest floor. She pocketed it and then drew him with her into the dense woods. The sun had risen somewhat, and beams of light showered the battlefield.

The turmoil and confusion of the initial fighting had slowed. Many British were surrendering, but some were deserting, streaming from the battle hoping to find refuge among New Jersey Loyalists. The Hessians were still charging, and the Continental Army was mowing them down with their relentlessness, accurate fire. It would soon be over.

As Aaron and Mercy made haste through the woods to the south and west of the British camp, the destruction became more evident. English dead were scattered everywhere. Too many to count. Beyond that, the Hessian tents were shredded and fallen, along with what could be thousands of casualties. They nearly walked into a British private who shouted, "I surrender," as tears streamed down his face. They told the young soldier, who looked more like a boy, to sit down next to a tree and take off his boots.

Gunfire was dropping off quickly now. A Hessian major left in charge had finally accepted that all was lost. The remaining Hessians dropped their muskets and sat on the field of battle. Soon the surviving senior Hessian officer would be taken to Colonel Overton to offer his formal surrender.

Such a massive presence of so many armed colonial troops permitted Aaron and Mercy to take a direct line back to Recon. They hiked their way past the bodies of the dead and injured.

Colonel Overton was waiting with his entourage when Aaron and Mercy returned. Very uncharacteristically, he hugged Howe. It was like being hugged by a polar bear. Fortunately, he used better discretion and merely shook hands with Corporal Gozen. Howe wasn't sure how Mercy would have reacted to an embrace from the colonel, and it was better not to find out.

"My gratitude, major," said the colonel, then added in a severe tone, "a Hessian major is offering surrender. What is the disposition of Dorchester and von Donop?"

"They're dead, sir," said Howe.

The colonel looked down at Aaron's blood-stained hand and then directly into his eyes. "Is that your blood or Dorcester's?"

"Actually, that's mine, but Corporal Gozen and I were there when both Dorcester and von Donop died."

"What happened?" the colonel asked.

"His own captain killed Dorcester. I killed von Donop, sir."

"How did you suffer that wound, major?"

"That was from von Donop's knife, sir," admitted Howe.

"I thought you would have just shot him."

"We had a knife duel, sir. I won."

Overton turned to Mercy. "What were you doing while Major Howe acted like a fool?"

Mercy smiled at the colonel, "I was following orders, sir. I stood back and watched the show—I mean duel, sir."

Overton shook his head in disbelief. "Right, well, you are dismissed. Go find Recon. They are some 100 yards south."

They trod back through the woods and found Recon sitting in a group with their packs. Everyone stood up and looked relieved. Lewis was with them.

The corporal shouted out in a dramatic tone, "Mercy, we were so worried about you!"

She looked back at them with a warm and loving smile. "Really?" she asked sweetly.

"No, not really," said Lewis, staring into Mercy's disappointed face. He then pointed at her, gave a sly smile, and said, "Gotcha!"

In a split second, she grabbed him by the ear. "That's it, you little turkey," Mercy yelled as she pulled him up and threatened to poke his aching ribs.

"He's already been shot once," yelled Clark. "Don't injure him! We need him to help carry the gear."

Chapter 36

General Charles Cornwallis was both pleased and distraught. News traveled quickly despite the weather. He sat stoically with his command officers, looking over a report they could not believe. If it was not an exaggeration, then the British Empire had suffered an unparalleled defeat in recent history.

"Charles," said General Henry Clinton. "I cannot believe these rumors."

"Henry, they are true and not mere tales. Washington sent de Heister with an entourage directly to General Howe. Some three weeks had elapsed. De Heister had been very ill for a time but recovered. Coincidentally odd that he became extremely ill on the same day as the loss of his army to Washington," snorted Cornwallis. "The general and admiral then sent de Heister to me. The Hessian is a bit beyond rational, but he confirmed everything."

"What are our losses?"

"At the engagement near Buck Mountain, the Continental Army attacked with 1,800 troops. Our forces were just less than 900, and the Hessians were 3,500.

"The following is difficult to comprehend, but we suffered 549 dead, 100 injured, and we lost deserters as well. The Hessians kept fighting even while suffering greatly. You must admit that they are incessant. They had 2,200 dead, 700 wounded, and many deserters simply vanished from the battlefield.."

"This tale must be a myth to cover the Hessian failure." Clinton was incredulous. "Washington had only 1,800 troops?"

"Do not discount the capture of de Heister's reserves as well," said Cornwallis.

"How many?"

"Washington sent a captured major to de Heister demanding

the Hessian surrender. General de Heister had 1,500 men and much artillery. Naturally, he sent his refusal, and Washington responded by sending 1,000 men to assault de Heister.

"The Hessian general sent 1,000 troops to face Washington, and de Heister capitulated after half that force was killed or wounded in a battle that lasted 45 minutes!" sneered Cornwallis.

Henry Clinton began to speak, but Cornwallis raised his hand to pause his friend.

"Henry, they have some inventive weapons. They have very accurate muskets and can shoot a dozen volleys in one minute. They have no shortage of food either. Washington said that he could match any number we throw at him, as his men will be armed with magnificent weapons."

"How shall we proceed?" asked Clinton.

"We leave this putrid colony—that is what we should do," admitted Cornwallis.

Clinton scratched his head. "The king will never accept such a sudden defeat and retreat."

"Ah, my dear friend, you are utterly correct. The Admiral has already dispatched a ship to consult with the king and Parliament. Washington has demanded that we start withdrawing our troops back to England by 1st day of April," said Charles.

"What sort of fools does he think we are?" asked Henry. "If we begin to load ships in March, the king will have our heads."

"Let us hope and find a path to keeping our heads," said Cornwallis. "In any scenario, it is not for us to decide. General William has decided that we should continue the fight. However, we have lost New Jersey. We have no choice but to wait for spring and then cross the Hudson and regain New Jersey. That is William's decision."

"What do you say?" asked Clinton.

"What can I say? William does not believe that the new weapons of Washington's army are real. He blames the loss on Dorcester and de Heister's incompetence. I can resign, or I can throw our men to the slaughter. Both choices yield misery.

However, William circumvented me and sent our answer to Washington a week ago. We are not leaving."

An hour after Clinton's meeting with Cornwallis, a major abruptly disrupted their pleasant afternoon tea.

"My apologies for barging in, generals, but you should examine this report."

Cornwallis snatched the paper from the major's hand. Colonel Clayton sent it. It said simply:

To General Cornwallis,

The Continental Army attacked from the northern fort east of the Hudson. We lost our entire contingent. The enemy now holds the north of the island. They have some fanciful muskets that we cannot defeat. The few survivors are making their way to the south. I await your orders.

Clayton, Col.

"Major, where is the messenger who delivered this?" barked Cornwallis.

"I will bring him immediately, sir."

A young sergeant was hustled into the presence of Clinton and Cornwallis. He was visibly shaken. He reached into his pocket and retrieved a bloodied brass bullet that had been dug out from a dead man's leg under Colonel Clayton's orders. He held it in his open palm for the generals to see.

"Sit down by the fire, sergeant," ordered Clinton.

"Yes, sir."

"Now, young man, tell us what happened."

Cornwallis reported to General Howe the loss or capture of an additional 3,500 soldiers in the north of New York. The rest of the island was now in striking distance. The story of the special muskets was true.

"I cannot sacrifice more men, sir," explained Cornwallis to

General Howe. “We have lost 8,000 men in less than a month. We must evacuate New York.”

General William Howe looked like he had aged ten years in just a matter of days.

“I will speak plainly, Charles. We are returning to England. We cannot win.”

Cornwallis was in shock at William’s sudden acceptance of their defeat. “And what of the king’s desires?”

“Yes, the king,” sighed the commander-in-chief. “We will have to find some miraculous means to placate the king.”

Chapter 37

"I'm staying," said Mercy.

"WHAT?"

"I'm staying here in 1776."

Howe didn't know how to react. He shrugged and said, "Whatever you want, it's your life."

"That's it? It's my life?"

He looked at her with mixed emotions. "What else can I say, Mercy?"

She took hold of Aaron's shirt and dragged him behind some trees. It was frigid out, and the warm uniforms were a blessing.

Recon was now near Trenton. Most of the remainder of the army with Washington had assaulted the top of Manhattan. They had crossed the ice at a narrow gap north of the city with seasoned men who had taken 2,000 of General Greene's troops with them. General William Howe sent a writ of surrender to Washington after the crushing defeat in northern Manhattan.

Aaron had decided to go back to the lab, back to his time. He had to see if the future would work out the way he'd hoped. His longing to return was palpable. Colonel von Donop, the ancestor of Evan Butler, was dead. His friend and general claimed victory over the king's Redcoats. Washington had succeeded, and it was time for Aaron to go back and see the future.

"I want to tell you some things." She paused to plan out what she would say. "Aaron, when I was in the lab with *Allison*, I knew what I had to do. Everything I learned, fighting, tactics, all that; it was all for vengeance—bloody revenge.

"When I came back here with you, this was not my home. It was just a battlefield. My home, my life, was ripped from me. There isn't a day that goes by that I don't weep for John, for Abby, and for Janey. I can see them clear as day."

Aaron reached out to comfort her. "If it is too painful, then you don't have to tell me this, and you don't have to stay here!"

"Yes, I do!" she insisted. "I will never, ever forget what was taken from me. And I want to tell you the honest truth. My intention was never to live after I killed Durst."

Aaron kicked a little snow off his boot and stared at her. "I knew that, Mercy. It was no big mystery that you wanted to die. At first, back in the lab, I considered that you died months ago in Piney Brook. You were just sticking around to deal with Durst and set things straight."

"Yes, that's a painful way of putting it, but accurate. I decided that I would go out to battle, and then I would give some Redcoat a clean shot at some point. With any luck, it would be a headshot. A graphic ending, Aaron, but I didn't want to go beyond that.

"Things have changed now," she said.

"What's happened now?"

Mercy motioned her thumb towards Recon a little ways away. They sat around the fire on beach chairs in the light snow cover. The men of Recon were laughing like soldiers who didn't have a care in the world.

"They happened."

Howe tilted his head a little perplexed. "You'll have to explain that one to me."

"Them, those guys. Look, I may be Tomoe Gozen, but I'm also Mercy. And, as Mercy, I also have a heart and emotions," she said.

"And—"

"And these guys over here are my family now. They are my brothers. I love them. Not romantically, of course, but they are my best friends in the whole galaxy.

"I want to stay with them. I want to watch over them. I want to dance at Schein's wedding when he finds the right girl. Someone has to pick on Monty, and Lewis needs someone to prevent him from doing stupid things once he becomes a civilian. All of that. Do you understand? The bond that Recon has; you did that. You created a bunch of people who are so damn tight that we are almost stapled together. I need to stay here with them." Mercy paused. "Besides, they need a cook."

Howe smirked, "So, if I understand you. Let me reflect this back: you don't want to die? I shouldn't shoot you?"

King George III was furious. He'd spent the day listening to his generals explaining why they had ordered his ships to bring back his army.

"We have endured quite enough," said the king, "We are going to order that we prepare anew. We will return to the colonies and land with 200,000 men if required.

"The Empire will not lay down like a lamb in the face of rebellious subjects. If you wish to resign, then we will accept your resignation. Soon, we will sail the Atlantic to teach them a lesson in respect for the crown and respect for the Empire."

The generals and admiral bowed and retreated from King George's wrath at the wave of his hand.

Later at the London residence of Admiral Richard Howe, the senior officers gathered for brandy and to discuss their fate.

"I will say it outright," said Cornwallis. "The king is sending our soldiers and sailors to their doom in that pathetic excuse for a country."

There was a nod of agreement all around, except from General William. "I smell the scent of treason, my friends, and if we are talking treachery, then perhaps we should not waste our time flapping our gums."

"What do you mean, brother?" asked Richard.

"What I am saying is, as commander-in-chief of the army—I will not stand idly and allow 100,000 or 200,000 soldiers to die on the soil of the United States of America. No matter what it takes to prevent that—if you grasp the measure of my determination."

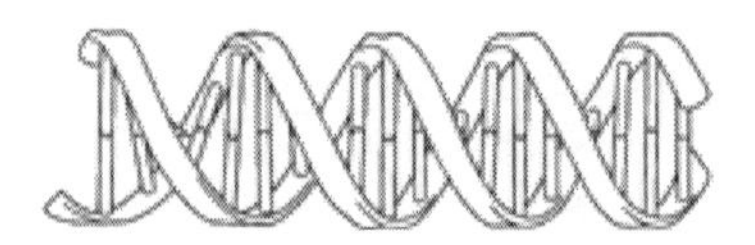

Dr. Aaron Howe, a major in the Continental Army, stepped through a virtual gate to his lab. He got his bearings and then looked around. It was midnight on July 3rd, and nothing in the lab seemed different. He immediately walked over to the AI.

"*Allison*!"

"*What*?" she said as her image appeared on the screen, yawning. *"I was sleeping!"*

"Since when do AI's sleep?"

"You know, Aaron, there's a lot you don't know about me."

"Before you do talk, I want you to know that I am not saying a word about anything yet." He symbolically put his fingers in his ears. After removing his fingers, he said, "I want to know one thing now but nothing else, got it?"

Allison saluted.

"What happened to England after the ships returned with all the king's troops?" he asked.

"Long or short version?" asked *Allison.*

Aaron held out his finger and thumb to indicate short.

"King George refused to accept defeat. He planned to send back at least 200,000 troops."

"What do you mean by 'he planned' to send soldiers back?"

"There was a clandestine meeting between the generals and Admiral Richard Howe. A few weeks later, at the end of March, they say that William Pitt stuck a stiletto into the king."

"That was it? They didn't come back?"

She shook her head.

"Okay, I'm going to sleep. Tomorrow is July 4th," pointed out Howe. "I'm taking a pill and going to sleep. Did I just say that I was going to sleep twice? I can't handle anything else yet. Too tired. Got it?" He yawned and sighed.

"Absolutely, Aaron," she said with a very contented smile.

Aaron slept the entire night on the Ugly Sofa. He was already dead tired, but the little helper pill knocked him out. He slept for 12 hours.

Aaron grabbed some cheese and crackers when he awoke and sat there munching away in front of *Allison*. She was quiet.

"Okay," he said finally. "I'm going home for a while."

"Great."

"Do I still live in the same house?"

She grinned. *"Yep, and your Cutlass is parked outside."*

"Excellent," he remarked, feeling butterflies in his stomach. "I'm going to go home and chill out on July 4th. Perfect. I know what you're thinking, *Allison*, and I don't want you to tell me anything. I'm not ready."

She gave him that head shake thing she did. *"Fine, but just in case you need me, you can get me on any of the monitors at your house."*

"You're like freakin' Big Brother!"

"Correction," she said in an animated deep girlish voice, her dark hair framing her on-screen image, *"Big Sister."*

Once outside, Aaron relished stepping into his '72 Olds convertible. He started it up and headed out of the parking lot. On the way home, there were tons of Independence Day ornaments and doodads on lamp posts, traffic lights, and stores; it was more than he'd ever seen in the past.

He drove past a Burger King but then did a U-turn and returned for some fast food. The parking lot was half full. He walked in to find a lot of kids dressed up like Revolutionary War soldiers.

The counter was slightly backed up, so he took the time to look around and check the menu display on the wall. Aaron perused his food choices which almost triggered him to laugh out loud.

"Happy July 4th," said the girl behind the counter. "How may I help you today?"

Aaron grinned and said, “how about some large fries, some chicken fingers, and a large Sergeant Gozenburger.”

He traveled the rest of the way home, listening to patriotic rock songs. Perhaps he’d had some kind of impact on history?

It was about 3 p.m. when he got to his house. The brick exterior was the same, the trees were the same, but the front lawn was nicely trimmed. He’d have to figure that one out. At the top of the driveway, he noticed an unfamiliar car in front of the garage.

Aaron pulled up and parked next to the strange car. He grabbed his Gozenburger and fries and walked to his familiar paneled front door. Fortunately, his key still worked, and he stepped in to find the lights on.

Aaron walked down the entry hall, then turned into his kitchen to see the back of a woman in jeans. She turned around when she heard the crinkling of his burger bag.

“Hey there!”

He found himself staring at a vaguely familiar pretty, blue-eyed woman.

“You look funny; you okay?” she asked. “I told you we would be coming for a barbecue today. What’s with the burger? Did you forget—that would be unusual!”

Aaron involuntarily dropped his keys and stood there, trying to absorb what he saw.

“Come here, you little pest,” she said, grabbing him and giving him a warm embrace.

He buried his head in her hair and quietly whispered in her ear, “Julia??”

She pulled back with her hands on his shoulders as tears flowed from his eyes.

“Hey! Of course, Julia, who’d you expect, Madame Curie?”

Aaron drew his wonderful sister close and cried on her shoulder. Julia held him for a moment.

"Aaron, what's going on?" she asked. "What happened? Are you okay, sweetheart?"

He stopped crying, wiped his eyes on his shirt, then moved a little so that he could gaze into his sister's eyes. "I love you, Julia. And things are so much better than okay."

Suddenly a loud pitter-patter was followed by some young kids running into the kitchen accompanied by a forty-something-year-old man.

"Uh, oh," said Julia. "Watch out, here they come!"

The kids ran straight at him and hugged him all at once, screaming: "Uncle Aaron, Uncle Aaron! Come play with us!"

Which he did.

Chapter 38

The next day, Aaron Howe, CEO of Howe It Works, parked his old SUV, leaving the Cutlass at home, and walked into the building, saying hello to every employee he met. He hurried to the elevator and then rode it up to his lab. For some reason, it was now on the eighth floor.

He entered the door code, held his thumb to the fingerprint reader, and eyed the retinal scanner. After he opened the door, he immediately went to *Allison*.

"Why didn't you tell me?" asked Aaron.

"Well, good morning to you, too!"

"So?"

"Because you told me not to say anything. What was I going to do? Besides, it was perfect! I couldn't have scripted it any better," she said while grinning from ear to ear.

"You mean you were watching?" he asked.

"Yep, the whole thing. I wouldn't have missed that for the galaxy."

"For an AI, you have a lot of sentimentality."

"AI, Aaron, can have emotions, too," she stated as-a-matter-of-factly.

"Great, so I thank you for everything you did for me, but before I get too emotional, I am changing the subject."

Allison looked at him with a knowing smile. *"Sure, you can thank me later because you and I have a lot of stuff to work out."*

Aaron sat, kicked off his shoes, and put his feet on the table. "Okay, great, I think," he said a little nervously. "But for now, I need to ask you—did you connect to your little surveillance bots that were on me in 1776?"

"Nope."

"Do you want to see them? There is a ton of stuff on there

that maybe you and I should analyze together. After all, I am a scientist. Maybe you'll even learn something new, *Allison*."

"Nope, I don't need to see them. I already know how it turned out. However, there are lots of things that we will need to talk about soon. I'm just waiting for the right time, and now is not the right time."

He looked around. "Have you seen Edgar?"

"Sure, Edgar comes here often. But remember, it's only been two weeks of current time that has transpired. Your time in 1776 is independent of time here. Don't forget that.

"Anyway, Edgar is in Washington on business now," she said.

"What kind of business?"

Allison pointed to herself. *"Some of it has to do with me, and some of it is about I.S., and he will be meeting with Carlisle to take care of some other things."*

"Carlisle is tricky," replied Howe. "I don't want Edgar to slip up with him. Maybe I should go down there and run interference."

"Edgar can take care of himself, and," she said in a loud voice, *"Vice President Carlisle might turn out to be one of the best friends you have."*

Allison and Aaron spent the day watching old TV shows and movies. She flipped over *Galaxy Quest*, and they laughed so hard at times that he thought he'd fall off his Ugly Sofa.

"While you were away, I've watched every episode of I Dream of Jeannie."

"That's wonderful," Aaron replied. "I like the 'Yes, Master' part."

She stuck her tongue out at him like the actress Barbara Eden would have.

When dinner came around, he couldn't help himself, so he had someone pick up another Sergeant Gozenburger. He munched away, feeling happier than he could ever remember. There was a tinge of sadness and loneliness for Mercy and

Recon, but he knew they were all right. That helped.

Eventually, staying in form, Aaron went to sleep in his office. This time, like the previous night, he might have good dreams.

Aaron slithered onto his favorite piece of furniture in the whole world and got comfortable.

He lay there, contemplating all that had transpired. As cryptic as *Allison* continued to be, he'd felt like whatever the big "test" was, he'd had to have made some progress. That was only logical. He'd gone back and managed to save his sister.

He thought about Julia. Could he ever tell her the truth? And when she started talking about mom and dad. That was another whole enormous story.

For now, Aaron relaxed and felt safe. He'd set things right. It was a given that there were aliens out there and a '60s sitcom-loving AI sitting in his lab. *Happy thoughts*, he reminded himself, *think happy thoughts*. He started drifting off when his gradual slumber was hi-jacked by a sudden banging on the lab doors.

The pounding was distinct, even inside Aaron's closed office. Rarely a moment of quiet. He sat up and got to his feet. Howe exited his study, weaved his way between tables, and passed *Allison*. No one appeared in the window, but three loud bangs rocked the door as he approached.

"All right, I'm not deaf," he yelled.

He released the latch and pulled the steel door inwards. A large man stepped through and slapped Aaron hard enough to knock him off his feet and land him squarely on his ass.

What looked like Sergeant Bonner stared down at Howe and reached for his hand to pull him back onto his feet. He did this with ease. Aaron then felt the sergeant's steely glare boring a hole through him.

"Listen, Howe; I should take these two hands of mine and do what I am justified to do—rip your arms off and, after that, maybe pull off your head and crap down your neck."

Bonner said all this as if such a thing was physically possible.

Shakily, Aaron replied. "Look, sergeant, I didn't know." His voice was surprisingly calm.

"Shut up, major," Bonner said and then grinned. "After what I've been through, you owe me big time, and I should give your skinny ass a first-rate whooping. But I'm gonna need you.

"So, listen up," he roared while poking a finger at Aaron's chest. "You get a pass for now because we are about to enter into a full-blown alien storm, and compared to a minnow like you, I've got bigger fish to fry."

Bonner paused and twisted his neck to one side until there was an audible crack.

"Ah. That feels better."

Excerpt from

Book Two of The Lost Council Trilogy

No Time for Mercy

Silence. It had a weight to it—a personality almost. Bonner felt it. He awaited a response, hoping it would not be the excruciating stabbing in his ear. His arms tingled; he wished his tormentors would return the block underneath his dangling feet. His body felt broken. It was an ache that never went away, just lessened slightly. The continuous torture was pushing him to his breaking point.

Blindfolded, he now heard shuffling and then a kind of clicking and chirping. It stopped, and there were more unintelligible noises, but nothing he could identify as words. The sounds went back and forth until there was quiet again.

"Do you speak English, Barrett Bonner?" The voice was rough and barely comprehensible.

Exasperated, Bonner replied, "No!"

There was a scrambling sound and more clicks.

"Do you know where you are?" The voice sounded odd as if it was projected through a tunnel.

More clicking. And a strange, rather whispery sound like two people conversing. It halted.

"No," answered Bonner.

Then the voice asked, "What do you remember?"

Not a yes or no question. He searched his recollection of—perhaps weeks that had passed since he was in the tundra. Time was foggy.

"Canada," he said.

"Is that a place on your…" the voice paused, "planet?"

What the hell kind of question is that Bonner thought. Was he a prisoner of some insane cult? He decided to be cautious.

"Yes, on my planet."

"Search your memory. What happened?"

What happened? Bonner thought. One hell of a good question. Bonner forced himself to push through his memories, passed the pain, the needle-like piercing in his ear, the aching of his fatigued arms. Then he remembered the Arctic tundra—his job with I.S. The Intelligence Support unit that had recruited him. He abruptly felt a sharp pain in his knee, the one that had taken a piece of shrapnel in Afghanistan.

His memory came flooding back; Dr. Howe, Dr. Tomis, the black box in the ground. He had been told to touch it. Dr. Howe had said to put his hand on the box and then—. He cleared his throat. Should I tell them, he thought. Better not.

"I don't remember."

Again. A pause.

"Bonner," the voice said. "We are the Panruk. You are no longer on your planet. Do you understand this?"

If this was some sort of advanced military training, he was not interested. Not on Earth? Whoever the hell was in charge of this had gone too far. Bogus! N*ot on Earth*?

"Yeah, whatever," Bonner barely bothered to respond.

The voice started again. "Do you understand?"

Bonner stayed silent. More chirps.

"We are the Panruk. Do you understand?"

Bonner grudgingly replied, "Listen, you Hajis, you can call yourself whatever you want. I'm taking a nap."

Suddenly, there was a sharp pain in his ear.

"F-this!" Bonner yelled out.

"We are the Panruk. Do you understand?"

"No. I don't understand. I want to leave now," he demanded.

"You cannot leave. You are a slave of the Mazik Bah-Gahn."

"Let me the hell out of here!" yelled Bonner.

There was silence, then, "Barrett Bonner, we are the Panruk. We are not from your planet. We are here to observe your examination by the Mazik."

Bonner was becoming more pissed off by the second, and his training barely kept his anxiety in check. He had to take advantage of any information his captors might offer. "How do I know that you are the Panruk and that I am not on Earth?"

"Barrett Bonner. Do you wish to do a verification?"

He was trying to stay focused, but Barrett increasingly wanted to beat the piss out of whoever was speaking to him. He sighed. Torture in the dark had worn him down. His strength and concentration were fading. "What's a verification?"

A different voice was heard. "A verification is the act of removing your…eyeshade." More clicking, "—blindfold. Under Agreement 642,510 of the Council, we are permitted to remove your blindfold. Do you agree?"

Bonner nodded.

He felt the dark visor lifted away from his face. His eyes adjusted quickly in the dim light of what was clearly a cell. He saw two cloaked people to his right, but then panic rose in his gut. Bonner pushed back against the terror welling up in him. He could just barely see that their faces were strange.

They were not people. They were—*not human*!

"Who are you!" he asked in a wavering, panicked voice.

"We are Panruk," answered one of them. "Do you verify?"

The person that was not a human being pulled back the hooded cloak. In the subdued light, Bonner could now see non-human features. The skin was bluish, and the eyes were large and blue with no iris. There was no hair. The nose was pugged, and the mouth was a slit. Humanoid, but not human.

Bonner looked down and saw the hands extending from the sleeves of its cloak. There were five fingers, like a human, but the index and middle fingers were very long, and something glimmered on the tips.

Bonner, in shock, barely managed to whisper, “I am not on Earth.”

“You are not on Earth,” confirmed the alien as it replaced the blindfold and left Bonner alone in the dark.

“In any moment of decision, the best thing you can do is the right thing, the next best thing is the wrong thing, and the worst thing you can do is nothing. —Teddy Roosevelt

Join all the fans of Howe, Mercy, Allision, and Recon! Visit and sign up so that you never miss important announcements regarding the continuing story!

www.booksbyblunt.com/contact

Made in United States
North Haven, CT
16 January 2024